# Praise for *The Wartime Sisters*

"Loigman's second novel portrays a sampling of the women whose roles were pivotal during the wartime manufacturing boom and highlights historic advances for women." —*Kirkus Reviews*

"With a perceptive lens on the challenges of whittling away grievances that have built up over the years, *The Wartime Sisters* is a powerful pressure cooker of a family drama." —*Booklist*

"With measured, lucid prose, Loigman tells a moving story of women coming together in the face of difficulties, both personal and global, and doing anything to succeed." —*Publishers Weekly*

"Readers will enjoy the heartfelt picture of women's daily life during wartime through the eyes of two extraordinary sisters. Recommended for historical fiction fans of Pam Jenoff and Kate Morton." —*Library Journal*

"Historical fiction fans will love *The Wartime Sisters*—a fresh take on the World War II novel." —*Real Simple*

"An emotionally honest story about the complexity of family." —*PopSugar.com*

"Loigman's commanding voice and crafty prose have been likened to celebrated author Alice Hoffman." —*Westport* magazine

"A heartfelt and poignant portrait of the complex bond between sisters, how our childhood roles define us as adults, and what dire consequences that can have, especially in times of war. *The Wartime Sisters* shows the strength of women on the home front: to endure, to fight, and to help each other survive."

—Jenna Blum, *New York Times* and international bestselling author

"An evocative home-front tale set against the backdrop of the Springfield Armory during World War II. Loigman skillfully chronicles the complex sibling bonds and rivalries, the secrets we keep, and truths that set us free. Loigman's strong voice and artful prose earn her a place in the company of Alice Hoffman and Anita Diamant, whose readers should flock to this wondrous new book."

—Pam Jenoff, *New York Times* bestselling author

"Loigman once again deftly explores the complexities, heartbreaks, and fierce endurance of family bonds. Even amid the great tension and fears of the Second World War, *The Wartime Sisters* reminds the reader that the harshest battles are often fought here at home, with those we love and are meant to trust most. A stirring tale of loyalty, betrayal, and the consequences of long-buried secrets."

—Kristina McMorris, *New York Times* bestselling author

"A riveting tale of sibling rivalry and the magnetic dissonance of family, filled with heart-stopping truths that are both tender and wise. One of my favorite books of the year."

—Fiona Davis, national bestselling author

"A powerful and moving story of secrets, friendship, and sisterhood. . . . Beautifully written, emotionally charged, and rich with historical detail, this novel and these sisters stayed with me long after I turned the last page."

—Jillian Cantor, author of *Margot* and *The Lost Letter*

"Complex and intricately woven, *The Wartime Sisters* is truly everything I love in a novel. Beautifully written, rich in historical detail, and anchored by two strong women who must reconcile their past—and their secrets—in order to survive. Loigman is a master storyteller and this novel had me from its very first page."

—Alyson Richman, international bestselling author
of *The Lost Wife* and *The Velvet Hours*

"*The Wartime Sisters* depicts the legacy of love and hurt between two sisters during an important historical time. Lynda Cohen Loigman's characters—as well as their shared home, the Springfield Armory of the 1940s—come to life in this sensitive, engaging novel."

—Elizabeth Poliner, author of *As Close to Us as Breathing*

## Praise for *The Two-Family House*

"It's hard to believe *The Two-Family House* is Loigman's debut novel. A richly textured, complex, yet entirely believable story, it draws us inexorably into the lives of two brothers and their families in 1950s Brooklyn, New York. . . . As compelling as the story line are the characters that Loigman has drawn here. None is wholly likable nor entirely worthy of scorn. All are achingly human, tragically flawed, and immediately recognizable. We watch them change and grow as the novel spans more than twenty years. Engrossing from beginning to end."

—Associated Press

"An outsider's look into a world filled with tension and mistrust—and most of all, secrets. It will make you rethink your own family history until you are left wondering—how much do you know about your own past? And how sure are you that, without warning, your world might not be blown apart?"

—Jewish Book Council

"This absolutely riveting book reads like a suspense novel. Although many clues are peppered throughout, the reader, like the families, is not invited to share in the shocking secret that binds the two women. The underlying complexities of friendship, the intricacies of marriage, and the disintegration of family are explored in this gem of a family saga. The characters are fully drawn, and the writing is superb. This is a book that is sure to become a popular choice for book clubs."

—Historical Novel Society

"*The Two-Family House* takes you on a tour of dysfunction and deep and abiding love in a way that reflects the entanglements that come with a close-living family. Its examination of generations of a family with their own high expectations to live up to resonates on several different levels. This very literary tale actually gives readers so much more than it may seem at first."　　　　—Bookreporter.com

"In her first novel, Loigman uses complex characters to deconstruct the anatomy of family relationships and expose deep-rooted emotions, delivering a moving story of love, loss, and sacrifice."
　　　　　　　　　　　　　　　　　　　　—*Booklist Reviews*

"Peeling back the layers that surround an irreversible, life-altering secret, this novel weaves a complex and heartbreaking story about lies and love, forgiveness and family. Written from alternating perspectives of the different family members over more than two decades, the deeply developed voices will bring tears and awe, settling snugly into the heart and mind. It's a reminder that love is always forgiving."　　　　　　　　　　　—*RT Book Reviews*

"Where Loigman excels is in capturing the time period—1950s Brooklyn. She draws gender roles accurately and nails the way family members, especially parents and children, inadvertently pierce one another with careless comments or subtle looks. As the story unfolds, we are reminded of how a split-second decision can reverberate for decades, even for generations. The real strength of Loigman's debut effort is her characters, to whom you find your loyalty shifting as the story unfolds."　　　　　　　—*The Jerusalem Post*

"In this spellbinding family saga, two women share a terrible secret that binds them for life—yet has the power to destroy everything they love most. With masterful control, Loigman boldly explores the anguish and joys of families united by blood and shared loyalties, even as they are divided by jealousy, passion, and mistrust. *The Two-Family House* is that rare, old-fashioned read you never want to end!"

—Cassandra King, national bestselling author of *The Sunday Wife*

"I read the short, gripping prologue, then immediately reread it to bask again in the delicious sense of mystery. *The Two-Family House* explores the impact of a split-second decision on the lives of two related families. I was fascinated by the intriguing blend of personalities as the characters experienced both tragedy and joy, inextricably bound together by blood and deception. With great skill and compassion, Loigman turns a story about complex family dynamics into a novel you won't be able to put down."

—Diane Chamberlain, *New York Times* and international bestselling author

"In *The Two-Family House*, young sisters-in-law are thrown together in a single home, where their children live as near siblings in what—on the surface—seems like an ideal life. Loigman plumbs the hidden world beneath the happy faces with insight, honesty, and compassion, and in doing so explores universal truths about family, love, and loss. I will certainly be giving a copy of this utterly charming novel to my own dearest sister-in-law."

—Meg Waite Clayton, author of *The Wednesday Sisters* and
*The Race for Paris*

"Two families, both living in one house, drive an exquisitely written novel of love, alliances, the messiness of life, and long-buried secrets. Loigman's debut is just shatteringly wonderful and I can't wait to see what she does next."

—Caroline Leavitt, *New York Times* bestselling author
of *Is This Tomorrow* and *Pictures of You*

## ALSO BY LYNDA COHEN LOIGMAN

*The Two-Family House*

# THE WARTIME SISTERS

## LYNDA COHEN LOIGMAN

ST. MARTIN'S GRIFFIN
NEW YORK

Published in the United States by St. Martin's Griffin, an imprint of St. Martin's Publishing Group

THE WARTIME SISTERS. Copyright © 2019 by Lynda Cohen Loigman. All rights reserved. Printed in the United States of America. For information, address St. Martin's Publishing Group, 120 Broadway, New York, NY 10271.

www.stmartins.com

Designed by Omar Chapa

The Library of Congress Cataloging-in-Publication Data is available upon request.

ISBN 978-1-250-14070-8 (hardcover)
ISBN 978-1-250-14072-2 (ebook)
ISBN 978-1-250-14071-5 (trade paperback)

Our books may be purchased in bulk for promotional, educational, or business use. Please contact your local bookseller or the Macmillan Corporate and Premium Sales Department at 1-800-221-7945, extension 5442, or by email at MacmillanSpecialMarkets@macmillan.com.

First St. Martin's Griffin Edition: March 2020

10  9  8  7  6  5  4  3  2

*For Bob, Ellie, and Charlie*

# Acknowledgments

Since the publication of my first novel in 2016, my world has expanded in ways I never could have imagined. I have met so many brilliant and generous people—not only in person, but through the magic of social media. It is an extraordinary thing, this book life that so many of us have chosen, and I will forever stand in awe of how it manages to forge friendships based on nothing more than a mutual love of the written word.

Thank you to my agent, Marly Rusoff, for her insight, her guidance, and her belief in my stories. Thanks to her partner, Michael Radulescu, for all of his support.

Thank you to my editor, Jennifer Weis, for encouraging me to dig deeper; to Sylvan Creekmore for her tireless assistance; and to the entire team at St. Martin's who brought *The Wartime Sisters* to life: Jen Enderlin, Lisa Senz, Brant Janeway, Jordan Hanley, Jessica Preeg, Jessica Katz, Sallie Lotz, and Olga Grlic.

Thank you to Kathleen Carter for her advocacy, her friendship, and her patience. Thank you to Ann-Marie Nieves for her marketing genius and positive energy.

Special thanks to Alex MacKenzie, the curator of the Springfield Armory National Historic Site, for his invaluable assistance.

Thank you to all of Alex's colleagues at the armory and also to Cliff McCarthy of the Springfield Museums.

Booksellers like Pamela Klinger-Horn make all the difference in the world. Thank you to all of the folks at Excelsior Bay Books in Excelsior, Minnesota, and to everyone at the following local bookstores: Scattered Books in Chappaqua, New York; The Village Bookstore in Pleasantville, New York; and Arcade Booksellers in Rye, New York.

Thank you to all the librarians, especially the folks at the Chappaqua library.

Warm thanks to everyone at the Jewish Book Council and to all of those who welcomed me to their communities through their festivals and author events.

I am so grateful to my fellow writers for their wisdom and inspiration. Warmest of thanks to these and so many more: Jenna Blum, Jamie Brenner, Jenny Brown, Jillian Cantor, Fiona Davis, Camille DeMaio, Abby Fabiaschi, Brenda Janowitz, Pam Jenoff, Susan Kleinman, Sally Koslow, Mary Kubica, Greer Macallister, Kristina McMorris, Louise Miller, Annabel Monaghan, Amy Poeppel, Alyson Richman, Susie Schnall, and Lauren Willig.

I owe so much of the success of my first book to the kindness of strangers who have now become friends. From the very beginning, Andrea Peskind Katz of Great Thoughts, Great Readers has been my cheerleader. Thank you to all the GTGR administrators and readers for their enthusiasm. A million thanks also to Robin Kall Homonoff and everyone at Reading with Robin, who have gone above and beyond to make me feel included in the bookish universe. Thank you to the Tall Poppy Writers for all of their support.

Thank you to the readers, the bloggers, the reviewers, and the bookstagrammers—too many to name, too wonderful for words.

There is no one more deserving of my gratitude than Elisabeth Bassin, whose special blend of brilliance, extrasensory perception, and editing prowess helped to make this book better than

I ever thought it could be. Special thanks also to Stephanie Marcus for her natural storytelling talent and attention to detail.

To my family and my friends, thank you for indulging me in my sophomore effort. I am so grateful to have all of you in my life.

This book is for Bob, for Ellie, and for Charlie. They are my heart.

Were half the power, that fills the world with terror,
Were half the wealth bestowed on camps and courts,
Given to redeem the human mind from error,
There were no need of arsenals or forts.

—*"The Arsenal at Springfield" by Henry Wadsworth Longfellow, 1845*


They split each other open like nuts.

—*"Sisters" by P. K. Paige, 1946*

# PART ONE

# Ruth

Brooklyn, New York (1919–1932)

Ruth was three years old when her sister was born. Like most first-born children, Ruth assumed her younger sibling would be a miniature version of herself. She would have straight hair, brown eyes, and a soft, gentle voice. She would love books and numbers, and the two of them would be inseparable.

It didn't take long for Ruth to realize her mistake.

When Ruth's mother felt up to it, she invited a small group of friends and relatives to the apartment. Packed into the small front room, nibbling on *kichel* and sipping glasses of tea, the visitors stared at the baby like tourists in a museum. "What do you call the color of those curls? Reddish like that—isn't there a name for it? And my God, those eyes! Who knew eyes could be so blue. *Keinehora*, Florence!" one of the cousins shouted. "You've finally got yourself a beauty!"

Ruth's mother was too distracted to notice the pitying looks her older daughter received from the downstairs neighbors. But Ruth had a glimmer of what the "finally" meant.

That evening, Ruth complained to her father about the fuss everyone made. He patted her head and told her not to worry.

"This is life, *mameleh*. People like babies. When babies grow up, people lose interest."

"When I was born, did they all say I was beautiful too?"

"Abso-lutely," he answered. "Such a *kvestion!*" Her father's accent was more noticeable when he was nervous or excited. It was especially conspicuous, Ruth knew, when he lied.

**To six-year-old Ruth's great disappointment, there was nothing** that Millie hated more than being read to. She covered her ears with her short, chubby fingers and held her breath dramatically until Ruth was silent. When Ruth expressed her dismay at her sister's tantrums, her mother brushed it off. "Not everyone is a bookworm like you are," she said.

When they were older, Millie would wait by the windows of their apartment, watching for activity on the sidewalk below. As soon as the neighborhood girls started their games of hopscotch or jump rope, Millie bolted out the door and ran down the steps to join them. It didn't matter that Ruth had just picked a puzzle for them to put together or that Millie had promised to play house with her after that. While Ruth sulked in her bedroom, her mother gave her some advice. "If you can't learn to let your sister be, the two of you will never get along."

The fact was, the two girls had little in common. Ruth liked to be early for school each day, but Millie dawdled in the mornings and made them both late. Ruth kept her half of their bedroom neat, while Millie's side was littered with paper dolls and crayons. With a different girl, such flaws might have drawn greater attention, but with Millie, no one seemed to notice or care. Their mother tidied the bedroom without a word of complaint, and no matter how late Millie was when she walked into her classroom, the elementary school teacher always marked her on time.

The sisters had opposite temperaments too—something it took Ruth longer to comprehend. Ruth was the steady one, disciplined and composed. She had always been proud of the way she could control her emotions, but eventually, she was made to understand that this wasn't a quality everyone admired. She learned this lesson at her great-aunt Edna's funeral, on a cloudy April morning just after she'd turned ten. Aunt Edna was their father's aunt—a woman they saw just a few times a year. She appeared mostly at holidays and the occasional Sabbath dinner. Ruth was sorry that she had died, but she didn't know the woman well enough to truly mourn her passing. Ruth sat quietly in the synagogue, half listening to the rabbi's words and wishing she'd been allowed to bring one of her books from home to pass the time.

Millie, on the other hand, was utterly bereft. Sandwiched between their mother and Ruth, the seven-year-old listened to the eulogy with the kind of concentration Ruth didn't know Millie could muster. When the rabbi spoke about Edna's childhood in Poland, Millie's sniffles turned to sobs and her whole body shook. Their mother tried to soothe her, but there was no calming the girl. Soon, her cries were so loud that they drowned out the rabbi's voice.

It was Ruth who took Millie by the hand and led her out of the chapel. It was Ruth who wiped Millie's eyes with the handkerchief from her skirt pocket and Ruth who made her blow her nose to stop the snot from running down her face. As they waited together in the synagogue's drafty vestibule, Ruth asked her sister why she was so upset.

"Why do you keep crying? You barely knew her."

"Because she's dead," Millie bawled. "She was a little girl like me, and then she got old and *died*."

"But she lived a long life. That's what the rabbi said."

"I don't care how long it was. I'm never getting old."

"You have to grow up sometime." Ruth hadn't meant for the words to come out sounding the way they did—more like a threat than a friendly observation.

Millie slid to the opposite end of the hard, wooden bench and stuck out her tongue. "Maybe *you* do," she said, "but I don't."

When the service was over and all the relatives gathered together at Edna's apartment, Ruth thought someone might thank her for calming the disruption her sister created at the synagogue. But instead, it was Millie who garnered all the praise. Mourners brought her plates of cookies and thick slices of challah, clucking to their mother about what a sensitive and sympathetic child she was. No one looked at Ruth or offered her a plate; no one complimented her quick thinking. On her way to the bathroom, she overheard a trio of women talking about her. "The older sister is a real cold fish," one of them said. Only later did Ruth understand what the term really meant. At the time, she'd only shivered and buttoned her cardigan over her dress.

**The more responsible Ruth proved to be, the more it was held** against her. Her exceptional report cards created such elevated expectations that when she received an A minus, her parents seemed disappointed. If she ever lost a hair ribbon or a button on her dress, her mother threw up her hands and complained about the waste. Meanwhile, Millie's poor grades were never discussed. And when Millie lost two library books—*books she hadn't even read*—her mother paid to replace them without a word of reproach. The fee was not inconsequential, and there was little to spare in the Kaplan household. But when Ruth grumbled about the cost, her mother defended her younger sister. "No one is perfect, Ruth. People make mistakes."

The discrepancy in treatment shaped Ruth's childhood. Years later, when she tried to explain it to her husband, she struggled for a long time to find the right words. Though Ruth's tiny transgressions were few and far between, they never seemed to escape her mother's notice. Any misstep Ruth made was a short, shallow wrinkle on an otherwise smooth and pristine tablecloth. Millie's slipups, by contrast, were like a full glass of burgundy tipped over onto clean white damask. To their mother's discerning eye, Ruth's wrinkles were conspicuous. But her sister's stains were overlooked and hastily covered—anything so that the meal could continue being served.

**The girls' teenage years brought more hurtful comparisons.** Even before she entered high school, Millie's curves and auburn curls turned men's heads on their block in Brooklyn. But with her pin-straight hair and even straighter figure, the only heads Ruth turned belonged to the balding, middle-aged men from her father's pinochle game. "Tell Morris we'll see him on Tuesday," they said.

By the time Millie turned thirteen, more than a few older boys had asked her for dates. To keep them at bay, their father enacted an ironclad rule: neither of his daughters was allowed to date before turning sixteen. While the rule was supposedly meant for both girls, Ruth's social life never required its enforcement.

One Friday afternoon, a few months after Ruth's sixteenth birthday, her mother was busier than usual in the kitchen. A pot of mushroom barley soup simmered on the stove, filling the room with a rich, earthy scent. Two fresh loaves of challah had been set out to cool. As Ruth did her homework at the small kitchen table, she watched her mother pull an apple cake from the oven.

"You're making an awful lot of food for just us," Ruth observed.

"We're having company tonight—Mrs. Rabinowitz and her grandson are coming." Ruth's mother looked away when she made the announcement, busying herself with the chicken she had left on the counter. She seasoned the skin with salt and pepper, all the while taking pains to ignore Ruth's fretful gaze. Though she had tried her best to make the news sound unremarkable, there was no way to disguise its significance.

"Her grandson?" Ruth questioned, chewing nervously on the back of her pencil.

"Mrs. Rabinowitz says he's a very bright boy."

"Well, if his *grandmother* said so, he must be a genius."

"Don't be such a comedian," her mother snapped, slamming

the oven door shut. "Now, put away your books and help me set the table. They'll be here in an hour, and I want everything ready. You'll have time to change your dress after."

"Why do I have to change?"

A weary sigh escaped her mother's lips. "You'll put on the blue dress and a little bit of lipstick. It's not going to kill you to dress up for company."

Ruth was so out of sorts that she hadn't even noticed her sister entering the kitchen. "We're having company?" Millie asked. "Do I have to change too?"

Their mother shook her head. "Not you. Just your sister."

**Ruth hated to admit it, but the grandson was handsome. His** lightly tousled hair was just a fraction too long, in a way that appealed to mothers and daughters alike. His build was athletic, but not overly slim. Ruth learned that he would be graduating from high school in a few months and starting at City College in the fall.

"Walter is one of the top students in his class," Mrs. Rabinowitz crowed.

"Very impressive," Ruth's father replied. "What will you study?"

"Mathematics, sir."

"Ruth is terrific at math," Millie chimed in. "They let her skip ahead so she could take the hardest class."

"Calculus?" Walter asked.

Ruth felt the heat of the soup rise upward toward her cheeks. "Yes," she answered.

"She might have to take a college math course next year," Millie continued. "The principal even wrote a letter to our parents about it."

"That's great," Walter said, smiling at Ruth. "You know, you're the first girl I ever met whose eyes didn't glaze over when I mentioned my major. Most girls think math is boring."

"Not Ruth," Millie said. "She's a whiz."

When their mother got up to clear the soup bowls from the table, Walter stood too and offered to help. "Sit, sit," she insisted, shooing him back into his chair. "Ruth will help me."

As soon as they were safely on the other side of the swinging door, Ruth's mother almost threw the bowls into the sink. "I told you," she whispered. "See how polite? And the two of you have so much in common."

"He does seem nice," Ruth admitted, smoothing her hair. Despite her initial misgivings, she felt herself being drawn into her mother's hopeful mood. "Should I go back and talk to him?"

"Yes. Send Millie in here to help me serve the chicken."

Later, it was decided that Walter and Ruth should walk to the drugstore to buy ice cream for the apple cake. "The cake isn't nearly as good without the ice cream," Millie said. "And the drugstore isn't far—it's just down the block."

"Of course," Walter agreed, making sure to hold the door for Ruth as they left the apartment.

She was delighted when they first set out. The evening air was warm, and the light from the streetlamps flickered softly on the sidewalk. But once they were away from her parents and Walter's grandmother, Ruth felt a not-so-subtle shift in the young man's mood. He became increasingly agitated, and his smile disappeared.

She tried to make conversation. "Are you excited to graduate?"

"I guess so. I don't know. Look, can I be honest?" Walter tugged at his shirt collar as if he were choking. "I don't want you to get the wrong idea."

Ruth's head began to spin with unfamiliar confusion. What was he talking about? Had she done something to offend him? She didn't answer right away, but Walter kept talking.

"I don't usually let my grandmother drag me with her to these dinners, but she can be awfully pushy sometimes, you know? And your mom's a good cook, so it wasn't half bad. But I don't want you to think that I'm asking you for a date."

Ruth bit her lower lip to keep it from trembling. She forced herself to answer so Walter wouldn't sense her disappointment. "Don't be silly," she lied. "I wasn't expecting anything like that."

"Phew." Walter exhaled. "I'm glad we understand each other. No offense or anything—you're just not my type. Of course, I figure I'm not your type either. From the way your sister was talking, you probably want to marry one of those Ivy League guys."

"Probably," Ruth agreed, suddenly exhausted.

On the way back from the drugstore, she stopped worrying what he thought of her. There was no way to change the outcome of the evening, so she decided to learn what she could from the humiliation. "Just out of curiosity," she decided to ask, "what kind of girl would you say *is* your type?"

Walter wrinkled his forehead and clasped his hands in front of his face. He leaned forward slightly, lost in his own thoughts. "Good question," he said as if she'd just won a prize. "My type is a girl who appreciates me, someone who likes to have fun and isn't too serious. I don't want her to be stupid, but I don't want to be with someone too intellectual."

"You mean, you don't want a girl you think is smarter than you?"

"Exactly!" Walter said, oblivious to her sarcasm. Ruth felt her hope melt away, like the ice cream in the paper bag she carried. "Of course, there is one more thing . . ." His voice trailed off.

"What's that?" Ruth asked, too far gone to care.

"It sure wouldn't hurt if she looked like your sister."

# Millie

Millie knew something was wrong as soon as they returned. There had been a quiet confidence in Ruth's bearing when she had set out for the drugstore, but when she got back to the apartment, the glimmer was gone. Millie watched, unsmiling, as Walter inhaled his dessert. When his plate was clean, he wiped his lips with his napkin, put his hand on his grandmother's arm, and told her it was time for them to head home. "I have a paper due on Monday that I have to get started. Thank you so much for the meal, Mr. and Mrs. Kaplan," he said. "Good luck with calculus next year, Ruth."

Puzzled, her mother turned to Mrs. Rabinowitz, but the old woman seemed equally taken aback. She lifted her shoulders upward into a shrug and raised her eyebrows as if to say, *I have no idea*. Ruth was the only one at the table who didn't seem surprised. After Walter left, she went into the bedroom and shut the door behind her.

Grandmother and grandson exited so quickly that Millie's father didn't even have time to get up from his seat. "Vat happened?" he asked, slapping his open palm on the table. "The little *pisher* bolted like a spooked horse!"

"Shush, Morris, please. Ruth can hear you." Millie's mother

cleared the plates with anxious efficiency. "Maybe my cooking didn't agree with him."

"Bah!" her father said. "Did you see how much he ate? It's a miracle he didn't choke!"

"Too bad he didn't," Millie muttered under her breath.

Her mother gasped and teetered on her feet, sending one of the plates she had been holding to the floor with a crash.

"Do you want to tempt the Evil Eye? God forbid *anyone* should choke in this house!"

"There's no such thing as the Evil Eye!"

"Don't raise your voice to your mother like that!"

They were all yelling now, bickering like children, despite the fact that Ruth was the one who should have been the most upset. The noise drew Ruth out from behind her closed door. When she saw the commotion, she skirted past the broken plate, retrieved the broom and dustpan from the back of the hall closet, and began to sweep up the shards. Her diligence shamed the rest of them into silence. Ruth had always been the best of them at cleaning up messes.

"I'm sorry, Ruth." Their mother was the first to speak. "I thought for sure . . . this time, after what Mrs. Rabinowitz told me . . ."

Her father shook his head. "He was a putz," he lamented.

Millie chimed in with her own observations, hoping to show her sister some support. "I didn't like him one bit, Ruthie. He wasn't nice, and he wasn't good-looking either."

"That's too bad," Ruth said coolly. Her words came out jagged, like the fragments she swept so neatly off the floor. "He certainly liked you. Apparently, you're just his type of girl."

Millie's stomach lurched. Ruth might as well have struck her with the handle of the broom.

"What are you talking about?"

"Did you have to keep talking about my math classes?"

"I wanted him to know that you have the same interests. I was trying to help!"

"Well, it didn't help at all. You made me sound like the dullest girl in the world! *'Ruth loves calculus, she studies all day.'* What kind of boy wants to ask a girl like that for a date? Meanwhile, you sat there and batted your eyes at him. No wonder he liked you better than me!"

"Batted my eyes? I barely even looked at him!"

"Well, he was looking at you!"

"That isn't my fault!"

"*Enough!*" Their mother's voice rang out over their shrieking, stunning the girls into temporary silence. After their father made them sit, the sisters glared at each other from across the dining room table. The evening had started with such high hopes, Millie thought—with silverware that gleamed and freshly pressed napkins, with a promising young man and a hint of romance for her older sister. But now it was over; all of that was gone. The silverware was sticky and the napkins full of wrinkles. The young man was indifferent—Ruth would not see him again.

"Of all the boys to fight over," their mother began, "that one isn't worth the aggravation. Believe me."

"I'm not fighting over him," Millie insisted. "I never wanted anything to do with him!"

Ruth crossed her arms over her chest and glared. Her rage was so fierce that it made Millie's eyes fill with tears. "*I didn't!*" Millie whined. "Stop saying I did! Mama, make her stop looking at me like that!" She lowered her head onto the table and sobbed. Why did Ruth always blame her when something went wrong? She had spent the entire evening complimenting her sister. She had thought Walter would be impressed, not put off or intimidated.

"Shush now, *mameleh,*" their mother said, patting Millie's back. Then she turned to Ruth. "I was sitting here the whole night, just the same as you. Your sister didn't do anything to get that boy's attention. Whenever she spoke, it was to say something nice about you. He must have said something on your walk to make you so upset."

"He said I wasn't his type. That I should marry an Ivy League boy."

Their father grunted. "He's not so wrong about that."

"Then he said he wanted a girl who wasn't so serious. And that he preferred a girl who looked like Millie."

Millie's head began to ache, her temples to throb. There was a long stretch of silence before her father spoke up. "Millie can't help the things the boy said. It isn't her fault his parents raised a schmuck."

Ruth uncrossed her arms and unclenched her jaw. "I know," she admitted, her voice softer than before. "I have to get used to it. It's just the way it is." She got up from the table and went back to sweeping. Her dustpan was almost full by the time Millie raised her head.

"What does that mean?" she wanted to know. The skin around Millie's eyes was swollen and raw.

Ruth didn't look up. She searched the floor for stray shards, for any broken bits she might have missed. "It means people notice you, but they never notice me. They like you better, they treat you differently, and there's nothing I can do about it. Everyone thinks you're special. Everyone goes out of their way to be nice to you."

"Not everyone," Millie said, her voice low and miserable. "Not my own sister."

# Millie

**Springfield, Massachusetts (June 1942)**

If it weren't for the fence, she would have thought she was in the wrong place—the view from Byers Street made the armory look more like a park than anything else. But the wrought iron fence had an unmistakably military air. It was at least ten feet high, pointed at the top, ominous and impenetrable. The fence ran the full length of the block, and as Millie turned the corner onto State Street, it seemed to go on forever.

Millie walked slowly so that Michael could keep up on his tiny, two-year-old legs. Although the walk was just a little over a mile, Millie wished she had splurged on a taxi at the train station. She felt conspicuous dragging her shabby suitcase up this half-empty sidewalk. There were no fruit sellers, no pickle men; there was no shouting of any kind. The silence made her uneasy. Back home in Brooklyn, the sidewalks were always crowded—no one ever noticed if an unfamiliar woman walked by. But here, the people she passed gave her strange looks and stared. By the time she turned onto Federal Street, she could feel a line of sweat running down her back. She smoothed her curls, trying to neaten the ones that spilled out from underneath her hat. She needed a visit to the beauty parlor, but there had been so little time before leaving, and she hadn't wanted to spend the money. She knew Ruth would notice.

Ruth had always taken note of Millie's shortcomings—every misspelled word in her school essays, every pimple on her chin. Surely she would see that Millie's hair needed trimming, surely her eyes would linger on the tear in Millie's stocking, and without question, she would notice the faded hat on Millie's head. It was the same hat Millie had worn when the sisters last saw each other five years ago—the hat Millie had purchased for their parents' unexpected funeral, and the same one she'd worn again a few weeks later at her wedding. It was, then and now, the only hat that Millie owned, and the fact that she hadn't been able to afford a replacement would be one more reminder of how much more successful Ruth's life had been than her own. Millie imagined the face Ruth might make when she recognized the hat: the tiny lift of her eyebrows and the pucker of her lips. Millie sighed and kept walking.

When they saw the guards at the main entrance, Michael cried for Millie to pick him up. Behind the pillared entry, a stately brick building ran the length of the entire block. At its center was a tiered double balcony with wide white columns and a painted railing. The building's effect was more collegiate than military. If not for the guards and the armory seals, Millie might have thought it was a university. She balanced Michael on her hip and greeted the guard.

Only after he found her name on the list was she able to breathe. She had left her home on the strength of the letter in her pocket, signed in her sister's dutiful hand. But when the man with the clipboard checked off her name with his pen, her lungs flooded with a relief she had not known she had been seeking. There would be no returning to Brooklyn—no more nights of uncertainty. She had left behind the noise, the crowds, and the piteous glances from the morning milkman. The guard made it official.

"I'll call up and let Mrs. Blum know you're here," he told her.

"Call up where?"

The guard pointed to the building behind them. "Administration. Mrs. Blum works in the payroll office."

"She does?"

"Yes, ma'am. We have a note to call when you arrive."

Ruth hadn't mentioned her job in her most recent letter, or in any of the letters that had come before it. Of course, there had been fewer than a dozen since the sisters last saw each other, and half of those had been mailed in the past six months—after the United States entered the war, and after Ruth learned that Millie's husband had enlisted. Ruth had written to say how pleased she was to hear of Lenny's decision. Wasn't it wonderful, she wrote, that they both had brave husbands who were fighting for their country?

Millie had resisted the urge to write back her true thoughts: that Ruth's husband, Arthur, wasn't "fighting" at all, and that he was, in fact, the farthest thing from brave. Yes, his degrees were impressive. But hadn't Arthur studied so hard, in part, to avoid having to fight? Hadn't he told her parents his calculated plan all those years ago at the kitchen table during one of their dinners? He would study hard and become an officer. The wars to come would be wars of science and technology, he insisted, and brains like his would be needed. He never intended to dirty his hands. And now, Millie knew, Arthur spent his days at the armory in laboratories and development meetings, perfecting the weapons he would never have to fire.

Of course, Millie hadn't written any of that. She wrote that Lenny was missing in action, that Brooklyn was becoming unbearable without him. She enclosed a photograph of Michael as well. *He is the sweetest little boy,* she wrote. A few months later, Millie was forced to write the unthinkable. *Lenny is gone.*

Ruth wrote back quickly, a letter filled with more practical suggestions than condolences. *We have an extra room for you and Michael. You can live with us and find a job at the armory. They need people desperately, as they are now running the factories twenty-four hours a day.*

It didn't take long for Millie to make up her mind. Her parents were dead, and she had no real friends left in Brooklyn. She needed a job, and her son needed a family. She would go to Springfield, she would work at the armory, and somehow, she would find a way to mend what had broken between her and her sister. What was it her mother used to say? *A seam sewn crooked is still better than a hole.*

After a few minutes, Ruth emerged from the building. Her dress, though cut in the latest fashion, hung aimlessly on her slender frame. Initially, she was more focused on her nephew than her sister. She tried to take Michael's hand, but he pulled it away and crammed his face up against Millie's shoulder.

"He's shy," Millie apologized, accepting Ruth's dry peck on her cheek. "Michael," she whispered into his hair, "this is your aunt Ruth."

"It's only natural," Ruth said. "He doesn't know me yet."

*You could have known him if you wanted to,* Millie thought. *If you ever visited us in Brooklyn, or if you ever invited us here.* It was unsettling to see her sister in this place, so far away from their childhood home. Millie motioned to the trees that surrounded them. "It's pretty here. So quiet too. I wasn't expecting it to look this way."

Ruth pointed to the other side of Federal Street. "The shops—that's what we call the manufacturing buildings—are across the street. Right now, we have more than ten thousand civilians working here." Ruth had always liked explaining things, especially to her younger sister. Nothing gave her more satisfaction than knowing all the answers. "But the officers and their families live on this side of the street, in Armory Square. Come, I'll show you."

Millie's head buzzed with the strangeness of it all. She had never heard of Springfield before her sister's move. The only places she knew in Massachusetts were Boston and Cape Cod. Now that she was here, everything was unfamiliar and unexpected. The square, for one thing—two football fields wide, with its manicured lawn, ancient trees, and tennis courts—how could she have known that the armory would be like this? She had pictured noise and dust, belching chimneys and bad-tempered foremen—not manicured shrubbery and sweet-scented breezes.

The perimeter of the square was dotted with houses and small buildings. When they reached the northwest corner, they stopped in front of a mansard-style home with a patterned slate roof. Two sets of stairs led to twin front doors, shaded under a generous porch that ran the length of the house.

"Is all this yours?" Millie asked. Her fingers tightened into fists as she lowered Michael to the ground. She had never imagined that her sister would be living in such an elegant place. *You have so much, and you never offered us anything. Only the one baby gift when Michael was born.*

"Just half. We're the door on the left, and another family has the right side."

Millie didn't say a word when Ruth showed her the fireplaces, the separate dining room, and the updated kitchen. She was silent when Ruth led her up the sweeping staircase and showed her the brightly lit bedroom she and Michael would share. She was so shaken that she forgot to be embarrassed when Ruth offered to help unpack her suitcase.

The clothes she had brought took up almost no room in the closet. "When your other things come, there'll be plenty of room," Ruth assured her. "It was smart of you to send them."

For the first time since their reunion, Millie found the strength to look her sister in the eye. "I didn't send anything," she said. "This is all we have."

A glimmer of understanding swept across Ruth's face, but she offered no real sympathy. "You have all you need," she insisted, "and once you have your job, you can always buy more."

"Yes," Millie agreed, choking on the words. She took off her gloves and placed them on the dresser before reaching up to unpin the hat from her head. Once the hat and gloves were off, she felt Ruth's stare last a bit too long.

"You still have the ring," Ruth murmured, surprised.

"Of course I do," Millie answered. She lifted her hand and glanced at the stone, a shimmering opal cabochon, round and iridescent, surrounded by small diamonds on a thick platinum band. It was too elegant for her, for the kind of life she led. She knew full well that she had no business wearing it. There were so many times she had been tempted to sell it, but it had belonged to her great-grandmother, and she hadn't wanted to part with it. She was glad she had it now, glad her sister would see that no matter how little she had, she had not yet sunk low enough to be forced to sell the heirloom. In keeping it, Millie thought, she had kept a small part of her dignity.

Ruth's eyes traveled slowly from Millie's hand to her head and back again. Her lips turned downward, forming a hard, familiar line.

"You need a haircut," Ruth said, unflinching. "And for goodness' sake, Millie, you've got to get yourself a new hat."

# Ruth

She and Arthur had set out for Massachusetts the day after Millie's wedding. For the entirety of the ride, the twins slept and Ruth cried. She cried for her parents, who had died a month before, together on a highway, speeding home to their daughters. She cried for all the words that had been left unsaid between them—all the *I love you*s that had never made it past her lips. She cried for her girls, who would never know their grandparents, who would never remember the smell of their grandfather's pipe or the taste of their grandmother's chicken soup. When she and Arthur arrived in Springfield, the buildings were too far apart, the streets were too quiet, and the grass was too green. The strangeness of the sights stalled her tears for a while, but when she walked into the house in Armory Square, she began to cry all over again. This time, she knew, they were tears of relief. *I can start over here,* Ruth thought. *Here, where no one knows me. Where no one knows my sister. Where no one will ask why I left her behind.*

In Brooklyn, Ruth hadn't paid much attention to her appearance. But in Springfield, she asked the other officers' wives where to get her hair done. She bought her dresses on sale from the shops they suggested and took note of the hats and the shoes that they wore. When Arthur asked if she wanted to take classes at the local college, she shook her head. "I want to settle in here first," she said. Her husband was surprised, but he didn't press. When Ruth met the other young wives at the armory, she didn't talk about the degree she had been pursuing at Brooklyn College. She didn't mention her studies or the accounting classes that had once consumed her thoughts. She put away her textbooks and bought women's magazines from the newsstand. As she fanned them out on her coffee table, she could hear her mother's voice. *You know, if you read a magazine every once in a while, like your sister, you'd have something to talk about with the other girls.*

Ruth invited other young mothers on walks to Forest Park. While they strolled through the grounds and walked their toddlers through the zoo, she let the others take the lead and steer the conversations. Some complained about their husbands, and others boasted about their children. Some asked for her recipes and others for her opinion on sink cleaners and cough syrups.

Despite Ruth's best efforts, however, real friendship eluded her. If she mentioned a book—no matter how well known—she was met with blank stares. After the war began in Europe, Ruth sometimes mentioned front-page articles from the newspaper. Wasn't everyone reading the same things these days? Wasn't everyone curious about when the United States might get involved? They were living at an *armory*, for goodness' sake! But most of the women didn't like to discuss it, and her attempts at serious conversation were met with uncomfortable silences. It wasn't long before Ruth found herself almost as overlooked as she had been in Brooklyn. Until she met Lillian Walsh.

Lillian moved to the armory in the winter of 1940, when her husband took over as the new commanding officer. On the day they moved in, Ruth heard the murmurings—the new colonel was tall and handsome; his wife blond and slim, like Carole Lombard. The day after their arrival, Lillian flooded one of the tennis courts and invited all the officers' families to an ice-skating party. Her four children set up tables around the makeshift rink's perimeter and served cups of hot chocolate to the gathering crowd. By the end of the party, Lillian knew everyone's name.

"Mrs. Blum," Lillian observed with a welcoming smile, "I think my youngest daughter must be the same age as your girls. Margaret just turned four."

"You're right, Mrs. Walsh. Alice and Louise are four years old as well."

"Four going on forty, my mother would have said. Please, call me Lillian."

"And I'm Ruth. If my mother were still alive, she would have said the same about the twins."

"You lost your mother too? Then you know how it feels. I just can't wrap my head around the idea that my children will never know her."

Ruth didn't answer, but she wondered how it could be that a woman she'd just met described her own feelings so accurately. After three years in Springfield, no one had bothered to ask Ruth much about her family. At first, she had been grateful—the last thing she wanted to discuss was her past. She had told no one of her parents' accident or her sister back in Brooklyn. But Lillian's small show of interest made Ruth realize how lonely she had been. She pulled her coat tighter against the winter chill and let herself imagine what it might be like to have this woman as her friend.

"I hope you'll come over to the house next Tuesday," Lillian said. "I was thinking of hosting a meeting to put together packages for the children overseas. They need clothing and supplies, warm coats and food. I have some other ideas too—get-togethers, concerts, maybe a book club."

Ruth did her best not to let her smile grow too wide. There was so much she wanted to say, but she didn't want to scare Lillian off by sounding desperate. "I'll be there," she said.

·     ·     ·

**After the skating party, Lillian began holding weekly meetings.**
She brought pianists in for concerts and held afternoon book clubs
once a month. All of the women wanted to be included, even the
ones who hadn't read a book in years. Lillian always set out her
best china cups and bowls of fresh flowers from the armory greenhouses. Everyone agreed that she was a flawless hostess—her first
Christmas party was such a success that people were still talking
about it twelve months later.

Perhaps that was why she insisted on having the party the
following year, even with Pearl Harbor so fresh in everyone's
minds. Some people argued that the festivities should be canceled,
but Lillian Walsh convinced them that social gatherings were important for keeping up morale.

The scent of fresh pine greeted Ruth and Arthur even before
they made their way inside the Walshes' home. The tree in the foyer
was at least ten feet high, and garlands of evergreen were wrapped
around the bannister and tacked above the doorways. Ruth took a
crystal mug of eggnog from the dining room table before she noticed that all the other women held glasses of champagne. The cin-
namon from the foam got caught in her throat after her first sip, and
she began to cough. Arthur was still patting her back when Lillian
and her husband came over to greet them. Lillian's ivory cocktail
dress was elegant and festive without being frivolous.

After Ruth stopped coughing, Colonel Walsh turned his full
attention to her. His height was intimidating, his gaze steady and
serious.

"My wife tells me you studied accounting," he said.

"Yes, at Brooklyn College, but I didn't finish my degree."

"Mrs. Blum, I'm not going to mince words. The armory has
orders to increase production immediately. By this time next year,
we expect to have over ten thousand employees. Those people
won't work if they don't get paid on time."

"Sir?"

"I'd like you to work in our payroll office. We need people with your accounting experience."

Ruth was flattered and surprised, but she told the colonel she'd have to think about it. She was even more surprised when Lillian showed up at her door with a freshly baked pound cake the next morning. Lillian's cheeks were red from the cold, but the cake was still warm.

"Patrick says they'll be rationing sugar soon," she explained. "I thought I'd better get my baking done while I still can." Ruth invited her in, and the two of them sat in the front room, drinking coffee and picking at their slices.

Over the course of her life, Ruth had known plenty of other women (her own mother included) who were just as determined and just as capable as Lillian Walsh. But she had never known anyone as patient. Ruth's mother would have told her to either take the job or stop kvetching, but Lillian wanted to understand what was driving Ruth's reluctance.

Together, they weighed the pros and cons. Ruth told Lillian how much she craved the stimulation that the work would offer, especially since the twins would be in school soon. She confessed her fear of what the other wives might say.

"Don't worry about them," Lillian assured her. "If I hear one bad word, believe me, I'll take care of it. And I'm going to make sure our meetings start at four o'clock from now on. The morning shift ends at three, and that way *all* working women can attend."

"But no one else works. You don't have to do that—"

"It's already done. Besides, we have other women coming to the meetings now—not just officers' wives."

Ruth shook her head. "I'm still not sure," she mumbled.

"What else is bothering you? Tell me, please."

"It's just that our family is already *different* from the others living here. I don't want to alienate myself further, that's all."

"Do you mean because you're Jewish? Ruth, no one here

cares. The only thing that matters is that we're all on the same side fighting for our country."

Despite Lillian's reassurances, Ruth wasn't convinced. The other wives had been cordial, but she had never felt like one of them. Some belonged to clubs where she knew Jews weren't welcome. Others gave her blank stares when she mentioned the name of her favorite Jewish bakery.

Still, she reminded herself, she felt no more comfortable with the women from her synagogue. When they first arrived in Springfield, she and Arthur joined Congregation Beth El on Fort Pleasant Street. Ruth knew it was something her parents would have wanted, and she hoped that within its walls, listening to the familiar prayers, she would find the sense of belonging she so desperately craved. But no matter how many services she and Arthur attended, she never felt at home.

"You're meant to do something more than just taking care of your girls," Lillian told her. "I'm not suggesting that being a mother isn't important. But Alice and Louise will be in school soon. I know you, Ruth Blum—you'll go crazy if you stay at home reading magazines. You're one of the smartest women I know."

A few weeks later, Ruth couldn't remember how she had filled her days before accepting the position. The work came to her more naturally than anything she could remember. Most important, it occupied her mind so that she didn't have time for the unpleasant thoughts and worries that so often consumed her: the war, her parents' death. Her brother-in-law. Her sister.

**Before Ruth started working, Millie had written to say that her** husband had enlisted. Ruth read the letter three times before handing it over to Arthur. He had been sitting at the kitchen table, rubbing at the spots on his glasses with his handkerchief.

"Enlisting could be a good thing for Lenny," he said. "It's a steady job, at least, and a steady income too."

"Maybe," Ruth said.

"Who knows? It's possible that he could find real success in the service. He could move up through the ranks, become an officer, make a real career. An experience like that can have a profound impact."

"People don't change that much, Arthur, not even in war. Do you really think it's possible for that man to stick with anything?"

"I don't know, but maybe this is a chance to reconnect with your sister. Lenny will be overseas soon, if he isn't already, and Millie and the baby will be alone."

"Michael isn't a baby anymore," Ruth said softly. "He's two years old now."

"Exactly. He's part of your family. I think you should write back to her—not only a New Year's card but a real letter this time."

"I don't know what to say."

Arthur gave her shoulder an encouraging squeeze. "Once you start writing, the right words will come to you."

He was wrong—the words didn't come. It took two long days of staring at a blank piece of stationery before she was able to reply. There was so much she could not say, so much she'd hidden for too long. Eventually, she managed to eke out a few short paragraphs, which, compared to the annual holiday card she usually sent, read like a novel. But there was a silence behind her sentences she could not seem to fill. She wrote what she could—how pleased she and Arthur were to hear of Lenny's enlistment, how the sisters might have a fresh start. She signed it *Sincerely* and forced herself to drop it in the mailbox.

Millie's reply came the next week, three full pages, signed *With love*. She wrote mostly about Michael and enclosed a small black-and-white photo.

It was the photo that changed Ruth's mind. At only two years old, the boy was the absolute image of his grandfather. Michael had Morris's eyes, his chin and hairline. Ruth kept the photo in her nightstand drawer, by her bed.

Months passed, and the sisters continued their correspondence.

When Millie wrote to say that her husband was missing, Ruth couldn't shake the feeling that Lenny would return unharmed. She assumed that he would cheat death as easily as he cheated at cards. But later, when Millie wrote to say that Lenny was gone, regret settled in Ruth's chest and would not let go. If it hadn't been for her, Millie might not be a widow. If it hadn't been for her, Millie might never have married at all.

So, Ruth invited Millie to Springfield, hoping to ease her own heart. Perhaps spending time with her sister would lighten her burden. Perhaps holding her nephew's hand would loosen guilt's grip. Perhaps the reunion would be painless and forgiveness would flourish between them. Perhaps the darkest parts of her memories would fade until they were forgotten.

**On the day Millie was expected, Ruth couldn't focus at her desk.** The lists of names and shifts that always seemed to calm her blurred before her eyes until the numbers made no sense. The volume of her task had always been a comfort, an assurance of importance, a promise of productivity. But today when she saw the stacks of papers in front of her, she felt overwhelmed for the very first time. The longer she sat, the more fretful she became.

It was just after one o'clock when the guard called to say that her sister had arrived. Ruth's shift ended at three, but she had planned on leaving early. As she tidied her papers, uncertainty took hold. On her way down the stairs, she clutched the bannister too tightly.

Her sister was standing in the shade, pointing out a bird to the boy in her arms. From a distance, Millie still looked like an eighteen-year-old girl, the undisputed beauty of their Brooklyn neighborhood. But when Ruth drew closer, she saw someone else: a haggard young woman in an out-of-date suit, with bags under her eyes and curls that needed trimming. Millie's hat, Ruth recalled, had been bought for their parents' funeral. After years of use, it was threadbare and limp, but the color of the wool still matched Millie's eyes—navy blue with a tinge of green.

What was the proper etiquette for such a greeting? What should her first words be to a sister not seen for five long years? Ruth's breathing steadied only when she realized that Michael's grip around his mother's neck made an embrace between the two sisters almost impossible.

Her nephew was, by far, the bright spot of their reunion. He looked even more like her father in person than in the photo, and though he spoke very little, his presence was a comfort.

Ruth walked them through the square until they got to her house. Millie seemed stunned by all that she saw—the tennis courts, the trees, and the house most of all. When she admitted that all of her belongings were in the one battered suitcase, Ruth was forced to bite her lip in order to stop herself from crying. She knew her sister's marriage to Lenny had not provided the wealth and glamour their mother had predicted for her younger daughter so many years ago. But even with that knowledge, Ruth had been unprepared for the case's meager contents.

As Ruth watched her sister struggle to fight back tears, regret took hold of her. Ruth wanted to say she was sorry for the distance between them, for the time that had passed. She wanted to pick up her nephew and smother him with kisses. She was about to say the words she had been thinking in her head when Millie removed her gloves to reveal the ring on her left hand.

Ruth had assumed that the ring was gone—sold, perhaps, or traded to pay off one of Lenny's debts. The sight of it now, on her sister's slim finger, brought back the memories Ruth thought she had banished. She tried to swallow the bile, but it stuck in her throat until all the pain and frustration came rushing back in a torrent.

"You need a haircut," she said. "And for goodness' sake, Millie, you've got to get yourself a new hat."

# Ruth

## Brooklyn, New York (May 1934)

Ruth's blind date waited in the dimly lit hallway holding a potted plant with thick, glossy leaves. "It's a rubber plant," he explained, holding it out to her. "*Ficus elastica*. I didn't know what direction your windows faced, so this was the safest choice."

The plant blocked most of his head, so Ruth couldn't get a proper look at him. But behind the leaves, she sensed a stocky frame and thick glasses. When he handed her the pot, the fingers that brushed against hers were soft.

"I considered roses, but this will last much longer."

"Of course," Ruth agreed. He was the first of her dates to arrive with a plant, and though she would have preferred flowers, she kept her thoughts to herself. When she invited him inside to meet her parents, he introduced himself with confidence. He was five years older than she was, already a man.

Her father stood immediately to shake his hand, but her mother was less friendly, standing off to the side and staring at the plant. Arthur mentioned the name of the restaurant where he had made a reservation. "Are you sure you two want to go out?" Ruth's mother asked. "Don't you want to eat here?"

"Thank you, Mrs. Kaplan. That's a very kind invitation. But I was hoping to take Ruth out. I promise to have her home early."

"You can have her until late," Ruth's father joked. "Go, enjoy yourselves. No need to rush."

"But, Morris, I made a brisket," Ruth's mother said, frowning. "Maybe Arthur doesn't know I made a brisket for dinner."

"*Mama*," Ruth interjected, trying to keep her tone light, "everyone in the building knows you made a brisket." The entire hallway smelled of braised beef and onions—a smell that was virtually impossible to ignore.

Ruth's father sensed her distress and led the couple to the front door. He gave his daughter a wink and patted Arthur on the back. "You'll come back for the brisket another time, yes?"

"Certainly, Mr. Kaplan. Another time for sure."

"There, Florence, you see? The man will come back. But tonight, they go out. So, the two of you, go." He used both hands to shoo them, like a pair of small children. "Eat slow!" he called out as he pushed them through the doorway.

They laughed about it later, when the waitress brought their food. "Please," Arthur said, his voice stern but his eyes twinkling. "Remember to eat slowly."

He told her about the master's degree he was getting at Columbia, and she told him about the classes she would be taking at Brooklyn College in the fall. She explained Brun's constant, and he explained electron microscopy. When he invited her to see his laboratory at the university, Ruth felt a bubble of excitement in the hollow of her chest. It was a perfect evening.

But when they returned to the apartment, her sister greeted them at the door. When Ruth saw Millie's face, her confidence turned to panic, and her palms began to sweat.

"Why are you here?" Ruth blurted out. "I thought you were babysitting."

"I was, but they came home early. Mrs. DeLuca wasn't feeling well." Millie turned to Arthur and held out her hand. When their fingers touched, Ruth wanted to scream. There would be no second dinner now, no visit to the laboratory. It was always the same, after her dates met her sister.

Walter Rabinowitz had been the first of many. Next came Bobby Weinstein, who had asked Ruth's permission to invite Millie to the movies. "I won't if you don't want me to," he'd said to her twice, as if somehow that would make up for the humiliation. After Bobby came Howard Hoffman, who had shown up with a box of chocolates—*for you and your sister,* he'd emphasized, to make sure she understood. Of course, neither of them had been as bad as Benjie Silver, who had tried to make a pass at Millie while Ruth was still in the room.

Miraculously, however, Arthur was different. He let her sister's hand drop immediately after shaking it. He didn't ogle Millie's chest or stare into her eyes. He didn't ask how old she was or try to say something clever. Instead, he turned his back to her and placed his hand on Ruth's arm.

"Would it be all right if I called you tomorrow?"

"Of course," Ruth answered.

"It's settled, then. Good night." He kissed her gently on the cheek and left without another word.

**When Arthur asked Ruth's father for permission to propose,** Mr. Kaplan opened a special bottle of whiskey he'd been saving. He raised his glass to the couple, said a prayer thanking God, and embraced the young man like a long-lost son. Ruth's mother, on the other hand, was considerably less ecstatic. "Maybe," she told Ruth later, in private, "he could lose a little weight before you have the wedding. And tell him not to talk about science so much."

Ruth was horrified. "How can you speak that way about the man I'm going to marry? He's going to be a *scientist*! He's brilliant and thoughtful. You should be proud to have Arthur as your son-in-law!"

"I am, I am. Of course I am. For you, he's a good match."

"For *me*? For me, but not for Millie—is that what you mean?

Just who do you think is going to marry her, Mama? A Rockefeller? A Rothschild? Or are you still holding out for the king of England?"

"Why shouldn't Millie marry a man like that? She only has to meet one."

"*You're* the one who saves the articles about all the royal weddings. Those marriages are arranged—they don't marry for love."

"You think you know everything? What do you know? When Princess Märtha of Sweden married Prince Olav of Norway, the newspaper said it was a real love match. So what if it was good for their countries too? People can marry for practical reasons *and* for love. Why couldn't your sister be like Princess Märtha?"

There was no sense in arguing. For years, their mother had filled Millie's head with pipe dreams and promises about the man she would marry. Whenever she spoke about Millie's extraordinary prospects, their father hid behind his newspaper and didn't say a word. Ruth, on the other hand, was vocal about her doubts. She had always been too practical to believe her mother's claims. *How is Millie going to meet these men, anyway? It's not like the Rothschilds are wandering around Brooklyn.*

**A week before the wedding, Ruth's mother took out her jewelry** box. She set the worn wooden case on the kitchen table and motioned for Ruth to sit down beside her. Inside the case was a collection of familiar gold and silver pieces. By most people's standards, they ranged from worthless to modest, but when Ruth had been young, she'd thought each one was priceless.

Her mother rummaged through the contents and handed Ruth a pair of clip-on earrings—two golden flowers with tiny garnet centers. "These are yours now," her mother said. "Your 'something old' for the wedding." Ruth had seen the earrings on her mother a hundred times—she wore them for every holiday, for every shivah call and funeral. *You should always wear a nice piece of jewelry to the cemetery,* her mother liked to say. *So everyone should know that you're not dead yet.*

Ruth fastened the flowers to her ears and kissed her mother's cheek. "You don't have to give them to me, Mama. They can be my 'something borrowed.' You can loan them to me for the day."

"What are you saying? That I can't give my daughter a gift? Besides, I always meant for you to have these earrings. We'll get them polished tomorrow, and they'll look as good as new. I'll take my brooch in too—you know, the one with the pearls. Now, where did I put it?" She picked her way slowly through the small mound of trinkets, but she couldn't seem to find the item she was seeking. "Oy," she huffed. "It's always the same. If I'm looking for something, it doesn't want to be found."

"Let me try," Ruth suggested, pulling the jewelry box toward her. She untangled the necklaces, pulled out the bracelets, and removed all the earrings until she reached the bottom layer. "Here it is," she said finally, handing her mother the pin—a simple golden circle surrounded by pearls the size of apple seeds. But before putting the other pieces back inside, Ruth spotted a black velvet pouch tucked into the corner. Made of the same fabric as the box's interior, it was easy to miss.

Ruth turned the pouch over onto her open palm. The ring that fell out was one she'd never seen before: thick, polished platinum, with a center opal surrounded by diamonds. Ruth stared at the ring for a long time before she spoke. It was obviously valuable—worth far more than the rest of the jewelry combined. "Where did this come from?"

"I never told you about that ring before? It was my grandmother Fanny's, from her first husband in Russia. He was a jeweler—much, much older than she was. Two days after the wedding, his favorite horse keeled over in the middle of the street. A week after that, he dropped dead himself. The jeweler's family told everyone that Fanny was cursed—all the bad luck was her fault, they said. Fanny was no fool—she knew she had no future in that *farshtinkener* town, so she booked her passage on a ship to New York the next day. She sewed her husband's watch into her coat pocket and that ring into her brassiere. She didn't tell anyone in New York that she had been married before. My grandfather didn't even know until my mother was born."

"And she kept the ring all that time?"

Ruth's mother shrugged. "She told my mother the ring reminded her to be strong. She came here all alone, and she built a whole new life."

"It's beautiful," Ruth said, holding it up to the light. "Why don't you ever wear it?" She set the ring down on the table, but her eyes lingered on the stone.

Her mother laughed. "Me? Where would I wear something so fancy? No, your sister is the one who will need that ring. After she gets married, she'll have dinners and parties . . ."

Ruth sucked in her breath. The clips from the earrings dug into her lobes, and the pain radiated outward until her whole head throbbed. "You've been saving it for Millie, then? Why am I not surprised?"

"Oh, Ruthie." Her mother frowned. "Don't get all worked up. You get the earrings, and Millie gets the ring. So, what's so terrible?"

Ruth unclipped the flowers from her ears and placed them next to the ring. Beside the magnificent opal and the glittering diamonds, the garnet specks and scuffed petals were lifeless and dull. Her disappointment gave way to despair. Ruth rubbed her ears—she could feel the dents in her skin where the posts from the earrings had pinched them too tightly.

"Ruth," her mother pleaded. "Don't take them off. They look perfect on you. Keep them on for a while."

But Ruth stood from her chair and left the earrings where they were. "No thank you, Mama," she answered. "They're uncomfortable."

**The night before the wedding, Millie kept Ruth awake, tossing** and turning and rearranging her pillow. Eventually, Ruth sat up and complained. "Millie, please," she snapped. "Stop making so much noise. If I don't get some sleep, I'll have bags under my eyes tomorrow!"

"How can you sleep? Aren't you even the tiniest bit nervous? You know, I read an article in *McCall's* that says it's perfectly natural for a young woman to be nervous before her wedding night."

Ruth groaned. "You've got to stop reading those magazines. You should be reading the newspaper."

"Newspapers are depressing. Anyway, aren't you excited for your wedding night? You know, because it's the first time you and Arthur are going to——"

"Millie! I'm not discussing that with you!"

"Why? Isn't that what sisters are for? Do you think it's going to hurt?"

"I said stop! Please!"

"Fine. I'll stop asking questions. I'll stop making noise. Would you like me to stop breathing too?"

"If that's the only way to get you to go to sleep!"

The next morning, Millie had forgotten all about their squabble. She woke smiling and cheerful, with offers to do Ruth's hair and makeup. It was well established that Millie had a talent for such things, so for the first and last time, Ruth told Millie yes.

Later that day, as Ruth stood under the wedding canopy, she was flooded with a joy she had never felt before. The man who stood next to her was intelligent and kind. He had chosen her for his wife, and he loved her unconditionally. Adding to her happiness—though she knew it was trivial—were the compliments she received from so many of the guests. Her dress was simple, but it fit to perfection, and Millie had worked wonders with her straight brown hair. Ruth knew it was customary to praise the bride's appearance at a wedding, but the truth was she had never felt beautiful before that day. She savored the sensation, so unfamiliar, so luscious—like a fruit she could not name from a distant, foreign land.

It didn't last long.

When the ceremony was over, Ruth waited on the receiving line between Arthur and her parents, accepting congratulatory handshakes and pecks on the cheek. Arthur's friends were polite, but they moved quickly through the bridal party, eager for the refreshments they knew would be waiting at the reception. Ruth thought nothing of it until she noticed the bottleneck—they had all suddenly slowed at the end of the line, taking their time as they fawned over Millie. On the way out of the chapel, Ruth overheard two of them talking.

"Did you see the bride's sister?" one of them said, and whistled. "How come Arthur never told us about *her*?"

"He's probably just sore," the taller one answered. "You know, because he didn't meet the pretty one first."

# Lillian

**Springfield, Massachusetts (June 1942)**

They first arrived at the armory in February, on a shroud-gray afternoon. The clouds provided a disappointing welcome, especially since their last day in San Antonio had been filled with brilliant sunshine. The children were quiet on the ride from the airport, until the driver—a nervous young corporal—rolled down his window and announced that the air smelled like snow. By the time they reached Springfield, a few flakes had begun to fall.

When the car finally stopped, the children scrambled out first, laughing and kicking at the snow on the driveway. "Welcome to the commanding officer's residence," the corporal said.

"It's huge!"

"Look at the porch!"

"Daddy, I want to live here forever."

Inside, the first thing Lillian noticed was the striking pattern of light-and-dark wood inlaid on the foyer floor. The second thing was the orphaned grand piano in the front half of the double parlor.

As soon as Patrick spotted it, he flashed his widest grin. "Well, look at that. Somebody left you a housewarming gift."

She swatted him on the arm and ran her fingers over the

keys. Every time they moved, they found something left behind: a chipped coffee mug covered with dust on a shelf, a stray moth-eaten sweater in the back of a closet. Whatever it was, and wherever it appeared, Patrick would point it out and declare it her "housewarming gift." More often than not, it was thrown in the trash. This time, however, she had gotten lucky.

It was always difficult at first when Patrick was reassigned, but Lillian tried to teach her children to adapt without regret. Each time he was given a new position, she baked a cake and hung streamers. She circled the new state in red on the family map and told them how excited she was for their upcoming adventure. For the most part, they believed her when she told them how fortunate they were. After all, her father had been in the military too. "I was lonely when we moved because I was an only child. But the four of you have each other. You're never alone."

As a child, Lillian had grown comfortable living in houses that weren't hers. As an adult, she had grown used to the borrowed feeling of other women's kitchens. She was an expert at fitting her children's clothes into the unaccommodating drawers of strangers, and there was no one more skilled at hanging family pictures on the left-behind hooks of other people's walls. Sometimes she wished that she weren't so good at it.

The truth was, the last thing Lillian ever wanted was to marry someone in the military. When she first met Patrick, she'd been twenty years old, a sophomore at Vassar majoring in art history. A nasty stomach flu had been raging through her dormitory, and one Saturday night, she was dragged along on a double date to fill in for a girl who lived a few doors down from her.

What she didn't know when she agreed to tag along was that both the other girl's steady beau and her own blind date were seniors at the United States Military Academy at West Point. When Lillian caught a glimpse of their gray uniforms from the top of the lobby stairway, she felt a wave of panic pass over her. The academy was less than an hour away, and the uniforms were distinctive.

She grabbed her friend's arm. "Katherine! You didn't say they were from West Point!"

"I know," Katherine said, mistaking Lillian's shock for excitement. "Don't you just love a man in uniform?"

Lillian descended the stairs slowly, racking her brain for excuses to return to her room. If she weren't such a terrible liar, she could have pretended that she had the stomach flu too. She thought about tripping on purpose—a twisted ankle would have been perfect—but in the end, she was simply too steady on her feet. There was no choice but to greet her date and to try to endure the evening.

She was cold to him—practically rude—but he wouldn't stop smiling at her. He asked about her art history classes, which painters were her favorites, what she hoped to do with her degree. She wanted to dislike him—to hate him, in fact. But his smile was never-ending, and his eyes were too blue. If an artist were to paint him, Lillian decided, the blue of his eyes would have to be made duller on the canvas—the actual shade was too vibrant to be real.

"What about you?" she asked, focusing on the menu to avoid his eyes. "What are you studying? I mean, besides peace treaties and sea battles?" He didn't answer right away, and when she looked up, he'd stopped smiling.

His friend answered for him. "Patrick is at the top of our class. They're sending him to MIT next year—the Massachusetts Institute of Technology. He's going to be an engineer."

"That's wonderful," Lillian said, but Patrick's smile didn't return. At the end of the evening, she wished she hadn't mocked him. She was sure she would never see him again, and though she wanted to be glad, she found herself thinking of him all the next day. When she asked Katherine for his mailing address at the academy, her friend's mouth fell open.

"I thought you didn't like him."

"I'm not sure I do, but I still want to apologize for the way I behaved."

"I'll write down the address."

*Dear Mr. Walsh,*
*Please accept my apologies for my remarks this past*
*Saturday. I have no explanation, other than that my*
*father's military career has influenced my thinking*
*in a way that isn't always fair to others. I am deeply*
*sorry if I offended you. I wish you all the best in*
*your studies next year. If you should ever find your-*
*self with some time to spare in Boston, I hope you*
*will consider a visit to the Isabella Stewart Gardner*
*Museum. I visited with my class earlier this year, and*
*it was extraordinary.*

*Best wishes,*
*Lillian Guilford*

His reply came quickly.

*Dear Miss Guilford,*
*Your apology is accepted. I suggest we avoid the subject*
*of fathers when we see each other again, which I hope*
*will be for dinner next Saturday evening.*

*Yours truly,*
*Patrick Walsh*

*P.S. I would be happy to visit the museum, but only*
*with you as my guide.*

They were engaged a year later. The fact that her father disliked him only made Lillian more certain that she had done the
right thing by saying yes.

# Millie

The first night in Springfield, Millie barely closed her eyes. In the morning, she was tired, but it wasn't exhaustion that made her want to stay in bed: it was the thought of facing her sister. When she finally got up, the house felt too quiet—there was no shouting from the street, no doors slamming down the hall. There were no morning smells either—no neighbors frying bacon, no fish peddlers under her window, no radio blasting from the apartment next door. She wondered whether anyone raised their voice in Ruth's house, whether her nieces ever shouted or pounded down the steps.

By the time Millie headed downstairs with Michael, Ruth and the twins were almost ready to leave. The girls were dressed identically in matching blue dresses with short puffed sleeves and red hair ribbons. Alice was shorter and stockier than Louise and insisted on pigtails instead of braids.

"Good morning," Louise called from the bottom of the steps. Alice echoed the greeting, but Ruth had no time for niceties.

"I left a note for you on the kitchen table. There's an extra key and directions to the child care center—it's on the other side of State Street, at the High School of Commerce. After you drop Michael off, go to the personnel department in the administration

building. That's the main building that we walked through yesterday."

"Today?" Millie steadied herself against the bannister and
tried to slow her breathing. The day had barely begun, and her
head was already pounding. "I didn't think I'd be starting so soon.
I've never left Michael with a stranger before."

If Ruth noticed Millie's dismay, she didn't acknowledge it.
"The mothers I work with say the facilities are excellent. He'll enjoy it; you'll see. Besides, it's right across the street. It couldn't be
more convenient."

"I'm sure it's very good. Maybe tomorrow—"

"Do what you like. It's up to you. There's oatmeal on the stove
and coffee in the percolator. Come, Alice. Louise, let's go." Ruth
opened the door and ushered the girls outside. She left Millie alone
without another word.

When the latch clicked shut, Millie felt a wave of nausea pass
over her. Yesterday, when she boarded the morning train from
Brooklyn, her nerves had been high, but her hopes had been too—
after all, Michael was finally going to meet his family. She had
known there would be tension; she had assumed some discomfort.
And yet, she had also believed that moving in with her sister would
be the first step toward forming a new friendship between them.
She was certain that after so many years away from each other,
she and Ruth would find some happy memories to share. But after
Ruth's comment last night and her indifference this morning, it
was obvious that she had no desire to reminisce. Loneliness had
followed Millie all the way from Brooklyn and had joined her, un-
deterred, at her final destination.

Once Ruth was gone, Millie moved freely through the kitchen.
She had been clumsy and awkward the night before, trying to help
her sister prepare dinner in the unfamiliar space. But today, the
spoons had lost their strangeness. The oatmeal in the pot was as
cold as her sister's parting words, but Millie heated it for Michael
and poured herself a mug of the left-behind coffee.

The cup of bitter liquid gave her courage. There was no use, Millie realized, in waiting for tomorrow. She would take Michael to the child care center today. She would visit the personnel department and secure a job as quickly as possible. As she helped Michael with his breakfast, she made herself a promise: she would not allow herself to grow too attached—not to the house, to the grounds, or to any of the people. She may have settled in Springfield, but she would keep her Brooklyn wits about her.

There was no telling how soon her sister's welcome might wear out.

# Millie

Millie's father disapproved of the way the neighborhood boys clogged up the sidewalk outside their apartment building. "They don't have homes to go to?" he asked his wife repeatedly. She tried her best not to smile, but most of the time she couldn't help it. "They're waiting for Millie," she told him.

"Let them vait!" he shouted, stomping his foot. "Until she turns sixteen!"

To be fair, it wasn't just the boys that her father disliked—he wasn't too fond of Millie's girlfriends either. Millie heard her parents arguing about it when they thought she was asleep.

"Morris, calm down. You can't keep her cooped up in the apartment all day. She wants to be outside with the other girls. They have fun together."

"What kind of fun? Those girls are no good. They come only because they see the boys walking by. But I see them whispering. I'm telling you, they're looking for trouble."

"They're just girls, Morris. That's what they do."

"Not Ruth! When she was fourteen, she stayed home and read her books."

"And now that she's seventeen, we worry that she stays home too much." Millie heard her mother sigh. "What can I tell you, Morris? It never rains but it pours. Millie is more high-spirited. She's a popular girl."

"Popular with who? Better she should be unpopular, like Ruth."

Millie thought she heard a rustle of blankets from across the room. Was her sister still awake? Had she heard their father too?

**In order to protect his younger daughter and keep her occupied,** Millie's father arranged for her to babysit every day for their neighbors. "I told Mr. DeLuca you'll help his wife after school. The woman isn't well, and the boys are too much for her. Paulie is four, and Nico is two."

Millie liked the DeLucas, but she was furious with her father for not asking her first. She crossed her arms over her chest. "I'm busy with my friends after school," she pouted.

"Listen to me, *mameleh*. This is more important than friends."

"What about my homework?"

"Since when do you worry so much about homework? You want to stay home and do homework, be my guest."

Millie groaned. "Fine. Do I get paid, at least?"

"With money? No. But it's a mitzvah, so yes."

"What does that mean?"

"A good deed comes with its own kind of payment."

Millie hated to admit it, but her father was right. It felt good to be needed, and the DeLuca boys needed her. They didn't care what she looked like—they didn't even notice. All they cared about was whether she knew the games they liked to play. She was good at pick-up sticks, but better at hide-and-seek—mostly because their apartment was the mirror image of hers, and she knew all the best hiding places from when she used to hide from Ruth.

Mrs. DeLuca needed her too, and not just to run around after the children. Her first language was Italian, and though her English was excellent, she sometimes asked Millie about expressions she didn't recognize in her newspapers and books. When Millie explained what *hit the sack* meant, Mrs. DeLuca snapped her fingers. "Of course! How lucky I am to know such a smart girl!"

Millie shook her head, surprised by the compliment. "I'm terrible at school. Ruth is the smart one. Not me."

"Why do you say this? Certainly, you are smart. How many other girls could do what you have done for us?"

"But I haven't done anything—I just play with the boys."

"Before you came to us, Paolo hardly smiled. Nico never talked. You taught them to say hello to the other children. You taught them to make friends. Now they know about baseball and marbles and tag. You make them laugh with the songs you sing to them. You make them smile with the stories you tell . . ."

"But they're just nursery rhymes and fairy tales. Things everyone knows."

"What everyone knows, not everyone can teach. Only a smart girl can do what you do."

**Over the years, Millie grew increasingly attached to the DeLucas,** but she found herself worrying more and more about their mother. Mrs. DeLuca was thin, and her once luminous skin had grown too pale. As the boys grew larger, she seemed to shrink alongside them. Millie began to stay longer at their apartment in the afternoons, and sometimes, after dinner, she would return to help Mr. DeLuca put the boys to bed. As the years passed, Mrs. DeLuca barely left the apartment. She slept in the afternoons and would wake, disoriented, to ask about her sons.

On the day Mrs. DeLuca died, Millie was only seventeen. For weeks, Millie had lain awake at night, listening to the poor woman's whimpering through the thin plaster walls. It was the last sound Millie heard before she drifted off to sleep and the first sound in her ears when the sun poured through her window. Ruth was already out of the apartment—married to Arthur and in her own home—so there was no one but Millie to hear. On the warm September morning when Millie woke to silence, she had a terrible feeling that Mrs. DeLuca was gone.

Later in the kitchen, Millie told her mother. "Should I go check on them?"

"Not until after school." Her mother was still in her housecoat, with a thick crown of curlers clinging to her head. "I'll be out this afternoon, but I'll leave a lemon cake for you to bring when you go."

Mr. DeLuca was a quiet, kind-faced man, not much taller than Millie. When he opened the door, Millie's fear was confirmed. He stared at her blankly, as if he had forgotten who she was. "My wife . . . ," he began, but he didn't complete the sentence.

Paulie and Nico threw their arms around her knees.

"Mama died," Nico whispered.

"Millie already knows," Paulie explained. "That's why she brought the cake. Isn't it, Millie?" His candor was a surprise, but strangely comforting. He was too young to have the kind of fear an older child would have. He knew his mother was dead, but he could not yet comprehend the finality of his loss. Millie patted his head, wishing more than anything that she could be his age again.

"Aunt Leora!" Paulie called out. "Millie brought cake!"

Their father's sister emerged from the kitchen. She had the same round face as Mr. DeLuca, but without any of the widower's humor or warmth. Though she visited frequently, her visits never lasted long. When she dropped off her casseroles or baskets of veg-etables, the only conversation she made with Millie consisted of complaints about the weather, the two boys, or both.

Over her dress, Leora wore her sister-in-law's favorite apron—the frayed yellow one that Mrs. DeLuca had used for her everyday cooking—not the blue one she had saved for holidays and guests. Millie felt a spark of rage ignite in her chest. Every smear of flour and every spot of coffee on the cotton told its own small story so that the smock had become as personal as a pair of shoes, as intimate as any undergarment. For Leora to wear it so soon after her sister-in-law's passing was, Millie thought, a treacherous act, a conscious betrayal.

"No cake until after dinner," Leora said. She took the plate from Millie and sniffed at the icing, but the boys wouldn't let go of Millie's legs.

"Mama can have cake now whenever she wants," Paulie muttered.

Millie was trying to think of how best to respond. Should she take the boys for a walk? Read them a story? Mr. DeLuca was oblivious to the four of them. He stared out the window, lost in his own thoughts, dabbing at his eyes with a handkerchief from his pocket.

"Boys, I need to speak to Millie alone. Keep your father company for a few minutes, please." Millie had no choice but to follow Leora to the kitchen, where the boys' aunt pulled out a piece of paper and a freshly sharpened pencil. "What time do the boys go to sleep?" Leora asked.

The flowered pattern on the kitchen wallpaper swam in front of Millie's eyes. She tried to blink away her confusion, but the question made no sense. Had she misheard Leora? Had she misunderstood?

"Excuse me?"

"Their bedtime? What is it? I want to write it down."

"They don't have a set bedtime. It would always depend on how Mrs. DeLuca was feeling and whether she was well enough to spend time with them in the evening."

"What time do they leave for school?"

"Mr. DeLuca tried to walk them over at eight, but it was later if he was up at night with his wife."

Leora rolled her eyes and put down her pencil. She untied the apron from around her waist and hung it on a peg to the right of the stove. Then she smoothed the front of her dress and motioned for Millie to sit down at the table. "Before she passed away, my sister-in-law insisted that I could rely on you. I can see, however, that she was mistaken."

Millie's cheeks grew warm. "What do you mean?"

"You don't seem to know much of anything about the boys."

Millie stared at the apron hanging on the wall and thought about the day, a few weeks earlier, when Mrs. DeLuca had worn it for the last time. She had been feeling good that morning, well enough to get dressed and cook a batch of arancini—fried rice balls stuffed with cheese and mushrooms. She had made them slowly so Millie could watch, and she had written down the recipe on a small card for her to keep. *Don't lose it,* Mrs. DeLuca had insisted, pressing the card into Millie's hands. *Life is so delicious,* cara. *If you start to forget, make these so you remember.*

Millie stood from her chair and straightened her shoulders. "I know *everything* about them. I know their favorite food is their mother's arancini. I know Paulie won't go to sleep until you kiss him twice on his forehead. I know Nico's favorite color is green and he likes to wear mittens, even when it's warm outside. I know—"

"Enough! I can't run this household on a list of favorite colors. I need to make a *schedule.*"

Millie felt as if she couldn't get enough air into her lungs. "You're moving in with them, then?"

"Of course I'm moving in with them. What did you think was going to happen?"

Millie hadn't been able to think past this moment, this terrible moment of unspeakable loss. She hadn't let herself contemplate what might come the day after. But she would do whatever possible to help the family go on.

"I can help you," she promised. "I'm good with the boys. I'll come every day. I'll come on weekends too."

"That won't be necessary. We no longer require your help."

Millie's hands began to tremble. "But I've been coming for four years. Paulie and Nico are used to me."

"The boys have to learn that I'm in charge now. Having you here will only make that harder for them to understand."

"But, you can't keep them from me. They *need* me."

"What they need now is structure. Only I can give them that."

"This isn't what Mrs. DeLuca would have wanted!" All the grief and hostility Millie had been trying to control came pouring out of her now in a torrent of tears.

Leora fumbled under the kitchen table for her pocketbook and wallet. She kept her eyes down to avoid Millie's gaze. "Of course, I will compensate you for this week's work. How much did they pay you?"

Millie walked over to the apron, still hanging from its peg. She ran her hand over the fabric until she found the patch of oil splatters from the day Mrs. DeLuca had made the rice balls for the boys. Then she took the apron down, folded it in half, and tucked it under her arm.

"They didn't."

# Lillian

**Springfield, Massachusetts (June 1942)**

When Patrick woke that morning, Lillian's heart swelled with sympathy. His eyes were as blue as the day she'd first met him, but dark gray circles had formed underneath them. How long had it been since he'd gone to bed before midnight? She ran her fingers through his hair and kissed his cheek. "Come outside for a bit before breakfast," she told him. "It's a gorgeous day. I want to show you something."

She led him behind the house to the edge of the garden where the grass was still damp from last night's rain. The top of the rose arbor spilled over with blossoms, like ice cream heaped on top of a too-small cone. A passing breeze licked at the vines, sending the scent in their direction.

"You look exhausted," she said.

He wrapped his arms around her and pulled her close. "It's a demanding position," he admitted quietly. "It doesn't stop for a minute. But I'm glad you brought me out here. The garden is beautiful in the morning."

Lillian pointed toward Pearl Street, toward the rows of long buildings that ran parallel to the road. "I've learned a lot about this place, you know. Behind the rose arbor are the storehouses, and behind the storehouses is the ballistics building. I know about the tunnel where they test the rifles too—sometimes the children ask me about the noise."

"Ah." Patrick nodded. "I bet they do."

"The point is, I could look past the roses and ignore them completely, but every day, I make a choice not to do that. I know those papers on your desk and every phone call you get is another order pushing you to make and do more. But when it becomes too much and you need a little peace, you can always come outside and sit here with me. We might hear the gunshots, but at least we can enjoy the flowers for a bit."

He smiled at her then. "I have an idea. Will you meet me at my office later? Say, twelve thirty? I want to take my beautiful wife out for lunch today."

"Why, Colonel Walsh." She laughed and kissed his cheek. "I thought you'd never ask."

**Lillian couldn't remember the last time she'd had lunch with** Patrick. The truth was, he had been working nonstop lately. The children tried to be understanding, but she knew how much they missed him when he didn't make it home for dinner or when he didn't get back to tuck them in at night. How different their experience was from her own childhood, when an evening without her father had been cause for relief rather than regret. Lillian remembered her own mother's reaction on the nights when her father phoned to say he was working late—how she would put away whatever pot roast or casserole she'd been preparing and start rolling out a pie crust instead.

The mood in the house would lighten instantly as Lillian's mother rummaged through the pantry to decide what kind of pie she would make. Blueberry? Lemon meringue? It didn't matter. All that mattered to Lillian was her mother's laughter, the way she hummed when she measured and sifted, the conspiratorial smile on her face when the two of them shared an entire pie for dinner. "Don't tell your father," she would say—as if Lillian needed reminding.

In contrast, Lillian vowed never to celebrate her husband's absence. She cooked the children's least favorite dishes when Patrick couldn't make it home: liver and onions, or cod with spinach. They would whine and hold their noses, but all would be forgotten the next night when Patrick sat next to them at the table.

Lillian's father hadn't liked Patrick, but that was no surprise. No matter that Patrick was at the top of his class at MIT. No matter that he earned promotion after promotion in the ordnance department. "He's not a real soldier," Lillian's father had sneered. She married Patrick anyway, in a quiet ceremony two years after they'd met. Lillian's mother had died many years before, and her father had sent word that he was too busy to attend. At the luncheon afterward, there had been two desserts—a traditional wedding cake and a strawberry rhubarb pie—her mother's favorite.

**As she entered through the administration building's rear door,** Lillian was so preoccupied thinking about Patrick that she walked right into a young woman who was on her way outside. The woman's purse and her papers fell to the vestibule floor.

"I'm so sorry!" Lillian said. "Please, let me help you." The stack of papers had scattered, so Lillian bent down to collect them.

"You're applying for a job?" Lillian asked, handing back the application forms.

"Yes . . . they told me to go to Building 27, but I'm not sure if it's this way or . . ."

"It's that one, right over there." Lillian pointed to a long brick building off to the right. "They'll give you an aptitude test when you get there, but it's nothing to be nervous about."

"That's what they said upstairs. But I'm nervous anyway."

"Oh, don't be. It's only to figure out what kind of job will suit you best. They'll check your hands, see how coordinated you are, things like that. Or so I've been told."

"Do you work here too?"

"Not officially. I really should have introduced myself properly in the first place." Lillian held out her hand. "Lillian Walsh—my husband is the chief commanding officer here. We live that way, at the far end of the square, to the right." Lillian pointed across the lawn, toward Byers Street.

"I'm Millie Fein. My brother-in-law is an officer here too. Arthur Blum."

"You're Ruth's sister! She mentioned that you would be staying with her. When did you arrive?"

"Just yesterday."

"And you're interviewing already? How industrious of you! You didn't want to work in the payroll office with Ruth?"

From the look on Millie's face, Lillian knew she'd said the wrong thing.

"Oh, no," Millie murmured. "I don't think . . . well, we never talked about that. Ruth is the one who's good with numbers. I'm probably better suited to something else."

"Well, every job here is important—we need all the help we can get."

"I hope so." The young woman clung to her papers and bit her lower lip. When her face turned pale and her shoulders began to shake, Lillian finally realized how close she was to tears. She'd been too busy asking questions to notice.

"Here, come with me. There's a bench right outside. Let's sit down for a minute."

In Armory Square, the air was still and warm. They sat together in the shade, under a canopy of leaves, while Lillian tried to think of a way to comfort Ruth's sister. When Millie pulled a handkerchief from inside her purse, Lillian couldn't help noticing that the buckle on the bag was about to fall off. The cuffs on Millie's sleeves had begun to fray.

Suddenly, Lillian was ashamed of herself. She remembered that Millie had lost her husband recently, and she hadn't even offered her condolences yet.

"I hope you'll forgive me. I'm so sorry I upset you."

"It's not you, Mrs. Walsh. Before I came here, I was at the child care center. It was the first time I've ever had to leave my son—he's never really been away from me before."

"If it makes you feel any better, most children cry and carry on the first few times their mothers leave."

"Michael didn't cry. He was thrilled with the toys and all the other children. In Brooklyn, he didn't have a lot of opportunities for that. No, I was the one who was upset by it all. I wasn't prepared for what it would be like. I wasn't prepared for any of this."

"I'm so sorry for your loss. Ruth told me about Private Fein."

At the mention of her husband, Millie transformed. She pulled back her shoulders, dried her eyes, and gathered her forms into a neat stack. "Please don't apologize. I'm sure that Michael and I will adjust very soon. I really should go for the aptitude test now, but thank you for sitting with me."

"Wait—I'm having some of the officers' wives over today at four o'clock. It would be wonderful if you could come. You can bring your son. The children will all be home, and they usually end up playing outside together. Maybe Ruth already told you about it?"

"No, but thank you. I'll try."

After Millie left, Lillian lingered in the shade, trying to decide who it was that the young woman reminded her of—was it her hair, perhaps, or maybe her lipstick? She was such a pretty girl—maybe it was a film actress or someone Lillian had read about in the newspaper.

It was only later, after lunch, that Lillian figured it out. She was passing the fountain in the square when it came to her—the melancholy eyes, the slightly forced smile. If Lillian thought back far enough, she could picture the same features on her own mother's face, most often after an evening at home with her father.

Lillian made up her mind before she reached her front door. She would do what she could to make Millie feel welcome at the armory. She would introduce her to the other women and make sure she had whatever she needed. She would be the kind of friend her own mother never had at all those lonely army bases.

No matter how many awful memories it dredged up.

# Ruth

Ruth couldn't understand Millie's hesitation that morning—the baffled look on her face when Ruth gave her directions to the administration building, the shock in her eyes when Ruth mentioned child care for Michael. What did Millie think was going to happen when she finally arrived in Springfield?

When she got to the payroll office, Ruth had a difficult time concentrating. Instead of focusing on her ledgers and the numbers in front of her, she pictured Millie lounging on the sofa and leafing through magazines. Ruth shuffled her papers and slammed the drawer of her desk.

"Is something wrong?" her coworker asked.

"Sorry, Maryanne. No, everything is fine."

As the clock ticked toward three, the idea of going home to her sister made her feel queasy. It was Tuesday—the day of Lillian's weekly meetings. Ruth had planned on skipping this week to make sure Millie was settled, but now she decided it would be better to attend. The twins would be waiting for her at the Walsh house anyway—it was the drop-off point for the corporals who drove the officers' children to and from the local schools. On Tuesdays, when their mothers gathered in Mrs. Walsh's living room, most of the children stayed and played together outside.

Like all good hostesses, Lillian Walsh was preternaturally aware of the whereabouts of her guests. She was at Ruth's side from the moment she entered the house, taking her elbow and ushering her through the foyer. Ruth could sense her giddiness from the grin on her face. "You'll never guess who I met this afternoon! Look!" She pulled Ruth into the light-filled double living room and pointed to a woman in a familiar navy dress. Ruth hid her dismay as Lillian led her toward her sister.

"Ruth! I'm so glad you're here." Millie had been looking at one of the photographs that sat on top of Lillian's piano, but when her sister approached, she put down the frame.

"What a surprise," Ruth murmured. "How did you find out about the meeting?"

"From me!" Lillian crowed. "I was on my way to Patrick's office, and Millie was heading to Building 27. We got to talking, and I invited her. Oh, Millie, I forgot to ask—how did the rest of the interview go?"

"It went well," Millie answered. "They said I'd be assembling triggers—at least at first. I told them I would start tomorrow morning."

Ruth's eyes widened. "You got a job today?" She had a hard time believing her sister had followed through on her instructions.

"I did. I dropped Michael at the child care center, just as you suggested. You were right—he loved it there. When I picked him up, he didn't want to leave. The only reason he stopped crying was because I told him he'd go back tomorrow." Millie pointed out the window to the Walshes' side yard. "He's outside with the other children now. Lillian's girls are looking after him."

"Isn't it wonderful how adaptable children are?" Lillian said. She checked her watch and scanned the oversized room. Two dozen women were scattered on sofas and conversing in small groups. "It looks like everyone is here. Excuse me just a minute while I bring out some trays."

"I'll help," Millie offered, and Lillian beamed.

"What a gem you are! People don't usually volunteer at these things." She winked at Ruth. "You know, if your sister is always this helpful, I might try to convince her to move in *here*."

"I'm happy to come too," Ruth offered, but Lillian insisted that only two sets of hands were needed. "Please, take a cup of tea and enjoy yourself." Ruth had no choice but to smile as Lillian led her sister away. The sight was all too familiar. When Millie had first started as a freshman at their high school in Brooklyn, girls who wouldn't deign to speak to Ruth had stopped Millie in the hallways. They had asked about her hairstyle and pulled her into corners for intimate chats—all while Ruth stood to the side, ignored or forgotten.

There had been no secret back then as to why the girls fawned over her sister. Millie had been strikingly pretty, easygoing, and cheerful. In high school, that had been enough for the other girls to make a fuss. But Lillian Walsh was not a shallow teenager. Ruth could only conclude that she had taken pity on Millie; there was nothing else to explain her sudden interest.

Ruth avoided conversation by pouring herself some tea from one of the silver urns set out in the dining room. Dozens of matching cups and saucers had been artfully arranged, along with bowls of thinly sliced lemon and small pitchers of milk. Aside from a handful of older women whom Ruth knew in passing—the wives of military suppliers located in Springfield—the crowd mostly consisted of the other women from Armory Square. The officers' wives wore dresses and spring suits in patriotic shades of reds, tans, and blues. Suit jackets were short-sleeved, with nipped waists and wide shoulders. A few of the women wore gloves, but most took them off or carried them in their purses—the afternoon had turned warm, and the air inside the living room was beginning to grow stuffy.

"Who was that woman you and Lillian were talking to?"

A familiar high-pitched voice cut through the hum of the crowd. Ruth recognized the speaker before she turned her head. She forced herself to smile. "Hello, Grace."

Grace Peabody always managed to be the most stylish woman in the room. A navy straw hat with a short, wispy veil was pinned carefully on top of her blond pompadour. She was the only one in pink—a dress of silk crepe, finished with a wide white collar and slim navy belt. No matter the temperature, Grace wore gloves; though her cotton-covered fingers were often curled into fists.

"Who was that?" Grace repeated. "Pretty, I suppose . . ." The other women in the room hadn't noticed Millie yet, but Grace had already managed to do a thorough evaluation. The grudging tone of her voice took Ruth by surprise. It had never occurred to Ruth that her sister's looks could be the source of someone else's resentment.

"That was my sister, Millie. She's come to stay with me."

"You never mentioned a sister."

The truth was, Ruth mentioned very little to Grace—she had earned her reputation as the armory's biggest gossip, and Ruth had always found it best to tell her as little as possible.

"Her husband was killed a few months ago. She arrived just yesterday from Brooklyn. I . . . haven't gotten around to telling many people."

"My condolences on your brother-in-law," Grace said mechanically. But her sympathy was swift. "How long is she staying?"

"Millie got a job at the armory this afternoon, so it looks like she'll be with us for some time."

"She's working with you in the administration building, then?"

"No. They've assigned her to the shops, assembling triggers."

Grace raised an eyebrow. "A lovely young widow on the front lines of production. How patriotic."

"Yes. Please excuse me. I really should try to find my sister now."

Ruth tried to slow her uneven breathing. She had known she would have to introduce Millie to the other wives eventually, but she'd been hoping to avoid those conversations for as long as possible. She didn't want to listen to Millie tell the story of Lenny's enlistment. She didn't want to hear the others praise his bravery or Millie's sacrifice.

Ruth carried her tea to the living room and found an empty chair. Around her, the steady sounds of spoons on saucers settled her nerves. She had just begun to relax when Lillian planted herself in the center of the room.

"Ladies, may I have your attention? I am happy to see so many of you this afternoon. We'll begin with a few reminders—our music club meets the first Wednesday of every month, and for those of you who knit, Susan's group meets tomorrow morning. No matter how warm it feels today, our soldiers will need gloves and scarves when winter comes. Now, before Caroline gives us an update on the war bond drive, I want to welcome someone new to our community. Millie, would you please come stand beside me?"

Bewildered, Ruth watched as her sister appeared and took her place next to the commanding officer's wife.

"I'd like to introduce all of you to Millie Fein. Millie recently relocated to Springfield from Brooklyn, New York, with her son, Michael. She's the sister of our own Ruth Blum—Ruth, would you stand so everyone can see you?"

With two dozen sets of eyes upon her, Ruth had no choice but to rise from her chair. She made a small wave with her right hand and promptly sat back down.

"Ladies, I believe we can all learn something from Millie's brave example and Ruth's generosity. When Millie lost her husband, Private Leonard Fein, a few months ago, Ruth offered Millie a home with her here. Not only did Millie's husband make the ultimate sacrifice for our country, but now Millie will be doing her part by joining our soldiers of production at the armory shops.

As we all know, this work is vital to the success of our troops. I encourage all of you to make her feel welcome."

When the applause died down, Millie was surrounded by women offering their sympathies and wanting to introduce themselves. While they squeezed Millie's hands and patted Millie's shoulders, Ruth turned away and went looking for the powder room. In the line that had formed, she spotted the back of Grace Peabody's hat a few women ahead of her.

"It's inappropriate," Ruth heard Grace complain. "Armory housing is for the immediate families of the officers, not for desperate relatives. What will be next? Renting rooms out to hobos?"

"I'm sure it's only temporary," another voice answered. Ruth couldn't see the speaker's face, but the tone was sympathetic. "Besides, Springfield has a housing shortage and the poor girl's husband just died. She isn't a hobo—she seems perfectly respectable."

"Respectable for now," Grace insisted. "But she's young and unmarried, and she's the only single woman living in Armory Square. How long do you think it will be before she starts noticing our husbands? How long will it be before they notice her back?"

"Did you see the look on her face when Lillian mentioned her husband? She's not looking for company. The girl is devastated."

"She may seem that way now, but just you wait."

Ruth decided to leave the line before Grace turned around— anything to avoid another confrontation. She walked outside and stood silently on the wraparound porch, trying to piece together the events of the afternoon. In just twenty-four hours, Millie had managed to topple Ruth's routine, to win over her only friend, and to incur the wrath of the armory's most unpleasant occupant.

Ruth had seen it before—tumult, then shock, followed by a string of too-late apologies. *I didn't mean to, Ruth, I had no idea.* It was the refrain of Ruth's adolescence, the song that played on repeat. It had been years since she had heard it, but she knew the tune by heart.

"Ruth? Are you all right? We were looking for you." Lillian tapped her on the shoulder, interrupting her thoughts.

"Sorry—I'm fine. It's so crowded inside."

"It certainly is," Lillian agreed, "and the heat doesn't help." She lowered her voice so only Ruth could hear. "I hope you're not upset with me. I realize I should have asked you first before introducing Millie to everyone. You may have wanted to do that yourself. I apologize."

"Don't be silly. You handled it much more gracefully than I ever could have."

"That's kind of you to say, but I hope I didn't step on your toes. Millie is so lucky to have a sister like you, especially after everything she and Michael have been through. You know, she told me that she met her husband when she was just seventeen. I'm sure he must have been a special young man."

Ruth paused before answering. *Special* was not the word she would have chosen for her brother-in-law, but she could hear the voices of her parents echoing in the back of her brain—lecturing, advising, whispering warnings. *If you don't have anything nice to say, say nothing at all; whatever you do, don't speak ill of the dead; speech may be silver, but silence is golden.*

If Ruth had felt free to be truthful, what would she say? That Lenny was charismatic, but rough around the edges? That his infatuation with Millie was heartfelt, but his ambition was lacking? That he was a man of limitations, some of which had been obvious to everyone around him, and some of which had been known to Ruth alone? It was impossible, she knew, to say such things. It was safer to stay silent, more prudent to agree.

"Yes," Ruth said when she finally opened her mouth. "Lenny was special. Of course he was."

# Millie

The day after Mrs. DeLuca died, Millie had nowhere to go after school except home. She longed to see Paulie and Nico, to play marbles with them on their kitchen floor. But Leora had made herself all too clear: Millie was not to visit, not even for a few minutes.

When the buzzer sounded, Millie jumped up from the couch, certain Nico or Paulie had snuck over to say hello. But when she opened the door, a delivery boy was waiting. He was a few years older than she was, she guessed, with dark wavy hair and an easy grin. He looked at her as if he thought she'd been expecting him, and the confidence in his expression made her blush. She had never seen a boy so handsome—he looked like the movie stars in *Photoplay* magazine.

"Can I help you?" Millie asked.

The young man held up a round, shiny box. "Delivery for Mr. DeLuca."

"What is it?" Other than pills from the drugstore down the street, she couldn't remember the DeLucas ever receiving deliveries.

But the young man didn't answer. Instead, he turned the box

around so she could see the printing. He tapped at the gold block letters. SOLOMON BROS. HAT SHOP.

"A hat?"

"Well, it ain't a telephone!" he tried to joke. "Sure, it's a hat." He cleared his throat for dramatic effect. "Open-crown homburg, black fur felt, five-and-a-half-inch crown, two-and-a-half-inch brim, lined in black silk. Your old man must have someplace important to be. Wedding, maybe?" He leaned forward slightly. "Not yours, I hope?" Despite his perfect features, his laugh was awkward and high-pitched, like the laugh of a child who knew he'd said the wrong thing. There was no way he could have known how mistaken he was. Mrs. DeLuca was dead, and her young sons were motherless. How could anyone laugh in the wake of such tragedy?

Millie threw back her shoulders and crossed her arms over her chest. "Mr. DeLuca is my neighbor, *not* my father. And the hat isn't for a wedding; it's for his wife's funeral. So try not to laugh when you make your delivery." She slammed the door in the young man's face before he could respond.

She had barely sat down when the buzzer sounded again. *I shouldn't answer it,* she thought. But what if it really was Paulie or Nico this time?

When she opened the door, his expression was repentant. "I shouldn't have joked like that," he said, his eyes serious and sad. "I'm sorry."

Millie went to shut the door again, but he reached his hand out to hold it open.

"Wait! Did you know her? The old lady that died, I mean?"

"She wasn't old. She had two little boys. She was . . . good to me." A lump rose in her throat when she tried to explain. Mrs. DeLuca had recognized qualities in her that no one else ever had. She had praised Millie's resourcefulness, her creativity, and her patience. She hadn't cared about Millie's appearance—she hadn't even noticed. She cared about Millie's opinions. She told Millie she was *smart.*

Before she could stop herself, Millie began to cry. The delivery boy reached into his pocket, pulled out a handkerchief, and offered it to her. It was rough white cambric, and Millie wasn't sure it was clean. But she took it from him anyway and dabbed at her cheeks with the scratchy square of fabric. When she was done, she tried to give it back. "Thank you," she said.

But the boy shook his head and turned in the direction of the DeLucas' apartment.

"It's all right," he said gently. "You can keep it."

**Millie's sixteenth birthday had fallen on a Sunday, and by** midafternoon, she had received half a dozen phone calls—invitations to the movies, to dances, and for ice cream. By evening, Ruth suggested that they take the phone off the hook. But their mother had refused, and the ringing continued.

Millie had to admit that it was exciting at first, but after a few months of dating, she grew discouraged. Her evenings always seemed to follow the same disappointing trajectory. A young man would show up at the door and shake her father's hand. By the time they reached their destination, he would be staring at her chest. In an effort to impress her, he would tell her about the sports he played or the clubs he ran at school. He might try to hold her hand or put his arm around her waist. Eventually, the conversation would turn to careers and college.

"You're lucky," the young man would say. "A girl like you doesn't have to worry about all that."

"What do you mean, a *girl like me*?"

"A girl as beautiful as you—it's a compliment, that's all."

The conversations varied, but the message was clear.

After a full year of dating high school boys, Millie was no longer interested. Unfortunately, the college-age men her mother set her up with weren't much better. The only real difference between them and their younger cohorts was that at the end of the evening, they expected something more than a peck on the cheek.

In the month leading up to Mrs. DeLuca's death, Millie gave up dating entirely. Young men still called, but she refused to come to the phone. Her mother was annoyed, but her father understood. "Florence, don't be such a yenta. Let the girl be. She'll call back all the *schmendricks* as soon as she's ready."

**On the Monday after Mrs. DeLuca's funeral, the delivery boy was** waiting for her. When the dismissal bell rang and Millie left school, she heard a group of girls buzzing just outside the double doors. *Did you see that boy standing at the bottom of the stairs? I swear he looks exactly like Douglas Fairbanks Jr.* When Millie saw that he was waving in her direction, she almost tripped down the flight of stone steps. The other girls sighed and went back to their conversations.

"Hi," he said easily, without a trace of embarrassment.

She was curious to know how he knew where to find her, but he didn't seem to think it was much of a mystery. "I asked around," he said, shrugging. "It wasn't hard to figure out."

"Do you go to school near here?"

"No, I'm all done with school."

"You graduated already?"

"That's one way of looking at it. Hey, do you want to get a Coke?"

A wave of dizziness washed over her, but she couldn't say whether it was from the afternoon sun or the intensity of his stare. She didn't answer.

She had spent the last month caring for a dying woman's children. She had tried to be a comfort, but the effort had exhausted her. In the last few weeks, the DeLucas had kept their shades drawn and the apartment lighting dim. By the end, Millie felt as if she'd been working in a tomb.

"The drugstore is on your way home," he insisted. "We'll be quick, I promise. Just one Coke." When he held out his hand, she was powerless to refuse him. It was an invitation out of the darkness, a reminder of the seventeen-year-old girl she still was. She wrapped her fingers around his and heard the girls behind her giggle.

It was only after they ordered their Cokes that she realized she didn't know his name.

"It's Leonard," he said, "but everyone calls me Lenny. You're Millie, right?"

"How did you know?"

"I asked the lady down the hall from you, when I delivered the hat. She told me your name, and then she warned me to stay away from you."

Millie pictured Leora's face and frowned. "But you didn't listen."

"I guess I don't like it when people tell me what to do." He flashed the same lopsided grin Millie remembered from the day they had met. "Besides, I got the feeling that the two of you weren't exactly friends."

"I babysat for the DeLucas for almost four years. Mrs. DeLuca was never really well, but this year she got worse—she was too sick to take care of the boys on her own. The day after she died, her husband's sister moved in with them. That was the woman you met last week. She told me she didn't want me to babysit anymore."

"She fired you? After four years? Just like that?" He shook his head angrily. "What a crummy thing to do."

Millie found his outrage enormously satisfying. The week before, when she'd told her family about the way she'd been dismissed, her mother had smiled and said she'd have more time to socialize. "You can finally return all those phone calls you missed. Who knows, sweetheart? One of them might turn out to be your future husband. Don't worry, I kept a list. You can start calling tomorrow."

Ruth's reaction was different, but no less infuriating. "Maybe now you can concentrate on getting a job for when you graduate," she said. Neither Millie's mother nor her sister acknowledged Millie's grief. Neither of them expressed even the smallest bit of sympathy.

"The worst thing is that she doesn't even want me to visit the boys. She said that if I come by, it will only confuse them." Millie could feel the tears starting to form, but she didn't want to cry in front of Lenny again. She wanted to say more, but she didn't have the words. How could she explain how lonely she was without the company of the DeLuca children to fill her afternoons? How could she explain the ache she felt in her chest when she walked home from school, knowing that no one was waiting for her, that no one needed her anymore?

*Stop thinking about Paulie and Nico. Stop being so sad. Whatever you do, don't make a scene.* Millie took a sip from her straw and forced herself to smile. "I'm probably going to die of boredom now that I don't have to babysit anymore. I have so much spare time now, and nothing to do."

Lenny spun a few degrees toward her on the red leather stool so that their knees touched. "Don't worry," he said. "I'll help keep you busy."

**A few weeks later, Ruth found out about Lenny from one of** Arthur's friends. "Anything you want to tell me?" Ruth asked on the phone. "Because Roger said he saw you with someone at the Sunday matinee. You shouldn't go around kissing people at the movies, you know. Even in the dark, people can still see. Do you want to get a reputation, like Shirley Gittleman?"

"Mind your own business," Millie snapped. She hung up the phone and went back to her magazine. Later on, when her mother asked who had called, Millie lied and told her it had been a wrong number.

Although Lenny lived in a neighborhood not too far from her own, Millie felt as if he were from a different world. He was Jewish, but he rarely set foot in a synagogue. He was smart, but he'd dropped out of high school when he was fifteen. He worked, but he changed jobs so often that Millie was never quite sure of his schedule. At twenty years old, he roamed the streets of Brooklyn with limitless freedom.

Millie didn't know any parents who would allow their son to drop out of high school. It was possible that Lenny's own parents wouldn't have tolerated it either, but his father had left soon after Lenny was born, and his mother had passed away the year he'd turned ten. For a while, Lenny had lived with a bachelor uncle, but now he shared an apartment with his older brother, Murray.

What set Lenny apart most from the other young men Millie knew was his seemingly endless network of friends. The first time he took Millie to the movies, one of his buddies was behind the box office window, and another was working the concession stand. Admission and popcorn were both free of charge. The next weekend at a Dodgers game, Lenny seemed to know every person who worked at Ebbets Field. The young man checking tickets waved them in through the gate, and another friend found them empty seats not too far from third base. She didn't question why it was that Lenny managed to get so many things without paying for them. He was outgoing and handsome—it made sense to her that people wanted to do him favors. Though she hadn't met his brother, she imagined him to be the same, especially since people were always asking Lenny to tell Murray they said hello. "Give your brother my regards," the peanut vendor at the baseball game said as he handed them free bags of nuts from his tray.

She tried to forget Ruth's warning about kissing Lenny in public, but she felt so self-conscious at the baseball game that she only let him hold her hand. At a dance the next weekend, he was far more persistent. After introducing her around to more of his friends, he took her hand without a word and led her to the dance floor. When he held her in his arms, the buzzing in her head blocked out the reluctance she knew she was supposed to feel. He didn't ask permission before his lips pressed against hers.

Afterward, she was surprised, not only by how grateful she

was for his silence, but by how easy it was to let go of the formalities she had always assumed were so important. She had spent too many months with her dying neighbor, and Lenny was bristling with life.

It didn't take Millie's parents long to start asking questions. Ruth was already married, and they recognized the signs. But the boys Ruth had gone out with were always boys that they knew. No one in their neighborhood had heard of Millie's young man, and he wasn't one of the college boys her mother had set her up with. They didn't know his family or what he did for a living.

"Invite him for Shabbat dinner on Friday," her father ordered.

"But he doesn't usually celebrate—"

"The boy eats, doesn't he? Tell him to come for dinner. Your mother and I want to meet him."

# Ruth

Millie's beau was late. By just a few minutes, but it set Millie on edge. She was picking her fingernails and chewing her bottom lip so intently that most of the lipstick was already gone. Ruth supposed that her sister wasn't used to waiting for men—her dates were usually early.

At exactly ten past six, the doorbell rang. Millie jumped up from her seat on the faded sofa, but their father motioned for her to stay where she was. Millie's mother, wearing her second-best dress, hurried in from her bedroom when she heard the door open. She had been checking on Ruth's twins, to make sure they were still napping. The scent of roast chicken hung in the air.

There was no mistaking the attraction between Millie and their guest. Ruth had seen plenty of young men try to catch her sister's eye, but when Lenny looked at her, Ruth could have sworn the lights flickered. He carried a bouquet of red roses, which he handed to Millie, and a box of their mother's favorite chocolates. "These are for you, Mrs. Kaplan," he said, presenting them. "Thank you for inviting me."

"Thank you, Leonard. Please, come in." Their mother's voice was measured—distant and cold. Lenny's wavy hair and chiseled jaw were straight off a movie screen, but Florence Kaplan wasn't going to be persuaded by good looks alone. She would need to know about Lenny's family, his education, and his prospects. If Lenny wasn't worthy, Ruth knew this dinner would be his last. Her beautiful sister was meant to marry a prince, and their mother wasn't about to let her settle for a pauper—no matter how handsome he happened to be.

"We understand that you've been spending a lot of time with Millie," their mother began.

"I'd spend more if she'd let me, Mrs. Kaplan. But Millie is dead serious about school."

Ruth began to cough. She could feel Millie glaring at her, but she couldn't help herself. The words were out of her mouth before she could think. "Serious about school?"

The truth was, Millie had asked Ruth about her college classes a few times. But when Ruth wanted to know why, Millie wouldn't say.

If Lenny noticed the tension between the two sisters, he didn't let on. Instead, he took Millie's hand and smiled at their parents. "Millie is the sharpest girl I ever met," he gushed. He stared at Millie's face with such adoration that it made Ruth embarrassed to be in the same room with them.

At dinner, he ate with gusto, complimenting the kreplach, the chicken, and the tiny potatoes. But he slurped his soup clumsily and picked up the drumstick with his fingers. When Millie's father asked if he had any plans for attending college, he shook his head and shrugged. "School's not for me," he said, unembarrassed, and Ruth watched her mother's face crumple into a frown.

But her father wasn't fazed. "It isn't for everyone," he agreed good-naturedly. "You're a workingman, then? What do you do?"

"Right now, I'm working a few different jobs, trying to figure out what'll be best. My brother wants me to work for him, but I want to see what I can do on my own first."

"What line of work is your brother in?"

"He sells soap flakes and detergents to the laundries and hotels all over the city. It's a big business."

"I'm sure it is. But you're still not interested?"

"Like I said, I want to see what I can do on my own."

Ruth's father nodded. "You want to be independent." He speared another piece of chicken from the platter with his fork while his wife gave him dirty looks from the other side of the table. For the rest of the meal, Ruth couldn't figure out what her father was thinking. Was he impressed by Lenny's pluck or disturbed by his lack of stability? His body language and expression were impossible to decipher.

Ruth's mother, on the other hand, made no attempt to hide her feelings. When Lenny spoke about delivering hats for Mr. Solomon, her frown grew into a full-blown scowl. "I'm sure you don't want to be a delivery boy forever, Leonard. What kind of future could there possibly be in that?" When Arthur mentioned yesterday's Dodgers game and Lenny remarked that he'd been in attendance, her mother huffed loudly and pushed her chair away from the table. "Who has time for baseball games on a weekday afternoon?" She returned from the kitchen a moment later with dessert, slamming down the cake plate with such force that the entire table shook. Ruth was surprised the glass plate hadn't cracked in two.

Millie said little and ate even less, and by the time the meal was over, she was as pale as the tablecloth. "Thank you for dinner, Mrs. Kaplan," Lenny said. "That was one of the best meals I ever had."

"I'm glad you enjoyed it," their mother managed to reply, but she spoke without smiling and with no trace of warmth. No mention was made of Lenny returning; no invitation was extended for another family meal.

Before he left the apartment, he made one last plea. "I want you to know, Mrs. Kaplan, I think that Millie is a terrific girl."

This time, their mother didn't bother to respond.

Ruth almost felt sorry for him. He wasn't the worst young

man her sister had dated. But he had no education and no plans for a career. He didn't come from money or even from a respectable family. No matter how much he liked her sister, Ruth knew their mother would never accept him.

When Millie left with Lenny to walk him down to the street, Ruth braced herself for her mother's commentary. It was as swift and as harsh as she'd known it would be. "An entire evening wasted! Wasted on *that bum*! I'm supposed to be impressed by a man who delivers hats for a living?"

"It's an honest day's work, Florence," Ruth's father said. "He's still a young man. At least he isn't a criminal."

"He's worse than a criminal! At least a criminal has a full wallet! This one has nothing! No education and no ambition!"

"Florence, stop shouting—you're going to wake the babies. Calm yourself down. Soon enough, they'll break it off."

"*Vos gicher alts besser.* The sooner the better."

After twenty minutes passed without Millie returning, their mother began to pace the living room floor. "How long does it take for a person to say goodbye?"

Arthur cleared his throat and pointed out the window. "They seem to be having a prolonged farewell."

Ruth rushed to the glass and pushed back the curtain. The September moon was so bright that it lit up the sidewalk, illuminating the pedestrians out for their evening strolls. Just below the window, Millie and Lenny stood together, their arms wrapped around each other and their lips pressed close.

"Morris!" their mother shouted as soon as she saw. "Morris! Do something!"

In order to minimize the scene, he asked Ruth to go down and break up the show. Lenny didn't make a fuss when Ruth approached, but Millie yelled at her sister as soon as he was out of earshot.

"Why did you make him leave? Did you have to embarrass me?"

"I embarrassed *you*? The whole neighborhood could see you!

Our parents are *mortified*." Ruth grabbed her sister by the elbow and pushed her into the entryway of their building.

"Let them be mortified. I don't care!" Millie yanked her elbow free and crossed her arms in front of her chest. Her voice echoed off the vestibule's dark walls, and Ruth worried that the whole building could hear them arguing.

"Millie, come on. He's a handsome guy, sure, but you must understand how wrong he is for you."

"Why? Just because our parents don't know his family? Get out of my way; I don't want to talk to you." She started walking up the stairs, with Ruth following behind.

"That's the least of it, Mil. Lenny didn't finish high school; he barely has a job."

"That isn't true—he has plenty of jobs!"

"Different ones every week! And who knows how long they'll last? Lenny isn't responsible, he isn't—"

"I'll tell you what he isn't," Millie interrupted. She stopped on the top step and whirled herself around. "He isn't *boring*!"

"Millie, please." Ruth lowered her voice and tried to speak calmly. "I'm worried for you. People will talk if you keep acting like this. A nice boy wouldn't grab you in public like that. You need to find a man who can control himself, a man who is steady, someone more like Arthur—"

"Like Arthur? Ha! It's not like *he* has a job! All he does is polish his glasses and do his stupid homework."

They had reached the third floor; the door to their apartment was at the end of the hall.

"You know Arthur has to study because he's in graduate school," Ruth said. "And Arthur is a gentleman—he would never have dreamed of kissing me in public like that."

"Well, maybe I don't want to be with someone like Arthur! Did you ever think of that? Maybe I don't want to be like you and marry some fat, dull man who only cares about memorizing formulas! Maybe I'd rather be with someone who *wants* to kiss me!"

Ruth heard the slap ring off her sister's cheek before she realized what she had done. She had never hit her sister before, not so much as a shove, not even when they were little. Millie's mouth hung open in disbelief.

"At least Arthur is kind," Ruth said. She entered the apartment before Millie could respond, and in one quick movement, she slammed the door shut.

# Millie

## Springfield, Massachusetts (June 1942)

Millie's first day of work was not what she had expected. She didn't mind the physical exam, but she found the fingerprinting unpleasant. The sensation of the ink on her skin, the way the technician forced her fingers into position, the nagging thought when the card was filed away that her person and existence had somehow been reduced to ten blurry orbs—all of it left her slightly nauseated.

She felt even more uncomfortable when they gathered her together with the other new hires to take the oath of office. It wasn't that Millie objected to the words—supporting the Constitution, defending her country—she believed in all of it. But saying the pledge out loud brought back memories of her first and only Girl Scout meeting, when Barbara Frankel's mother singled her out with a nasty comment right after the troop learned to recite the Girl Scout promise. When Millie returned home from the meeting, she told her mother she wasn't going back.

"You can't quit," her mother pleaded. "I already paid for your uniform."

"I'll pay you back."

Millie's mother closed her eyes and shook her head. "You're going to put me in an early grave, you know that?"

"Ma, those girls aren't nice, and neither is Mrs. Frankel. She told the whole troop my uniform was too tight up top and that I had to wear a cardigan over it from now on."

"You're being too sensitive. Mrs. Frankel is very civic-minded. She told me she organized a community project for the troop next week."

"You know what the project is? We're all supposed to meet at Frankel's Butcher Shop and help them clean the back room!"

"So? It's a mitzvah!"

"Ma! All Mrs. Frankel wants is unpaid labor! And she humiliated me!" Millie flung herself on the bed while her mother left the room, muttering something about trying to get a refund for the uniform.

**It was only after taking the oath, while they were standing in line** to have their photographs taken for their identification badges, that Millie began to relax. There were at least fifteen people in front of her, most of them women. She had been afraid of standing out, of being too young or too old, but as she examined the other faces, Millie realized that there were men and women of every age in the windowless room. Behind her were two high school girls, chattering loudly about their new jobs as messengers. Next to her was a stout woman in her forties, holding a cloth-covered picnic basket, and farther in line, a man who could have been Millie's grandfather.

From the front of the room, an announcement was made. There would be a short delay while one of the corporals was sent for more film.

The woman ahead of Millie placed her basket on the floor.

"Careful," she warned. "I wouldn't want you to trip on that."

"I won't," Millie said. "You were smart to bring lunch. I didn't think of it."

The woman chuckled, revealing oversized dimples and a playful smile. "There's no lunch in there, *cara*. Believe me, I wish there was. It seems like we may be here for a long time."

"It does," Millie agreed. She must have looked back at the basket a little too long, because the woman lifted it from the ground and removed the cloth cover to reveal the contents. Tiny glass jars of oregano, minced garlic, and dried basil were tucked inside, along with a dozen other jars of herbs and spices Millie did not recognize. The smells wafted toward her, fragrant and savory, flooding her nostrils with the scent of old memories.

"I'm starting work at the cafeteria today," the woman explained. "So, I brought all my spices." When she unfolded the cloth, Millie saw that it was an apron.

"You're a cook?" Millie asked.

"That's what they tell me! But the cafeteria just opened, and I don't know what's on the menu. All I know is, I can't cook without an apron, and I like to wear my own."

"Wearing someone else's apron is like wearing someone else's shoes."

The words came out before she could stop them, and Millie was sure that the cook would think she was crazy. Instead, the woman smiled as if she understood. She took one of Millie's hands in both of her own. "I know just what you mean."

"I'm Millie Fein."

"Arietta Benevetto. Any chance you're working in the cafeteria too?"

Millie shook her head. "They'd never want me—I'm useless in the kitchen. But I had a neighbor back in Brooklyn when I was young—Mrs. DeLuca—and she tried to teach me. She was the most wonderful cook."

The people ahead of them began to move. "They replaced the film," someone announced.

The line went quickly after that, and soon the photographer was ready for her. One of the assistants handed Millie a card to hold beneath her chin with a five-digit number printed on in it bold type—"The number for your badge," the photographer explained. He told her to smile, but the scent of garlic that lingered in the air made her think again of Mrs. DeLuca. There was an instant directly after the flashbulb went *pop*—when the promise of blindness turned everything black—that Millie let herself imagine her neighbor's face. But the colors of the world intruded quickly on the darkness, and the picture in her mind faded too soon.

When the photographer was finished, Arietta waved at her from across the room. "Come visit me in the cafeteria," she called out. "I promise to cook something delicious for you!"

**On the other side of Federal Street, the inside of Building 103** smelled like lead and steel, sulfur and grease. The molten hum of machinery was everywhere at once, high pitched and low, rolling and relentless. Millie felt it in her chest when she entered the room—a warehouse-sized space filled with tables, machines, people, and parts. The tangy taste of metal crackled on her tongue like Coca-Cola bubbles. She felt her fingers tingle from knuckle to tip.

The gang boss noticed her hands before she even began. "Tiny," he noted. "Perfect for triggers." She was told to leave all jewelry at home, to tie up her hair, to wear comfortable shoes. Some of the women wore coveralls, but trigger assembly didn't require special clothing.

She was given pamphlets on safety and was warned about accidents—lost fingers and limbs, hair caught in the teeth of unstoppable gears. She was lectured on nutrition, on staying healthy for work. *Every missed day in the shop means less equipment for our troops.*

Just when she thought the orientation was over, another officer was brought in to speak to them. *Never discuss your work at the armory—you never know who might be listening. As soldiers of production, we must guard against saboteurs and foreign spies. Loose lips sink ships. Always be vigilant.*

By the time Millie was shown to her place at one of the

wooden tables, there were only a few hours left on her shift. Her assembly station was crowded with wooden boxes filled with the different components that made up the trigger mechanism of the rifle. The woman at the station to her right was to be her instructor, but for the next two hours, Millie never once looked up from the table to see her face. The woman's voice and her hands were all that existed, both smooth and certain, synchronized and calm. The woman's fingers and lips tapped out their own rhythm, and all Millie could do was to follow along.

*Here, this is the housing. No, hold it like that. Ejector spring clip— it's tricky, I know. The trigger guard here. Now you line up the holes. The safety, the hammer, the pin, is it flush?*

At first, Millie wasn't convinced that she was up to the task. The metal was cold, and the pieces fought against her touch. But by the end of the shift, her hands began to make peace with the parts. She promised herself she would go faster tomorrow.

Millie only knew the shift was over because the woman to her right said so. She knocked her knuckles on the wooden table, gave Millie a pat on the arm, and said, "It's three o'clock now, dear. Time is up. You're done."

Only then did Millie look up to see the woman's face. She was older than her voice, with round cheeks and soft wrinkles under dark brown eyes.

"Hello," the woman said. "I guess it's time we met?"

Millie let out a groan. "I'm so sorry," she said. "I can't believe I was so rude. I got so caught up, I didn't even introduce myself—"

"Oh, don't worry." The woman laughed. "It happens all the time. The first day of work is like that for a lot of people."

Millie stood from her chair and held out her hand. "My name is Millie Fein. Thank you for all of your help."

"I'm Delores," the woman said. "Welcome to the armory."

# PART TWO

# Ruth

Over time, a carefully choreographed routine evolved between the two sisters. The dance was wordless and intricate, full of side steps and skirting, avoidance and circumvention.

When Millie was in the living room, Ruth usually avoided it. When Ruth sat on the porch, Millie stayed inside. Millie kept clear of the kitchen while Ruth prepared dinner, and Ruth helped the girls with their homework while Millie did the dishes. They listened for each other's footsteps, each heeding the heartbeat of the other.

"I'm glad you're getting along better," Arthur observed.

"We stay out of each other's way, that's all," Ruth corrected him.

"I think it's more than that," Arthur said. "You seem more relaxed."

Ruth supposed he was right. A person could get used to anything, really. The suffocating sensation she woke with in the morning began to dissipate slowly as the weeks went on. But she suspected that the change had more to do with her nephew than with her sister.

It didn't take long for Michael to get used to her. In just a few days, he was giving her shy smiles, and after a week, he insisted on sitting next to her at breakfast. He looked so darling when he woke up in the morning, with his messy curls and baby-pink cheeks. Her heart almost broke when she saw the threadbare pajamas he wore, his round little knees visible through the thin striped cotton.

One day after breakfast, he wrapped both of his arms around Ruth's neck. "Roof," he cooed, nuzzling his head into her shoulder. Ruth's heart swelled as she kissed him on the cheek.

"He asks for you in the mornings now, when he wakes up," Millie told her.

Ruth didn't answer, but when Millie and Michael were both out the door, she stood in front of the kitchen sink and cried. For the rest of the day, she could smell Michael's hair and feel the press of his small body against her own. She imagined her father and Michael together—the sweet little boy on his grandfather's knee. She wondered whether she should encourage Arthur to spend some time with him, but she worried about the consequences that might result.

That afternoon, Ruth took a walk to clear her head. The twins had been invited to a friend's house after school, so she was in no rush to get home. She followed State Street toward the river and made her way to the entrance of Forbes and Wallace on Main Street. Ruth rarely shopped at the department store. She found its eight floors—each as wide as a city block—overwhelming, and it was much too expensive for everyday purchases. But something— guilt or restlessness—propelled her through the front doors.

"No, thank you," she repeated as she pushed her way past the saleswomen offering eye creams and lipsticks. A labyrinth of glass cases filled with powders and perfumes occupied the front half of the first floor. The constant chatter of overeager customers was magnified tenfold as it bounced off the walls. When Ruth finally made her way to the back of the store, she asked the elevator operator to take her up to the boys' department. With its dim overhead lighting and carpeted floors, it was a haven from the chaos below.

A middle-aged man with neatly parted hair showed her the selection of boys' pajamas. Ruth chose two sets—one in pale blue cotton for summer, and one in forest-green flannel with white piping for fall. Both looked like shrunken versions of the pajamas Arthur wore—collared shirts with buttons on the front and draw-string pants, cuffed at the bottom. The salesman folded the minia-ture clothes with such precision that Ruth was mesmerized. After wrapping each set in crisp white tissue paper, he tucked them gen-tly inside a glossy cardboard box.

It was only when she was outside that she began to have doubts. The pajamas were too expensive . . . she should never have spent so much . . . the flannel might be itchy . . . Millie might refuse the gift. The walk home felt endless, and when Ruth finally arrived, she ran upstairs and hid the box in the back of her closet. That night, she could barely sleep.

The next morning, Ruth brought the box straight to Millie's room. If she waited, she knew she was sure to lose her nerve. Millie wasn't quite dressed when she opened the door, and Ruth handed the box to her before she could speak.

"I bought these for Michael yesterday," Ruth blurted out. "Two pairs of pajamas. I thought he might need them. I hope you don't mind."

The look of surprise on her sister's face filled Ruth with shame. "Of course I don't mind," Millie answered. "Thank you."

# Millie

Millie thought about telling her sister the truth on her first day in Springfield. She had already surrendered so much of her pride by arriving with nothing but a half-empty suitcase. What difference would it make to give up what was left, to say to her sister: *Our mother was right about him all along*?

But the travel had been grueling, and Ruth had been difficult to read. The next morning had been no better, and Ruth's hasty goodbye left Millie no opening in which to tell her story. By the end of the second day, Millie had forgotten the speech she had practiced on the train ride.

A few days later, the words came back to her: *He could never keep a job. We could never hold on to an apartment. When he started working for his brother, things only got worse. Half the time, he didn't come home in the evenings. When he did, he was drunk. After Michael was born, he promised to change. When he left to enlist, I thought things would get better.*

She wanted to tell the truth, but with each day that passed, she became more confused. At first, Ruth's demeanor made Millie believe that there was no chance for a sincere reconciliation between them. Ruth was offering shelter, but not a real home. And then, Ruth surprised her with those pajamas for Michael. It wasn't just the gift, but the thoughtfulness of the gesture. It was the tone of Ruth's voice and the kindness in her eyes. It was the way she looked at Michael, with such love and delight, so that for the first time in years, Millie felt hopeful. If it truly was possible to repair the rift between them, Millie didn't want to risk ruining that by bringing up the past.

**After a month in Building 103, Millie was as fast as Delores. They** had been right about her hands—they were nimble and quick. Over time, the calluses on her fingers hardened and her smooth palms turned rough.

Eventually, she learned the other women's names and stories. She was not the only single mother, she was not the only younger sister, she was not the only person who had come from somewhere else. Together at the tables, the women formed a kind of sisterhood—their hands moved in unison, and there was safety in synchronicity.

At least once a week, a group of them purchased lunch in the new cafeteria. Millie didn't go for the first several weeks—she hadn't wanted to spend the extra money when it was just as easy to bring a sandwich from home. But after a month, she grew desperate for a change of scenery. The others promised that the food was cheap and delicious. "They have the best macaroni and cheese—come with us, you'll see."

When they reached Building 111, Millie could hear the clapping and foot-stomping even before they walked inside.

"Arietta must be singing," Delores explained. Millie knew that the Works Progress Administration arranged for lunchtime concerts all around the armory, but she had never heard the WPA musicians receive such loud applause.

Inside the cafeteria, a stocky brunette stood on top of a milk crate, blowing cheerful kisses to a raucous crowd. Millie recognized her as the woman she had met her first day of work, the one holding the basket of spices on the photography line. Cheers of "Encore! Encore!" filled the small space.

"Enough now. *Silenzio!*" The singer laughed. "This next one will be my last song for today." The tune was slow and easy, the words like honey on her tongue.

> Although some people say he's just a crazy guy
> To me he means a million other things
> For he's the one who taught this happy heart of mine to fly
> He wears a pair of silver wings.

Her voice took the crowd away from the industrial lighting and the smell of frying meat. It made them forget the monotony of their jobs and the aching of their muscles. It made them worry less, for a moment, about their sons and nephews, their cousins and their friends, all fighting far away.

*Who cooks in a cafeteria with a voice like that?*

Arietta held the last note like a lover in her arms. People forgot what they were eating. They forgot they were supposed to be eating at all. Millie closed her eyes and imagined she was at one of the nightclubs in New York she had read about in magazines— the Copacabana, maybe, with its red velvet chairs and candlelit tables.

When she opened her eyes, Arietta was in front of her, smiling from ear to ear. "Well, look who's here!" Millie couldn't remember the last time someone seemed so happy to see her.

"You said you were a cook!" Millie said. "Not a singer!"

"I'm a cook who sings," Arietta admitted. "Or maybe a singer who cooks. It's Millie, right? How's the new job? When you didn't come in, I thought maybe you had quit."

"Oh, no, I'd never do that. The work has been good. And I'm sorry I didn't come sooner. It's been so busy."

Arietta flashed a conspiratorial grin. "Don't worry, *cara*—I know all about that. Listen, I've been working on something new for the menu. If you come back next Wednesday, it should be ready to try. I think you're going to like it."

"Of course I'll come."

"Sorry to run, but if I don't turn off the oven, my biscuits are going to burn. See you next week!"

By the time lunch was over, Millie's stomach was full and her heart was lighter. On the walk back to the shop, there was a spring in her step and a grin on her face. If Ruth had seen her from a distance, she wouldn't have recognized her.

For the first time in a long time, Millie had something to look forward to.

# Arietta

Arietta Benevetto was born in New Haven, Connecticut, on December 31, 1899, ten minutes before midnight. Her father's employer, the prominent theater owner Sylvester Poli, shared her New Year's Eve birthday and took a special interest in her. When he received word of her mother's departure from the world a few hours after Arietta's birth, Poli shook his head in sorrow and allowed his tears to fall freely. "In the short time that she has been alive," he sighed, "this motherless child has aged a century."

Arietta's father was one of Poli's most valuable builders. He was told to take all the time he needed—paid, of course—to arrange for both his wife's funeral and his daughter's continued care. Between family, friends, and the wives of Poli's employees, half of the Italian women in New Haven lined up to help. They passed Arietta from lap to lap, smothering her with kisses and tears, while her father, bewildered and grieving, found himself drowning in a sea of polenta and new marriage offers. He accepted the former and rejected the latter with all the grace he could manage.

Meanwhile, the women couldn't get enough of the baby. Each tiny coo that escaped from her lips made their sympathetic hearts burst with pity and pride. Every woman who saw her insisted on holding her, and every woman who held her insisted on feeding her. Not one of them thought about keeping track of how many bottles she was offered, however, so by the time Arietta was two months old, she was the fattest baby any of them had seen. Her extraordinary size only made them love her more.

Her father never remarried. Instead of igniting desire, the steady stream of women in and out of his small house made him tired. He longed for quiet days when he could be with his daughter alone, away from the flock of women that surrounded her. As the years went by, the number of ladies pledged to care for Arietta dwindled to a devoted group of three. These women were affectionately known as "the Aunties" or, as they taught Arietta to say, *Le mie zie.*

Arietta was five years old the first time her father heard her sing. When he opened the front door one Friday afternoon, he heard music coming from the back of the house. Assuming it was the radio, he followed the sound to the kitchen where the Aunties sat around the table on a set of mismatched chairs. No one noticed him at first. The radio was off, but there was his daughter, standing on top of a wooden milk crate in front of the stove, singing with her eyes closed. The Aunties had curled her hair and topped it off with a pink satin bow.

Arietta's voice was light and comforting, like summer rain on a cottage roof. It was not the voice of a child but that of a natural performer—expressive but precise, swelling to crescendo at the perfect moment, dropping to a whisper when the melody required. It was impossible to listen and remain unmoved.

By the time the song was over and Arietta opened her eyes, her father was weeping. The sight of him in distress frightened her, and she began to cry as well. Wet round tears rolled down her pink cheeks, and in her haste to go to him, she teetered on her wooden box and fell to the ground. He was at her side in an instant, lifting her from the floor into his arms.

"Papa, why didn't you like my song?"

"I liked it very much." He wiped his eyes with his sleeve and tried to smile.

"Then why are you crying?"

The Aunties shuffled in their seats, uncomfortable bearing witness to such an intimate scene.

Arietta's father was a simple man, but he had always tried his best. He read his daughter stories and took her on walks around their neighborhood. He bought her dolls when he could afford them and slept on a chair beside her bed when she had trouble falling asleep. Still, he had never spoken to her about her mother before. It had always been too painful.

"I'm crying because the song you sang reminded me of your mother."

For her whole life, Arietta had been afraid to ask any questions about the woman who had given birth to her. Sometimes the Aunties spoke of her, but always in hushed tones and never when they thought she was listening.

"Mama liked to sing?"

The excitement in Arietta's voice, the simple pleasure she took from saying the word *Mama*, broke her father's heart all over again. "Of course. You get your beautiful voice from her."

Arietta buried her face in her father's shoulder. At the table, the Aunties held each other's hands and mouthed silent prayers of gratitude.

**When Arietta first met Millie, she was overcome with the desire to** make the girl smile. There was something about her—a worn-out sadness that was only magnified by her shabby attire. And that look on Millie's face when she talked about her apron! It was enough to break Arietta's heart. When Millie mentioned her childhood neighbor's cooking, Arietta decided that the best way to cheer her up would be to start with her stomach. After all, weren't the women from her church still talking about the time her lasagna cured Father Bianchi? The doctors at the hospital insisted the priest would be dead from pneumonia in a matter of days, but after two helpings of Arietta's lasagna, his cough disappeared and his temperature returned to normal. If lasagna could bring Father Bianchi back from the brink of death, who knew what it might do for a healthy young woman?

The problem was, Millie never showed up at the cafeteria, and Arietta had no way of tracking her down. She knew the girl's first name, but she didn't know which shop Millie worked in or where she lived. After weeks went by with no sign of her, Arietta figured she'd probably never see the melancholy young woman again.

She kept busy with work—the cafeteria manager hadn't known he'd gotten a cook *and* a singer when he hired her, but he caught on soon enough. "I'm two for the price of one," she told him. "People used to pay good money to hear me sing, back when I was young and on the circuit. I may be older and my dress size may have gone up a few notches, but believe you me, I can still belt out a tune."

Any skepticism the manager had was dispelled on Arietta's first day. Not only did the customers praise her cooking, but they loved the entertainment as well. On the days she performed, people bought extra food so they could stay longer to listen. Workers in dusty jumpsuits ate their lunch standing against the wall because all the seats were filled. "You're better than any singer on Broadway," one of the older men told Arietta. She was fairly certain the man had never been to Broadway, but she was touched by the sentiment just the same.

Millie finally walked into the cafeteria a month after they first met, while Arietta was in the middle of one of her favorite songs. Arietta spotted the girl on the hot food line at the beginning of the second verse. Millie looked a little better—her face had filled out some, and she stood a bit taller. Still, sorrow flickered in her eyes like a half-hearted flame. Arietta wished there had been more time to talk, but she made Millie promise to come back the next week. "I've been working on something new for the menu," Arietta said.

She could have sworn the girl's mouth curved upward then, the closest thing to a smile she had seen on Millie's face yet.

The next day, Arietta approached her manager, Mr. Fitzgerald. "Listen, Fitz, I've got a new recipe for next week. Lasagna. It'll be a big hit, I promise."

Mr. Fitzgerald raised a pair of bushy eyebrows. "What did you call me?"

"Fitz. Isn't that what everyone calls you?"

"Only the fellas call me that." Fitz straightened his tie and rubbed the top of his balding head. He was at least six foot three, but he was pouting like a child.

"Oh, come on." Arietta winked. "I thought we were friends by now."

"I guess so," he said. "Listen, is it spicy? I'm not sure folks will go for something so exotic."

"You never had lasagna before?"

"Nope."

"I'll make some at home and bring it in tomorrow. Once you taste it, I guarantee you'll be begging me to put it on the menu."

That evening, Arietta adjusted her recipe. She knew Fitz would give her grief if she told him how much meat she would need—between rationing and costs, he would never agree to it. So, she cut the beef in half and used store-bought noodles instead of homemade. As she layered the ingredients, she pictured the Aunties shaking their heads at the modifications.

After her shift the next day, she set a large piece of lasagna on a flowered china plate that she had brought from home. Fitz traced the edge of the dish with his index finger and whistled. "Where'd this plate come from?" he wanted to know.

"That's what you're looking at? How about you look at what's *on* the plate?"

"I feel like I'm eating in a fancy restaurant."

Once she realized he was trying to pay her a compliment, Arietta's irritation with him faded. "I wanted you to be in the right mood when you tasted it—to feel like you were having a home-cooked meal."

"That was awfully nice of you."

"Yeah, well, I happen to be a very nice person, in case you hadn't noticed."

Fitz blushed then, the blotchy red of his neck rising slowly to the tips of his ears. "I've noticed," he said. He didn't say another word until the lasagna was gone.

**"What do you think?" Arietta asked Millie the next Wednesday.** "Is it as good as your neighbor's?"

"Better! How did you learn to cook this way?"

"Oh, *cara*, that's a long story—too long to tell during my shift anyway. Hey—how about you and me head over to the Loew's Poli for a movie on Friday night? Or maybe the Paramount? Then after, I'll tell you how I learned to cook."

"I'd love to, but I have a little boy at home. He's almost three. I don't go out much in the evenings."

"Maybe your husband could stay home with him and let you have a night to yourself?"

Millie held her fork in the air, as if she had forgotten what to do with it. When Arietta realized, she sucked in her breath.

"I'm so sorry—what a dope I am! No wonder you've been so blue. Listen, bring your little boy on Friday, and we'll go see a picture together. The Bijou is always showing Abbott and Costello films—he'll love it. Or maybe one of the new musicals."

"I've never taken Michael to a movie before. You really wouldn't mind if I brought him along?"

"Of course not!" Arietta smiled and stood from her chair. "Time for me to head back to the kitchen. I'll meet you and Michael in front of the Bijou on Worthington Street, Friday at six. And after the movie, I'll tell you all my secrets."

# Lillian

Well after midnight, Lillian woke to the sound of sirens. Patrick bolted out of bed and down the stairs to use the telephone. Within seconds, the children burst into her room, the younger ones wide-eyed and the older ones confused. Margaret and Peter got under the covers with her while Frances and Thomas stared out the window and tried to figure out where the flashing lights were headed.

After the phone call, Patrick hurried to get dressed. "I need to go," he said, pulling on his trousers. "The field service building is on fire."

"What? But they didn't even finish building it yet!"

"They think a tarpaulin caught fire from one of the lamps—half of the building is in flames already. They called in the city firefighters because we can't contain it on our own." He was still buttoning his shirt when he walked out of the bedroom. "Don't wait up," he called out. "I don't know how long I'll be."

The sirens kept coming, one after the other, so that Lillian was sure every fire truck in Springfield had been called to fight the blaze. She lost track of when the children finally fell asleep, though she guessed it was somewhere between two and three in the morning. She was making coffee in the kitchen when Patrick finally got home.

"It's a mess," he told her, his voice gravelly and tired. His eyes were ringed with dark circles, and the lids were swollen. A filmy layer of ash coated the top of his head, and the smell of stale smoke wafted off of his clothes.

She wished there were something she could do to help him. "You need to take off those clothes and eat some breakfast. Do you have time for a few hours of sleep at least?"

"There's too much to do. I'm heading up to shower, and then I've got phone calls."

"Should I cancel my meeting? It's Tuesday, remember?"

But Patrick shook his head. "Don't change it for me. I'll be out of the house until late tonight anyway." He took a swig from the coffee mug she'd pressed into his hands. "Besides," he said, doing his best to make light of the situation, "if you cancel, Fred Peabody's wife will have a fit."

**When it came to gathering information, Grace Peabody didn't like** waiting. She marched over to the commanding officer's house shortly after breakfast to find out what Lillian knew about the fire. She spotted Lillian in the garden at the back of the house, standing on a stepladder, pruning the rose arbor. Thanks to the Works Progress Administration, there were plenty of skilled gardeners on staff at the armory. In most areas, Lillian deferred to their expertise, but ever since her first spring in Massachusetts, she had made an exception for the roses in her yard.

Though it was barely past nine, not a single hair was out of place on Grace's well-coifed head. If she had been up late because of the sirens, no one would have known; her face was as smooth and unblemished as always, and her blue summer suit was impeccably pressed.

"Lillian! What on earth happened last night?"

Lillian held her shears firmly, at just the right angle, and made a careful cut to a branch. "Good morning, Grace. How are you?"

"Exhausted. I couldn't fall asleep again after the sirens."

Lillian nodded, but she stayed put on top of the ladder, snipping and shaping and cutting back the deadwood. She could feel Grace losing patience with each minute that passed.

"Can't you let the gardeners take care of that?" Grace hinted.

Lillian climbed down the ladder, tossed the trimmings into a bucket, and tucked her gloves into her apron pocket. "I could," she said, "but I prefer to do it myself."

"Tell me, what did Patrick say about the fire? What do they think caused it? Are they sure it was an accident?"

"Of course it was an accident. What else could it have been?"

Grace crossed her arms over her chest. "Don't you read the papers? It could have been saboteurs—like those German spies they caught off the coast of Long Island last month. A fire like this is exactly the kind of thing they were planning. With the field services building gone, the overseas shipping is going to be interrupted. Isn't that what the Germans want? And the Japanese and the Italians? I'm telling you, Lillian, there could be spies right here in Springfield."

"I'm sure the fire wasn't set intentionally. And I find it hard to believe that Springfield is harboring German spies."

"Don't be naive. They could be anywhere. They could be working at the armory, at any of the shops. What do we really know about all of these new workers anyway?"

"Every new employee takes an oath of loyalty."

"So? Anyone can say the words. It's easy to lie." Grace took a step forward and lowered her voice. "Do you know what Fred told me? They had *Italian* food in the cafeteria last week. They hired a new cook, and that's what she's been serving."

Lillian bit her lip to keep from laughing. "There's nothing sinister about Italian food, Grace."

"You know as well as I do that Italians have been declared enemy aliens—"

"Only those who haven't become citizens yet. And everyone knows that declaration is meaningless. Springfield is full of Italian Americans. Their husbands and sons are fighting for this country and risking their lives just like everyone else."

"Fred told me the enforcement in California is strict. Italians aren't allowed to work on the waterfront or live near defense plants. They can't have radios either."

"It's not like that here."

"Well, maybe it should be! For all we know, that new cook is a sympathizer. Think about how easy it would be for her to poison the food. You must tell Patrick to look into her background."

"I'm afraid Patrick doesn't have time to monitor the cafeteria menu." Lillian snapped her fingers. "But if you're really that concerned, we could meet there for lunch. The atmosphere may not be as elegant as Steiger's Tea Room, but from everything I've heard, the food is excellent."

"I don't think you're taking this seriously, Lillian."

"I'm sorry you feel that way. Now, if you'll excuse me, I have to get ready for my guests this afternoon. I'll see you at the meeting, Grace." Lillian tucked her shears under her arm. "Have a lovely day."

# Ruth

**Brooklyn, New York (April 1937)**

When she and Arthur were first married, Ruth hoped for a fresh start. She wanted a space of her own, a chance to live life out from underneath Millie's shadow. But the shadow's reach turned out to be longer than she ever thought possible—stretching from her parents' apartment to the one she shared with Arthur, twenty blocks away. Her new downstairs neighbors went to church with the De-Lucas, the couple across the hall had a son in Millie's class, and the widow next door was an old family friend. Every one of them knew her parents and her sister. There was no place in Brooklyn where Ruth felt she could hide. Besides, even if the new building had been full of strangers, there was no way to avoid her mother's visits and phone calls.

*Jerry Polikoff keeps begging Millie to go to the movies, but she refuses.*

*Your sister got four phone calls during dinner, and your father was so angry, the steam was pouring from his ears.*

*Millie and I had a free lunch at the automat. A gentleman in a suit insisted on treating us.*

When the topic of conversation was Millie and her suitors, Ruth's mother could stay on the phone forever. But whenever Ruth spoke up about her own daily life—the classes she was taking or the books she was reading—her mother found a reason to end the discussion. There were chickens and vegetables to prepare for dinner and all kinds of important errands to run.

Ruth's pregnancy did nothing to detract her mother's focus from Millie's love life. Apparently, Ruth's morning sickness and swollen feet were even duller conversation topics than her books and classes. When the babies were born, not much changed. But when the twins were a year old, Millie met Lenny, and suddenly the tone of Ruth's mother's voice shifted. Where once her mother had been irritating but hopeful, now she sounded bitter and less sure of herself.

Her mother wanted to forbid Millie from seeing Lenny altogether, but Ruth's father had a more philosophical approach. "Forbidden fruit is always the sweetest. Wait a little longer. She'll get bored with him soon."

"So, I should do nothing and let her make a spectacle of herself? People will start to talk if she keeps up with him this way!"

"You remember what I told you about my oldest sister, Hilde? How she took up with a man my father didn't like? My father thought he could stop them—he screamed and he hollered and cursed the man to his face. But Hilde stole my father's horse and ran off with the man anyway. She left no note, no way for us to reach her. No one from our village saw where they went. The rabbi told us to sit shivah, and we never saw her again."

"Morris, how many times do I have to hear that story?"

"Ach, so? Sue me for talking. *Es iz laichter tsu hitn a zak flai eider a farlibte maidel.* It's easier to guard a sack of fleas than a girl in love. You want to be like my mother and sit shivah for your daughter?"

**Soon, the number of phone calls Ruth received from her mother** doubled—long, angry rants about Lenny being unsuitable. "I raised your sister to marry a prince, and she's throwing herself away on that good-for-nothing bum!" When Ruth tried to defuse her mother's rage with stories about the girls—Alice had said a new word and Louise had learned peekaboo—there was always someone at her mother's door or something burning in the oven.

Ruth longed for a change, for some kind of escape. When Arthur first mentioned that he'd been offered a job at the Springfield Armory, Ruth burst into tears. Naturally, he assumed she was upset about leaving Brooklyn. What he failed to realize, and what Ruth had been forced to explain, was that her tears were born of joy instead of despair. The job in Massachusetts was the answer to her prayers. In Springfield, no one would know anything about her family. In Springfield, no one would know she had a sister at all.

Ruth's preference was to leave New York as quickly as possible, but the armory's new metallurgy lab was in the process of being built, and Arthur's job wouldn't begin for another six months. They would have plenty of time to break the news to her parents.

"Springfield? Who knows from Springfield?" her mother had said.

"It's a nice city, Florence, and a very good position." Arthur tried to be reassuring, but Ruth's mother wore her anxiety like some women wore the wrong color lipstick—it was far too loud and took forever to wear off.

"A job making guns? I thought you were a scientist! What does a nice Jewish scientist need with guns?"

"It isn't just guns. I'll be working in the laboratory, testing raw materials, figuring out the most efficient methods of manufacturing. It's important work, important for the country's future—"

"Is there a synagogue? A kosher butcher? What will you eat?"

Ruth resisted the urge to remind her mother that neither their lunches at the automat nor their dinners with neighbors had ever been kosher and that, aside from weddings and holidays, they rarely attended services.

"Springfield is a big city; there are plenty of Jews there. Believe me, they have everything!" Arthur scratched the top of his head and tried to stay calm.

Ruth's father wasn't critical, but he seemed uncertain. "I don't know much," he admitted. "But Springfield isn't Brooklyn."

Ruth never had the chance to tell him, but her father had been right.

**At some point, though Ruth couldn't say exactly when, their** mother began refusing to speak Lenny's name out loud. When Millie was in earshot, she referred to him as *the Boyfriend*, and when Millie was absent, she called him *the Bum*.

By April, Ruth's mother had spiraled into a full-fledged panic. Lenny was supposed to be a distant memory by then, but Ruth's father's plan had backfired. It was already Passover, and they were still dating.

"Your sister wants me to have the Bum over for seder. But that isn't all. She wants me to invite the Bum's brother too!"

Ruth had walked over to her parents' apartment after breakfast. The twins fell asleep on the way, and they were still dozing in their carriage when Ruth's mother began her tirade.

"Mother, shhh! Lower your voice. The girls were up half the night, and they need to nap."

"Fine, fine. I'll whisper, but believe you me, I feel like screaming."

"I don't know—maybe it will be good for you to meet Lenny's brother. You're always saying how important it is to meet a man's family. Aren't you curious?"

"About the Bum's brother? Absolutely not. But what choice do I have? You know the rule. *All who are hungry, let them come and eat. All who are needy, let them come and celebrate with us.* Your sister *knows* I can't say no on Passover. That's why she asked."

Her mother was quoting from the Passover Haggadah—the booklet they read out loud every year during the seder. In addition to instructions and prayers for the holiday meal, the Haggadah told the story of the exodus out of Egypt. Ruth didn't say it to her mother, but she had been thinking about it as well, especially the part about the flight from bondage. *Now we are slaves; next year may we be free.* Ruth was hoping to flee herself, wasn't she? Hoping for her own kind of freedom, from her family and her past.

On the morning of the seder, Lenny's brother sent flowers—a massive arrangement of white tulips and roses. Ruth's mother called her immediately after it was delivered. "It's too big," her mother complained. "I almost had a heart attack when I opened the door. Now I have to rearrange the table."

"He's trying to impress you," Ruth said. "Were they from Abel's shop?"

"The card wasn't from there. It must be a different florist, but I don't know which one."

"What did the delivery boy's uniform say?"

"He wasn't wearing one. I tried to give him a tip, but he refused to take it. He was a little fidgety, if you want to know the truth."

When Murray Fein showed up that evening, he was not what Ruth expected. For one thing, he was closer to thirty than twenty. She assumed he would be a duplicate of Lenny, but his expression was harder and his temperament more subdued. In his custom-tailored suit and expensive silk tie, he looked wealthy and capable—a far cry from Ruth's first impression of his brother.

Once the meal was under way, the differences between the men became more pronounced. While Lenny drained his cup of wine in sloppy gulps, Murray took small sips. While Lenny talked about baseball, Murray talked about business. While Lenny complimented the meal repeatedly in a desperate effort to ingratiate himself, Murray chose his words carefully and said them only once.

During the seder, it was traditional to take turns reading out loud from the Haggadah. But Lenny struggled so painfully with the Hebrew that Murray interrupted. "I apologize," he said, addressing their father. "Lenny was very young when we lost both our parents. The uncle who took him in didn't see the need for him to continue his Hebrew lessons."

"Or to finish high school, apparently," their mother snapped. The words were spoken with such scorn that Ruth almost gasped out loud. Her mother had always been difficult, but she had become even more shrewlike lately—nagging and shouting, banging kitchen pots and pans. This latest comment was proof of her decline.

Millie stood from her chair and threw her napkin on the table. "Mama, stop it! You're *ruining* the holiday!"

Ruth glanced at their father—the peacemaker of the family—but it was Lenny's brother, Murray, who spoke up first. "Please," he said calmly, holding up one hand. "Don't blame your mother. She isn't wrong. Please, sit." His voice was like marble, smooth and cold. His eyes were unblinking—almost hypnotic.

Millie sat back down.

"If anyone is to blame for Lenny quitting school, it's me," Murray said.

"C'mon, Mur, you know that's not true," Lenny moaned in protest.

"The truth is, if our mother were alive today, she would be ashamed of us both. Education was important to her. So was family." Murray refolded his napkin and placed it neatly beside his plate. "Our father ran off when Lenny was a baby, and our mother died when Lenny was ten years old. I was eighteen; I had just finished high school. I was offered a good job in Chicago, so I took it and left. There were too many bad memories in New York. But I never should have left my brother. To this day, I still regret it."

"You don't need to explain," Millie started to say, but Murray kept talking.

"The uncle I left him with wasn't fit for the job. It was fine at first, when Lenny was still little, but when he got bigger, the uncle lost interest. I sent money every month, but the kid didn't see any of it; Lenny was forced to take care of himself. He stopped going to school so he could pick up odd jobs. He was sixteen years old by the time I found out. When I realized what was going on, I came back for him."

Ruth watched her mother as she listened to Murray's speech, but if her mother felt any pity, it wasn't discernible. Ruth's father, on the other hand, was visibly moved. He patted Murray on the back and shook his head sadly. "It's a tragedy when children lose their parents so young," he said. Millie gave her father a small, grateful nod. For the rest of the meal, her mother didn't say a word.

The next morning, Ruth's phone rang earlier than usual.

"I didn't sleep all night, not for a minute, not even for a *second*."

"Then why do you sound so happy?" Her mother's voice, in fact, was eerily cheerful—high pitched and giddy, like an overexcited child's.

"Because right before sunrise, it came to me like a flash. The perfect solution to get your sister away from the Bum."

"Well, I'm glad you feel better, but I can't talk now. The girls are crying for breakfast, and I have to get them fed—"

"You don't want to hear my idea?"

"Fine, but tell me quickly. I really have to go."

Years later, when Ruth thought back to that awful conversation, she remembered her mother's words like two hands around her throat.

"You can take your sister to Springfield with you."

# Lillian

**Springfield, Massachusetts (August 1942)**

When the residents of Springfield complained to Lillian about the heat, it was all she could do not to laugh in their faces. Just now, when Grace Peabody said she thought it was hot enough to fry an egg on the sidewalk, Lillian wanted to tell her that if she dropped an egg in Texas in the middle of August, it would already be hard-boiled by the time it hit the ground.

But before she could speak, her daughter Margaret began screaming. "*Mommy!* Peter is splashing me!"

Lillian walked to the edge of the swimming pool and bent down so that her face was only inches from her son's. "Peter, do you think I can't see what you're doing? That's your second warning. I want you out of the pool."

"But I don't have a towel."

"And whose fault is that? Didn't I tell you to bring them?"

"Yes, ma'am. Sorry." Peter dragged his skinny frame out of the water and stood to the side, shivering in the shade. "Do you want me to go get the towels now?"

"For goodness' sake, Peter, stand in the sunshine. I'll get the towels; I don't want you dripping all over my clean floor. Grace, would you mind keeping an eye on them for me? I'll be back in a few minutes."

From beneath her perfectly tilted straw hat, Grace Peabody nodded her consent.

The pool was small and secluded, surrounded by privet hedges and centered behind two of the officers' homes. Anyone strolling through the main part of Armory Square would never have known that it existed.

Lillian followed a short path past a row of fruit trees, made a left at the garden, and then a right at the greenhouse. Stone piers with lights marked the entrance to her driveway, which she followed straight ahead to her back door. The air was heavy with the scent of overripe roses clinging to the trellises and drooping off the vines.

The towels were waiting just where she'd left them—in a forgotten pile, next to a bag of peaches. As she retraced her steps and headed back to the pool, Lillian made a mental note to ask the gardeners about her tomato plants—the ones in her victory garden were brown and limp.

She could hear Grace shouting even before she could see her. *What has Peter done now?* It wasn't her son, however, who was the object of Grace's reprimand, but a very small boy—no older than three. His mother knelt beside him, rubbing his back. As Lillian got closer, she recognized the young mother as Millie Fein. Her hair was tied back with one of the red bandannas issued by the Women Ordnance Workers.

"Millie! Is something wrong?"

When Millie realized who it was, her face flooded with relief. "Lillian!"

Grace frowned. "You two know each other?"

"Of course we do. Millie is Ruth Blum's sister. I'm sure you remember her—I introduced her at one of our meetings in June."

There was no doubt in Lillian's mind that Grace knew who Millie was; she wasn't the kind of woman to forget a face so quickly.

Still, Grace wasn't above *pretending* to forget, especially when the face belonged to someone like Millie—someone young and pretty but without social connections.

"Yes, of course," Grace murmured. "I hadn't realized that the two of you were still in touch."

Lillian bent down next to Michael. "Would you like a peach?" she asked, holding one out to him. "It's from a tree near our house. Peter! Come over here and say hello to Michael. I want you to take him to the shallow end of the pool and sit in the shade with him while he finishes his snack. When he's done, you can take him swimming."

Peter grinned. "You mean you're going to let me go back into the pool?"

"As long as you behave." When the boys were out of earshot, she turned to Grace. "Now, then, is there some sort of problem? I could have sworn I heard some raised voices when I was walking through the hedges."

Grace pursed her lips. "This pool has always been for the exclusive use of armory officers and their families. It is for residents only, not for civilian workers or their children."

"Millie is a member of Officer Blum's extended family," Lillian said. "And, since she lives with her sister, she is also a resident."

"She works at the *shops*," Grace answered. "Look at her badge. This pool is *not* for shopworkers."

"I'm sure you're not suggesting that you are superior to our shopworkers, Grace. Because that would be like saying you were better than our soldiers—better than the men who risk their lives for our country."

"That's not what I mean, Lillian, and you know it. This pool is for officers and their *immediate* families. If we let Millie in, where does it end? Is Ruth's third cousin going to be here next week? Or Millie's friends?" Grace kept her voice low so the children wouldn't hear, but her tone was unyielding. "I didn't want to have to say this, but I can see that you're going to make me spell it out for you.

You're ignoring the obvious health risks to our children! It's polio season, and swimming pools are prime breeding grounds. I've read a dozen articles at least, and they all say so. We don't know who Millie's son is associating with, what germs he's being exposed to, what diseases he could spread—"

"Stop it this instant! That is *enough*!" Lillian was certain that no one had ever shouted at Grace before—for a moment, the awful woman was stunned into silence. But Grace regained her composure quickly.

"Madeline, Clara, time to leave now." The command was unambiguous; Grace's voice was firm. The always-obedient Peabody girls climbed out of the pool, buckled their sandals, and wrapped their towels around their waists.

"I hope you and your *friend* enjoy the afternoon," Grace said. "It's gotten too warm for us, I'm afraid."

Lillian slipped her arm around Millie's shoulder. "Funny how some people can't take the heat."

# Millie

**Brooklyn, New York (August 1937)**

Despite the rising temperature outside, Millie's mother insisted on cooking. When Millie told her to sit and relax for a while, she dismissed the suggestion with a wave of her hand. "Hot or cold," she grunted, "people need to eat."

"But no one wants soup in weather like this. It's an inferno in here."

"Who said anything about soup? I'm making stuffed cabbage."

"Oh, Mama," Millie groaned. "That's even worse." Millie leaned against the counter, fanning herself with a day-old newspaper, while her mother separated a fat, green cabbage into leaves. A pot of salted water bubbled on the stove. As the leaves began to boil, the sour smell of cooked cabbage overwhelmed the room.

"I need some fresh air," Millie said.

"So, go down to the drugstore and get some ice cream with your friends. You can pick up some aspirin for me while you're there."

Millie hadn't mentioned it to her mother, but she hadn't seen much of her girlfriends lately. They'd stopped calling her for plans when she and Lenny had gotten serious, and when she'd asked them about it, they had only made excuses. *You're always out with him. You're never home when we call.* And then there were the rumors she knew they'd been spreading: that Lenny was faster than the boys in their own crowd and that Millie had gotten in over her head. She'd heard the talk in the bathroom when no one realized she was inside the stall; she'd heard the whispers in the hallways when they thought she couldn't hear.

The truth was, since her graduation, Millie had been thinking of ending things with Lenny. On the day she first met him, she had been drowning in grief—not just for Mrs. DeLuca but for Nico and Paulie as well. She had been alone and lonely, with far too much free time. Ruth was already married, and the tiny bedroom the sisters had shared felt suddenly cavernous. When Lenny knocked on her door, it felt like fate—he was handsome and funny, the perfect cure for the emptiness that swirled inside her. Lenny gave her a glimpse of the world outside her tiny neighborhood—parts of the city where people didn't know her, where no one thought of her as Ruth's flighty younger sister.

But lately, she'd been feeling increasing moments of uncertainty—small doubts that festered in the back of her brain: the nervous way Lenny laughed when he spoke about his job, the shrug when she asked where he'd been, the vacancy of his stare at her high school graduation when one of her teachers asked where he went to college. She had no doubt that Lenny loved her, but she began to question whether that was enough. What was the proverb her mother was always quoting? *Love is sweet, but it tastes better with bread.*

**On the way to the drugstore, her light summer dress felt like a** thick woolen coat. By the time she reached the soda counter, it clung uncomfortably to her skin.

"Millie! How is your summer so far?" Beverly Botnick was sitting at the soda counter with two other girls from Millie's high school class. The three of them were dressed alike, in pastel skirts and white blouses. Each wore her hair in a neat ponytail.

"Hot," Millie answered, forcing a smile. She'd been hoping to avoid Beverly and the others—they were the same girls who had dropped her so abruptly that spring, the ones who had gossiped and spoken behind her back. "How are all of you?"

"Oh, we're swell. Joyce just got engaged—Joyce, show her your ring. I don't start college until the first week of September, so I have all summer to help her look for dresses. And Audrey is starting a new job next week. She's going to be the receptionist at her uncle's law office."

Millie felt an ache in the hollow of her stomach; suddenly everyone she knew had plans for the future—plans that had fallen into place as neatly and crisply as Beverly's shirt collar.

"Tell us about you. Everyone wants to know what's next for the *famous* Millie Kaplan. Are you still dating the hat salesman? I don't see a ring . . ."

"Yes." Millie nodded. "Lenny and I are still together."

"Poor Jerry Polikoff." Beverly snorted. "You know it broke his heart when he saw you necking at the movies. But he's with Leslie Schwartz now; they're practically engaged."

"You should get engaged too!" Joyce insisted. "It's been so much fun, planning the wedding. David is in medical school, so he doesn't have much time to help, but my mom says it's probably better that way."

"Thanks, but Lenny and I aren't in any rush."

"Not *yet* anyway," Beverly muttered under her breath.

Millie cleared her throat. "I've been thinking about taking some classes."

"College, you mean? Well, that's a surprise, coming from you."

"Shhh, Beverly." Joyce elbowed her friend. "I think that's great, Millie. Really, I do."

The air in the drugstore felt suddenly stifling. Noises from every direction roared in Millie's ears—the jingle of the doorbell, the ding of the cash register, the constant buzz of customers and clerks back and forth.

"I'm so sorry," Millie murmured. "I have to get back home."

She stumbled through the doorway, gasping for air, and sped down the sidewalk back toward her building. When she entered the apartment, she found no relief—just the sulfurous stench of cabbage that had been cooked for too long. Millie ran to the bathroom and vomited in the toilet, her head pounding from a terrible mixture of heat and humiliation.

When she finally finished, her mother was waiting, as oblivious to her distress as she was to the smell of the dinner she was preparing.

"How are the girls? Did you remember to pick up the aspirin for me?"

Millie shook her head. "I'm sorry," she answered. "I was having so much fun, I completely forgot."

**When her father came home, he opened all the windows. "Your** mother is a wonderful woman," he said, "but only a meshuggener makes stuffed cabbage in this heat."

Millie flipped through the pages of her magazine. "After a few hours, you won't be able to smell it anymore."

"Tell that to Mrs. Bernstein downstairs. You should have seen the look she just gave me." He sat down next to his daughter and loosened his tie. "What's the matter? You forgot how to smile today, maybe?"

Millie wondered how honest she should let herself be with him. He was different from her mother—more open-minded. Certainly, he was more accepting of other people's flaws. He didn't seem to hate Lenny the way her mother did, but then again, he'd never said anything nice about him either. More and more,

Millie found his lack of commentary puzzling. From somewhere in the kitchen came a metallic clang: the lid from the stewpot falling to the floor. It shook her from her reverie, and she shut her magazine.

"Papa, what do you really think of Lenny?"

Her father raised his eyebrows. "You met him, when? Last September? Why is my opinion so important all of a sudden?"

She had thought he would answer her question and be done with it. But clearly, it was going to be a longer conversation. "I know that Mama doesn't approve of him. She thinks that Lenny isn't good enough for me. But you and I both know how unrealistic she is. She has a crazy fantasy about who I'm going to marry."

"Your mother is a wonderful woman. She only wants the best for you."

"I know she does, Papa, but she takes it too far! You saw how she treated Lenny at Passover. She won't even say his name out loud!"

Millie's father took a handkerchief from his pocket and wiped his forehead. "Your mother is a wonderful woman—"

"Stop saying that already! Please, just be honest. You *must* like Lenny more than she does, or you would have forbidden me from seeing him. But you never say anything, good or bad. Please, Papa, tell me: Do you think he's a good match for me?"

Her father's lips curved into a faraway smile. "Ach, *mameleh*, I'm flattered that you want your father's opinion, but believe me when I tell you, you're asking the wrong person."

His answer only made her more confused. Why did he have to speak to her in riddles? Why did he have to make this so difficult?

He rose from the couch and kissed her gently on the forehead. "You ask me this question—you say, 'Papa, tell me.' But how can one person tell another person her heart? When I introduced my sister to your mother, they didn't get along. Did I ask my sister what to do when I wanted to propose? Of course not; I knew the answer she would give me. I knew I loved your mother, and that was enough. When it comes to love, nothing good comes of asking for someone else's opinion. Love is something you have to decide for yourself."

# Ruth

After her mother revealed her grand plan, Ruth prepared a mental list of reasons why Millie couldn't come to Springfield. First, Ruth had no idea what their assigned housing would be like. There might not be enough room for an extra adult. Arthur would have to check with his superiors to see if non-immediate family members were permitted to stay.

There were other issues, of course—whether Millie could find a job in a city where she didn't know anyone; whether leaving her friends would be too difficult. When Ruth's mother rang her doorbell a few days later, Ruth was ready.

"Don't you think Millie will be homesick if you make her leave Brooklyn?" They had settled in Ruth's kitchen to box up her grandmother's china. Though Ruth's departure was still a few months away, she was trying to pack whatever she could in advance.

Her mother rolled her eyes. "Trust me, Millie will be happier away from the Bum, even if she doesn't know it yet." She took a sheet of newspaper from the stack on the floor and laid it open on the wooden table. Then she set a single plate on top of the center crease and folded the paper neatly over the porcelain.

"Come on, Mama. Lenny isn't *that* terrible. Daddy doesn't seem to mind him as much as you do."

"Your father has a soft spot for orphans and strays. He's too sympathetic, that's what he is. The Bum could never support a family, he's nothing but a *pustunpasnik*—a loafer."

"What about his brother? Murray is successful. He'll probably bring Lenny into his business soon."

"I don't like the brother. He has a smile like a crook, shifty eyes like a ganef."

"A crook and a thief? Do you know how you sound?"

"You think I care what I sound like? I know what I know. Get me another stack of plates, will you? There, the smaller ones. I'm done with these."

"You can't deny how much Lenny is smitten with Millie. He's completely in love—you see the way he looks at her?"

"I'll tell you what I see, Ruthie. I see a man with no steady job, no education, and no ambition. I see someone who cancels dates for no reason and who forgot your sister's birthday. Did he show up the next day with a million excuses and a fancy present all tied up in a bow? Sure, sure, of course he did. But that isn't love, not by a mile. He looks at your sister like a cat looks at a mouse. He doesn't want to take care of her—he wants to gobble her up."

"Well, I'm just surprised you'd want Millie to go to Springfield. When I said *I* was moving there, you acted like it was the North Pole." Ruth pulled the gilt-edged bowls down from the cabinet while her mother continued wrapping the plates.

"Better to live in peace at the North Pole than to stay here with that no-goodnik."

"Well, I can't take her with me right away, Mama. I don't know where we'll be living, I don't know if we'll have room, I don't know if she'd even be *allowed* to live with us."

"Just have Arthur tell them she's coming."

"Mama, don't you see? Arthur can't *tell* them anything. They tell *him* what to do, not the other way around."

"So, you'll go and settle in, and we'll bring her in a month. By that time, it should be fine. I'm sure you'll have room."

"I don't understand why you think she'll listen to you. If she really loves Lenny, she's not going to leave; if anything, she's going to want to stay here and marry him."

"Marry him? *Marry* him?" Her mother's face turned purple. "Your sister will marry the Bum over my dead body!" The plate she was holding came down with a *snap*, like the splitting of a seam or the tearing of a page. Suddenly, her mother's eyes filled with tears.

Ruth couldn't remember ever seeing her mother cry. She hadn't cried at Aunt Edna's funeral or when their neighbor passed away. She hadn't cried at Ruth's wedding, not even when Arthur stomped on the glass under the chuppah. She hadn't cried when the twins were born.

To see her mother so vulnerable made Ruth uneasy. "Mama, don't cry. I'm sure we can fix it. I have some glue somewhere—just give me a minute to find it."

Her mother's face crumpled. "You think I care about a plate? You think I'd cry over an old dish? No, Ruthie. No. If your sister marries Lenny, then I'll have something to cry about. If she marries him, mark my words: that man will break her heart."

# Millie

**Springfield, Massachusetts (September 1942)**

For the next few weeks, Millie couldn't get Grace Peabody's voice out of her head. *Diseases.* Millie knew Grace was wrong about Michael getting the other children sick, but still, she lay awake at night, worrying. It wasn't polio she was afraid of but something else entirely.

"Do you have a pediatrician for the girls?" Millie tried to sound nonchalant when she asked her sister the question.

"I take them to Dr. Gibson, here at the armory. Why? Is Michael coming down with something?"

"No, he's fine. But I was thinking that he should have a doctor in Springfield, just in case."

It had been years since Millie shared anything private with her sister. Ruth had invited her into her home, she had tolerated Millie's presence, but their connection was tenuous, their adult bond barely formed. Theirs was a détente of domesticity, held together with tacit understandings and unspoken boundaries. The sisters spoke of the weather, of laundry and dinner. There was safety in the mundane. But personal concerns were a potential minefield.

Millie started out slowly. "I'm not sure you ever knew this, but

Lenny's father died of a heart attack when he was very young—it was after he had already left Lenny's mother. And Lenny had some . . . issues with his heart too. I'm worried that the problems might be hereditary."

Millie hadn't overestimated her sister's affection for her son. No matter how Ruth felt about sharing Millie's personal burdens, she rose to the occasion when it came to Michael.

"He should have a checkup," Ruth insisted. "I'll call Dr. Gibson first thing tomorrow."

**"This is going to feel cold,"** Dr. Gibson told Michael. He placed the stethoscope against the boy's tiny chest and listened for what seemed like an eternity. Then he moved the instrument to Michael's back and listened again. Millie began to speak, to ask how much longer, but the stern-faced physician silenced her with a single finger placed over his lips. For the next few minutes, Millie forgot how to breathe.

When the doctor was finished, he gave Michael a quick pat on the head. "Everything sounds normal," he told Millie. "Now, let's talk about vaccines."

Michael was still sniffling from the shot when she carried him out of the building. Back at the house, Ruth looked nervous when she saw the tears, but Millie calmed her fears. "His heart is fine. Dr. Gibson gave him a shot, that's all. A vaccination."

"Thank God," Ruth said. She leaned toward her sister and gave Michael a kiss on the cheek. "Come in the kitchen. I made some molasses cookies; one of the girls in the office gave me the recipe."

They followed the warm, sweet smell toward the back of the house. But when they got to the kitchen, a pitiful moan escaped from Michael's throat. It was a different kind of sound from the wail he had made in the doctor's office. He buried his head in Millie's shoulder and sobbed uncontrollably.

"Michael, what's wrong?" Ruth was confused, but Millie knew

the reason for her son's outburst. A single red balloon was bobbing in the air over the kitchen table, the string tied to the back of the chair where Michael usually sat. Ruth must have picked it up from one of the merchants in town.

Millie handed Michael to Ruth and untied the balloon. She carried it through the kitchen's back door and let go of the string. It flew up and to the west, a crimson cloud in an otherwise clear blue sky. When it was no longer visible, Millie made her way back inside.

"All gone," she told Michael. "I promise. All gone." She took him from Ruth and rocked him in her arms, cooing and shushing and humming in his ear. After he calmed down, he took one of Ruth's cookies and nibbled it slowly until it was gone.

"I had no idea he was afraid of balloons," Ruth said softly. "I'm so sorry."

Millie forced a smile to defuse the tension. "Don't worry about it," she said. "How could you have known?"

# Millie

**Brooklyn, New York (November 1937)**

They had been married for a month when Lenny began working full-time for his brother. "What's the job exactly?" Millie wanted to know.

But Lenny wouldn't discuss the details. "Deliveries, sales, wherever they need me. Whatever Murray wants." Though he worked longer hours than ever before, Lenny didn't seem to be earning any more money. He grew sullen and angry when she asked for a grocery allowance, and he accused her of shopping at expensive stores.

"But my mother always bought her meat at Frankel's," she protested.

"I don't care where your mother bought her brisket," he grumbled. "His prices are too high. Find somewhere else."

Lenny began staying out later and later in the evenings, until one night he simply didn't come home. At two in the morning, when he still hadn't shown, Millie decided to call Murray. Her brother-in-law answered on the very first ring, almost as if he'd been waiting by the phone.

"Murray? It's Millie. I'm sorry to call so late . . . I wanted to see whether you'd heard from Lenny. He hasn't come home."

"Millie? Is that you? Sweetheart, go to sleep. There's nothing to be nervous about. Trust me, he's fine." Murray sounded unconcerned.

"But where could he be? Is he still at work?"

"Listen to me, Mil. He got stuck on a job. I'm sorry he didn't call you to say he'd be late. I'll talk to him about that for next time, I promise. Now, go back to bed. And don't be worried."

Before she could respond, Murray hung up. Instead of calming her, the conversation only made her more anxious. She wrapped herself up in one of her father's old sweaters and settled on the sofa in the front room. The couple was still living in her parents' apartment, but Millie knew that the arrangement would not last much longer. They couldn't afford the rent—not by a mile—and the landlord's sympathy was beginning to fade.

She was still on the couch when Lenny stumbled in a few hours after sunrise with blood on his collar. "Are you hurt? What happened?" She had her arms wrapped around him before he could answer, checking his body for bruises, pressing her head into his chest. His shirt reeked of cigarettes, but she didn't care. When she was certain he was unharmed, she burst into tears.

"Geez, would you stop bawling? Work ran late, and then some of the guys invited me to their poker game. I got a bloody nose, that's all." Lenny wriggled out of her embrace and flung himself on the sofa, where he slept like a dead man for the rest of the afternoon. The next day, he acted as if nothing had happened.

The second time he disappeared was a few months later, after they had moved to a smaller apartment in a noisier neighborhood. Lenny told her he was stuck making deliveries in Queens. After a day and a half, when she didn't hear from him, she used her neighbor's telephone to call Murray again.

This time, her brother-in-law sounded mildly annoyed. "There's nothing to worry about," Murray said smoothly. "A couple

of my trucks broke down, that's all. I sent Lenny and the guys to
New Jersey for some new ones."

"But how long does it take to go to New Jersey? He's been
gone since yesterday morning."

She could tell Murray didn't appreciate being confronted.
"You like asking questions, don't you?" he said.

"I think I'm entitled to know where my husband is," she
snapped.

"Millie," Murray cooed, "listen to me. You're a newlywed, so
of course you're upset. A beautiful new bride should never spend a
night alone. It's my fault for sending him out on that job. What can
I do to make it up to you?"

His tone was so condescending that she wanted to scream.
But she would not give him the satisfaction of raising her voice. She
would take a page from his book and reveal absolutely nothing.

"Just tell your brother to call," she said. This time, Millie was
the one to hang up first.

When Lenny returned two days later, the smell of cigarettes
on his shirt was mixed with the scent of ladies' perfume. Millie
found two matchbooks from a Philadelphia nightclub in his jacket
pocket. When she handed them back to him, he threw up his hands.

"You accusing me of something?"

"I'm not accusing you of anything. I didn't know you were in
Philadelphia, that's all."

"We were all over the place—New Jersey, Philly. I lost track
after a while. What's the big deal?"

The disappearances continued. Millie thought they might
stop after Michael was born, but they only became more frequent.
Lenny would be gone for a night or two or sometimes three and
would return smelling of women, of liquor, and lies.

The last time she called Murray, a different man answered.
"Hello?" the voice shouted. "Whaddya want?"

"This is Millie Fein, Murray's sister-in-law. May I speak with
him, please?"

After a pause, the man returned to the line. "Murray said to tell you Lenny is fine. Stuck on a job. He'll be home tomorrow."

"If I could speak to my brother-in-law for just a minute—"

"Sorry, lady," the voice said. "Murray can't talk."

**Before the attack on Pearl Harbor, Lenny had been gone for three** days. The evening after President Roosevelt declared war, Lenny walked through the door of their tiny apartment, shaved and sober, with a half-crushed bouquet of flowers and a wallet full of cash. Millie was sitting at home with Michael, hungry for news and straining to hear her neighbor's radio through the thin plaster walls of their apartment. This time, Lenny smelled of soap and witch hazel. His clothes were clean and his shoes freshly shined. He had come directly from the barber, he said, which was where the bouquet of flowers got crushed. "I left them on a chair, and someone sat on them by mistake."

This time, she actually believed him.

Usually when Lenny got home after one of his sprees, he got into bed and slept the day away. This time, he was bursting with energy—swinging Michael in the air and tickling the little boy until he was howling with laughter.

Lenny took them to the coffee shop down the block for dinner, and afterward, he bought Michael a red balloon. Millie tied it to Michael's wrist so it wouldn't float away, and the whole time they walked, Michael stared up at it. A thousand stars hung in the clear night air, and the moon was brighter than Millie could ever remember. Lenny carried Michael up high on his shoulders, and when they got home, Lenny tucked him into bed. Watching Michael fall asleep in his father's arms almost made her forget all the other nights she had sat up waiting for her husband.

Lenny spoke while Michael slept, of his plan to join the army, of his desire to rise up in the ranks and to make something of himself. He wanted to fight for his country, he said, the greatest country in the world. He had never thought much about being Jewish before, and he hadn't been inside a synagogue for at least a decade, but that night, he spoke of his ancestors and the faraway places his people had come from—Poland and Russia and towns with no names. "I never really thought that stuff mattered before," he confessed. "If I was Jewish or Catholic or whatever, you know? But if you're Jewish over there, they can take away your business even if you've never been to a synagogue. Hell, they can put you in jail even if you don't believe in God."

Millie didn't say much; she tried only to listen. She wanted so much to understand her husband, to know what he was thinking. More than anything in the world, she wanted to believe he could be a success.

She was so elated the next morning that she wrote a letter to Ruth right after Lenny left for the recruiting office. *Lenny is joining the army. I've never seen him so excited.* Although pride prevented her from revealing the whole truth of her marriage, she poured all of her hopes into her words. She didn't write about their dismal living arrangements, Lenny's failed jobs, or her own awful loneliness. She wrote only happy news, only her most positive thoughts. She asked about the girls, about Arthur, about Springfield. There was more she wanted to say, but she had already filled the page.

Millie took Michael for a walk and dropped the letter in the mailbox. She bought groceries with the money Lenny left her and spent the rest of the afternoon roasting a chicken and making an apple pie.

By the time Lenny returned to the apartment that night, he was drunk and the chicken was cold. The stench of whiskey wafted off his new shirt, now crumpled and stained. At first, Millie thought he had been celebrating, but the look on his face told her he had been drowning his sorrows.

She was afraid to ask, but she couldn't help herself. "What happened?"

She had seen Lenny angry before, plenty of times, but she had never heard his voice so brimming with rage. "I'll tell you what happened! I went down there and filled out all their damn papers. I answered all their stupid questions for nothing!"

"Are they sending you to the Pacific? Is that why you're so upset?"

"They're not sending me anywhere! The goddamn doctor said I have a heart murmur. A heart murmur! Can you believe that? I'm healthy as a horse!"

"Did he say what kind of heart murmur?" Millie tried not to let the panic she felt creep into her voice.

"How the hell am I supposed to know? The idiot stamped my papers and told me to see a cardiologist. One doctor ruins my life, and then he tells me to go see *another* doctor!"

"We'll go tomorrow. I'll go with you."

"Are you kidding me? I'm not going to any more doctors."

"But what if you need medicine? What if you have what your father—"

"Jesus Christ, you're gonna start in with me about my father now? Just shut up, will you? *Shut up!*"

Years before, when Ruth had slapped her that first night Lenny came for dinner, Millie hadn't seen it coming. She had been so surprised that she had barely registered the pain—the shock of the act overshadowed every physical sensation. But this time, the opposite was true. Millie knew what was about to happen before Lenny raised his arm. She could see the movement in her mind, she could feel the air push forward from the back of his hand through the space between them. She felt the sting of the impact before his knuckles hit her cheek, and when it was done, there was only a sick sense of relief. He left the apartment without a word, without a single backward glance, so spent from the deed that he didn't even have the strength to slam the door on his way out.

The next morning, all that was left of Lenny was the deflated red balloon. When Michael saw the shriveled sphere, empty and lifeless on the worn wooden floor, he flung himself down next to it and cried.

# Lillian

**Springfield, Massachusetts (September 1942)**

The hammering started precisely at seven. An enormous grandstand had been constructed in front of the main arsenal building the day before, but the finishing touches were made that morning. At least a dozen men were draping the platform with red, white, and blue bunting, oversized American flags, and ribbons. More than a hundred folding chairs were being arranged underneath the covered area, with a special section up front for presenters and guests of honor. The freshly painted podium—a glossy white lectern adorned with the armory seal of two crisscrossed cannons—was placed in the center, facing what soon would be a crowd of thousands.

The festive atmosphere extended to the Walsh breakfast table, where Thomas, their oldest, had just taken a seat. Between bites of toast and gulps of milk, he questioned his father about the ceremony. "Frances said the mayor is giving a speech. Who else is coming?"

Before the colonel could answer, Frances swept into the kitchen waving the morning edition of *The Springfield Republican*. Her ponytail was knotted with a tight red bow, and her knee socks clung obediently to the tops of her calves. "Honestly, Thomas, don't you ever read the paper?" She recited from the front page. "The Army Navy 'E' Award for Excellence in production will be presented by Major General Thomas J. Hayes, chief of the industrial service of the ordnance department." Then she tossed the paper at her brother's plate.

Thomas scowled, but took his turn reading. "Also attending will be Major General Sherman Miles, commander, first service command; Captain Arthur Atkins, representing the commandant of the first naval district; Brigadier General H. R. Kutz; and Captain Gerald Strickland."

Lillian felt a lump in her throat as Thomas read the last name. "Gerald Strickland?" She coughed. "Are you sure that's the name?"

"That's what it says. Right here in black and white."

**From their seats on the platform, Lillian and the children could see** all the groups of workers filing into Armory Square. The men were clean-shaven, in sweaters or suits, and the women had abandoned their bandannas and coveralls for carefully set waves and Sunday-best dresses. By the time everyone assembled, at least five thousand people filled the grassy campus. The mayor of Springfield and half a dozen captains and generals held seats of honor in the grandstand's front row. The renowned color guard from Fort Devens was on hand, marching in formation for the cheering crowd. Every member of the guard held an armory-made M1 Garand rifle.

Lillian was especially proud when General Hayes spoke about the number of women at the armory.

*In paying tribute to the armory employees, I am not unmindful of the big part that the girls and women of this plant have played and are playing. Without women in war industry, our production objectives could not be reached.*

When the pennant was presented, a steady stream of applause filled the square. Patrick and the guests of honor were ushered to the side, and the giant E banner was raised on the flagpole in the center of the green. Afterward, Patrick introduced Lillian to the visitors, including a white-haired and solemn Captain Strickland. He had the same rutted features she remembered from her youth—the same untrusting eyes, the same tightly clenched jaw.

The captain studied her face, his frown deepening. "You're Malcolm's daughter," he observed. "I suppose it's Mrs. Walsh now?"

"Yes, sir, it is."

"And those are your children? How old are they?"

"Margaret is our youngest—she's six and a half. Thomas, our oldest, just turned thirteen—the same age I was when we last saw each other."

"Your father did the right thing by sending you away. After that business with your mother, it was the very best thing for you."

Lillian bit her lip hard to keep herself from answering. What did this man know of what her mother endured? *The best thing for me,* she wanted to say, *would have been a childhood free from men like you and my father.* Instead, she changed the subject. "Will you be joining us for refreshments back at the house?"

"No time, Mrs. Walsh. Not a minute to spare. I'm not sure why all those generals have so much time for socializing, but some of us have to get back to Washington. Give your father my regards."

"Have a safe trip. Children, let's go." As she led them away, she felt Margaret tugging on the bottom of her skirt.

"Who was that, Mommy?" her youngest whispered.

"Nobody, sweetheart. Just an old friend of my father's."

**As a child, Lillian had been dragged to more military events than** she cared to remember. During World War I, her father had been gone for over a year, and when he finally returned, there had been parades, presentations, and dinners of all kinds. In an effort to save money, her mother sewed most of their dresses. She worked late into the evening, cutting fabric, pinning pleats, and ironing seams. Some mornings, Lillian would find her hunched over the sewing machine, snoring softly next to a pile of muslin. Only later did she realize that her mother hadn't fallen asleep there by mistake—that even a pillow of pins, if located far enough away from her father, held secret comforts a young girl couldn't comprehend.

When Lillian was twelve, there had been a banquet her father insisted they attend. He hadn't said what it was for, but from the way he went on about it, she knew it was important. Lillian's mother worked on their dresses for a month—long formal gowns in complicated styles.

On the evening of the banquet, Lillian and her mother got ready in Lillian's bedroom. Lillian was allowed to wear a drop of her mother's perfume, and by the time she was zipped into her pale blue gown, she felt like a princess. Her mother was stunning in long-sleeved green brocade, perfectly cut to showcase her slim figure. While they waited for Lillian's father, hope hovered in the air between them. Surely he would be complimentary; surely he would be proud to escort his wife and daughter to the officers' club that evening.

But when Lillian's father finally entered the living room in his dress uniform, he barely looked at them. He made his way over to the bar cart in the corner and poured himself a full glass of scotch. Prohibition was in effect, but he still had his sources. "Why are the two of you dressed like that?" he asked.

There was a long stretch of silence, so deep that Lillian felt she might drown in it.

"We're dressed for the banquet," her mother answered. "It's tonight, isn't it?"

"Of course it's tonight. But it's for officers only."

Her mother lit a cigarette with shaking hands. "Last month, you said Lillian and I were expected to attend. You said the event was formal and that we'd need gowns."

Lillian's father shrugged. "The general changed his mind. His mother-in-law is ill, and his wife went to California to take care of her. I told you before, it's officers only."

"You most certainly did *not* tell me. If you had *told* me, Lillian and I wouldn't be dressed like this. If you had *told* me, I wouldn't have spent the last three weeks sewing gowns that would never see the light of day." Lillian's mother began pacing across the living room floor, taking puffs from her cigarette.

"I don't appreciate your tone, Evelyn. I'm positive I told you. If you think I'm going to apologize just because you're too flighty to remember our conversations—"

"Flighty? That's a first. I haven't forgotten one word you've said to me, *ever*. Believe me, there have been plenty of times that I wish I had."

"I said to watch your tone." Lillian's father was practically growling now, stepping closer to her mother with long, lurching steps. His eyes were unblinking, fixed on Evelyn with a furious glare. Lillian watched her father put down his drink, watched his fingers curl into fists, watched his pupils turn black as he took another step—

Lillian jumped up from the sofa and grabbed her father's arm. "Daddy, don't you like my dress? Didn't Mom do a wonderful job?" She spun around and around, feigning delight in the swish of her skirt and the lift of the ruffles. The twirling made her sick to her stomach, but she forced herself to smile.

"You'd better take it off before you ruin it," her father said. He downed the rest of his drink in one quick gulp before depositing the empty glass on the bar cart. There was no further mention of the dresses or the banquet. He didn't even look at her as he made his way toward the foyer. "I'll be home late," he snapped just before he slammed the door.

# Ruth

Ruth wished she didn't have to sit on the platform for the award ceremony. She would have preferred to stand in the crowd with her colleagues from the payroll department, but all the other wives had places on the dais. The truth was, she was more at ease with her coworkers than she was with the women she saw at Lillian's weekly meetings. Her office mates admired her for the qualities she was proudest of: her attention to detail, her painstaking efficiency. But women like Grace Peabody didn't care about those things; they were more interested in her hairstyle and her housekeeping skills. Sitting next to Grace, self-doubt nagged at her, causing even more discomfort than the folding chair beneath her.

From her elevated seat, Ruth spotted her sister in the crowd, engrossed in conversation with a full-figured brunette. The woman was older than Millie by at least fifteen years, but they seemed content in each other's company, like old friends. Ruth assumed the woman was Arietta, the cook from the cafeteria whom Millie had mentioned.

From a distance, Millie's beauty was more evident than ever: her copper curls, her complexion, her hourglass figure. She wore a green knit dress—the first new clothing she had purchased in years. When the afternoon clouds parted, a narrow patch of sunlight fell across Millie's face, illuminating her from above. She threw her head back and laughed, unaware of Ruth's gaze. It was the freedom of her movement, the simple joy in her laughter, that made Ruth remember the girl Millie once was and the woman she might have become if their mother's dream had come true. Who would Millie be now if their parents hadn't died? Who would Millie be now if Ruth had told her the truth?

"That's your sister, isn't it?" Grace pointed into the crowd. "Over there, in the green?"

Ruth stiffened. "Yes, that's Millie."

"I saw her at the pool last month. Or didn't she tell you?"

Something about Grace's tone made Ruth hesitate. "No . . . Millie didn't mention seeing you there. I do know Michael enjoyed swimming this summer."

"Swimming in the pool reserved for officers, you mean?" The tone was unmistakable this time.

Ruth didn't answer. The last thing she wanted was an argument. Her social status was fragile enough—a battle with someone as outspoken as Grace Peabody would only reinforce her position as an outsider.

It was easy enough to stay silent during the program, to clap when the others clapped and to smile at the speeches. Ruth could ignore Grace then; she could overlook her sideways glances and pursed lips. But she dreaded the moment when the ceremony would end. She dug her nails into her palms and tried to think of a reason to leave early—a migraine, perhaps? Some kind of appointment? But though she racked her brain, she knew it was hopeless. She would have to stay in her seat until the speakers were finished.

Afterward, Grace wouldn't leave her alone. "Has Arthur told you anything more about the fire? Fred doesn't believe what they're saying about an accident. He's convinced it was arson."

"Arson? What do you mean?" She was grateful they had moved on to a different topic, but she couldn't think of where this new conversation was headed. The fire was old news as far as she was concerned. It had happened weeks ago, and the cleanup was well under way.

"Arson. Sabotage. Most likely by German sympathizers. Fred thinks it was probably someone new to the armory. Someone with access to the shops and the square. Maybe even a resident." Grace's eyes drifted back to the crowd on the lawn, back to the area where Millie had been standing.

"A resident? But the only residents at the armory are officers and their families."

"And their guests, of course. People who come to stay for extended periods of time."

Ruth's head began to pound. She could feel her knees shaking.

"By the way," Grace continued, "isn't that the Italian cook your sister is with? Your sister seems awfully chummy with her."

"The cook? I've heard that she's very popular with the cafeteria customers; she sings for them at lunchtime. She's supposed to be quite talented."

"I couldn't care less about how talented she is. Tell your sister to be more careful about the company she's keeping."

# Millie

## Springfield, Massachusetts (October 1942)

Every month, Millie looked forward to the day *The Armory News* came out. Some of the younger women she knew flipped right to the personals pages, where engagement and wedding announcements flooded the columns. But most read the monthly booklet cover to cover—even the armory bowling team scores. The first few pages consisted of updates on the war: recent battle news and pieces about the troops. But further in, there were all sorts of hand-drawn cartoons, poems, and essays about armory life.

Millie's favorite articles were the ones about her coworkers: spotlight pieces accompanied by photographs. She was fascinated to learn that someone in the heat-treat department was, at one time, a world-renowned harpist. And that the armory's very first female bus driver spent her life before the war driving across the country.

"There should be a piece about Arietta in the newsletter," Millie said the next day, to no one in particular. In the trigger assembly area, conversations bounced around like baseballs during team warm-up—carelessly tossed and dropped at random. Millie's days were filled with chatter that was interesting enough to move the day along but never particularly significant or personal. No one pressed her for the particulars of her life in Brooklyn or for any of the details about her husband. Building 103 wasn't the place for intimate discussions.

"Why Arietta?" The voice came from behind her, but Millie didn't turn around. She kept her eyes on the hammer springs at her fingertips and moved the small, steel spirals into place the way she had been taught.

"She has such an interesting background," Millie answered. "Did you know Arietta's father helped to build the Poli theater? It used to be a vaudeville house, and she sang there when she was younger. I can just picture her in costume, standing under the lights on that stage."

Another voice, from Millie's left, joined the conversation. "I can only picture her on a milk crate in the cafeteria."

Someone to her right chuckled. "Me too."

From the station across from her, Delores chimed in. "The *News* is always looking for story ideas. Go over and talk to them. See if they'll do an article."

The next day, Millie couldn't stop thinking about Arietta. If it weren't for her, Millie never would have found the library on State Street, and she and Michael never would have discovered the zoo in Forest Park. Arietta was always looking out for her—pointing out sales for whatever Millie needed and bringing her to the stores where she'd find the best deals. At the Morse and Haynes Shoe Shop, Arietta secured a discount by pointing out Millie's armory badge. "I'm sure you don't charge defense workers full price," she said to the owner. The next thing Millie knew, he'd taken 10 percent off her bill.

Millie had had girlfriends before, but none like Arietta. In fact, the more she thought about the girls she had been friendly with in high school, the more she realized how little most of them cared. Not one of them visited after her parents died. Not one of them sent a card when Michael was born. In the back of her mind,

Millie had always known those girls were happier to see her fail than succeed.

Of course, Millie hadn't necessarily been a wonderful friend either. She'd been caught up with the DeLucas and, after them, with Lenny. She hadn't gone out of her way for any of the girls she'd known back in Brooklyn. But now, Arietta's example made her want to do better. She would make a visit to the newsletter editor tomorrow, and then she would invite Arietta over for dinner. It was the least she could do to repay her friend's kindness. Ruth had discouraged guests, but Millie would be firm. She had spent her first few months in Springfield trying to fit into her sister's life. She had folded herself up like a torn scrap of paper, end over end, making herself small. She had tiptoed and whispered and confined herself to corners, all the while taking up as little space as possible. But she was done with all that. It was time for a change.

After all, how much more could she possibly lose?

# Arietta

Across the street from the armory's main gate, Federal Square bustled with activity. Three separate shifts kept the shops running twenty-four hours a day. People came and went in a steadily moving stream, with no differentiation between daylight and darkness, and the city of Springfield was happy to accommodate them. YMCA dances began at midnight for those working the three-to-eleven shift. Movie houses showed films at nine in the morning for people just getting off work. Federal Square was never silent and its people never still. A small, grassy courtyard greeted workers upon entry, but the area consisted mostly of manufacturing buildings—enormous brick structures that shivered and groaned with movement and sound.

In contrast, Armory Square was an oasis. Every time Arietta walked the grounds, she marveled at the manicured lawns, the spotless walkways, the space, and the quiet. The center was an open field, while the north and south edges were lined with small buildings. Most were individual homes occupied by officers and their families, but one served as a hospital, and another held shared quarters for lower-ranking personnel. The storehouses and garages, larger and less charming, were tucked behind the houses and gardens, hidden from view.

The house Millie lived in was more spacious than Arietta had imagined, with high molded ceilings and patterned parquet floors. She wondered whether all the houses in Armory Square were as nice as this one inside, but she decided to keep her questions to herself.

From the instant she met Ruth, Arietta could see that her assumptions had been wrong. She had thought the two sisters would look more alike—have the same mannerisms, perhaps, or share certain features. But where Millie was soft, Ruth was all edges. Ruth was attractive in the way certain women could be with enough time and effort, but natural beauty like Millie's eluded her. If she had met them separately, Arietta would never have guessed that the two women were related.

Ruth apologized for Arthur's absence. "He's been working so late these days that he almost never makes it home for dinner. But I'm sure the children would love to hear about your career on the stage. How old were you when you first started singing professionally?"

"I sang at my church when I was very young, but my father wouldn't let me sing in Mr. Poli's shows until I turned fifteen."

"Did you enjoy it?"

"I did, for a very long time. Of course, my experience was different from a lot of the other performers'. I didn't travel as much as most of them—my father wouldn't allow it. I worked out of New Haven until we moved to Springfield, and then my travel was limited to the Northeast and New England. When my father got sick, I stopped singing so I could take care of him. My mother died when I was born, so there was no one else to help."

"It must have been difficult for your father when your mother passed away."

"Yes." Arietta paused, unsure of whether she should continue.

"Millie mentioned that you lost both of your parents in an accident a few years ago. Please accept my condolences."

"Thank you," Ruth mumbled. Silence settled over their meal like a dense gray fog.

Twenty minutes later, Ruth excused herself from the table and went upstairs to lie down.

Arietta took a second helping and made a few jokes to lighten the mood. Dinner at Millie's was turning out to be more complicated than she had expected. When Millie told her about the tension she'd been having with her sister, Arietta had assumed that the problems stemmed from tight living quarters. But after seeing the house, she knew space was not the issue. Surely, the sisters' struggles weren't born from proximity.

In fact, from everything Arietta observed, the conflict between Millie and Ruth began long before Millie's arrival in Springfield. The pain in Ruth's expression ran too deep to be new. The hurt on Millie's face wasn't novel or fresh. It had evolved over time, with a scar-like permanence. Dinner didn't last long after Ruth left the table. The children were cranky, and Arietta didn't want to overstay her welcome.

She made it back home just in time for her favorite radio program: *The Victory Parade of Spotlight Bands*. The familiar bugle call echoed through her living room as the announcer introduced the guest for the evening.

*For the fighting sons of freedom, the Coca-Cola Company presents* The Victory Parade of Spotlight Bands! *Tonight, tomorrow night, every night, Monday through Saturday, the Coca-Cola Company sends the greatest bands in the land to entertain the soldiers, the sailors, the marines, and war workers.*

The program was a diversion, but even after it ended, Arietta found herself still thinking about dinner with her friend. She closed her eyes, trying to recapture the moments around the dining room table. There was something in Ruth's furtive glances and in Millie's agonized avoidance that bound the two of them together in a way she hadn't first noticed. There was an ache behind their smiles, a palpable longing—the same expression her aunties used to have before her father broke his silence and finally decided to speak openly about her mother. It was then that she realized the burden the sisters shared: each had a secret she was keeping from the other.

# Lillian

For the most part, Lillian enjoyed living at the armory. She took comfort in her volunteer work, in the meetings, and in war bond drives. But there were certain aspects of being the commanding officer's wife that she did not enjoy. Dealing with women like Grace Peabody was one. Business dinners with manufacturers were another.

Patrick's position at the armory meant that the two of them were forced to entertain more often than they liked, not only with military higher-ups who badgered Patrick with impossible quotas but with civilian businessmen who pestered him for contracts and then tormented him with overdue shipments. Tonight, they would be spending their evening with the latter.

Roy Crawford's company supplied the armory with sodium cyanide, the chemical compound used to case-harden steel. In Lillian's opinion, Crawford was the worst kind of dinner companion—the kind who spent the evening giving unwanted advice. He had never served in the military, and he knew nothing about weaponry, rifles, or any of the issues involved in their production. Despite his lack of knowledge, however, there was nothing he enjoyed more than forcing his opinions on others. He started out innocently, with questions about his own shipments. "Where's the storage facility these days? How's the ventilation system?" But after a few drinks, he began to engage in a steady stream of criticism. "Can't you make the damn rifles any faster, Pat?"

"It's not that simple, Roy," Patrick answered through gritted teeth. "The M1 is the product of years of research and design. It's been tremendously successful. You know that."

"Well, then, you're going to have to demand longer hours from your people."

"The armory already runs twenty-four hours a day, seven days a week."

"Hmph."

Mrs. Crawford sipped at her champagne and smiled. She was dull, pasty, and overdressed in a blue satin cocktail dress and heavy fur stole. It was Lillian's job to engage her in conversation, but tonight, she could barely think of anything to say.

The Hotel Kimball dining room was expansive and elegant, painted in muted tones of rose and gray. Coffered ceilings and patterned carpets warmed the space, while crystal fixtures provided a golden glow that flattered even the most anemic of complexions. Lillian wondered if that was why Mrs. Crawford had chosen the restaurant.

"Tell me, Mrs. Walsh, where is it that you're from? I thought your husband mentioned the South the last time we met, but you have no accent at all."

"My father was in the military too, so we moved around quite a bit. We jumped all over the South, but when I was thirteen, I was enrolled at a girls' boarding school in Connecticut."

"That explains the lack of accent, then. It must have been very hard on your mother to send you away. I could never have sent my girls away at that age."

"Unfortunately, my mother had just passed away. Given the circumstances, boarding school seemed to be the best choice."

"I'm so sorry, dear. Was she ill?"

"Patrick tells me you have a new grandson," Lillian gushed, changing the subject. "You must tell us all about him!"

**Lillian's aunt Catherine, her father's only sister, arrived on the** base just in time for the funeral. She'd shown up without flowers, casseroles, or soothing words, but with a stack of brochures for girls' schools in New England.

To be fair, boarding school had been Lillian's idea. Elated by the suggestion, her father passed on the task of choosing one to his sister. The Littlefield School in Connecticut was one of the few to accept students midway through the year. One of Catherine's acquaintances knew someone on the board.

Her aunt took her shopping for a simple black dress that she could wear to her mother's funeral. The saleswoman tried to give Lillian a reassuring smile as she wrapped up the purchases: the somber new dress, a pair of black pumps (Lillian's first), and a navy wool coat that her aunt insisted would be suitable for Connecticut winters.

For the rest of the week, Catherine was given free rein. She went through Lillian's closet, and Lillian's mother's, compiling a suitable wardrobe for a "Littlefield girl." Her aunt also filled a suitcase for herself—stuffed to overflowing with handbags and jewelry and the most beautiful of the dresses Lillian's mother had sewn. Lillian didn't say a word—she was too grief-stricken to object.

A week after the funeral, Aunt Catherine left, and Lillian and her father began their trip north. They drove for eighteen hours straight, stopping only for quick meals and trips to the bathroom. Lillian slept for much of the way, and when she wasn't asleep, she pretended to be.

"This is it," her father said as they turned into the school's driveway. Large stone pillars and snow-covered hedges framed the paved circle where he put the car in park. He pulled two suitcases from the trunk, set them in front of the large white-columned building, and returned immediately to the driver's seat. The process took only a minute, and he hadn't even bothered to turn off the engine.

"You're not going to walk me in and meet the headmistress?"

"You're a big girl now, Lillian," her father said, shifting the gears. "I'm sure you can handle this on your own."

"Am I coming home for Easter?"

"We'll see," he mumbled before driving away.

After witnessing the send-off from her front office window, the headmistress whispered some instructions to her assistant. When Lillian entered the office fifteen minutes later, she was greeted with a plate of cookies and a pot of hot chocolate instead of the customary tepid cup of tea. It wasn't until a month and a half later, when another new girl matriculated, that Lillian understood: she was an object of singular pity. Having a dead mother was one thing, but combine that with a father who never visited or called, not even on his daughter's birthday, and everyone—the headmistress, the teachers, and all the other girls—took notice. Lillian never knew if they were being nice to her because they liked her or because her family situation made her too tragic to treat poorly. On some days, Lillian was grateful for their kindness, but on others, it only made her feel more alone.

**She didn't go home for Easter, which was probably just as well.** Almost a dozen girls had stayed behind at the school, and after morning services at the chapel, they gathered together in the dormitory to gorge themselves on jelly beans and chocolate eggs. The other parents had sent packages, but Lillian's mailbox was empty.

"Have some of ours," the girls insisted. "There's plenty." But the sight of all the candy only made her stomach turn. Lillian didn't know the girls well enough to explain, and even if she did, what would she say?

The previous year's Easter had been the hottest she could remember. Lillian's mother had placed the turkey in the oven early, and by the time they got back from church, the inside of the cramped ranch house had been sweltering.

"Why's it so hot in here?" Lillian's father barked. He slid off the jacket of his uniform, revealing the sweat stains that had spread under his arms.

"It's the oven, Malcolm. It heats up the whole house," her mother explained.

"Then turn it off!"

"I can't turn it off now. The turkey hasn't finished cooking."

When he retreated to the master bedroom, Lillian assumed that was the end of it, but an hour or so later, he emerged to complain about the eggs she was decorating.

"You've used up a dozen eggs with this nonsense. It's a waste!" He grabbed one of the eggs out of Lillian's hand, but the dye was still wet, and some dribbled onto his shirt. "Damn it!" he shouted, flinging the offensive orb across the room.

Lillian's mother swept the bits of shell and yolk off the floor. "Sweetheart, why don't you go outside? You can have your Easter hunt now; I hid some treats for you."

"But we always do it together."

"Go on, sweetheart. Please."

With the help of a few garden benches and some plantings, Lillian's mother had made the most of their tiny backyard. For Easter that year, she had truly outdone herself—there were lollipops tucked into the flowerbeds, chocolates nestled in the roots of the willow tree, and painted eggs hidden in all of the bushes. After she filled her basket, Lillian sat on one of the benches, sucking on a lollipop and listening to the shouting that was coming through the windows. She returned to the house only after she was sure that her father was gone.

She found her mother in her bedroom, seated at her dressing table with a pile of glass jars and tubes laid out in front of her. When her mother turned her head toward the door, Lillian gasped. Underneath her mother's left eye, a bluish bump had begun to form. "Don't be upset," her mother said calmly. "These things happen sometimes. Once I get this covered up, you won't even notice."

Lillian dropped the Easter basket and ran out of the bedroom. She had always suspected something was wrong with her father. Her mother had tried to blame his behavior on the war, claiming he hadn't been the same since returning from World War I. But Lillian knew the war was just an excuse. Her father had been a bully long before that.

When her mother was finished camouflaging her face, she coaxed Lillian out of her bedroom with a too-cheerful smile. "I know you're not in the mood for your candy," she said, "but I have an idea." She placed all of the chocolates into a large glass bowl and melted them over a pot of warm water. Eggs, vanilla, and heavy cream were added, and the mixture was set aside long enough to roll out a fresh piecrust.

After the pie cooled, Lillian and her mother sat on the bench outside with two plates and two spoons. The temperature had dropped, and a soft breeze blew by, drying what remained of Lillian's tears. She hadn't eaten all day, and she should have been starving, but the pie was too sweet and the filling too rich. Lillian couldn't keep down a single bite.

After that day, her mother stuck to fruit fillings. She never made chocolate cream pie again.

# Millie

The letter arrived in early November. It was the first piece of mail Millie had received since she'd moved. When she saw the return address, her throat began to tighten. The letter came from Brooklyn—from the DeLuca boys' aunt who had fired her all those years ago.

> *Dear Millie,*
> *I am writing to you in the care of your sister. If you are no longer in Massachusetts, I hope she will forward this to you.*
>
> *Perhaps you have heard that my brother remarried. His new wife is a widow with a son of her own, and the boys seem to enjoy their new little brother. Sharing a house with two children was already a burden on my nerves, and the addition of a third was too much for me. I live a few blocks away now and see the family every weekend.*
>
> *Last Sunday, our supper was interrupted by an*

*unexpected visitor. My brother didn't know the man, but I recognized him immediately.*

*Leonard did his best to be charming at first, but he became sullen and angry after he realized we had no information as to your present whereabouts. I did not mention what I knew of your trip to western Massachusetts. (I found out from your mother's friend Mrs. Shapiro, who spotted you at the train station several months ago.)*

*I'm sorry to say, but I never trusted your husband. He kept unusual hours when he lived with you next door, and I could not help but overhear his many late-night outbursts. I could only assume that you did not want him to know of your recent relocation, but I wanted to make you aware of his search.*

*Please give my regards to your sister.*

*Sincerely,*
*Leora DeLuca*

With shaking hands, Millie tore the letter into dozens of tiny pieces. She hadn't heard from Lenny since the day he had left, almost a year ago. She had tried to contact Murray, but no matter how many times she called, the voice on the other end of the line insisted that she had the wrong number.

She had known when Lenny hit her that something in him had broken. He'd been angry before; he'd been dishonest and mean. But that night, he had crossed an invisible line. He must have known that he could never make it right with her again. He must have known she would never look at him the same way.

Mr. Solomon, the owner of the hat shop where Lenny once worked, took pity on her and hired her as a sort of assistant. The phone hardly ever rang, but he let her bring Michael, and sometimes she would rearrange the hats in the window. Every once in a while, she caught Mr. Solomon staring at her son and shaking his head. One day she had asked him, in a whisper, what he knew.

"Lenny and his brother owe a bunch of money," Mr. Solomon explained. "An awful lot of money to an awful dangerous fella."

"So, you don't think they're coming back?"

"Millie, sweetheart, from what I've heard, I'd be surprised if either one of them is still alive. I hate to say such things, but it's better maybe that you should know. So you don't get your hopes up."

Night after night, she waited and wondered. Was her husband truly gone? Would she ever know for sure? A year later, the bits of paper in her wastepaper basket told a story that she could never have anticipated.

"Mama!" Michael was calling from downstairs, eager for her attention. She had taken too long in her room, and he was growing impatient.

"I'm coming!" Millie unpinned her identification badge from her dress, smoothed back her hair, and tried to slow her breathing. Her brain raced with new worries about what to do next. She had always consoled herself with the fact that she hadn't spoken any strict falsehoods to her sister. Lenny had disappeared, and she'd written that he was gone. He had abandoned them, and she'd written that she was alone. Still, she had omitted the most difficult truth of all. In her heart, Millie knew she should tell her sister everything.

But as she headed downstairs, her certainty fell away. Step after step, doubt consumed her. *Remember how quickly Ruth left after our parents died, how she deserted you after the wedding, and how she barely looked back? What's to stop her now from throwing you out?*

She could hear Michael whining—hunger made him irritable. When she walked into the kitchen, he let out a groan. "Mama, why is everyone sad today?" he asked.

Millie had been lost in her own private thoughts. But when she looked at the faces around her, she saw that Michael was right.

Ruth looked ill—like she had eaten something spoiled—and the girls were sniffling and rubbing their eyes. It was rare for Arthur to drink alcohol with his dinner, and yet tonight, he had a full glass of whiskey in front of him.

"What's wrong? Why is everyone so upset?"

It was Arthur who answered, his voice steadier than his hands. "I'm being sent out of the country for a little while."

"Six months isn't a little while," Ruth snapped.

"We're setting up an ordnance outpost in North Africa. The rifles have been having some slight malfunctions—parts have been seizing up. It happened back in Singapore with the heavy rains, so it may be the humidity or a lubrication issue. In any event, they're sending a few of us over to evaluate and come up with some solutions."

Millie chose her words carefully. "I'm sure you'll be far away from the front lines. And six months will go by before you know it." She took the children's plates and packed them with fish fillets, carrots, and rice. She made sure the water glasses were filled and helped Michael cut his food. For the rest of the meal, she tried to keep up the conversation, but Ruth barely spoke and hardly touched her plate. When dinner was over, Millie stayed behind to do the dishes.

She was almost finished when Arthur returned to the kitchen with a freshly filled glass of whiskey. His hair was slightly mussed, and his dark-rimmed glasses were slipping down his nose.

"May I speak with you for a moment?" he asked.

"Of course."

Since her move to Springfield, Millie had barely spent any time with her brother-in-law. Her distance had been purposeful; she knew enough of Ruth's jealousy to stay as far away from him as possible. Despite their lack of contact, however, it was clear to her that Arthur was a good husband and father. She knew her sister and her nieces would be devastated by his absence.

"Millie, I'm not a particularly spiritual man. I don't go to synagogue much or even think about it really, but now . . . now that I'm going to be away, I feel as if maybe there was a reason you came to live with us."

She had never heard her brother-in-law speak this way before. "What do you mean?"

"You're the only one who can understand what Ruth will be going through. You know what it feels like to wait for your husband." He downed the rest of his drink in one long swallow. "Don't get me wrong—I expect to make it home, safe and sound. But if anyone could possibly help Ruth while I'm gone, it's you."

Why did he have to ask this of her now? She had been so close to telling the truth, so close to unburdening herself. But now was not the time to add to her sister's troubles. The revelations of Leora DeLuca's letter would have to wait. Millie found herself frustrated but utterly relieved.

"You will take care of her, won't you?" Arthur pleaded.

She didn't trust herself to speak, so she nodded in agreement. *You mean, take care of my sister the way she took care of me?*

# Millie

Millie's parents were going to Philadelphia for a third cousin's wedding, and Millie would be staying in the apartment alone. She had never stayed by herself—not even for one night—and her mother was beside herself.

"Why can't you stay with one of your girlfriends?" she demanded before they left. "Who wouldn't want you?"

"Beverly is at school, and Joyce is too busy planning her wedding."

"Hmph. I don't understand why you don't go to your sister. You shared a room together for all those years—"

"Mama, please. The twins are sick, and Ruth doesn't want company. I'll be perfectly fine on my own, I promise. I'm eighteen years old. It's just one night. And Mrs. Bernstein is downstairs if I have an emergency."

There had been additional discussions before her parents left—*Keep the door locked, the toaster unplugged; if you think you smell gas, call the police; absolutely no visitors, and don't think I don't mean business because Mrs. Bernstein has big ears and big eyes, and if she notices anything fishy, believe me, we'll know.*

When they were gone, Millie crept into her parents' bedroom and pulled a hand-sewn muslin bag from the back of the closet. Inside was her mother's wedding dress—cream-colored lace turned fragile with age. For as long as she could remember Millie had admired it, but her mother had always discouraged her interest. *Compared to the gown you'll have one day, this is just a pile of rags.*

Millie stepped into the dress and buttoned it up the back as far as she could—the fabric strained over her chest, but she pretended that it fit. From the front at least, the girl in her mother's mirror was a picture-perfect bride—it was only when she turned that the flaws became visible. After a few minutes in the gown, the lace began to scratch her skin. Carefully, she pulled it off, and returned it to the closet.

She thought about calling Audrey or Joyce, but she worried that neither of them would come to the phone. She hadn't seen them once since the drugstore that summer, and she still hadn't received an invitation to Joyce's wedding.

Lenny called sometime in the late afternoon, but she lied and told him she was going to Ruth's for dinner. Other girls in her situation would have invited him over in a heartbeat, but Millie refrained. In the past, she had assumed that Ruth's "rules" were rubbish—*nice girls don't smile at strangers, nice girls don't wear tight skirts, nice girls don't go around kissing men on street corners.* She'd argued with her sister and called her a prude. But the truth was, Beverly's comments at the drugstore had bothered Millie more than she wanted to admit. She didn't want to give the gossips any more ammunition, and besides, she still hadn't decided how she felt about Lenny. Her conversation with her father hadn't helped one bit.

So, for the rest of the afternoon, Millie listened to the radio and read her mother's copy of *Gone with the Wind*. At dinnertime, she fixed herself a cold chicken sandwich. She was already in her nightgown when the clock struck nine.

It was almost eleven when Lenny showed up, tapping so quietly at the door that she almost didn't hear him. "I didn't want that

lady downstairs to hear the buzzer." He grinned. "But I figured
you'd be home from your sister's by now." His jacket was crumpled, his eyes were bloodshot, and Millie recognized the faint smell
of liquor on his breath. When he leaned forward to kiss her, she
took a step back. "You can't come in now. I'm about to go to sleep."

"Aw, Millie, please? Lemme stay for a little? I just wanna talk."

"We can talk tomorrow, Lenny."

"I can't wait until tomorrow!" When he began to raise his
voice, Millie pulled him inside. "Shh!" she hissed. "Do you want
the whole building to hear you?"

"I'm sorry, I'm sorry," he muttered over and over. "I didn't
mean to yell—I had a coupla drinks."

"More than a couple. You can barely stand. Go ahead and sit
down, but just for a minute."

He fell onto the sofa, still whining his apologies. "I needed the
drinks so I'd have the nerve to ask. Millie, do you love me? Because
I sure love you. I think you're the most beautiful girl I ever met."

"That's sweet, but I think we should talk about this another
time."

"Nooo," he moaned. "I need to know now. Please, Millie, do
you love me? Because if we got engaged, your mother would know
I'm serious. If I was her son-in-law, she'd have to like me." Lenny's
eyelids fluttered, and his words came out garbled. "Wouldn't that
be terrific?" He reached out a hand to stroke Millie's cheek, but his
fingers were clammy, and she brushed them away. If he had been
more alert, he might have been insulted, but he giggled as if she
were playing a game.

It wasn't supposed to be like this.

For most of her life, Millie's mother had spun stories
about the kind of man who would propose to her one day. The
gentleman/millionaire/prince among men would be like one of
the Rockefellers—only Jewish, of course. He would have degrees
from Columbia or possibly Harvard and would come from a large
and prominent family. Tall and handsome, most likely—but even

if not, his clothes would be so well made that they would do the job for him. He would wear a gold watch, but no other jewelry, and he would smell of expensive cologne.

Most important of all, this miraculous man would dedicate his life to making Millie happy. He would shower her with gifts, adoration, and praise. His proposal would be planned well in advance, and would take place in an elegant restaurant or perhaps a garden. When he asked her to marry him, he would kneel down beside her, take her hand in his, and gently slip the ring on her finger. There would be champagne, of course, in crystal glasses. He would swear his devotion and promise to love her forever.

Meanwhile, the man in front of her could barely keep his eyes open. Soon his head drooped backward and he began to snore. She tried to shake him awake, but he was out cold. Was this the man she should choose for her husband? In the silence that surrounded her, she could hear her father's voice: *Love is something you have to decide for yourself.*

"Wake up. Do you hear me? You have to go home!"

She tried to pull Lenny to a standing position, but his body was too heavy for her to move. Disgusted, she left him on the couch, retrieved her book from the bedroom, and went into the kitchen to brew a pot of coffee. She would try to wake him again soon, and he would need it then.

Millie should have had a cup of the coffee herself, because half an hour later, she began to drift off. She lay her head down on her book and let herself dream about the wedding her mother had promised. In the dream, her gown was long and made of shimmering white silk. The room was filled with gardenias, and violins played. Her parents were on either side of her as she walked down the aisle, and at the front of the room, under the chuppah, was a man in a tuxedo waiting for her. She couldn't see the groom's face, but she knew he was smiling.

At around three in the morning, she woke to the sound of screaming. *"What are you doing here? Where is my sister?"*

Millie lifted her head from the table and rubbed her eyes. Her back ached and her legs were cramped, but she hobbled out of the kitchen and into the living room. Her sister stood over Lenny in a red-faced rage.

"How could you, Millie? How could you spend the night with him like this?"

"Ruth, calm down. I didn't invite him. He showed up on his own—he tried to propose. But he was drunk, and then he passed out and I couldn't move him."

Ruth sank slowly to the floor and began to weep. Millie knew that finding Lenny in the apartment was a shock, but her sister's reaction was far too extreme—there had to be something else to explain her behavior. A kernel of fear began to grow in Millie's chest.

"Ruth?" she asked softly. "Why are you here? Did something happen? Can you tell me what's wrong?"

Millie turned to Lenny, who was finally awake. "You should fix yourself a cup of coffee in the kitchen," she suggested. "I made a pot a few hours ago."

"Sure," he agreed, relieved to have been given a task. "I'll go do that."

Once he was gone, Ruth began to speak. The words poured out of her like water through a partially clogged faucet: a trickle and then a gush, soft and then loud. "Papa called me after the wedding. He said they were going to come home early. Mama didn't like the hotel room—you know how she is. She told Papa she wanted to sleep in her own bed. The police showed up at my door around two in the morning . . . they sent Officer Wexler because he knows Papa. He said there was an accident. A car crash in New Jersey . . . they're not sure who was at fault. It doesn't matter anyway."

Millie heard Ruth's words, but she couldn't process their meaning. Her head began to pound. "I don't understand . . . did they bring them to a hospital? Should we go to see them? Where are they?"

"There is no hospital. Mama and Papa are dead."

Millie shook her head. "No. No, that can't be. They must have the wrong car. They must have the wrong people."

"It was the Schwartzes' car—the one Papa always borrowed. The license plate matches. Arthur went with Officer Wexler to New Jersey to . . . identify them. He said I shouldn't go . . . that it's better not to remember them that way."

"What should we do?" Millie moaned. "Ruth, what should we do?" Tears burned her cheeks, and she could not get enough air. She fell to her knees just as Ruth rose from the floor. Even in the haze of her grief, Millie felt the transformation—Ruth's reclaimed composure, her newly minted armor. Without a single word, they fell into old patterns: as Millie grew more agitated, Ruth became calm. Millie wanted to change course, but she didn't have the strength.

"I don't know," Ruth answered. "We'll decide tomorrow. Listen to me, Millie. I can't stay much longer. I had to get my neighbor out of bed to come over and watch the girls—they've been sick all week, and they keep waking up. Mrs. Klein is too old—she won't be able to lift them out of their cribs. I need to get back. Do you want to come home with me? You can sleep on our sofa."

Millie still hadn't answered when Lenny returned from the kitchen. From the look on his face, she knew he'd heard every word.

"Millie?" Ruth repeated. "I know that you're devastated. We both are, believe me. I wish I didn't have to go, but Arthur won't be home for hours. Do you want to come home with me? Please, you need to decide."

Millie began to rock back and forth, slowly, on her knees. Her eyes were half closed, and her teeth were chattering. Lenny took the afghan from the sofa and wrapped it around her. She could feel the weight of it, but it provided no warmth.

Ruth bent down and took hold of her shoulders. "Millie? Can you hear me?"

"I can stay with her," Millie heard Lenny offer. "I'll sleep on the couch."

"Millie?" The pitch of Ruth's voice rose higher and higher. "Is that what you want? Tell me what you want to do. Answer me, please."

But Millie couldn't answer. She couldn't even think. She closed her eyes and let her mind drift away. She must have fallen asleep, but it was sleep without rest, a fits-and-starts slumber marred by terrible dreams. When she opened her eyes the next morning, she was still on the floor, though someone had tucked a pillow under her head and covered her with an extra blanket. When she sat up, she was surprised to see Lenny resting on the sofa.

Her sister, on the other hand, was nowhere to be found.

# Lillian

Every month, Lillian read *The Armory News* from cover to cover. Sometimes Patrick contributed a letter or an essay, but Lillian preferred the lighter pieces, especially the cartoons. She was always surprised by how many pages were filled with reports of social gatherings or just plain gossip.

As she flipped through the November issue, one picture in particular caught her eye—a pretty young woman in her early twenties, clad in an elaborate gown and feathered headpiece. Her hair was swept back, and her round cheeks were rouged. Next to it was another photo, taken twenty years later, of the very same woman in a plain workday dress.

> It is a pleasure to introduce Miss Arietta Benevetto, an accomplished vocalist who has performed in theaters all over the East Coast, including Springfield's own Poli's Palace. Arietta was born in New Haven, Connecticut, where her father, Mr. Salvatore Benevetto, was a master builder for none other than Sylvester Poli himself. Miss Benevetto's talents were discovered by Mr. Poli when

she was only five years old, and she began performing regularly at the age of fifteen. She shared the stage with many prominent vaudeville celebrities, including Shirley Booth.

Today, Miss Benevetto is our most popular cook at the armory post restaurant, working the weekday lunch shift. Those of us who frequent the restaurant are fans of her macaroni and cheese and baked beans. Recently, Miss Benevetto's homemade lasagna was added to the menu, and it is now the cafeteria's most requested item. Miss Benevetto performs regularly for cafeteria customers on Wednesday afternoons. Often, the WPO orchestra accompanies her. Tables are packed, with many regulars standing during their lunch break to hear her perform.

Outside of the armory, Miss Benevetto is a member of the choir at St. Ann's Church in West Springfield.

This had to be the cook Grace Peabody mentioned months ago—the woman Grace suspected of poisoning the food. How ludicrous it was to think that this lovely woman would ever be capable of such an act. Lillian thought about Arietta all afternoon, and she decided to visit the cafeteria the following Wednesday.

In the administration building where Patrick worked, Lillian had always blended in easily. Women wore their best dresses, and there was no need to worry about catching a bracelet in a typewriter or losing a finger to an adding machine if you didn't remove your rings. But in the cafeteria, she felt overdressed and conspicuous. Her suit and her jewelry set her apart. As she waited in line, the two young women behind her stared at her shoes and whispered.

Lillian watched the men and women pour through the double doors, some of them in coveralls, and others in work dresses or shirts. The more she watched, the more she noticed the slowness of their gait and the bags under their eyes. She wondered how many

of the men had worked more than one shift and how many of the
women had been up with crying babies the night before.

Federal Street—the road that separated the shops from where
she lived—was not merely a street but the widest of chasms. Lillian
kept mostly to the west side of the street, to the park-like sanctuary of Armory Square. After lunch, she would make her way home
on the well-tended paths, past the tennis court, the greenhouses,
and the charming homes of the other officers.

But on the east side of the street, in Federal Square, the armory was a place free of fountains and privet hedges. It was there
and at the Water Shops where the difficult work was being done,
where thousands of women and men performed the most grueling
of tasks. Inside the brick storehouses and the factory buildings—
that was the heart of armory production. Her trip to the other side
of Federal Street was a journey to another world.

"Mrs. Walsh!"

Lillian spotted Millie Fein waving from halfway across the
room. Like most of the other women, Millie wore a simple dress
and flat, lace-up shoes. She gestured to an empty seat at her table.
Lillian hurried through the crowd and set down her tray.

"Thank goodness you saw me! Is it always like this? I can't
believe the crowd!"

Delores introduced herself and shook Lillian's hand. "Wednes-
days are always busy, but none of us has ever seen this many people
before."

"It must be the write-up in *The Armory News*."

Before Millie could chime in, a balding man in a worn suit
placed a wooden milk crate on the floor a few feet in front of them.
A cheer went up from the crowd.

"Hi, folks," the man said, giving his tie a nervous tug. "We've
sure got a big turnout today. So, ah . . . you've all been waiting
patiently, and I do appreciate it. Let's see . . . the musicians are all
set up, and Arietta is going to come out in a minute. Oh, and when

you're done eating, please make sure to bring your trays up to the front."

It wasn't exactly a rousing introduction, and for a moment, Lillian wondered whether she'd made a mistake in coming. Her doubts continued to linger after Arietta emerged from the kitchen. The cook looked nothing like her glamorous photograph in the newsletter. Her cheeks were ruddy from a long morning spent at the stove, and her brow glistened with perspiration. She wore a well-used floral apron over her dress, which was tied around her back in the limpest of bows.

It was when she took off the apron that Lillian's misgivings faded.. Not because of what was underneath—a plain navy shirt-dress pulled too tightly around the middle—but because the grace of the gesture transformed the singer completely. The most refined Manhattan socialite removing a velvet cloak at the opera could not have been more elegant than Arietta removing her smock. Her bearing was suddenly regal, and her harried flush of exhaustion became a crimson glow of anticipation. Reflected in the singer's heavy-lidded eyes, the low-wattage bulbs dangling overhead could have been mistaken for stars.

Arietta walked confidently to the front of the room, cued the musicians, and stepped onto the milk crate. Eager diners shushed one another as a silky ballad filled the air.

As the cook sang, Lillian felt the mood of the room lighten. She felt her own heartbeat slow and the tension in her shoulders evaporate. When she looked at the other diners, they were smiling and still. The last note came too soon, and when the song ended, Millie and Lillian rose from their chairs to join the others in a standing ovation.

Arietta beamed as the diners sat back down. "How about we liven things up a bit? See if you know this one." She began the next song with no music at all, belting out the opening and swaying side to side. Lillian was surprised by how many people sang along.

He's 1-A in the army and he's A-1 in my heart,
He's gone to help the country that helped him to get a start.
I love him so because I know he wants to do his part,
For he's 1-A in the army and he's A-1 in my heart.


A few songs later, Arietta stepped off her crate. There were shouts for "one more" and pleas from the crowd, but back in the shops, the machinery was waiting. The hands that clapped now were needed to straighten barrels later. Reluctantly, the patrons went back to work.

Once the crowd dispersed, Lillian asked Millie to introduce her to her friend. "Your performance was sensational!" Lillian told the cook. "I know you must be busy, but I have two questions for you. The first has to do with our annual Christmas party. Patrick and I host it at our home every year, and I was hoping you'd agree to sing for us."

"I'm flattered to be asked—I'd love to. What's the second question?"

Lillian paused. "I've been thinking about putting together a much bigger concert, not just in the cafeteria but an event that every employee would be able to attend."

Arietta whistled. "Everyone? That would mean a concert for thousands of people, ma'am."

"Yes. It will have to be outside, so we'll need to wait until the spring, when the weather is more accommodating. It will take a lot of organization, but it would be wonderful for morale."

"And you'd like me to sing at it?"

Lillian smiled. "Well, with all your professional experience, I was actually hoping that you might help me to plan it."

Arietta threw her head back and laughed. "Shows you what I know," she said. "I thought you were going to ask for my lasagna recipe."

# Ruth

## Springfield, Massachusetts (December 1942)

After Arthur left Springfield, Ruth couldn't sleep. Her husband was halfway across the world, facing dangers she couldn't even imagine. The less she slept, the more anxious she became. Her concerns became clouded, and the nonspecific nature of them only agitated her more. In the past, she had always known where to focus her energy—what exactly to worry about and when to worry most. But her husband's new life was too unpredictable. Should she worry about the airplane, the gunfire, or disease? She had no way of knowing where to focus her feeble prayers.

When Arthur's first letter arrived, she devoured it in minutes, then read it repeatedly until she knew every word. He wrote of the weather, the people, and his daily tasks. His words, like her worries, were vague and unsatisfying, but too many details would never get past the censors.

The second letter was like the first, but by then, she'd realized that the contents didn't matter. An envelope from Arthur meant that he was alive, that his base hadn't been attacked, that he hadn't become ill. She saved the two letters in her top dresser drawer, and at night, in the dark, she put them under her pillow.

In the mornings, she was irritable and curt with the children. Not only with the twins but with Michael as well. The affection she had earned from her tiny nephew was eroding bit by bit, like stones at the shore.

The girls turned to Millie for their small daily needs. She became the one to pack their lunches and to braid their hair in the mornings. Hurt and relief twisted together in Ruth's chest, and she was filled with an unfamiliar sense of gratitude toward her sister.

In the payroll office, the other women tried to be sympathetic, but they weren't sure of what to say. It seemed to them that Arthur was in a unique position of privilege and safety. Their own friends and relatives were overseas too—enlisted men, not officers—bound to go and do whatever they were told. Ruth couldn't bring herself to complain or share her fears about her husband's post. She tallied the numbers on her lists and ate lunch alone at her desk.

A few weeks into Arthur's absence, at the beginning of December, Ruth's colleagues began discussing their preparations for Christmas.

"We're picking out a tree this weekend."

"I swear I have no idea what to get for my mother-in-law. She's impossible to buy for."

"Steiger's is having a sale on perfume. I get that for Jerry's mother every year. The bottles are pretty too."

"When is your holiday, Ruth?" one of the younger women asked. "What's it called again?"

"Hanukkah. It's . . . oh my . . . the first night is tonight." *How could she have forgotten?* "It lasts for eight days," she explained.

"I remember now. And you light all those candles. Well, at least your husband isn't away for Christmas. Now that would *really* be awful."

Ruth didn't respond.

The longer she sat at her desk, the more guilt she felt about forgetting the holiday. She had always prepared a big family dinner for the first night of Hanukkah, with potato latkes, brisket, and her mother's honey cake for dessert. One year, she had even tried to make a batch of homemade *sufganiyot*, but the traditional jelly doughnuts had come out greasy and flat. The honey cake was easier, and no one seemed to mind.

She and Arthur gave the girls a small gift for each night. They were nothing elaborate—a rag doll, a jump rope, a book, or some hair ribbons. But with Arthur away, she had forgotten to buy presents. She hadn't even purchased the small bags of chocolate Hanukkah gelt the girls loved so much.

When her shift ended, Ruth put away her pencils and shook off her lethargy. She pulled her coat tight against the icy December wind and walked west on State Street in the direction of the river. Main Street was crowded with holiday shoppers. Outside Johnson's Bookstore, a young mother consoled a weeping toddler. "You're too little for that now," she told him. "Maybe when you're older." He'd been pointing to an archery set on display in the window, but his mother took his hand and led him away.

Inside Johnson's, young children in various stages of anticipation waited for a chance to meet Santa Claus. A line of weary parents attempted to maintain order, drying tears for some and begging for patience from others. The older children gave up their turns to sit on Santa's lap—they had come solely for the gold-painted keepsake coins that the store gave out every Christmas. A picture of Santa was on the front side, and the back read, *Lucky Coin from Santa Claus, Johnson's Bookstore.*

Ruth picked out books for the children—*Betsy-Tacy and Tib* for Alice, *The Moffats* for Louise, and *Make Way for Ducklings* for Michael. She bought two watercolor paint sets for the girls and a wooden pull toy that the clerk suggested for her nephew. The line at the cash register was longer than she had ever seen it, so by the time she completed her purchases, it was already past five o'clock. The butcher on Dwight Street seemed as far away as the moon, and Ruth was too tired to attempt the trek so late in the day. Dinner would be leftovers—no brisket, no latkes.

She practiced her excuses on the long walk home: the rush
at work, the crowds, a sore throat that still nagged. She would
promise a holiday feast for tomorrow. The girls would be disappointed.

But when she opened her front door, she heard laughter coming from the back of the house. The unmistakable smell of frying
latkes filled the foyer, and the dining room table had been set with
her good china. Her mother's silver menorah was displayed on the
sideboard, polished to an unrecognizable shine.

"Mommy!" Louise called out happily. "We're teaching Arietta
how to play dreidel! Come see!" Inside the kitchen, the children
were gathered around the table, each guarding a small pile of pea-
nuts for the game. They held their breath as Millie's friend spun a
small wooden top. When it fell to one side, the children cheered.

"That's the *nun* again, right? So I get nothing?"

"Nothing!" Michael yelled, and the girls giggled.

At the stove, Millie was tending to an enormous batch of potato pancakes. She lifted the last of the latkes from the oil with her
spatula and laid it on top of a heaping golden pile.

"When did you learn how to make those?" Ruth asked. "You
never used to watch when Mama made them."

"I've had a lot of holidays on my own." Millie shrugged. "I had
to learn."

Ruth's lower lip began to quiver. "I forgot about Hanukkah,"
she confessed. "If one of the girls at work hadn't asked me about it,
I never would have remembered. I rushed to get a few presents, but
the stores were so crowded—I almost gave up. It doesn't feel like a
holiday without Arthur here." Ruth felt a sob rising up in her chest,
threatening to ruin the holiday mood.

Millie put down her spatula and took Ruth by the hand. "Not
in front of the girls," she said. They had barely reached the dining
room when Ruth began to cry—tears as unexpected as the meal
her sister had prepared. If Millie was surprised by her sister's rush
of emotion, she hid it well. "Arthur will come back to you," Millie

insisted. "I know he will. In a few months, he'll be back and it will feel like he never left."

"I'm sorry." Ruth sniffled. "It's not fair for me to cry to you about my husband being away. You haven't cried or complained once since you moved here. If something happened to Arthur . . . well, I wouldn't be able to handle it as well as you have. I don't think I could ever be as brave as you've been. I don't know how you do it."

Millie let go of Ruth's hand and smoothed her apron over her skirt. "Surviving isn't the same as being brave," Millie said. "Sometimes a person doesn't have any other choice."

# Millie

Hanukkah ended a few weeks before Christmas, just in time for the Walshes' annual holiday party. Millie hadn't planned on attending—the party was only for officers and their wives—but Lillian insisted. "If it weren't for you, I'd have no entertainment," she told her. "Besides, I want you to be there."

Millie wasn't convinced that Ruth felt the same way. She'd been grateful to Millie for helping her with the girls, but the tension between them hadn't fully evaporated. Like mist after a rainfall, it hung in the air.

Still, Millie agreed to go, if only to hear Arietta sing. "First, come over to my house," Arietta encouraged. "We can look through my dresses together and pick something to wear."

The day before the party, Millie visited the house on Walnut Street. "It's so unfair." Arietta grumbled, poking through her closet. "All a man needs is one uniform. You put him in that, and poof—he's ready! Meanwhile, women have to fuss to find just the right outfit, and there's still no guarantee that anyone will notice."

"Mr. Fitzgerald certainly notices *you*," Millie said.

"Ha! Fitz only cares about the cafeteria sales. Sure, he might glance my way when I'm singing. But that doesn't mean anything; everybody looks when I sing."

"It's not only when you're singing. Last week, you were chopping onions when I came by—you should have seen how he was looking at you then."

Arietta popped her head out from behind the closet door. "While I was chopping *onions*? Are you sure?"

Millie winked. "It could have been carrots. Potatoes, even. Come on now, go back in that closet and find something to wear. You said it yourself—everyone watches when you perform. You have to look perfect."

Arietta laughed. "You think I'm looking for a dress for *me*? I already know what I'm going to wear. I'm looking for *you*. Last year, the nicest young woman rented out the front bedroom—pretty, well dressed, and exactly your size. She ran off to get married and left a stack of clothes behind. I asked around for an address, but I never could find one. I heard she's living on a dairy farm up in Vermont, so I guess she doesn't need her fancy dresses. I gave a few of them away, but I kept the best two. I just need to find them." Arietta's head was back inside the closet. "Here they are!"

She pulled out two cocktail dresses—one in brilliant blue and the other in black satin with padded shoulders and a fitted skirt. "The blue is gorgeous with your eyes," Arietta insisted. "You'll really stand out."

"In that case, I'll wear the black. I'd rather blend in."

**Downstairs, the babysitter had just arrived. Ruth was upstairs,** still getting ready, so Millie gave the sitter a few instructions and kissed the children good night. "We'll be right across the square, at the commanding officer's house."

She called up the steps. "Ruth? We should get going!"

Ruth descended the stairway like a slowly sinking ship. She had touched up her makeup, but there was no disguising the bags under her eyes. There had been no letter from Arthur that week.

Colonel Walsh had assured her that the outpost was safe and that Arthur and the others were making steady progress. Still, even with his reassurance, worry took its toll.

"You look beautiful," Millie said, but the compliment didn't improve Ruth's mood. They walked across Armory Square without speaking, heels tapping on the paths and the patches of frozen grass. A waxing winter moon hung silently above them, lighting up the old arsenal like a medieval fortress.

The Walshes' lengthy porch railing was draped with garlands of pine. Guests crowded together near the entrance, removing coats and stoles. Men in uniform lingered by the door, patting each other on the back, while their wives walked farther into the entrance hall for warmth.

"Ruth!" A tall man carrying a taller glass of whiskey bent down to give her sister a kiss on the cheek. "What's the news from Arthur? How's our man doing?"

"Nice to see you, Fred. From what I can tell, they're keeping him busy. His letters don't say much, just what you'd expect."

"Well, they won't keep him long. Try not to worry too much. He's the smartest of all of us—he'll work out all the kinks and be home before you know it."

"I hope so."

"Now, who is this lovely young woman you've brought with you?"

"This is my sister, Millie. Millie, Fred Peabody. You may have met his wife, Grace, at one of Lillian's meetings."

Fred's smile was too wide, his teeth were too white, and Millie didn't like the way his eyes lingered on her chest. He held her hand tightly, running his thumb back and forth across the top of her wrist. When she pulled it away, his smile vanished. "That's right," he said. "I remember Grace mentioning something about your sister."

"We met at the pool," Millie murmured. "She was there with your daughters."

"The girls love to swim. Or at least they used to——toward the end of the summer, they stopped going to the pool. In any event, Grace isn't here. She decided to take the girls to her family in Boston for the weekend."

"What a shame that she's missing the party," Ruth said.

"It's probably better this way." Fred drained his glass in one long swallow. "Now I can talk to all my colleagues, stay as late as I like. Take time to get to know some of the new faces." He stared at Millie as he spoke.

"Ruth, shouldn't we find Lillian now, to say hello?"

"Yes, of course. Enjoy your evening, Fred."

Millie whispered in Ruth's ear as she led her away, "I don't like that man. There's something about him . . ."

"Fred likes to drink. I'm no fan of his, but Arthur works with him, so I try to be congenial."

The dining room overflowed with potted poinsettias and tall white candles. An untouched bowl of eggnog sat in the center of the table, along with trays of stuffed celery sticks and platters of canapés. A glossy smoked ham, beautiful but forgotten, rested on a silver tray next to a crystal dish of olives.

"It looks like a magazine photo," Millie observed. "Not a meal." She wished she had eaten something before she came.

Ruth nodded and gestured toward the others in the room. "Have you seen the size of these women? They don't eat anything."

"Mama would hate this party." Millie laughed. "Too much liquor and not enough food."

"She'd leave early for sure," Ruth agreed. "And then go home and make a casserole."

Millie couldn't remember the last time she had shared a joke with her sister. It finally felt like the two of them were on the same side.

When Ruth said her goodbyes only one hour later, the disappointment Millie felt took her by surprise. "Don't leave," Millie entreated, but Ruth was firm. "I'm tired, but you should stay and hear your friend sing. Enjoy the rest of the party."

Soon, Arietta sat down at the Walshes' grand piano. It was impossible to believe that she was the same woman who had been baking biscuits in the cafeteria kitchen just a few hours earlier. Instead of a faded apron, Arietta wore a taffeta dress the color of garnets. Silver satin heels took the place of her dull brown loafers, and her hair was swept up with rhinestone pins instead of her Women Ordnance Workers bandanna. Millie held her breath as Arietta began. The shopworkers in the cafeteria loved Arietta on their lunch breaks, but who knew how the officers in Armory Square would receive her?

She needn't have worried. The minute Arietta's fingers touched the keys, the room fell silent. The gems in her hair sparkled in the candlelight. When she began to sing, even the most cynical of guests fell under her spell.

When she was finished, Millie made her way over to congratulate her. "You were fantastic!" Millie crowed. "They absolutely loved you! Did you hear how they clapped?"

"Aw, thanks, Mil, but it might just have been the champagne. There's nothing like a few drinks to loosen up a crowd." She lowered her voice. "Take that one, for instance, over there by the bar. The music is over but he's still swaying."

Millie turned to see Fred Peabody filling another glass. "Oh, *him*," she said, rolling her eyes. "I met him earlier. His wife is out of town, and he's making the most of it."

"He certainly is. I don't like the look of him."

"Would you be upset if I headed back home? Ruth left a little while ago, and I don't want to stay too long."

"Don't worry about me, hon. Mrs. Walsh wanted to introduce me to a few people. I'll do a little meet and greet, and then I'm heading out too."

**On the walk home, the cold air helped to clear Millie's head. She** thought about Ruth and their interaction that evening. After a childhood of bickering and a hostile adolescence, they had entered adulthood almost estranged. Was it possible that now, with so many losses behind them, they could enter into a new stage of acceptance?

Millie was so lost in contemplation that she didn't hear the footsteps gaining speed behind her. The night sky had grown cloudy, and the path ahead was difficult to see. When a hand reached for her shoulder, she spun around and screamed. Even in the dark, she recognized his teeth.

"Mr. Peabody!"

"Call me Fred," he said, still smiling. He didn't apologize for frightening her half to death. He didn't acknowledge that there was anything strange about following her outside and grabbing her in the dark.

"I saw you duck out early, and I thought I'd . . . walk you home."

"That's really not necessary. My sister's house is right over there. Practically spitting distance. She's waiting up for me."

Fred Peabody shifted in his uniform, cracked his knuckles twice, and flashed what he must have thought was a charming grin. "It's still early. Maybe you'd like to get a drink. I know a place we could go."

"Thank you, but it's already past eleven, and I need to get home to my son."

He put one hand on her shoulder and reached around her waist with the other. "Come on now. Don't be that way." Millie struggled to break free, but he only pulled her closer. The stench of alcohol on his breath filled Millie's nostrils.

"Take your hands off her!"

The voice took him by surprise, and when he loosened his grip, Millie stomped on his foot with the heel of her shoe. Fred Peabody yelped and spun around. "Who the hell is that?" he growled into the darkness, squinting until he recognized the figure in front of him. "You're the singer from the party. Why don't you mind your damn business?"

"This *is* my business. But if you'd like me to ask Colonel Walsh about it, I'd be happy to." Arietta walked in front of the officer and placed herself between him and Millie.

"You say one word to Walsh, and I'll make you wish you hadn't." Fred spat onto the ground and glared at Millie. "You think I didn't know who you were before your sister introduced you? My wife warned me about you, about *both* of you. I wonder what Walsh would think about the two of you being in cahoots."

Arietta crossed her arms in front of her chest. "What are you talking about?"

"You don't think that big fire set itself, now do you?" He smirked. "Pretty suspicious, probably set by some new employees. Spies or sympathizers, folks who've got gripes."

"That fire was months ago, and everyone knows it was an accident. You're crazy."

"I'm a well-respected officer is what I am. And at the Springfield Armory, that means something. You think anyone will take your word over mine? Who do you think the people here will believe? An officer of the armory——or a fat *wop* cook and a dumb *kike* whore?"

After Fred limped away, Arietta walked Millie to her front door. "We should tell Ruth what happened," Arietta insisted.

But Millie shook her head. "I don't want her involved. Arthur and Fred work together."

She didn't tell Arietta about Walter Rabinowitz or Bobby Weinstein. She didn't mention Howard Hoffman, Benjie Silver, or any of the others. She didn't speak the names of all the boys her sister blamed her for——the ones Ruth accused her of smiling at or flirting with or worse. Millie didn't want to tell her sister what Fred Peabody had done because a part of her was terrified that Ruth would blame her once again. Perhaps her dress had been too tight, perhaps her manner had been too coy, perhaps the perfume that she wore had been too enticing to resist.

Since Millie had moved to Springfield, she and Ruth had come a long way. There had been hints of affection, even a bit of shared laughter at the party. But Millie was only too aware of her sister's changeable moods. She had seen Ruth turn on her too many times before, and she knew her sister too well to make the same mistake again.

Besides, when it came to men, Ruth had never been forgiving.

# PART THREE

# Millie

Millie wished she hadn't bought that new pair of heels in December. She had gotten them on sale, right before Christmas, but now that shoe rationing had gone into effect, she regretted the choice. Her work shoes weren't sturdy enough for the ice on the streets. She should have bought boots—warm, heavy boots for this endless Massachusetts winter.

In Brooklyn, the snow had been more submissive—deferring always to the buildings, the trolleys, and the bridges. Here in Springfield, however, the snow asserted itself. It filled the streets and the sidewalks with no apologies, taking up space and stretching itself out on the lawns and the squares like a smug, self-satisfied cat.

Luckily for Millie, Building 103 was never cold. There were too many people, too many machines, too much metal, and not enough time. The pressure to produce gave off its own kind of heat—not only the daily quotas and the numbers on the supervisors' clipboards but the constant war chatter from the radio and newspapers. For the first time in history, the president of the United States had traveled by airplane on official business—Roosevelt had flown to Casablanca, Morocco, for a strategy conference with Winston Churchill. Speed and efficiency were on everyone's minds. General Eisenhower had just been selected to command the Allied armies in Europe, battle plans were being made at an unprecedented pace, and the workers in Building 103 had sworn to keep up. They had signed a "Victory Pledge" mere months before—a promise to produce, a vow to push onward. When Millie read the words, she felt proud to sign her name. There was comfort in being counted, in standing up to say, *I'm here.*

The work itself was tedious, unquestionably so. But for a woman like Millie, the work occupied the empty space her losses had created: her parents, her sister, her husband, her home—all of them absent, most of them gone. Putting triggers together filled her days with purpose. Hour after hour, she pushed the pins into place, weaving memory and metal to prove her worth and ease her sorrow. As she worked, she wondered about the other women at the tables. What secret stories did they tell themselves while their hands were occupied but their minds were free to wander?

**When she first left the building that February afternoon, Millie** welcomed the rush of fresh air on her face. Her feet were frozen, but the sun poked through the clouds. The walkways across Federal Square were slathered with melting slush and the refrozen detritus of the most recent snowstorm.

Millie moved slowly over thawing patches of ice, keeping her head down so she wouldn't miss any slippery spots. She was so focused on the ground beneath her that she didn't look up, even after she passed through the gate.

"Millie!"

A passerby might have thought the man calling her name did so out of concern after watching her fall. But the truth was that the fall happened only after her name was called. The truth was that the sound of the voice caused a shift in her equilibrium—a sudden disintegration of her center of gravity. The afternoon sun flashed off the piles of snow lining Federal Street so that the dust specks in the air looked like pinpricks of light. She was temporarily blinded by the glittering particles and undone by the voice shouting into the wind. "Millie!" it called, and her chest thundered with fear. At the sound of her name, her body betrayed her, and she fell to the pavement in a muddled heap.

She came to a minute later, surrounded by a flock of women she recognized from the shops. She had taken quite a spill—was she hurt? Did anything feel broken? But she shook her head. She was sure she was fine. They helped her up from the ground, and as she struggled to right herself, she saw him across the street, waiting for her. He was leaning on the iron fence that outlined Armory Square, a fence so black and cold that he blended in against it. That he hadn't approached when she had fallen—hadn't bothered to walk across the street to be sure she was unharmed—did not surprise her.

She inched across the street, knees throbbing, back aching. Part of her wanted to run in the opposite direction, but she forced herself to walk toward him instead. As sore as she was, she held her head high.

"Rough spill," he said, but he didn't sound sympathetic. He was still handsome as anything, with that dark, shiny hair and Hollywood smile. But his face was newly flawed by a raised scar across his right cheek—inflicted, Millie assumed, by an unforgiving acquaintance.

"I've been through worse," she said. "What happened to your face?"

It was a question she wouldn't have dared to ask him back in Brooklyn, but in the bright light of Springfield, his imperfections were glaring. He frowned at the question, surprised she had noticed.

"Nothing." He shrugged. He motioned to the workers pouring out of Federal Square. "So, you work there now?"

"Yes."

"How's the pay?"

"It's fine. Listen, Lenny, what do you want?"

"Jeez, Mil, why the rush? That's not very friendly. I thought we could catch up a little, thought you might be happy to see me."

She wanted to scream. *Happy to see you? What kind of man disappears for a year and shows up out of the blue without any warning? What kind of man lets his wife think he's dead and never even asks about the son he left behind?* Anger Millie hadn't known she was capable of seared its way through her, but she couldn't afford to cause a scene. There were too many people she recognized walking by, too many familiar faces who might ask questions later. No one at the armory knew her husband was alive. She owed some of them explanations—her sister and her friends—but no good would come of strangers finding out first. "I have to go," she said firmly. "I'm late for an appointment." She began walking toward State Street, but Lenny pulled her back.

"Listen," he said, "I didn't come to make trouble. I just want to talk and maybe borrow a little cash."

She should have known that there would be nothing noble about his return. "I don't have any money. You left us with nothing but a pile of bills, remember? It's going to take a long time before I can pay them all off. Besides, if you need money so badly, why don't you ask your brother?"

Lenny's eyes clouded over. "Murray is dead."

It was true, then, Millie thought, what Mr. Solomon had told her. The brothers had been in trouble with some dangerous people. Lenny was probably lucky to have gotten away with just the scar. "I'm sorry," she said. "I know how close you were."

Lenny blinked a few times and squared his shoulders. "Yeah, well, what's done is done." He glanced nervously at the gloves on her hands. "Hey, how about that ring I gave you? The one I proposed with? You still have that?"

"My grandmother's ring? Of course I still have it." His eyes lingered desperately on her wool-covered fingers. "I'm not wearing it now, though. We're not allowed to wear any jewelry on the job. One girl almost lost a hand when her charm bracelet got caught in some gears." She took off her gloves. "See for yourself."

"But you have it, you said. You know where it is. You could get it for me if you wanted to, right?" Lenny pushed his hands deeper into the pockets of his coat and shivered. "I'm really in a bind, Mil. The guys Murray owed . . . I'm still on the hook. If I don't give them something soon, I don't know what they'll do. Murray used to say that ring was worth a fortune."

When Millie didn't answer, he continued to plead. "Listen, Mil. I know I was a crummy husband. I started drinking too much. I stayed out all the time. When the war started, I thought the army would be a fresh start. But when they wouldn't take me, I didn't know what to do."

"That isn't an excuse for abandoning your family. I thought you were dead!"

He kicked at a pile of slush by his feet. "Whaddya want me to say? I'm sorry, all right? When I started working with Murray, everything got mixed up." He reached one hand around her waist and tried to pull her toward him. "You missed me, though, didn't you? Tell me you missed me."

The truth would have taken too much time to explain. She missed the young man who had knocked on her door back in Brooklyn, the one who'd rescued her from loneliness after Mrs. DeLuca had died. She missed the man who had looked at her like she knew all the answers—who had seen something more in her than just her good looks. She missed the man Lenny had been the night before he'd tried to enlist: the hopeful soldier-to-be, the one with purpose and pride. But she could never miss the man who had taken his place: the man who blamed her for his bad luck, the one who drank and disappeared, the one who hit her and showed up broke with nothing but excuses.

Millie pushed his hand from her waist and shook her head. "No."

He began to whine then, like a child who'd lost a toy. "You *gotta* help me, Millie. If you gimme the ring, I'll get out of your hair. I'll get outta town, and I won't bother you again. I swear it on my grave. It'll be like you never knew me."

To give him the ring would be to give up a part of her history. But her desire to have him leave was greater than any sentimentality she could muster. What was a piece of jewelry compared to her peace of mind? What wouldn't she give up to secure her son's safety? Of course, Lenny might come back, even if she gave him what he wanted. But what choice did she have other than to trust what he told her? If the men Murray owed were to hurt Lenny again, she didn't think she could live with the guilt of knowing she might have prevented it.

"Fine," Millie agreed. "Meet me back here tomorrow and I'll bring it with me. But after that, I don't ever want to see you again."

Lenny leaned forward to kiss her, but she stepped to the side. He hid his frustration with a plastered-on smile. "You look good, Mil, real good. I knew you'd come through. I swear you won't be sorry."

A gust of winter wind blew through her thin coat. *I already am.*

# Ruth

After the holidays, Ruth quit her job. She was too concerned about Arthur to do any of her work properly, and she wanted to make sure she spent enough time with her daughters. Word of her decision spread quickly among the other wives.

"I don't know how you managed to keep that position for *so long,*" Cecily Abbott said to her at the tail end of one of Lillian's meetings. "It must have been terribly tedious." Mrs. Abbott had the most seniority among the wives, having lived at the armory for the longest of all of them. She was in her late fifties, stout and silver-haired, with a fondness for entertaining and speaking her mind.

"Ruth did the armory a great service," Lillian insisted. "We are all grateful to her."

"I don't doubt for a minute that it was the patriotic thing to do. But now that Mrs. Blum is finished with her professional duties, I assume she will have more time for socializing with the rest of us." She turned to Ruth. "I'm having a baby shower for Captain Baxter's wife tomorrow, a luncheon at my home. She's such a sweet thing—I'm sure you'll want to join. I'm adding your name to the list. We start at noon."

**The next morning, Ruth dressed carefully in a soft blue wool suit** with a matching velveteen hat. Her stomach churned with nervous energy, and she changed her lipstick color three times. "You're ridiculous," she told herself as she reapplied her makeup. "You've known these women for years, and they've never been particularly nice to you. They're not your friends, so stop worrying what you look like."

But she had never been invited to Mrs. Abbott's home before, and despite the last-minute nature of the offer, she was flattered. To be included meant more to Ruth than she wanted to admit. What would she have given, back in Brooklyn, to have been asked to some of the high school parties that Millie had attended?

After she was dressed, Ruth went to Forbes and Wallace to buy a baby gift. The line for gift wrapping took forever, and she had to rush back so as not to be late for the party. She hurried along the sidewalk, checking her watch, and waited impatiently to cross at the corner. Ruth noticed a man staring from the opposite side of the street, but when she looked in his direction, he ducked his head and turned. By the time she crossed the street, the man was halfway down the block. He was too far away for her to get a good look at him, but there was something about his gait she found strangely familiar—was it the bend of his knee or the tilt of his head? She wanted to call out, or to follow him, but she had no time for foolishness. She had someplace to be.

When she arrived at Mrs. Abbott's, Ruth's mind was still racing. Inside, the gathering was more intimate than Lillian's meetings—there couldn't have been more than ten women in all. A formal luncheon had been set out in the dining room, complete with crystal goblets, cloth napkins, and handwritten cards to mark each guest's place. Grace Peabody was seated directly to Ruth's right. The silk dress she wore was the same one Ruth had seen in the window of Forbes and Wallace that morning.

Ruth was certain that Grace would ignore her completely, but as the luncheon continued, it was obvious that Grace was anxious to tell her something. When the conversation turned to nursery decorations, Ruth felt a hand on her shoulder and a voice in her ear.

"I saw your sister yesterday, outside the main gate. She was talking to a very rough-looking young man."

Ruth reached for her water goblet. "Probably someone she knows from the shops."

"He wasn't a shopworker. They were arguing."

Ruth had grown tired of Grace's preoccupation with her sister. Despite having every financial and social advantage, Grace still seemed to see Millie as some kind of threat.

"I don't see why my sister is any of your concern."

"*Everyone* who lives in Armory Square is my concern."

Ruth refolded the napkin on her lap. Laughter filled the room as one of the women told a story about the first time she asked her husband to change their baby's diaper. *I told him if he refused, I'd have a chat with his superiors. "What's it going to be, Paul?" I told him. "Active duty or diaper duty?"*

Grace droned on. "Armory Square isn't for everyone, and your sister seems to be associating with all the wrong people. First the cook, and now this thug. She'd be better off if you sent her back to Brooklyn."

The clatter of silverware rang in Ruth's ears. Send her sister back to Brooklyn? She would never admit to Grace how much she had once wanted to do that very thing. She flinched at the words, banishing from her thoughts the awful notion that she and Grace had something in common after all.

**Ruth left as soon as the last gift was opened, thanking Mrs. Abbott** profusely on her way out the door. Millie's shift ended at three o'clock, and Ruth wanted to ask her about the man Grace had mentioned. How many other people had noticed Millie with him? Hadn't her sister learned anything from what happened in Brooklyn? Ruth remembered the first time she'd heard about Lenny—when Arthur's friend saw Millie kissing him at the movies. The last thing Ruth wanted was a repeat of that.

She said hello to the guards, all of whom she knew, and told them she was waiting for her sister's shift to end. "If you don't mind, I'm going to plant myself right here," she said, leaning against the back side of one of the pillars. "It's the best place to stay out of this wind."

"Stay as long as you like, Mrs. Blum," they told her.

Workers streamed in and out of Federal Square; the shifts were turning over, and the street was congested. Even among the crowd, Ruth was able to spot her sister, with her forest-green coat and reddish-brown curls. Ruth expected Millie to turn left and make her way toward the child care center, but instead, she stood still, watching and waiting. After a few minutes, a man in a shabby black overcoat approached her.

From where Ruth stood, it was impossible to see his face, so she walked through the gate to get a better view. When she finally could see his profile, she let out a gasp. It was Lenny, Millie's husband. He was alive.

Ruth raced down the sidewalk, dodging people on every side. "Excuse me," she murmured, pushing past them all. Millie opened her purse and pulled something out, but Ruth barreled into her and caught her wrist in midair. Her sister was frozen in place, too shocked to speak. When Ruth looked down, Millie's engagement ring was in her hand.

"If it isn't my favorite sister-in-law," Lenny said, amused. He pulled a match from his pocket, cupped his hand to guard it from the wind, and lit a cigarette that he had plucked from behind his left ear.

People whooshed past, wrestling for space on the sidewalk, oblivious to their dilemma and to Ruth's racing pulse. Ruth stepped away from her brother-in-law and shoved her hand into her pocket. Through her glove, she could feel the scourge of the opal.

She wished—not for the first time—that she had never seen it that day in her mother's jewelry box.

Ruth looked to her younger sister for some kind of explanation. The wind had whipped Millie's curls into a mop of tangles, and tears had sent thin rivulets of mascara running down her cheeks. "I got a letter in December saying Lenny was alive," she whispered. "But I couldn't tell you then. Arthur had just been sent to Africa, and I didn't want to make you any more upset—"

Lenny coughed loudly and sputtered on his cigarette. "Art got himself shipped off to *Africa*? I wasn't good enough for Uncle Sam, but they sent *Arthur* into action?"

"Shut up!" Millie snapped.

Ruth sucked in her breath. "What do you mean you weren't good enough for Uncle Sam?"

"Goddamned heart murmur," he muttered. "At least that's what the doctor said."

The truths Ruth thought she knew were crumbling around her. "I don't understand," she said to Millie. "In your letters, you wrote that Lenny was *dead*."

"I wrote that he was gone. *Gone*. And he was. When the army wouldn't take him, he left us for good. And then Mr. Solomon from the hat shop heard he was in trouble. He said Murray and Lenny had probably been killed."

"They got Murray." Lenny grimaced. "The old man was right about that." He tapped at the scar on the side of his face. "I got away with this—my souvenir."

Ruth held her tongue, unsure of what to say. There were so many questions churning in her brain, so much she needed to discuss with her sister. "My condolences on your brother," she said to Lenny. "But right now, I need to speak to Millie alone. Come, Millie. We're leaving."

"There you go again," he growled, "ordering everyone around."

"Excuse me?"

When he answered, his voice was high pitched and mocking. *"Come, Millie, we're leaving; Lenny, propose to her; Lenny, say this; Lenny, do that.* I did everything you told me, Ruth, and where did it get me? Murray was right—you're a sneaky, selfish bitch!"

Millie's lower lip began to tremble. "What are you talking about?"

Lenny's eyes were glued to Ruth as he continued his tirade.

"You said your parents wanted me to have that ring! They wanted me to have it so I could propose to Millie. I did what you said, and now you *owe* me. If you don't hand it over now, I'll make you wish you had!"

"Ruth," Millie whispered, "just give him the ring. He'll leave us alone then. He promised he'd go."

But stubbornness or pride or guilt held Ruth back. Her brain began to buzz with the beginnings of a plan. She pointed behind him toward the armory's main gate. "See those guards over there? I know every single one of them. If you don't leave right now, I'm going to have them arrest you."

Lenny flicked the end of his cigarette onto a slushy patch of sidewalk and pressed it into the snow with the heel of his shoe. "You can't arrest a guy for talking," he said. "Go ahead and try."

Ruth walked toward the gate and shouted to one of the guards, waving her hand to get his attention. "Charlie! Would you mind coming over here, please?"

"Sure, Mrs. Blum! I'll be over in a minute!"

Ruth's confidence swelled. She delivered her terms to Lenny in a steely monotone. "Listen to me and do exactly as I say. Turn around, walk to the station, and get on a train. If you don't, I'll tell Charlie and the other guards about you—about how much you hate your country because they wouldn't let you fight. I'm going to tell them that you've been asking us questions about armory business, about shipments and timetables and all the things spies like to know. Did you know there was a fire here last summer, by the way? They say it could have been sabotage, and I'm going to tell them I

think it was you. After they get a look at your record, they'll believe everything I say. You'll be rotting in a federal prison for the
rest of your life."

Lenny's jaw dropped. "You wouldn't lie like that. You don't
have any proof. You'd never get away with it." But as the guard
came closer, Lenny looked less sure of himself. Slowly, he backed
away and turned toward State Street. "This isn't over."

By the time the guard reached them, Lenny was gone.

# Millie

Millie tried to wipe away her tears when the guard approached, but her cheeks were splotchy from crying, and her eyes were glazed over from the shock of what she'd just heard. Ruth, on the other hand, was eerily calm.

Despite the guard's youth, his presence brought order to the scene. The front of his uniform bore gleaming brass buttons, and even in the slush, his shoes kept their shine. After one glance at Millie, he pulled a handkerchief from his pocket. "Here you go," he said softly, pressing it into her hand. "You look pretty shaken up. That friend of yours left quick. Can I do anything to help?"

She bit her lip to keep herself from crying again. "I'm fine," she lied. "But he wasn't our friend." To Ruth, she said, "I need to pick up Michael. We'll talk later."

As she sped away from her sister, Millie's breathing grew steadier. Distance brought relief; the farther away she was from Ruth, the better.

It wasn't like Millie to show up unannounced on Arietta's doorstep, but after retrieving Michael from the child care center, she couldn't bear the thought of returning to Armory Square. She stood on the steps of the small house on Walnut Street, knocking on the chipped paint and hoping her friend was inside.

It was already past five, sunset was approaching, and Millie knew that Ruth would be wondering where she was. *Let her wonder,* Millie thought. *I can't stand beside her right now, pretending nothing has changed.*

It was Friday night, and Ruth would be lighting the Sabbath candles soon. In the past, she had observed the tradition haphazardly—sometimes remembering and sometimes not bothering for months at a time. But now that Arthur was gone, the ritual had become fixed. Millie found Ruth's sudden burst of observance self-serving and insincere. If God was keeping tabs, what counted more—Ruth's spurt of weekly prayers or the lies she had told? Millie hadn't had enough time to piece together all that Lenny had said, but one thing at least was perfectly clear: Millie may have kept an important secret from her sister, but Ruth had been keeping plenty of her own.

She knocked again on the door, more forcefully this time.

"You're too early!" Arietta shouted from inside the house. "You can't come in now. I'm not ready yet!"

Millie was confused. "Arietta? It's me."

The cook opened the door wearing a bulky blue bathrobe. Her hair was wrapped in curlers, and her face was covered with cold cream. "Millie! Thank goodness! I thought you were Fitz! He's not supposed to pick me up until seven thirty."

Michael took one look at Arietta's face and began to cry.

"Uh-oh," she said. "I must look worse than I thought. Let me go wash this off."

By the time Arietta returned from the bathroom, Michael was calm. He sat on the living room sofa next to his mother, pointing to the comics from a newspaper he had found. There were always extra newspapers and magazines scattered around the house, left by the female boarders who rented the bedrooms upstairs. Arietta kept a large crystal bowl filled with foil-wrapped candies on the side table. "The girls go through these like locusts," she said. She unwrapped one of the candies, handed it to Michael, and ushered Millie into the hallway so she could speak to her alone.

"Tell me what's wrong," the singer insisted. "And please don't say, 'Nothing.'"

"Everything is fine; I just thought we'd stop by."

Arietta didn't press. "Listen, I'll make you and Michael some dinner, and you can stay as long as you like. Fitz and I can go out another night. The dance will be too crowded anyway; I heard they sold a couple of thousand tickets at least."

Millie clapped her hand over her mouth and groaned. "The dance! I can't believe I forgot about it! You have to go! Please—if you cancel because of me, I'll never forgive myself."

"Fine, I'll go. But we'll eat something first."

"You can't start cooking! You have to get dressed!"

"I made a pot of lentil soup yesterday; all I have to do is put it on the stove."

The soup was warm and savory, and there was thick crusty bread from Mercolino's bakery for mopping up what was left in their bowls. After they finished, Arietta wouldn't let them leave. "Stay a little longer, will you, until Fitz picks me up? You can answer the door so I can make an entrance."

**Fitz declined Millie's invitation to take a seat in the living room. He** preferred standing, he said, holding his corsage box as if she might try to wrestle it from him. She had never seen anyone look so nervous. But when Arietta appeared at the top of the stairs, Fitz's face warmed and came to life at last. His eyes sought Arietta's with a younger man's anticipation, as if his only desire was to love and protect her. It was the way Millie's mother had always wanted a man to look at *her*.

How could she have understood in the hastiness of her youth what those who loved her best had wanted her to know? She had been too lonely to imagine that a man could offer more than the passion and excitement that Lenny had provided. In his arms, she had found solace; in his kisses, new life. It had been unthinkable to her that it could cease to be enough.

But if her parents had known what love was supposed to be, hadn't Ruth—already married to Arthur—known it too? Ruth had disapproved of Lenny at first. She had thought he was wrong for her; she had said as much to Millie's face. But that summer before their parents had died, Ruth had softened toward him. And after the accident, Ruth had sworn that their parents had as well. *Papa always liked Lenny; he just never really spoke about it. Mama was tougher, but even she knew how much Lenny loved you.*

Millie had wanted to believe everything Ruth told her: that Lenny had won her parents over in the end; that before they passed away, they had recognized the goodness in him; that marrying Lenny and staying in Brooklyn was absolutely what their parents would have wanted her to do. Millie had trusted Ruth completely; she had followed her advice. Of course, the marriage hadn't worked out happily in the end, but Millie couldn't hold her sister responsible for that.

Could she?

# Ruth

**Brooklyn, New York (September 1937)**

Their mother started up with Ruth again the day after Millie's graduation. *What about bringing your sister to Springfield? Did Arthur ask about the housing yet?* As the summer wore on, Ruth knew she needed a plan—anything to make Millie stay in New York.

Ruth tried to help Millie look for a job, but it was difficult to find anything she was qualified to do. Her grades were poor, and she hadn't bothered to take the typing or stenography classes their high school offered. No one was optimistic about her securing employment anytime soon.

With so much else to worry about, Ruth gave up on pressuring Millie to end things with Lenny. Besides, Millie was too stubborn to listen to anyone's advice—even their parents had begun to see that. They stopped bad-mouthing the Bum when Millie was in the room, and eventually, they stopped mentioning him altogether. Their father was still confident that the romance would run its course, but their mother's anxiety had been escalating since June. "Stop telling me how your daughter is going to get tired of him!" she shouted at her husband. "The Queen Mother must have thought the same thing about her son, and then he went crazy and gave up the throne. He was the *king,* Morris. The king of England! Until that Simpson woman got her hooks in him and made him break his mother's heart!"

When July came around, Ruth tried a new tactic—what if she began praising Lenny instead of criticizing him? She began mentioning his best qualities when Millie was in earshot—Lenny was fun-loving and exuberant; he was outgoing and affable. One Saturday, after lunch, their mother pulled Ruth into the hallway. "Why so many compliments for the Bum?" she demanded.

"Shh. Don't you see? If you insult him or act like he doesn't exist, it just makes her want to be with him more. I'm doing the opposite. Why don't you try it?"

"And pretend that the Bum is some kind of prize? No, thank you!"

"Suit yourself, Mama. But it might actually work. Besides, he isn't *all* bad."

"Do you hear what you sound like?" her mother hissed. "That's why I don't lie. Do it enough, and you start believing your own words."

**When Ruth had found Lenny in the apartment the night her par-**ents died, her chest had constricted with white-hot rage. Anyone could see how much he'd been drinking. The air all around him reeked of cheap liquor. Just who did he think he was, showing up like that?

She should have known that Millie would fall apart after she heard the news; she should have known that she would have to be the strong one, like always. She'd allowed herself one moment—*one moment*—of weakness. But when Millie became hysterical, Ruth's moment was over. When Millie fell to the floor, Ruth picked herself up off of it. It wasn't just her sister she had to take care of; the twins were sick with fever and up every few hours. She'd woken her elderly neighbor to stay with them for a while, but Ruth couldn't trust that the woman would be able to take care of them. Ruth had asked Millie to come back to the apartment with her, but her sister was in shock, completely unresponsive. Ruth had no choice but to leave her with Lenny. He was sober by then, and he had promised to stay.

She wasn't happy about it, of course, but what choice did she have? She called Millie the next morning, first thing, to check on her. Arthur stayed home with the girls, and Ruth ran to help Millie pack. Of course, Millie would have to stay with them now—where else could she go?

Ruth decided not to tell Millie all the details of the phone call she had had with her parents before they drove home from Philadelphia. It was true that her mother hadn't liked the hotel—she had told Ruth as much in no uncertain terms. "How do I know the sheets here are clean? I can't sleep on a pillow other people have slept on."

But there had been more to the phone call that Ruth didn't reveal. "You know," her father had whispered so her mother wouldn't hear. "I met a man from Chicago who knew Lenny's brother."

"Small world," Ruth answered. "What did he say?"

"If it's the same Murray Fein, he was a real *shakher-makher*—a wheeler-dealer—running liquor to the hotels."

"Are you going to tell Millie?"

"There's nothing to tell. When Prohibition ended, he gave up the business. Murray is in soap flakes now, just like he told us. Still, I'm not going to be sorry when your sister ends it with his brother."

"Do you really think she will?"

"Ach, who knows? A few weeks ago, she asked if I thought Lenny was a good match for her."

"What did you say?"

"I said not to ask me. I said my opinion didn't matter."

"Why didn't you just tell her that you don't approve of him?"

"Sweetheart, when I have nothing nice to say, I keep my mouth shut."

"All right, Papa. Be careful driving home. It's very late—don't fall asleep."

"You think I sleep anymore? Ach, not me. *Klaineh kinder lozen nit shlofen; groisseh kinder lozen nit ruen.*"

"I don't know what that means."

"Small children don't let you sleep; big children don't let you rest."

**The funeral was a blur. As usual, it was up to Ruth to make all the** decisions. Contacting the relatives, coordinating the service, selecting the caskets, purchasing the cemetery plots. She took care of it all in between caring for twin toddlers while Millie stared at old photographs and cried on the couch.

After the burial, they went back to their parents' apartment to sit shivah with their neighbors and the out-of-town relatives. Ruth worked frantically in the kitchen, arranging platters and making coffee so that everything would be ready. In between setting out the silverware and folding the napkins, she fielded the inevitable questions from the twins. Alice and Louise had only just turned two, but even they were old enough to know something was amiss. They wandered around the apartment calling for their grandparents, unable to understand that Bubbe and Zaide would never return.

Millie emerged from her bedroom an hour or so later, once most of the visitors had already arrived. Her bluish-green eyes were heavy with tears, and she had tied back her auburn curls. With her impeccably pale skin and sorrowful expression, she was a vision of heartache, a goddess of grief. Their father's pinochle group cleared a place for her on the sofa, and a half dozen relatives flocked to her side. Mrs. Shapiro from the synagogue brought Millie a plate of kugel, and Mr. Gluck offered her a freshly made cup of coffee. It was Great-Aunt Edna's funeral all over again, with everyone praising Millie's sweetness and sensitivity. Ruth stood to the side, rearranging the napkins. She was a mourner forgotten.

"There you are." Lenny's brother, Murray, had snuck up beside her. "Please accept my condolences. Your parents were fine people." Murray's expression was stony, but when he shook her hand, his fingers were warm. A gold watch peeked out from underneath the cuff of his shirt, and his fingernails had been buffed to an impeccable shine.

Ruth didn't know that a man could have such well-groomed hands. In his black silk suit and matching black tie, Murray seemed accustomed to attending funerals. Ruth wondered about what her father had told her. What kind of business was Murray in really?

"Thank you for coming."

"Your father was a mensch. I'll never forget his kindness when I told him about our mother."

"He was a compassionate man."

They were interrupted by sobs from the center of the room, where Millie held court from her seat on the sofa. A new crowd of mourners had gathered around, patting and consoling her as if she were a pet.

"Millie seems to be taking it awfully hard."

The look on her face must have given her away. Maybe she rolled her eyes inadvertently, or maybe her cough was a little too abrupt. Whatever it was, Murray took notice. His lips curved upward into a small, sly smile.

"I understand completely. Don't forget: I happen to be the older sibling too. I know what it's like to be the responsible one." He motioned around the room and lowered his voice. "I'm assuming that you took care of arranging all this? You planned the funeral and the burial, yes? The little one was probably too distraught to help you?"

Ruth stared into Murray's unblinking eyes. How was it possible that this man should be the first person to understand?

"I don't mean to overstep," he continued, "but I've been through this before. I'm the one paying the bills, helping Lenny find jobs, smoothing the rough spots so he doesn't get upset. 'Course,

I'm eight years older than him, so that accounts for some of it. I forget sometimes how young he is."

"I'm only three years older than Millie."

Murray took a step closer and whispered into her ear, "I imagine sometimes it feels like more, though, doesn't it?"

His breath was too warm, the gesture too intimate.

"If you'll excuse me, I'm going to brew another pot of coffee." She had been caught off guard; she had revealed too much. Her mother would have cautioned her to be more careful. *Don't air your dirty laundry in public,* she used to say.

Once the coffee was made, Ruth slipped down the hall and into her parents' bedroom. Her father's felt slippers peeked out from under his side of the bed, and his pipe waited patiently on top of his nightstand. Ruth lay on top of the bedspread and breathed in the scent of the Blue Carnation perfume that clung to her mother's pillow. She felt the hum of activity on the other side of the door, but inside the bedroom, it was quiet and peaceful. How many days had it been since she had slept? Two or three now? She couldn't remember. Her eyelids fluttered shut, and she let sleep overtake her.

She hadn't been out for long when the door swung open. In her half-awake haze, Ruth recognized the voices of Arthur's cousin Gary and his wife, Sheila.

"Oops!" Sheila whispered. "Ruth is resting in there." Sheila thought she had shut the door, but the latch didn't click, so Ruth could hear the rest of the couple's conversation from out in the hallway.

"That room could do with a good sprucing up." Sheila's voice was low and raspy, her tone condescending.

"Shhh! What if Ruth hears you?"

"She's *asleep*! Trust me, Gary, she can't hear a thing. I suppose they won't be keeping this apartment for much longer. Millie can't live here alone—she moved in with Ruth."

"Lucky for Arthur." Gary whistled.

Sheila's chuckle filled the air like cigarette smoke. "There's no way I'd let a girl like Millie live with *us*. Too much temptation. Of course, Arthur is different. After all, he married *Ruth*, didn't he?"

"Even so," Gary said, "he's still a man. Did you see him comforting Millie at the cemetery? How he put his arm around her? I'm telling you, Sheila, it's only a matter of time. Come on, let's get out of here. I need to find that bathroom."

The conversation was over, but Ruth didn't budge. A blanket of dread spread itself over her, weighing on her chest so that she could not move. A few days ago, when she'd been told of her parents' accident, she had felt as though her worst possible fear had come true. But now she understood there were even worse fears lurking, lying in wait for just the right moment. Now she understood there were further places to fall.

Though far too premature, the death of her parents was part of the natural order of life. But the horror that Sheila and Gary predicted was neither natural nor inevitable. If it ever came to pass, it would be more than Ruth could bear—a terrible culmination of all the smaller indignities she had suffered over the years.

Ruth struggled against the doubt that wrapped itself around her, flung it aside, and rose from the bed. From inside her mother's closet, Ruth pulled out the jewelry box, opened the lid, and removed the black velvet pouch. She smoothed back her hair and pinched her cheeks for color. By the time she left the bedroom, the crowd in the apartment had thinned.

She found Lenny in the dining room, leaning against the wall, deep in conversation with her father's pinochle buddies. Her fingers rubbed against the soft velvet pouch in her pocket. In her mind, the ring inside it was a talisman of hope, a gem that had traveled across oceans and decades to guide her toward her future and guard her from harm. If her great-grandmother were alive, surely she would agree.

"Come with me," she told Lenny. "I have something to give you."

# Millie

Millie had never felt more alone than when Ruth walked out the door the night their parents died. Lenny had sobered up quickly after Ruth revealed the news—Millie was vaguely aware of him asking if she wanted tea, giving her his handkerchief, bringing another blanket. She was unable to answer; she kept her eyes closed. Eventually, she fell into a nightmarish sleep, dreaming of a childhood outing with her sister.

Ruth had just turned twelve and Millie was only nine when Gertrude Ederle became the first woman to swim across the English Channel. The newspapers couldn't get enough of her—she was only twenty years old, and a real New York girl, like Millie and Ruth. When Ederle returned to New York from England, her home city planned a ticker tape parade in her honor. The sisters begged their father to take them into Manhattan, but their mother was afraid one of the girls might get lost.

"I'm taking them, Florence. It's a historic event. Besides, the girls have never been to a parade," their father said.

"So what?" their mother snapped. "I've never been to prison. But that doesn't mean it's a good idea."

The crowd was enormous—over two million people—and the ticker tape fell like snow in the summertime. At first, Millie loved it, her father holding her high in the air as he walked up Broadway. But when he got too tired, he put her down and she had to walk. She was too small to see anything—she could barely see the sky.

The walk back to the subway was the worst part of all. Their father said he'd go in front, to clear a path through all the people. He told the girls to stay behind him, to hold hands and stick together. But after a while, Ruth got frustrated with Millie's slow pace and let go of her hand. Millie screamed for her sister, but Ruth didn't look back.

Eventually, a policeman saw her crying and put her up on top of his shoulders. Millie spotted Ruth's yellow dress half a block ahead of them, and the policeman ran through the crowd to reunite the trio. Afterward, their father bought ice cream cones for them and made them promise not to tell their mother what had happened.

**The day after their parents' death, Ruth came over early in the** morning. "I'm sorry I had to leave last night," she said. "But you'll stay with us for now, and then we'll figure out what to do." After she helped Millie pack a small bag of clothes, the two of them left for Ruth's apartment.

Millie liked sleeping with the twins in their bedroom. Their steady breathing was a comfort, and she felt less lonely. But once the funeral was over and the week of sitting shivah had passed, Millie wasn't quite sure where she fit into the household's daily routine. Ruth was moody and difficult to read. Arthur was kind, but he was preoccupied with preparations for his new job in Springfield. Millie assumed she would move with Ruth's family to Massachusetts, but her sister hadn't said much to clarify the situation.

The first Friday after the mourning period ended, Ruth invited Lenny over for a family dinner. The invitation caught Millie entirely by surprise. "I thought you were still upset with him. Because of the way he showed up at the apartment that night."

"No," Ruth assured her. "Lenny has been wonderful. Look at how he took care of you. Mama and Papa would be grateful."

Millie's eyes began to tear. "Do you really think so?" she asked.

While Millie ruminated, Ruth began swiping at the furniture with a feather duster. She had been unable to sit still since the day of the funeral. "Millie, I need to tell you something," she said. "I didn't want to bring it up before, but I think it's time now. The night Mama and Papa died, when they called me on the phone to say they were coming home early, Papa said some other things too."

"What do you mean?"

"Maybe he got caught up in the wedding festivities—you know how everyone is always so happy at weddings . . ." Ruth mumbled her words from behind the china cabinet. "And he ran into someone too. Some man who knew Lenny's family."

"Oh?" Millie answered. "What was his name? Can you come out of there, please? It's hard to hear what you're saying."

When Ruth finally emerged, her face was red. "Cobwebs," she stammered, waving the duster in the air. "I don't remember the name, but he must have said something nice about Lenny's mother. Anyway . . . before he got off the phone, Papa told me that he thought Lenny might be a good match for you."

The hairs on Millie's arms stood on end. "That's what he told you? Those were his exact words? A good match?"

"I think so. Anyway, he said he thought he could convince Mama to give Lenny a second chance."

Millie wished Ruth would stop cleaning for a minute. Was it possible that her father had liked Lenny all along? Had he been so afraid of contradicting his wife that he had kept his thoughts to himself? Had he wanted Millie to make up her mind on her own? Either way, Millie was stunned into silence.

"I know it's surprising," Ruth said, without looking up. "But now that they're gone, I thought you should know."

**A few weeks later, Lenny invited Millie to dinner at a restaurant—** not one of the shabby joints he frequented with his buddies but an elegant establishment known for its white linen tablecloths and crystal chandeliers.

When Lenny arrived to pick her up at Ruth's apartment, he wore a new silk tie and a freshly pressed suit. There was an impish grin on Ruth's face when he came to the door, a funny little smile Millie had never seen before.

"Have a nice time, you two!" Ruth sang out when they left. Her voice was so high pitched that she sounded like someone else.

At the restaurant, the maître d' held Millie's chair out for her and, once she was settled, laid her napkin on her lap. A waiter filled their water goblets from a sterling silver pitcher, slowly, so as not to spill a single drop. Millie marveled at the crystal, the flowers, and the china. She had to stop herself from touching the rose-shaped mounds of yellow butter—she couldn't imagine who had sculpted them and how much time it had taken. Another waiter appeared with a bottle of champagne she didn't remember Lenny ordering.

"I think there's been a mistake," she murmured, confused. But when she turned to ask Lenny, he was already kneeling on the carpet. The ring he held out to her caught the light from overhead so that the center opal appeared to be glowing from within. The stylish patrons surrounding them turned their heads and gasped before a reverential hush fell over the dining room.

It was a scene taken straight from one of Millie's mother's fairy tales, at once surprising and hauntingly familiar. Only after the applause, when the ring was on her finger, did Lenny explain to her the story of the gem he had given her. It had belonged to her great-grandmother, and Millie's mother had been saving it. "Your sister gave it to me," Lenny told her. "She said your father would have wanted me to give it to you."

Once order was restored, the waiter returned with the steak for two: a massive hunk of meat that he carved right in front of them. Millie turned her head away as the knife cut through the flesh—it was too rare for her taste, soft and undercooked. With sterling silver tongs, the waiter served them both, but Millie left her portion untouched and nibbled on a roll. Eventually, she transferred the slices to Lenny's plate; he devoured them quickly, as if he had somewhere else to be.

By the end of the meal, the other diners lost interest in them. The butter roses were whisked away, and the leftover champagne grew warm and flat. Millie tried to find the waiter to refill her water goblet, but she couldn't catch his eye, no matter how many times she tried.

Later, when Ruth asked about her evening, Millie found it difficult to find the proper words. She tried to picture the restaurant in her mind so she could describe it to her sister—to recall the maître d', the waiters, and the patrons. But when Millie shut her eyes to summon the scene, all she could see was a cold pool of blood, left from the steak, on her white china plate.

**They were to be married in one month, in the rabbi's study at her** parents' synagogue. Millie wanted to wait, but living alone in her parents' apartment would have caused a scandal, and moving to Springfield temporarily didn't make sense. Besides, Lenny begged her to have the wedding as quickly as possible. "I don't want us to be apart anymore," he insisted.

Millie wished her parents could be there to walk her down the aisle. She wished she still had some close girlfriends to serve as bridesmaids at the ceremony. She knew her reservations were normal under the circumstances. But she was plagued by other doubts that were more troubling: she wished Lenny would get a steady job, she wished he sounded more interested when he spoke with Ruth and Arthur, she wished he cared less about baseball and more about his career.

At night in her cot, listening to the twins' breathing, misgivings clouded Millie's mind and kept her awake. She stared at her ring finger—the finger of a stranger—and wondered how she had come to this place in her life. A year ago, she had been a confident young woman. But now, contemplating her marriage, she felt like a frightened child.

# Lillian

## Springfield, Massachusetts (February 1943)

It was a quarter to eight when Lillian and Patrick made their way up the steps of the Springfield Auditorium. Though they were among the first to check in for the On to Victory dance, guests would be arriving at all times throughout the evening. To ensure that all defense workers could attend, the event would be in full swing until three in the morning. Armory workers on the 11:00 P.M. shift would go directly from the dance to their jobs in Federal Square. The people they relieved would change out of their coveralls and arrive at the auditorium by midnight.

Before Lillian and Patrick passed through the sculpted bronze doors, they stopped to watch a spectacle unfolding on the street below. A horse-drawn wagon overflowing with hay had just pulled over at the bottom of the steps. When the horses came to a halt, a handful of men in jackets and ties jumped off the bales and onto the pavement. The women, hindered by their dresses and evening shoes, shimmied slowly out of the wagon with the help of their escorts, taking care to remove any stray bits of straw from their hair and décolletage.

Patrick chuckled at the sight of the group. "I suppose that's one way to get around the gasoline rationing."

Inside, the massive hall was filling up quickly. Jack Teagarden's fourteen-piece orchestra was on the stage, and people who weren't dancing were tapping their feet to the music. Women wore anything from formal gowns to skirt sets. Some men were in uniform and others in suits—a few were even decked out in shiny tuxedos. Volunteers walked around selling raffle tickets for war bonds, while others carried clipboards and took down names for the jitterbug contest. During a pause in the music, an announcement was made that one lucky young woman would be chosen as the Women Ordnance Workers girl of the evening.

By ten o'clock, Lillian was desperate to sit. The dance floor was packed, and her feet had been stepped on by more strangers than she could count. Patrick walked her upstairs to the balcony, where they found some empty seats overlooking the dance floor. Once she was settled, he promised to return with Coca-Colas for both of them.

A group of young women sat in the row behind her—dateless, it seemed, and hoping to be noticed. Between bouts of nervous laughter, they spoke longingly about the young men they wanted to dance with. Their conversation reminded Lillian of all her high school dances—the ache of anticipation and the inevitable disappointment.

Attendance at all Littlefield School dances had been compulsory and regarded as essential to every girl's social education. Dresses had been scrutinized for appropriate necklines, and white gloves had been required. The first time a young man approached Lillian at one of the gatherings, he stuttered so badly that she barely understood him. She thought it would be cruel to ask him to repeat himself, so she stood and took his hand, hoping that his mumblings had been an invitation to dance. His palm was warm and damp, like the wet socks her roommates left on the radiators in their dorm room.

Littlefield held most dances with its brother institution, the

Wolcott Ellsworth Academy, just down the road. Unlike some of her classmates, Lillian didn't roll her eyes when a boy stepped on her foot or lost track of the music. She never made faces when a young man approached, no matter how many pimples he was plagued with or how far his ears stood out from his head. As a result, she became a popular partner, especially for the shyer of the Wolcott Ellsworth young men.

There had been only one instance during all her time at Littlefield when Lillian had refused a young man asking for a dance. It had been in the fall of her senior year, during an event with the Farragut Military Academy. The Farragut upperclassmen had traveled north from Virginia for a tour of West Point, and a dinner dance in Connecticut had been arranged by the headmistress.

Lillian's head began to ache when she heard the news; her father had attended the Farragut Academy. On the morning of the dance, she visited the nurse, but her temperature was normal, and she was sent back to the dorm. "I'm sure you'll perk up," the nurse told her with confidence.

Lillian wore her least-flattering dress and refused the other girls' offers to help with her makeup. "At least brush your hair," they begged. But Lillian had no interest. "It's fine the way it is."

In the end, it hadn't mattered. There were twice as many boys as girls in attendance, and in the bright light of the gymnasium, there was no place to hide. Before long she caught the attention of the very group of boys she'd wanted most to avoid: the wisecracking ones—the ones who took sips from the flasks they had hidden in their pockets and returned from the bathroom smelling of cigarettes. Before she could blink, the tallest and handsomest of them was standing in front of her.

When asking for a dance, the boys from Wolcott Ellsworth were always polite. They bowed at the waist, extended an arm, and stuttered their way through *May I have the honor?* or *Would you care to join me?* They wore braces on their teeth and navy suits with scuffed shoes.

But this boy, in his uniform, was a completely different species. His teeth and his shoes were of an equal, blinding shine. He did not bow or even bend, and he kept his hands in his pockets. His invitation to dance was more command than request.

Lillian searched the boy's face before she answered. There was something familiar about it, but nothing redeeming. "No, thank you," she said finally, assuming he would retreat. But he stood there and glared, eyes blazing and furious. "I'm not feeling well," she said, to try to save his feelings.

Before she could say more, the other boys from his group formed a circle around her and stared, open-mouthed, at the girl who had dared to refuse their friend.

"It's fine," the boy announced, pretending to be gracious. "I didn't really want to dance. I was just being polite, since we grew up together."

"What do you mean?" Lillian asked. "Do we know each other?"

"You *are* Lillian Guilford, right? We went to school together. My dad was the doctor on base." He paused and narrowed his eyes. "You honestly don't remember me?"

"I'm sorry, but no."

She couldn't figure out what bothered him more—her refusal to dance or the fact that she'd forgotten him. He ran his hand through his hair and flashed an angry grin. She knew from his expression that something cruel was coming.

"You know," he said, stepping closer and feigning concern, "you seem really confused. You should probably go to the infirmary or something." He turned his back on her then and motioned for his friends to follow. "Her mother was nuts too," he said, loud enough for everyone to hear. "Hung herself from a rope off their kitchen chandelier."

Later, at the infirmary, the nurse took her temperature again. "One hundred and three," she announced, sounding surprised. "I guess you were coming down with something after all."

# Arietta

Arietta felt guilty leaving Millie to go to the dance. But she had been looking forward to her date with Fitz all week, and she worried that if she canceled, he'd be too discouraged to ask again. She was grateful when Millie insisted that they go.

The truth was, Arietta had never had much luck with men. The ones she met backstage were always waiting for the chorus girls, and even when they complimented her singing, she knew the roses they carried were not meant for her. There had been that one time, back in New Haven, when a greasy-haired young man handed her a half-crushed bouquet, but only after the girl he'd been waiting for breezed by on the arm of an older patron wearing an expensive silk suit. Embarrassed, the young man had pressed the flowers into Arietta's empty hands. But before she could thank him, he'd bolted for the back door.

Her Aunties assured her that the right man would come along one day to sweep her off her feet. "If he can lift me," Arietta would joke, patting her round hips and forcing a smile. By her teens, she had managed to slim down considerably, but she would never have the long legs or wispy waists the dancing girls had. Their fringed flapper dresses, meant to hang loose and sway, pulled tight around Arietta's stomach and tugged at her thighs.

When she turned twenty, the Aunties passed away in a single sad month, like a row of trees cursed with fast-moving blight. As she watched them wither away, she was left with a newfound appreciation for her own powerful figure. She wondered whether her size might be the font of her musical abilities and whether an attempt to reduce it might diminish her vocal gifts. Eventually, she stopped comparing herself to the girls in the chorus.

She took to the stage with a renewed sense of confidence, singing of heartache and lost love so believably that her audiences were moved to tears. She didn't need a real broken heart to convince them. And while she certainly longed for a love of her own, the adoration of the crowd helped to dull her disappointment.

When her father took ill, she stopped performing to care for him. Before his last breath, he squeezed her hand. "One day you will meet a good man who loves you the way I loved your mother." She hoped he was right, but by the time she began working at the armory, she was certain he'd been mistaken. Good men didn't look at her that way, and the bad ones didn't either. She was forty-two years old when Fitz began looking, and all she could do was hope that he was one of the good ones.

They had a bit of a choppy start when she arrived at the armory restaurant. "Only the fellas call me that," he said when she had referred to him as Fitz. "I'm not sure folks will go for something so exotic," he insisted when she had told him about her lasagna. But once the awkwardness passed, they had settled into a routine. Now, no matter what she was doing—checking the stove or rinsing pots, she could feel his protective gaze upon her. If she raised her head to smile at him, his neck and his ears turned red from embarrassment.

*That man is forty-five if he's a day,* Arietta thought. *What is he so afraid of?*

Every Monday, Arietta prepared piles of biscuits and mountains of baked beans for the lunchtime crowd. The kitchen usually smelled of warm molasses and Worcestershire sauce. But one Monday in February after she pulled the pans from the oven, she was overcome by the smell of limes and sandalwood. It didn't take her long to figure it out: Fitz was wearing a new cologne.

He looked different too. His eyebrows had been tamed, and he'd taken special care with his shirt. When he tugged at his tie, Arietta had an inkling. She tried to look encouraging as he struggled with what to say.

"I was hoping . . . you'd go to the dance with me this Friday."

"The 'On to Victory' dance, you mean? I'd love to."

"You would?"

"Don't look so shocked."

"Sorry. I'm happy you said yes, that's all." He'd been shuffling his feet, staring down at his shoes, but after Arietta accepted his invitation, he took a step closer. Fitz took her hand in his gently, as if he thought he might break it.

Arietta's apron was stained, and her hair was mussed, but the warmth of Fitz's fingers made her feel beautiful and young. She closed her eyes for a moment to savor the sensation. When she opened them, she could have sworn that the biscuits smelled like roses.

**Arietta's gown for the dance was uncharacteristically plain—a** muted shade of blue without sparkle or embellishment. She kept her curls loose, framing her face, and the makeup she chose was soft and subdued. There was no need for false eyelashes or a costume this evening—all she wanted was to be an ordinary gal out on the town with her date. She relished the feeling of Fitz's arm looped through hers as he guided her carefully to the middle of the dance floor.

"Front and center," he said, smiling shyly. "That way everyone can see my dance partner."

For a man his size, he was surprisingly light on his feet. After thirty minutes, Arietta grew winded, but Fitz spun her in circles without missing a beat. When her toes turned numb, she begged for a break. "Can we take a breather, just for a bit? I'd love to freshen up," she told him.

"Of course," Fitz said. "I'll grab us some drinks."

The ladies' room was even more congested than the dance floor, with women of all ages swarming the small wall mirrors to neaten their hair and powder their noses. Arietta was reapplying her lipstick when a well-dressed blonde squeezed in beside her and stepped on her foot. Instead of apologizing, the blonde jostled Arietta further, pushing and elbowing as if Arietta didn't exist.

"Excuse me," the cook said, catching the woman's eye in the mirror. "If you give me a little room, I'll finish up in a jiffy."

The woman in the mirror glared back but didn't budge. A flicker of recognition passed over her features. "You're the cook from the armory cafeteria, aren't you?"

"That's me, all right. Have we met before?"

"Certainly not. My husband is an officer." The stranger's tone was belligerent, but Arietta made an effort to remain polite. "Well, then, maybe you recognize me from the Walshes' Christmas party?"

"I didn't go, and my husband left early. Fred said the entertainment was *awful*." She smirked.

The insult, combined with the mention of her husband's first name, left no doubt in Arietta's mind as to who this stranger was. She had to be Fred Peabody's wife, Grace.

The wisest course of action would have been for Arietta to walk away—to find another mirror or another bathroom entirely. But Fred Peabody's threats still rang in her ears. She could picture his angry face; she could hear his slurred voice. *You say one word to Walsh, and I'll make you wish you hadn't.*

"Funny," Arietta said, her brown eyes glued to the reflection of Grace's blue ones in the mirror. "I remember your husband staying late that night."

"You must be thinking of someone else."

Arietta should have stopped, but she couldn't help herself. "I don't think so. I'm good with names. Captain Fred Peabody—tall man, dark hair. He had too much to drink, but that probably doesn't surprise you. He made some very inappropriate remarks to my friend Millie."

Grace snapped her compact shut. "I'm good with names too, and I *know* Millie Fein. There's no way Fred would have been talking to her. He knows better than to waste his time on trash."

Arietta pushed forward to reclaim her spot at the mirror, intentionally knocking Grace off balance. Grace's compact exploded as it hit the tile floor; bits of glass and powder flew into the air like shrapnel. Grace scowled and pointed a gloved finger at Arietta. "You're going to regret this," she said. "And your friend is too."

# Millie

It was easy sometimes to forget about the war. Easy to let a tiny tragedy in an ordinary day eclipse the greater horror of a global calamity. Easy to let the fear of a personal confrontation obscure the vaster dread of battles halfway across the world.

It was easy to forget, when men and women were dancing and orchestras were playing, that other men and women were fighting and dying. Easy, when she held a sleeping child in her arms, to forget the other children awake in places she'd never heard of, children who were hungry and frightened and cold.

It was easy, much too easy, to think only of herself and the smaller war that waited on the other side of her sister's front door.

**The air in the foyer was heavy with frustration. Ruth's hair was in** disarray, as if she'd been tugging at it, and she was still wearing the apron that she'd worn to cook dinner. She looked several years older than she had that afternoon.

"Where have you been? I've been worried to death!"

"Shh. Michael is asleep. We were at Arietta's for dinner."

"I thought maybe Lenny came back for you, that he hadn't

left town after all—" Ruth paced the floor as she blurted out the words.

"I need to put Michael to bed. We can talk about this in the morning."

"This can't wait until tomorrow. Come down when you're done."

What was it Lenny had said? *There you go again, ordering every-one around.*

When she returned, Ruth had made her a hot cup of tea—a kind of peace offering, Millie supposed. But she would not be taken in by the sweet, fragrant liquid, no matter how inviting or comforting it was. She carried the cup to the sink and poured the contents down the drain. Then the sisters stared at each other across the wide kitchen table, each waiting for the other to break the peace first. Their truce had come to an end—there was no way around it—and the only way forward was to barrel straight through. Millie decided to wait for Ruth to begin.

"You should have called to say you'd be late. I don't think you understand how worried I was."

"You didn't seem worried before, by the gate. Calling the guards and threatening to arrest Lenny. You seemed awfully sure of yourself then." Millie thought Ruth seemed surprised by her tone.

"You can't possibly be angry that I told him to leave!"

"I'm not. I wanted him to leave as much as you did. Which is why I begged you to give him what he came for—to give him my ring so he'd leave us alone."

"I couldn't do that."

"*Why?* Why couldn't you? And what did Lenny mean by all those things he said? What have you been hiding?"

"What have *I* been hiding? *You're* the one who lied about Lenny joining the army! *You're* the one who lied about your husband being dead!"

"I didn't lie to you when I wrote that he enlisted. Lenny went to the recruiting office, just like I said. I put my letter in the mailbox before he came home." Remembering that day, Millie's eyes filled with tears. "You should have seen how excited he was. He promised to be back early so we could celebrate together, but when he finally came home, it was late and he was drunk. They said he had a heart murmur, but I knew he was humiliated. We had a terrible argument—he hit me, and then he left. He had disappeared before, so I was used to it by then. But after that night, I knew he wasn't coming back."

"He hit you?" Ruth leaned forward and put her head in her hands. "Why didn't you tell me?"

"Tell *you*? Are you joking? All of my life you made me feel like a failure. You waved your report cards in my face. You laughed at the magazines I read. You were good at *everything*. I thought I could be good at marriage, at least. How could I admit that I had failed at that too?"

"If you had told me what was happening, maybe I could have helped. I could have visited—"

"Visited? You never came back to Brooklyn *once* after our parents died! You left the day after my wedding and never looked back. You didn't even come when Michael was born! I wrote you long letters, and you sent me back postcards. The only time you seemed interested in us was when I wrote that Lenny enlisted. After that, I was afraid to tell you the truth because I didn't want you to freeze me out again."

"So, you're saying it's all *my* fault? You're blaming me for your lies?"

"What if I am? You've been blaming me for my looks since the day I was born!"

"Do you think it was easy having you as my sister? Do you think it was pleasant having relatives and friends and every boy I ever dated forget I existed when you waltzed into the room? Do you think I liked fixing all your homework and cleaning up your messes?"

"I never asked you to do those things! I was a child!"

Ruth pounded the table with her fist so hard that it shook. "You were *eighteen* when our parents died! *You* got to grieve! *You* had the luxury of mourning our parents and running to your room whenever you felt like crying. I was left alone to make all the arrangements—to speak to the rabbi, to tell all the relatives. And I did it all with two toddlers on my hips. Do you have any idea what it was like to pick out coffins for our parents? Of course you don't, Millie, because I did it *for* you!" The words flew out of Ruth's mouth like arrows rushing toward their mark.

"I didn't know how to do any of those things—"

"I didn't either, but I did them anyway! *That* is what it means to be an adult—choosing to be capable when you'd rather fall apart; forcing yourself to stand and speak when you'd rather lie down and cry; taking care of your little sister because everyone knows that she's the sensitive one and you're the cold fish."

Millie stared at Ruth, wide-eyed. "I didn't ask you to take care of me," she mumbled.

"Well, our parents certainly did." In the wake of her frenzy, Ruth grew suddenly calm. Her eyes turned murky and gray, like the sky before a storm. "Mama showed me the opal ring the week before my wedding. I couldn't believe my eyes when I saw it—that beautiful jewel mixed in with all of her schlock. She was always going on about you marrying a millionaire—I guess I don't have to tell you; you know what she used to say. She was saving that ring for you, of course. She said you would be the only one who would have an occasion to wear it. Then she gave me her funeral earrings—those gold-plated clip-ons she always wore to the cemetery. I didn't find out until later they weren't even real gold. What did it matter? They were hideous either way."

"I'm sure she didn't mean to hurt you."

"She didn't mean to, but she did. I was never going to be worthy of wearing that ring. I was never going to be glamorous or impressive enough. Mama always thought I was too serious. She thought Arthur was too . . . too serious and too fat. When he first told her about the job in Springfield, you should have seen the face she made. Springfield was *nowhere* to her—dull, just like me. But once you graduated from high school, she got it into her head that you should move there with us. It was the best way she could think of to separate you from Lenny."

Millie shook her head. "She never said anything about that to me."

"Of course she didn't. She knew you'd never agree to it, but she was going to figure out a way. She wouldn't let it go. She didn't care that I had a husband I wanted to start a new life with. She didn't care that it might be nice for me to have a fresh start for once. I spent that whole summer thinking up reasons why you should stay in Brooklyn. And then they died. The morning after, when things were clearer, I knew you'd have to come with us. I couldn't leave you alone in New York. And when you moved into our apartment, I thought, *Well, this is what it's going to be like. I'll be taking care of Millie now for the rest of my life.* I convinced myself it would work out. I didn't have a choice.

"After the funeral, when you came out of your bedroom during the shivah, it was like the Red Sea parting. All those people in Mama and Papa's apartment ran to your side to kiss you and comfort you. They brought you drinks and plates of food and told you how sorry they were for you. I was invisible again. Again! Like always! I went to Mama and Papa's room to rest, but then I overheard Arthur's cousin talking about us. About how I was a fool to let you move in with me and Arthur, about how he would be . . . tempted. They said it was inevitable. It was just a matter of time. And I knew it wouldn't be long before I became invisible to Arthur too." A staggering wail escaped from Ruth's lips. Sobs poured from her chest, racking her body until she could no longer speak. "He was the only one who ever chose *me*. I couldn't lose him too."

Millie had never seen her sister so completely unmoored. She didn't know how to respond. Eventually, Ruth composed herself and rose from her chair. She paced the length of the kitchen, speaking as she walked. "I took the ring from Mama's jewelry box, and I gave it to Lenny. I told him that our father would have wanted him to have it. I said he should propose again—a real proposal this time, romantic and elegant, the way Mama would have wanted."

Millie's head began to pound. All the small mysteries were beginning to make sense. "You lied to him," Millie murmured. "And you lied to *me*. Papa never said that he approved of Lenny, did he? You wanted me to get married so I would stay in Brooklyn."

"Yes."

"When he proposed at the restaurant, it happened the way Mama used to tell me it would. You planned it that way, didn't you? You told Lenny what to wear, how to kneel down, what to say?"

"I gave him some advice."

Millie felt her jaw tighten, her body stiffen with rage. "I had been thinking of breaking it off with him before then, did you know that? All that summer, I had been thinking of ending it." Millie thought back to the night of the proposal—the restaurant where Ruth must have made the reservation; the champagne Ruth must have reminded Lenny to order. Revulsion welled up in her throat. "You tricked me with the ring. You tricked me with the proposal. You tricked me into marrying him so you could be free!"

From upstairs came a thud and then Michael's drowsy wail. Her shouting must have woken him—he was always a light sleeper. Millie searched Ruth's frozen face for a hint of remorse, but all she saw was a stranger, a face she barely knew, so she ran from the kitchen and up the stairs to Michael's room. He had kicked off his covers, but she tucked them back around him and shushed him softly in the dark until both their heartbeats steadied. She was about to curl up beside him when she heard voices coming from the foyer.

Millie tiptoed down the hallway, to the top of the staircase. Below, two men in uniform were speaking with her sister. The first was a guard she recognized from the main gate, but the second, whom she didn't know, wore an officer's uniform. As she walked down the steps, the officer stared.

"Millie Fein?" he asked. "I'm Captain Richard O'Brian, head of Armory Intelligence. I'd like you to come with me, please, to answer some questions."

Ruth spoke, her voice high pitched and shaky. "I don't understand why this can't wait until tomorrow. It's almost midnight, for goodness' sake! If you really need to talk to her, why can't you do it here? Just go in the living room—it's right through that doorway."

But the intelligence officer would not be swayed. "As I said before, ma'am, this is an urgent matter regarding armory security. I need to question Mrs. Fein in private, and it may take some time."

Millie held up her hand to end the debate. "It's fine, Ruth. I'll go with them."

The truth was, Millie had no more strength left to protest. The revelations of the evening—Lenny's appearance and Ruth's lies—had taken their toll on her, mentally and physically. Her thinking was muddied, and her mind was a blur. She had been struggling and screaming for too long; she could not start again now, not with these men. Besides, leaving with them meant a respite, however brief, from thinking any more about the events of her past.

"I have one question," she said as she pulled on her coat. "Does this mean you're arresting me?"

"No, ma'am," Captain O'Brian said. "We just want to ask you some questions."

At the mention of arrest, Ruth grew even more agitated. She placed herself intentionally between her sister and the door. "Millie, you don't have to go with them. They can't drag you away like this!"

"Calm down," Millie said. "You have nothing to worry about. You don't need to take care of me anymore."

# Lillian

The phone in Patrick's office began to ring just as they walked through the front door. "Patrick, grab that, please, before it wakes the whole house." Lillian was used to her husband's evening phone calls, but they had left the dance at midnight and it was well past that now. She slipped out of her shoes and waited to find out who had called.

From the hallway, it didn't sound like standard armory business. Her husband's voice was gentler than usual—soothing, in fact. Whoever he was speaking with must have been upset. When the conversation ended, she heard him dial another number. A moment later, he returned to the foyer looking confused. "That was Ruth Blum. You're not going to believe this, but Dick O'Brian just took Millie Fein into custody for questioning."

"*Now?* Why on earth would he do that? He's the head of intelligence—what could he possibly want with Millie?" Suddenly, she snapped her fingers and let out an angry groan. "Damn that Grace Peabody," she muttered under her breath.

"What are you talking about? What does Grace have to do with this?"

"Listen to me, sweetheart. You've got to get Dick on the

phone. I'm willing to bet that Grace is involved in this somehow. For months, she's been spreading rumors about that fire being a sabotage. I'm sure she called Dick and accused Millie of something."

"Why would she do that? What could Grace possibly have against Millie?"

"Jealousy, for starters. Grace doesn't like attractive women, especially when they're a good ten years younger than she is. With a husband like Fred, it's not hard to see how she got that way. But it's certainly no excuse for the way she behaves."

Patrick shook his head. "The results of the investigation were crystal clear—the fire was an accident, pure and simple."

"Grace doesn't think so. Can you call Dick's office?"

"I just tried a minute ago, but he isn't answering his phone."

Lillian threw her evening shoes into the hall closet and pulled on an old pair of boots. There was no time to change her dress, but at least her feet would be comfortable.

"Put your coat back on, Patrick. We'd better get over there."

**A February moon hung low in the sky, casting an eerie glow on all** of Armory Square. The hallways of the administration building were dark and deserted, but when they reached the second floor, a slim line of light shone from under one of the doors. Patrick rapped his knuckles twice and then entered without an invitation.

The room was poorly lit, drafty, and cold. Millie hadn't removed her coat, and neither had the grim-looking gentleman sitting across from her. Captain O'Brian was older than Patrick, but no more than fifty. He took notes on a pad with a silver fountain pen, which he set down when he stood to shake Patrick's hand. "Colonel Walsh, Mrs. Walsh. What brings you over here so late?"

"We were wondering the same thing about you," Patrick said. "Couldn't your questions for Mrs. Fein wait until the morning?"

"Normally, yes. But I received a series of phone calls this evening, and I thought it best to speak with Mrs. Fein immediately."

"Let me guess," Lillian said. "Were the calls from Grace Peabody, by any chance?" From the look on Captain O'Brian's face, Lillian was certain she was right. "I'll take that as a yes." She reached her hand out to Millie, pulled her to her feet, and put one arm around the shivering girl. "Captain O'Brian, let me assure you that whatever Mrs. Peabody suggested, Mrs. Fein had nothing to do with the fire last summer. She is an armory resident and a loyal worker in our shops. She is the sister-in-law of one of our finest scientists. She also happens to be my personal friend and a friend to our entire family."

"I appreciate that, Mrs. Walsh, but you must understand that we need to take any allegations of sabotage seriously, no matter how far-fetched."

"Listen here," Patrick interjected. "Since when did you start bringing young women in for questioning in the middle of the night? This interrogation is officially over. Whatever questions you have left, you can ask tomorrow during daylight hours in my office. Are we clear on that, Captain?"

"Yes, Colonel Walsh, sir. Of course."

**The next day, after dinner, Lillian pulled Patrick aside. "I told** Millie that she and Michael can stay here with us for a while."

Patrick raised his eyebrows, but he didn't object. "Did she and Ruth have some sort of falling-out?"

"It's complicated, but yes. I take it that things have been uncomfortable between them for some time, but after what happened yesterday, Millie doesn't feel like she can stay. She was planning on moving in with Arietta—you remember, the singer from our party? But if she stays there, she and Michael will be sleeping on the couch. Arietta rents a few bedrooms, but they're all filled for now. I told Millie it was ridiculous for her to live like that when we have so many empty bedrooms here."

"I'm not saying no; it's your decision to make. But don't you think it looks odd to have her living with us? It sets a strange precedent, Lillian—one I'm not excited about repeating."

"I know, Patrick, but this is a special set of circumstances. I had a long talk with Millie today. I promised that I'd keep her situation confidential for now, so I'm not going to tell you all the details of what she's endured. For such a young woman, she's been through a great deal. She . . . she reminds me of my mother, Patrick. That's really all I want to say."

A look of concern passed over his face. "That bad?" he asked softly.

"Different, but I'd like to help her if I can. It will only be for a few months. One of Arietta's boarders is moving out then."

Patrick kissed Lillian on the forehead and wrapped his arms around her. She felt lucky to have him, lucky to be married to a man who could stand with her in silence, a man who didn't demand explanations for every choice she made.

# Ruth

Ruth heard a loud thump followed by a series of softer ones, as if someone or something had fallen down the stairs. "Is everyone all right?"

"I'm fine," Millie answered, but Ruth could hear the irritation in her sister's voice. When Ruth reached the foyer, she understood why. Millie had been carrying her suitcase down the steps when the top latch had come undone and everything inside it had spilled out.

"The handle was already broken," Millie murmured. "It was only a matter of time before the latch fell apart too." She rested the now-empty suitcase at the bottom of the steps and began to pick up the scattered clothes.

"I don't understand," Ruth said. "Why are you packing?"

Millie busied herself folding the clothes, trying to avoid her sister's gaze. "Mrs. Walsh invited me and Michael to stay with her for a while. She has an extra bedroom for us. We'll move tomorrow."

Ruth swayed slightly before reaching for the bannister. "You have a room here."

"It would be better if we stayed somewhere else for a while. This living arrangement has become uncomfortable for all of us."

Millie spoke calmly, without a trace of emotion. The words sounded rehearsed, as if she were reading a part.

But Ruth refused to play along. "What are you talking about? A shopworker can't just move into the commanding officer's house."

"I was going to move to Arietta's, but she has too many boarders and no spare beds. Lillian has plenty of empty rooms. She insisted."

"You're my sister. You're supposed to live here, with your family. What do you think people will say if you move? It will be humiliating."

"Really?" Millie snapped. "For me or for *you*?"

"That isn't fair! I didn't ask you to leave!"

"Maybe not yet, but history has a way of repeating itself." Before Ruth could answer, Millie gathered the rest of her clothes and ran up the steps, back to her bedroom. The only thing left was the broken suitcase. Scratches on the sides had worn off almost all the color, the corners had caved in, and the latch had disintegrated. That it had survived the trip from Brooklyn in one piece was, Ruth decided, nothing short of a miracle.

Ruth went to bed early, but sleep would not come. All she could think of was the worn-out suitcase—something once so essential, now rendered obsolete. She pushed off her covers and tiptoed into the hallway. A few minutes later, she found what she was looking for pushed against the back wall of the upstairs linen closet. The suitcase was five years old, but it looked practically new. She pulled it out from its resting place, blew off the dust, and carried it down the hall to Millie's bedroom door. She knocked several times, but Millie didn't answer, so Ruth left the suitcase on the floor outside her sister's room.

For the rest of the night, Ruth stared at the ceiling. She finally gave up sometime after twelve and retreated to the kitchen for a hot cup of tea. When the morning light woke her, she was still at the table, her head down on the wooden top with a dishrag as her pillow.

She stretched out her shoulders, achy from the awkward position, and hitched up her robe so she wouldn't trip on the steps. Upstairs, the hallway was quiet. When Ruth peeked inside Millie's open bedroom door, she saw that all traces of her sister and her nephew were gone. All that was left was a note on the bed and her sister's opal ring propped up against the pillow.

> *I don't want this anymore, but I think you should keep it. Thank you for the suitcase.*
>
> > *Your sister,*
> > *Millie*

This time, Ruth was the one left behind.

# Millie

**Springfield, Massachusetts (April 1943)**

Inside the commanding officer's house, Millie breathed more easily. It wasn't only the kindness she was shown or the absence of Ruth's icy stares in the mornings, but something Arietta had said when Millie told her about Lillian's offer: *There's no safer house in Armory Square.*

The truth was that Millie had been afraid ever since Lenny had reappeared. The scar on his face hadn't been the only change she had noticed. There was a hunger inside him now, a desperation that she heard in his laughter and saw behind his eyes. Ruth's threat may have shaken him, but Millie knew that his hesitation in contacting her again would only be temporary. Unless Lenny found the money that he needed elsewhere, time would embolden him, and he would return.

For the first few years of their marriage, no matter how many days he stayed away or how drunk he was when he reappeared, Millie honestly believed that one day Lenny would change. *Think of all that he went through without a father or mother. He never had the kind of love my parents gave me. He'll come around—I know he will. All he needs is time.*

Only after he struck her was she able to see her mistake. How naive she had been to let it go on this long; how blind she had been to all of the signs. The only thing worse than the shame of her mistake was the feeling she'd had in the moment just after his hand struck her cheek. It was a feeling she had never dreamed that Lenny could awaken in her—a fear so consuming she felt as if she couldn't breathe.

The night he had hit her, she had barricaded the door with the flimsy table from their kitchenette and stayed awake keeping watch. She knew Lenny could have shoved the table aside, but placing it in front of the door gave her a small bit of comfort. As the months passed and Lenny showed no signs of returning, Millie's fear began to fade, like freckles in the winter when the sun was out of sight. But when he appeared in the middle of Federal Street, snickering at her clumsiness and making his demands, fear gripped her again and wouldn't let go. For now, she may have earned a slight reprieve, but she had a terrible feeling that Lenny would be back.

So, Millie clung to Arietta's words because they made her feel secure. She stayed in the Walshes' home not only to get away from her sister but because she wanted to believe that behind its brick walls and tall garden hedges, she and Michael would be safe.

*"Peter!* Half of my morning newspaper is missing!" Millie could hear Colonel Walsh's booming voice all the way from the kitchen.

Millie and Michael reached the bottom of the staircase just as Peter Walsh rushed past. Still chewing on his toast, the ten-year-old waved a section of *The Springfield Republican* above his head. "Morning!" he yelled. Before he shut the front door, he called over his shoulder, "Hey, Michael—wait 'til you see the new boat I made. We'll test it on the pond this afternoon!"

The "pond" was the fountain that sat in front of the commanding officer's house. Round and shallow, it was the perfect place for paper boat sailing. Peter was an expert at folding the fragile vessels, but unfortunately for Colonel Walsh, he was a stickler for quality.

"I can't use yesterday's newspaper," he liked to tell his father. "Today's paper is crisper. It floats better."

When she and Michael first moved, Millie was so intimidated by Colonel Walsh that she could barely speak when he entered the room. The fourteen-year age difference between them might as well have been forty. She found his voice too stern and his posture too straight. Plus, every day, Ruth's parting words echoed in her head—who did Millie think she was, moving in with the commanding officer's family?

Over time, she grew more comfortable, not because of anything specific he said but because watching him interact with his family made her realize that no matter his title, Patrick Walsh was, first and foremost, a devoted father and husband. Their household was messy and raucous and loud. With four children to wrangle, it was rare that a morning passed without a scuffle, some spills, and a good amount of shouting. But even when he yelled, Millie could tell that Colonel Walsh was never truly angry.

It was the colonel, after all, who taught Peter to fold the boats that required the sacrifice of his early morning newspaper. It was the colonel who showed Margaret the proper way to hit a tennis ball; the colonel who helped Thomas learn to calculate the circumference of a circle. And how many evenings had Millie seen him with Frances, their two heads pressed together over a book, discussing politics and war and a thousand other things? When Millie saw how the colonel looked at his children—the combination of amusement and awe on his face—she ached for her own son and for what she knew Michael would never have.

The longer she lived with them, the more Colonel Walsh tried to include Millie in their family dinner conversations. She knew he only wanted to be kind, but she was reluctant to participate. Lillian would shake her head at him when he pushed too hard, and most of the time, he would back off or change the subject. But one evening after the children were excused to do their homework, he tossed his napkin on the table and looked Millie in the eye.

"Millie," he said, "I'm hoping you can help me with something. Can you think of anything we can do to reduce turnover in the shops? Too many women are quitting after just a few months on the job."

"You shouldn't put Millie on the spot like that," Lillian scolded. She took a sip of tea and raised her eyebrow at her husband.

"But I could use Millie's input."

"Patrick—"

Millie didn't want to be the cause of a tussle between them. "I don't mind," she answered. "I think . . . I think a lot of the girls start out excited, but the work can be tedious, and they feel disconnected."

Patrick leaned forward in his chair. "What do you mean, disconnected?"

"I assemble the trigger mechanism, and someone else straightens a barrel. Someone else polishes the gunstock, and so on and so forth. But each one of us is completely separate from the other. I see thousands of triggers every day, but I've never seen all the rifle parts put together."

Colonel Walsh rocked in his chair and drummed his fingers on the table. Had she offended him? There was no way to tell.

"You know," he finally said, "you raise a good point." He stood from his chair with a smile on his face. "Both of you, come with me. I have an idea."

Colonel Walsh's office was located to the right of the front door, just off the foyer and across from the living room. The door was usually closed, and though Millie had glimpsed into the room a few times, she had never been inside. A massive wooden desk stood in the center, buried under books and bulky stacks of papers. Cabinets and bookcases adorned the back wall, crafted in once gleaming mahogany that had dulled over time. Inside, the air was heavy, serious, and solemn, like the sanctuary of her old childhood synagogue in Brooklyn. It was a room full of history, a room that knew the work that accompanied war.

244 Lynda Cohen Loigman

Colonel Walsh walked around to the back of his desk and moved two of the highest piles of paper to the floor. Under the piles was a leather blotter, and under the blotter was a small brass key that fit one of the vertical cabinets along the back wall. Colonel Walsh opened the cabinet and pulled out an armory-made M1 Garand rifle.

Millie had never seen him with a weapon in his hands before. She glanced over at Lillian to see if she felt the change, but the colonel's wife was nonplussed; the firearm did not faze her.

"So," Colonel Walsh said, "I take it you've never held one of these?"

Millie shook her head. She still remembered her mother's words when she had first learned about Arthur's new job at the armory. *What does a nice Jewish scientist need with guns?* She wondered what her mother might think if she knew Millie worked there too.

"Let me show you something." The colonel laid the rifle down on top of the paper piles and pulled the operating rod back to inspect the chamber. "I don't keep it loaded," he explained, "but I always like to check." Then he flipped the gun over, pulled the back of the trigger guard with two fingers, and swung it upward. The next thing Millie knew, he had pulled the entire trigger housing from the bottom of the rifle.

"Does this look familiar?" he asked, handing it to her.

"Of course—I've made thousands of them." She was amazed by the ease with which it separated from the rifle. "I didn't realize it could all come apart like that."

"Well, I've had lots of practice. Once the trigger group is out, the stock comes free from the rest of the rifle like this." He tapped the rear of the wooden stock on his desk to loosen it and pulled the stock free from the receiver in one swift motion. Next, he showed her how to remove the follower rod and spring. He pushed the follower arm pin out of the left side of the receiver and lifted the magazine slide and follower out of the magazine well. He flipped the receiver over and pulled out the operating rod. The last part he removed was the bolt. "That's about as far as we usually go for cleaning," he said. "And then we put it all back together again."

As Millie watched the reassembly, she couldn't help but stare. "It's like the different parts of a jigsaw puzzle," she mused. "When you pull it apart that way, it's easy to forget that it's a weapon at all. It seems so . . . simple."

Her choice of words made Colonel Walsh laugh. "It may seem simple, but I assure you, it's not. The best scientific and engineering minds in our country worked for years to create it."

"I wish the other girls could see this. They have no idea . . ."

"I'm going to see what I can do about setting up some demonstrations," Colonel Walsh said. He held the rifle out to Millie. "Would you like to hold it?"

She reached for it without thinking. It was heavier than she had expected, but even more surprising was the way it felt in her hands: comfortable, easy, like the most ordinary thing in the world. Millie held it up to eye level and aimed at the bookcase, the way she'd seen soldiers and cowboys do in movies.

Colonel Walsh grinned. "You look like a natural. You know, if you ever feel like getting in some practice, we happen to have a terrific rifle club here—more than fifty members now. They meet Wednesday evenings at the Wonder Rifle Range in Indian Orchard. There are plenty of female members."

"I'll think about it," she murmured. She passed the rifle back to Colonel Walsh, but once she let go, her hands felt strangely empty.

**A week later, one of the corporals who drove the Walsh children** to school delivered a letter with the rest of the Walshes' mail. When he gave her the wrinkled envelope, Millie's knees began to shake. There was no mistaking the handwriting.

The letter was short—just a few spiteful lines.

*Dear Millie,*
*You probably had a good laugh after I left. But like I*
*said before, this isn't over. You and Michael can't stay*
*away from me forever. The next time I see you, I won't*
*be so nice.*

*Lenny*

Millie felt the panic she had worked so hard to contain come rushing back to her in an instant. Her mind raced with possibilities about how to protect herself and Michael. They could leave Springfield that evening, they could move somewhere new—there were other defense plants, other factories and places where women like her might find work. Lenny wouldn't be able to find her if she told no one where she was going. She could cut off all ties and start over again.

But if Lenny returned and came looking for her, Ruth would have to be the one to tell him that she had gone. Ruth would never give him the ring; she would never succumb to his demands. And Lenny would not believe that Ruth didn't know where Millie was. Who knew what he might do if Ruth made him angry enough? The idea that he might harm her sister set Millie's temples throbbing.

That settled it, then—she would have to stay. She would need to gather her strength for an uncertain future and for the possibility that Lenny could return. To prepare herself properly—well, Millie had an idea, one she was absolutely certain her mother wouldn't have approved of.

Millie Fein, a nice Jewish girl from Brooklyn, was about to join the Springfield Armory Rifle Club.

# Ruth

When Millie first came to Springfield, it seemed to Ruth that the
five years they'd been apart hadn't altered her at all. Millie's hair,
her clothes—even the ring on her finger—were exactly the same
as they always had been. Michael was an addition, of course, but he
looked so much like their father that even he seemed familiar.

But now, when Ruth saw her sister from afar, Millie seemed
changed. It wasn't merely her shorter haircut or the newish dress
she wore but the confidence with which she carried herself. Her
composure caught Ruth entirely by surprise.

Of course, Alice and Louise had asked a lot of questions about
why their aunt and their cousin had moved out of their house. Ruth
tried to answer as honestly as possible without getting into too
much detail. *No, Millie and Michael aren't going back to Brooklyn. Yes,
they moved to the Walshes' house. Millie and I argued, but of course we
don't hate each other. Sometimes sisters fight—don't the two of you know
something about that?*

Despite the anger between them, Ruth and Millie agreed that
the children should see each other often. Millie dropped Michael
off at Ruth's a few afternoons a week, and Alice and Louise went to

the Walshes' as well. The twins were used to the house—all of the armory children played at the Walshes'.

Ruth and Millie were polite but distant, and Ruth assumed that her daughters were old enough to understand the subtleties of their relationship. She was wrong, of course—her daughters didn't understand. Instead, they asked when their aunt and cousin were coming for Passover. In their innocent minds, it was all so simple: Millie and Michael were family, and families always spent the holidays together.

**Before Ruth left Brooklyn, she had set aside the most meaningful** of her parents' possessions—all the things she didn't trust Millie not to lose or break: the silver kiddush cup their parents had drunk from at their wedding, the leather-bound album their mother had filled with family photos, the seder plate they had used for every Passover meal she could remember. Ruth wrapped these items— plus a dozen or so more—in old sheets of newspaper and packed them in boxes. Not once did she consider asking Millie's permission before taking them to Springfield.

Now, as Ruth set the table for the holiday meal, the sight of the seder plate stretched her heart with a shame that was long overdue. When their parents had died, she had taken what she wanted. She had known that Millie was too distracted to notice.

The seder plate's hand-painted letters brought back their father's voice, and Ruth could almost hear him recite the familiar words. *This is the bread of affliction which our ancestors ate in the land of Egypt; let all those who are hungry, enter and eat thereof.* Five years had passed since she had heard him lead the seder, five years of holidays without her mother, her father, or her sister by her side. She had thought that this year Millie would be at her table, but after their argument, she hadn't been brave enough to suggest it.

For the rest of the day, Ruth worked on dinner preparations, chopping apples for the haroseth and grating potatoes for her kugel.

She set the stove at simmer to keep the soup warm and filled a small bowl with salt water for dipping the parsley. When everything was ready, she called the girls into the dining room.

No matter how savory the smells that wafted in from the kitchen or how sparkling the silver was under the candlelight, it was difficult to celebrate without Arthur at the table. She and the girls made miniature sandwiches of matzo and horseradish, they recited the ten plagues and lined their dinner plates with dots of sweet purple wine. But the Passover story was somber and slow.

"Mama?" Louise asked. "Who should read next?" They had come to the passage about the four kinds of children and the best way to teach each one about the holiday. *Blessed be He whose Law speaketh distinctly of the four different characters of children: the wise, the wicked, the simple, and the one who hath no capacity to inquire.*

When she was young, Ruth remembered, she had always insisted on reading the passage about the "wise" child. She was the older sister, after all—it made perfect sense. The ritual had continued into her adulthood, and for every Passover she could remember, she had read the same words. Millie had always been irritated by what she perceived to be the injustice of the tradition. "Where does that leave me?" she asked year after year. "Am I wicked or simple or unable to ask?"

Ruth never answered, but depending on the year, she had different opinions. There were times she believed that Millie truly *was* wicked—that she intentionally flirted with Ruth's dates just to be spiteful. Other times, she would have said that her sister was simple—too caught up in her movie magazines to read a newspaper or a book. But after their parents died, Ruth changed her mind again—Millie was too incapacitated by grief to question anything at all. And Ruth had used that to her own advantage.

"Mama?" Louise tried to get her attention again. "Should I read the wise child, or should Alice do it?"

The sweet wine turned sour in the pit of Ruth's stomach. She couldn't bear the thought of her girls arguing the way she and Millie had. She never wanted to treat one of them differently from the other. From the day the twins were born, Ruth had dressed them identically. She had fed them the same foods in the exact same amounts, and she had put them to bed at the same time every evening—even if one of them was still wide awake. She had been so intent on treating her daughters equally that she refused to spend time alone with either of them. She was afraid of separate smiles, separate laughter, separate love.

When they were babies, it was always easy enough to manage, easy to pretend that her girls were the same. But now, at almost seven years old, they had distinct personalities, and there could be no more disguising the differences between them. Alice was the artist, always drawing and sketching, never without a pencil or a crayon in her hands. Louise was outspoken, quick-witted, and funny. She liked to take things apart, but not to put them back together. Ruth's love for them was equal, but over time, it became clear that her two daughters required different treatment to thrive. Alice needed encouragement and time alone to create. Louise needed guidance and steady supervision. Ruth tried her best with both of them, but she was overwhelmed by guilt. She could not bear to make the same mistakes her own mother had made. She knew all too well the power a mother might wield, the harm she might inflict in the name of protection or love.

"Let's skip the passage about the children," she said. "I'm going to go open the front door for Elijah." Holiday tradition mandated that a cup of wine be poured for the prophet Elijah and that the front door be opened to allow his spirit to enter.

When Ruth approached the front of the house, she heard a creak on the porch. She dismissed it as the wind; it was too late for unplanned visitors. Ruth twisted the brass handle to pull the door inward, but she felt another hand turning and pushing from the outside. She stepped backward, pulse racing, drenched in sudden fear. Could Lenny have dared to return to Springfield? By the time she thought to shout, the stranger had pushed his way inside. It was too late to bar his entry, too late to keep him out.

He looked different from the last time she had seen him—thinner and tired. His face was dark with stubble. Only his glasses were the same.

"Arthur!" Ruth gasped. "My God, Arthur! You're home!"

# Lillian

Lillian had been writing and calling the men in charge of *The Victory Parade of Spotlight Bands* radio show for months, but they would give her no assurances. Then, without any warning, at the beginning of April, she received a telephone call with the extraordinary news: in exactly one month, Benny Goodman—the King of Swing—would be performing at the armory.

Lillian was accustomed to planning large events. As a military wife, she was used to extended timelines, to organizational delays, to the never-ending process of obtaining government approvals. But live radio, she learned, was a last-minute business. Though she'd been frustrated and skeptical waiting for news, when it finally came, she felt a burst of adrenaline. The limited amount of time in which to get everything done only sharpened her focus.

Lillian needed access to the telephone and a place to organize her papers, so she began doing her work at Patrick's desk. He balked slightly at first when she moved some of his files, but soon enough, he was referring to the room as "our" office. Inside, Lillian was comforted by the solidity of the shelves and the spicy scent of Patrick's pipe that lingered in the air. Most of all, she loved the silence that billowed peacefully around her when the door was shut tight and she was alone. She felt safe in that space, content and peaceful.

It was a far cry from what she had felt in her father's old office, the one time she had entered without his permission.

**When Lillian was seven years old, she borrowed a copy of** *The Wonderful Wizard of Oz* from her library. World War I had just begun, and even the librarians were on edge, recommending fantasy and romance to anyone who walked through the doors.

Those days, Lillian's prime occupation was finding the perfect spot in which to read her books. But the day after she checked out *The Wonderful Wizard of Oz*, noise and distraction seemed to follow her everywhere. Unfortunately, her bedroom was next to the kitchen, where her mother was humming loudly through dinner preparations. Lillian sat on the sofa in the living room for a while, but the lighting was dim, and no matter how hard she tried, she couldn't block out the ticking of the grandfather clock. She moved to the tiny backyard next, but by the late afternoon, the warblers showed up, and she was forced to go inside to escape their constant chirping.

As the afternoon wore on, Lillian couldn't stop thinking about how empty and quiet her father's office was. It was only an extra bedroom that her father had claimed, but it was far from the kitchen, far from the birds, and if she shut the door all the way, she wouldn't hear the grandfather clock. She had over an hour until he got home from work.

Lillian creaked open the door and tiptoed inside. The room was off limits, but what would be the harm? She made herself comfortable in the cracked leather chair and basked in the silent space behind the desk. Before long, she was immersed in the pages of her story, so engrossed that she didn't hear her father come in.

"What are you doing in here?"

She slammed the book shut, jumped down off the chair, and

stood in front of him with her knees shaking. "I didn't touch anything. It's so quiet in here, and I wanted to read."

"You wanted to read?"

Her voice dropped to a whisper. "I thought you wouldn't mind."

He took a step closer and grabbed the book from her hands. She was about to protest but she held her tongue.

"What have we here?" he asked, tapping the cover. "*The Wonderful Wizard of Oz*. Aren't you a little young for this book?"

For a moment, she believed he was excited about her selection. For a moment, she mistook his sarcasm for pride.

"Some of the words are hard for me, but when I don't know what they mean, I look them up in the dictionary."

"In that dictionary over there?" He nodded in the direction of the bookshelf under the window.

"Yes," she repeated. "I look up the words."

She was completely unprepared for the pain that shot through her arm when he grabbed her by the wrist and dragged her toward the bookcase.

"You told me you didn't touch *anything* in this room," he growled. "But if you used this dictionary, you were lying." When Lillian looked up at him, his eyes had clouded over. He looked past her, through her, as if she weren't there.

"I won't lie again, Daddy. I promise I won't!"

"You're damn right you won't."

His lips, pale and slimy, formed a callous grin. In one swift motion, he let go of her wrist and pushed her backward into the corner of the desk. He was just about to strike her with the borrowed book when Lillian's mother ran into the room.

"Malcolm! Put that down!"

It was as if her mother had turned off a switch, her voice breaking the spell Lillian's father was under. He blinked a few times and threw the book on the desk.

"I'd better not see you in here again," he said. When he walked out the door, Lillian's mother asked where he was going.

"I'm not staying here. I'll eat at the officers' club."

Lillian never finished reading *The Wonderful Wizard of Oz*. She returned it to the library the very next morning.

# Millie

Millie would never forget the first day she entered Building 103—the taste of metal in the air, the ceaseless ringing in her ears, the sense of purpose that ran through her fellow workers like an electric current. But she was never more grateful for her job at the armory than in the days after she received Lenny's letter. Her fingers flew through the motions until her knuckles grew numb. She lined up the holes; she steadied the springs. Her hands took over so that she didn't have to think. She hummed softly as she worked, and her worries fell away.

But when each shift was over, her fears returned. When she shut her eyes at night, she was haunted by Lenny's image—by the scar on his face and the emptiness behind his eyes. Some nights, sleep came, but it was always interrupted. She would wake in the shadows to increasing darkness: the shock of Lenny's smirk when he waited for her on Federal Street, the threat behind the words of the letter he had written.

But even those thoughts were not the most troubling. As bad as they were, there was worse to contend with, visions that roused her with heart-stopping clarity: Lenny trying to take Michael away from her for good, her little boy's screams as a stranger assailed him.

**The only person Millie recognized at her first meeting of the rifle** club was Charlie, one of the guards from the armory's main gate. He was the same guard Ruth had summoned the day she had confronted Lenny, the one who'd offered Millie his handkerchief and asked if he could help. Ever since that day, whenever Millie passed through the gate, Charlie made a point of greeting her and Michael. He would wave or tip his hat and bend down to shake Michael's hand. "Good morning, sir," he would say with mock formality. Michael would repeat the greeting with a solemn look on his face, while Charlie would wink and share a smile with Millie.

Away from work and out of uniform, Charlie appeared more youthful; he couldn't have been more than a few years older than she was. She had wondered what his hair was like under his hat—it was darker than she'd supposed and curlier on top. His face seemed rounder, hearty and whole, and when he spotted Millie waving, his mouth widened into a grin.

"Hello," she said brightly, happy to see him.

"Fancy meeting you here," Charlie answered. Carefully, he handed her an armory-made rifle. It was familiar in her hands, a not uncomfortable feeling.

"This is only the second time I've held one of these," she confessed.

"Really? What made you want to join the club?" He was genuinely curious, so sincere in his expression that she almost considered telling him the truth.

*Because my husband is still alive and sending me threatening letters. Because if I don't give him what he wants, I'm afraid he might come after me or try to take away my son. Because if he shows up again, I want to be prepared.*

"I wanted to learn something new," she said. Millie turned

the rifle over, the way Colonel Walsh had shown her, to get a better look at the trigger housing. "I wonder," she said, thinking out loud. "What if the trigger on this rifle is one I made myself, one I put together at my table in the shops? There's no way to tell, but what if it is?"

The expression on Charlie's face was a mixture of admiration and curiosity. He didn't dismiss her question; he didn't find it strange.

"Gee." He whistled softly. "Wouldn't that be something?"

# Ruth

Arthur knew nothing of what had occurred between the sisters—he had no idea that Lenny had risen from the dead or that Millie had moved across the square to live with the Walsh family. Though Ruth had written to him often, the series of revelations and events that had occurred during his absence had been far too complicated for her to put down on paper.

Once the girls were in bed, Arthur took a hot shower and shaved off his beard. Underneath all the stubble, his round face had turned angular, and beneath his bathrobe, his soft middle was gone. He held himself taller. *Like a soldier,* Ruth thought.

Ruth had placed some clean pajamas on the bed for him to wear, but the bottoms were so large that they fell off his waist. Ruth couldn't help her laughter, but Arthur wasn't smiling. Naked before her, he took a step closer and pulled her tightly toward him with unfamiliar strength. The shock of his desire, of his mouth over hers, made her forget everything else, including her sister.

Afterward, she told him all of what had happened, confessing her sins with his arms wrapped around her. "I lied to them both. I pushed for that wedding. I didn't want Millie to come to Spring-field with us."

"But Millie agreed. Marrying Lenny was what she wanted. You didn't force her; it's not like you held a gun to her head."

"If she had come here with us, she might never have married him. She might have met someone else. She might have been spared all that pain."

"Maybe, but then Michael would never have been born." Arthur tightened his embrace and kissed her again. "You can't change the past, Ruth. You can only move forward."

In the next few days, a newfound closeness developed between them. Arthur held Ruth's attention now in a way he had not before. Certainly, she had thought about him while he was away—pacing the floors and worrying for his safety. But now her thoughts were layered with curiosity and desire. There were sides to her husband that she had never anticipated, a passion that he'd only recently revealed. He reached for her now with a boldness that stunned her. On his second day home, while she was stirring a pot of oatmeal on the stove, he slipped his hands around her waist and pushed aside her hair. The fervor of his kisses on the back of her neck put her in such a stupor that she lost track of her surroundings. The oatmeal burned so badly that she was forced to throw away the pot.

In the weeks after Arthur's reappearance, her thoughts were consumed with him. Was this how her sister had first felt about Lenny? Back in Brooklyn, Ruth hadn't been able to understand the kind of power such attraction could hold over anyone. But now that she'd finally tasted it herself, a new kind of sympathy bubbled up inside her. She wished she could tell Millie that she finally understood what had drawn her to Lenny in the beginning. But she was too embarrassed to admit how little she had known, how limited her view of love had once been.

**"Fred and Grace asked us to have dinner with them tomorrow."**

"Fred and Grace *Peabody*?" Ruth put down her toothbrush, shut off the faucet, and followed Arthur into the bedroom.

"Why do you sound so surprised?"

"You've been working with Fred for more than five years, and you've never socialized with him before."

He kicked off his slippers and slid under the blankets. "You know we have drinks after work sometimes. What can I tell you? He wants to take us out to celebrate my homecoming."

"Can't you get out of it? Tell him we're busy?"

"I don't understand. Why don't you want to go?"

"I'm not sure I can stomach an evening with Grace. She's a terrible gossip, she's rude, and she's a snob. And since Millie came to live with us, Grace has only gotten nastier. I'm not sure what exactly she has against Millie, but she's certainly made no attempt to hide her feelings." Ruth chose not to mention her nagging suspicion that Grace was involved in Captain O'Brian's decision to question her sister.

Arthur leaned over and kissed the back of her shoulder. "Don't worry, I'll make sure that Grace behaves at dinner. Besides, Grace's feelings about Millie don't matter. Your sister doesn't live with us now, remember? The fact is, she isn't your responsibility anymore."

Ruth knew Arthur didn't mean to be cruel, but she found herself blinking back the tears anyway. "Are they taking us to the Colony Club, at least?" she asked. If she had to spend the evening with Grace and Fred Peabody, she hoped it would be at the private eating club in the old Wesson Mansion. Ruth had walked past the French-style château on Maple Street a dozen times, but only members and their guests were allowed inside.

"Fred booked us a table at the Hotel Kimball."

"That will be nice." She had a feeling that she and Arthur weren't Colony Club material; nobody talked about it, but she doubted that the club allowed Jews as guests. Arthur was kissing her neck now, stroking her hair. She put aside her disappointment and turned her attention to her husband.

**The next day, Ruth chose the most fashionable dress in her** closet—a slim-fitting sheath in smooth black satin. When she went through her jewelry box to choose a pair of earrings, her eyes lingered on the ring that Millie had left behind. The center opal beckoned from inside its diamond nest, and Ruth felt her frustration rise to the surface. *Your sister is the one who will need that ring. After she gets married, she'll have dinners and parties.*

*Mama always underestimated me,* Ruth thought. *She thought Springfield was dull and that my life would be dull too.*

She wondered what her mother would have to say now, if she could see where Ruth lived and how Arthur had changed. In his newly tailored uniform, he was barely recognizable—broad-shouldered and strong, like an officer out of a movie. Ruth lifted the ring from the box and placed it on her right hand. With all of the expensive jewelry Ruth had seen Grace wear—the diamond brooches and the double strands of pearls—even *she* didn't have anything that could compare to the ring. It was dazzling, unique—a perfect accessory for a night on the town. Ruth would wear it to dinner, just this once.

At the hotel, Grace was as glamorous as ever—swishing into the dining room fifteen minutes late with a new fur stole draped over her shoulders. She had refused to let the coat check girl stow it away, preferring to let everyone admire it instead. She gave Ruth a once-over, markedly unimpressed, until she noticed the ring perched on her finger. "What an exquisite piece," Grace remarked. Ruth held out her hand, as obedient as a child, and waited while Grace examined the opal. "I don't think I've ever seen a setting like that. Where did you find it?"

"It's been in my family for generations."

"That makes sense." Grace smirked. "It doesn't look like something you would pick out for yourself."

Fred ordered champagne to toast Arthur's return and later had the waiter bring a full bottle of scotch. Grace gave him a look, but Fred wouldn't budge. "We're *celebrating*," he insisted, downing his third glass. "This man survived the *war*. He's entitled to a drink."

"Then why are *you* the one polishing off the bottle? Last time I checked, you weren't the one overseas."

"We all have our battles to fight," Fred said bitterly. "Some are just a little bit closer to home than others." He poured himself another glass, and Arthur tried to change the subject to the new Pentagon building. Grace took out her frustration by guzzling the champagne.

When the meal was over, Fred insisted on walking back to Armory Square. He wanted some fresh air, he said, and time to stretch his legs. But before long, he wandered far ahead of their group, leaving his wife behind for Ruth and Arthur to contend with. Grace was woozy from the champagne, so Ruth stood on one side of her and Arthur on the other, their arms looped through hers to help pull her along. They were waiting to cross at the corner of Chestnut and State Street when Ruth spotted Arietta and her sister walking toward them.

When she caught Millie's eye, Ruth felt her face turn pink. She knew how it must look—her arm linked with Grace's, as if they were friends, chummy ones, even. Ruth's first thought was to let go of Grace's arm, but she knew that if she did, Grace might topple to the ground.

"Hello," Millie said, approaching the three of them.

Arthur answered first, without any awkwardness. He was immune, Ruth realized, to the guilt that plagued her. Grace was mercifully silent; her eyes were half closed, and she swayed slightly on her feet. She was much too far gone to recognize anyone.

"Is she ill?" Millie asked. "What's wrong with her?"

"She's had too much champagne."

Arietta crossed her thick arms over her chest. "What a shame," the cook said. "It must have been quite a celebration." Hostility hovered around her like steam over a soup pot. *This isn't what it looks like,* Ruth wanted to explain. *Grace isn't my friend. We don't even like each other.* But anything she said now would sound contrived.

"We just saw *Casablanca* at the Bijou," Millie said. "You would have liked it, Ruth. It was beautiful, but so sad." The sorrow in her sister's voice made Ruth want to linger, but Grace began to mumble, and Arthur said they should get back.

Ruth was about to ask if Millie wanted to walk home with them, but Arietta spoke first. "Let's grab a cup of coffee, Mil, and maybe a slice of pie?"

Millie nodded wordlessly and gave Ruth a small wave goodbye.

Ruth lifted her left hand to return the gesture, forgetting, for a moment, the ring on her finger. A streetlamp overhead illuminated the opal, and Ruth watched as the jewel drew Millie's eye.

Ruth was mortified. "I've never worn it before tonight, Millie, I swear. It was just this once," she mumbled. "I promise."

It would have been easier if Millie had caused some sort of scene—if she had shouted or cried or stomped away in a huff. But she was no longer the impulsive girl that Ruth remembered, and her silence was more painful than any outburst could have been.

"Don't worry about it," Millie said softly. "It looks good on you."

# Arietta

When the afternoon lunch crowd cleared, Arietta told Fitz she had an errand to run. She took off her apron, pulled out her compact, and carefully painted on a fresh coat of lipstick. The fact that her dress smelled of the Tuesday lunch special couldn't be helped.

In Armory Square, the spring grass was luxuriant. Shrubs of golden forsythia lined the narrow walkways, and the leaves on the trees were a buoyant shade of green. Two men she did not recognize were hitting balls on the tennis court, and a group of women had gathered for archery practice. They stood, strong and straight in the center of the square, squinting at their targets in the afternoon sun. Arietta held her breath as they pulled back their bows. She had no time to linger, however, so she pulled herself away and continued along the path to where Ruth's house was waiting.

Millie's sister seemed puzzled to find Arietta standing in her doorway. "Didn't Millie tell you? She and Michael don't live here anymore."

"I know," Arietta answered. "I came to speak with you."

With its bright yellow wallpaper and cozy wood-trimmed

fireplace, Ruth's living room should have felt more cheerful. But gloom gathered in every corner, invisible to the eye, coating the sofas and tables like dust. Ruth was the same. On the surface, she had multiple reasons to be happy: her husband had returned to her, ahead of schedule and unharmed; she had two beautiful daughters and a large, lovely home; she was intelligent and respected—her colleagues in the payroll department were still bemoaning her resignation. Yet despite all her blessings, her misery was palpable. Arietta wondered whether it was due to Millie's absence.

She decided it was best to be straightforward. "I'm worried about Millie," the cook began. "Lenny sent her a letter. It came last week."

Ruth frowned when Arietta said Lenny's name out loud. "So, she told you about him, then? I wasn't sure."

"Millie told me everything after I was questioned about the fire."

"I didn't realize Captain O'Brian brought you in too."

"Well, I didn't get dragged out of my house in the middle of the night the way Millie did. He didn't come to see me until the next afternoon."

"What did the letter say?"

"It was a threat, mostly. Lenny said he'd be back and that he wouldn't be as nice the second time around. From what Millie told me, he's in a bad spot."

"Lenny was always a bit of a lost soul; he went from job to job, he didn't have any real ambition. Still, he was always devoted to my sister. I never thought he would mistreat her. I never thought he could be dangerous."

"Well, it sounds like he's changed."

Ruth's tone turned defensive. "Do you think I don't know that? I *saw* him, Arietta. I spoke to him myself."

"I understand. I don't pretend to know anything more about

Lenny than you do. But his letter isn't the only reason I came. I also wanted to talk about your friend Grace Peabody."

"Grace *isn't* my friend. I know it may have looked like that when you saw us the other night, but our husbands work together, and that is the extent of our relationship. Fred invited us to dinner to celebrate Arthur's homecoming. Besides, I really don't see how this is any of your business—"

"It's my business—and yours too—because of the way Fred Peabody attacked your sister."

"What are you talking about?"

"The night of the Walshes' Christmas party, he followed her outside and grabbed her before she made it home. If I hadn't come along, I don't know what would have happened. He wasn't happy to have been caught, that's for sure. He said that if either of us reported it, we would both be sorry. Millie didn't tell you; she didn't want you to get involved."

Ruth's face drained of color. "Are you sure it was Fred?"

"I'm positive. The same way I'm positive it was Grace who called Captain O'Brian to accuse Millie and me of sabotage."

"How could you be so certain that was Grace?"

"Because I had a run-in with her inside the ladies' room at the Victory dance. She said some awful things, and I told her what a jerk her husband was to Millie. She told me I would regret saying what I did and that Millie would too. A few hours later, O'Brian took Millie into custody. Do you really think that was only a coincidence?"

"I . . . I don't know what to think." Ruth placed her hand on her stomach as if she might be sick. "Millie attracted a lot of attention from men when we were young. She got herself into some . . . uncomfortable situations."

"Look, I don't know what 'situations' you're talking about, but Millie didn't ask for Fred Peabody to follow her home."

"You don't understand. My past with Millie is complicated."

"I don't give a damn how complicated it is!" Arietta had lost patience with Ruth's flimsy excuses. "I came here today because I want to protect Millie and I thought that as her sister you would want to do the same. I never dreamed for a second that I would need to convince you." She reached for the doorknob to let herself out. "You need to figure out whose side you're on."

# Lillian

## Springfield, Massachusetts (May 1943)

They decided to have the concert on Armory Hill—the soft-sloping area behind the old arsenal. Everyone in Springfield was clamoring to attend, but tickets were limited to armory employees and one guest each. Even with the restrictions, more than five thousand people were expected.

Security was a major concern, of course, requiring all kinds of coordination among Captain O'Brian, the armory guards, and the Springfield police. It was decided that concertgoers would enter through the gate on the corner of Byers and State streets, in the hopes that the smaller entry point would make for a more orderly entrance. With spies and saboteurs on everyone's minds, tickets would be carefully checked, and extra guards would be posted.

Lillian supervised the construction of an elevated stage where the featured entertainers, orchestra, and production crew would assemble. But as the concert date grew closer, she began to worry about the weather. The early-May evenings had been unusually cold.

On the morning of the concert, the newspaper predicted a gusty evening, with temperatures dipping into the forties. Lillian

called the carpenters and asked them to erect canvas flaps on the
sides of the stage to protect the performers from the wind. The
rest of the afternoon was a blur of activity, from greeting the crew
to wiring and sound checks. The head producer arrived late and in
a terrible mood. He had just gotten word that his opening act had
canceled.

Ignoring Lillian, he turned to his assistants, a trio of young
men clutching clipboards and pencils. "Get me *somebody*! Anybody!
I don't give a damn who it is, do you hear me? We need an opener
to warm up this crowd! We go live at nine thirty—we only have
five hours!"

The last-minute snafu had thrown the men into a panic, but Lillian knew exactly who to call. She cleared her throat to get their attention. "I have someone," she announced. "A singer—she's perfect."

The men looked up from their clipboards in unison and stared.
"Who is she?" the producer asked. "What's her name?"

"Arietta Benevetto. She's a cook at the armory, but she used
to sing professionally. You might not know her, but everyone in
Springfield does. If you put her on the stage, the audience will go
wild."

"You want a *cook* to open for the King of Swing?" He was
mocking her, she knew, but she didn't care. This man's idea of ca-
tastrophe was a vacancy in his show. She knew too many men—her
husband included—who were all too aware of what real catastro-
phe was. She wasn't about to be intimidated by someone who flus-
tered so easily.

"She's not just a cook, and it seems to me that she's your only
option. So, what will it be? Yes or no?"

**A few hours later, Lillian walked home to get dressed. She fixed**
her hair and makeup and set out clothes for the children. "Daddy
will walk you over before the concert starts. I have seats saved on
the side of the stage for all of you. It's going to be cold, so wear your
winter coats."

"Our winter coats?" Margaret whined. "But it's already spring."

"It may say spring on the calendar, but it's going to be freezing. Now, be a good girl and do as I say."

Lillian was on her way out the door when Millie returned.

"I just came from Arietta's," Millie said, beaming. "I don't know how you convinced them to let her perform, but she's absolutely beside herself! I promised I'd go back and help her finish getting ready. Michael is going to stay over at Ruth's tonight. I was surprised, but she offered to have him stay."

"You know, I've been so busy, I haven't even asked—how have things been between you and your sister?"

Millie raised her shoulders in a good-natured shrug. "Lillian, you don't have time for this now—you have a show to put on! We can talk about me later."

"Do you promise? You're a part of our family now, you know. If you ever need to talk, I hope you'll come to me."

"I appreciate that. But you need to go!"

"Just do me a favor and be careful tonight. With five thousand people wandering around, there are bound to be a few rotten apples in the bunch."

"Don't worry about me. Fitz and I are going to watch Arietta together."

"All right, then." Lillian smiled. "As long as you're not alone."

# Millie

The evening was unusually chilly for spring, but most people were so excited that they barely even noticed. What did a little bit of wind matter anyway? They would have braved a blizzard to see the King of Swing.

People began pouring through the gate more than two hours before the show—thousands of workers and guests waving their tickets at the guards. The radio program would be broadcast live at nine thirty, but the opening act would entertain the crowd first. Millie marveled at Arietta's ability to stay calm. After all, she was about to sing for the largest crowd of her career.

Millie and Fitz waited with her behind the stage until it was time for her to make her entrance. Since the concert was outside, there were no dressing rooms. Arietta wore a heavy coat and scarf until the very last minute to ensure that her body and her voice stayed warm. Her satin shoes sank into the dirt, and the bottom of her gown grazed the newly mowed grass. Millie worried that it might be an inauspicious beginning.

But when the announcer called her name, Arietta was ready. Beneath the frumpy coat and scarf was a shimmering red sheath, cut just low enough in the front to showcase a double strand of pearls. Arietta threw her shoulders back and flashed a confident grin in Millie's direction. "Wish me luck." She winked and blew Fitz a quick kiss before she climbed the stairs.

"Isn't she something?" Fitz sighed.

"She certainly is," Millie agreed.

Millie was grateful to have Fitz by her side. Without the benefit of his height and bulky frame, she doubted whether she would have been able to make her way through the mob. They finally found an area where the crowd was slightly thinner and settled in a spot with a partial view of the stage.

Fitz was anxious to get closer but reluctant to give up the place they had already secured. "I think I see a spot up ahead with a better view!" he shouted. "I'll come back in a minute and let you know."

Only when he was a few feet ahead of her did she fully realize the folly of his plan. As tall as Fitz was, he disappeared from Millie's sight. She scanned the area in front of her, trying to pick out the top of his head or the slope of his shoulders, but there was no way to spot him in the crush of the crowd. Before the concert began, Millie thought she might run into Charlie. But if she couldn't find Fitz, there was no hope of finding anyone. She began to feel uneasy.

Her apprehension lessened as soon as Arietta took the stage. When the announcer explained that she was not merely a singer but a cook at the armory cafeteria as well, the roar of the crowd was absolutely deafening. Arietta smiled and waved until the hollering died down. Then she took two steps forward and cued the band leader. As the music swelled, she began her first song.

Millie had never been prouder of her friend. She knew Arietta could woo any audience, but to watch her command a crowd of thousands was something she couldn't have imagined. She began with "Moonlight Cocktail"—one of Millie's favorites—and moved on to other songs Millie recognized from her repertoire. Five thousand sets of eyes were glued to the stage until it was time for the cook to sing her final number.

"It has been my absolute honor to perform for you tonight," Arietta said into the microphone. "Before I go, I'm going to sing one last song. This tune was made famous by Mr. Benny Goodman himself. Now, I know you're used to hearing Peggy Lee do these vocals, but I hope you won't mind if I give them a try." A familiar melody wafted through the air, and the audience grew silent.

> You had plenty money, nineteen twenty-two
> You let other women make a fool of you
> Why don't you do right, like some other men do

Millie had never cared for the song. She found the tune ominous and the lyrics unnerving. Until that moment in the evening, Arietta's performance had captivated her completely. But now, Millie's mind began to wander. A sudden gust of wind cut straight through her coat, and she felt an overwhelming desire to get away from the crowd.

Millie pushed past the people around her, her panic rising with every elbow and shoulder that blocked her path. Layer by layer, she made her way through the mob. When she finally reached the edge, she walked in a circle around the back of the stage until she found a tree to lean against. She could still hear the music, but at least she could breathe. She leaned her body forward, shut her eyes, and put her head between her knees to stem the wave of nausea that ran through her.

"Fancy meeting you here," said a voice in the dark. It was what Charlie had said when she'd first seen him at the rifle club, and in the minute before she lifted her head, she thought it might be her friend. But when she opened her eyes, she saw she'd been mistaken.

The first thought she had was that the song had somehow conjured him. The second was that he was almost unrecognizable. The scar on his cheek was even more pronounced, and his face was a pulp of greenish-blue bruises. His nose had been broken in who knew how many places. What Millie had once thought to be the most handsome face in Brooklyn was now a hollow remnant, the face of a ghost.

She stepped away from the tree, but her legs were shaky. "How did you get through the gate without a ticket?"

"What's the matter?" He smirked. "You're not happy to see me? I met a gal last night—sweet little broad. I showed her a good time, and she gave me a ticket. It was easy enough to ditch her once we got inside."

Millie knew just the kind of woman who would fall for him— young, overeager, too easily impressed with a tough guy from New York. The poor girl was probably looking for him right now, calling his name into the wind, wondering where he was.

"But there are so many people here. How did you find me?"

Lenny began to chuckle—he was as surprised as she was. "Damn if I know. When I saw the size of the crowd, I figured it was hopeless. But when that last song started, I looked up and— *bam!*—there you were, walking away from the audience all alone." He took a step closer, but he was no longer laughing. "I guess I was meant to find you, Millie. Isn't that something? Now, what do you say you play nice and give me that ring."

She held up her hand. "I already told you, I don't wear it anymore."

The pain when he grabbed her wrist ran all the way up her arm. He pinned her against the tree and pressed his face to hers, so close that she could smell the cheap whiskey he'd been drinking. *Just like old times.*

"I'll bring you the ring tomorrow," she promised.

"Ha!" The spray of his spittle on her neck made her shiver. "Do you really think I'm stupid enough to fall for that again? This time, I'm not letting you out of my sight until you give it to me."

She tried to pull away, but his grip was too strong. "What happened to your nose?" she asked, pretending to be concerned. "Did those fellows come after you again?"

"Don't worry about me. I can take care of myself." He fingered his scar and then pulled out a small blade. "I've got protection now," he hissed. "Hey, how'd you like a nice little scar to match mine? I bet I could give you one almost as pretty." He drew a flask from his pocket and took a few gulps.

*Think, Millie, think.* She contemplated bringing him to Ruth's house for the ring, but the idea of leading him to Michael was far too risky. Who knew what kind of argument Ruth might start if she saw him, or what he might do with that knife if he got angry. She couldn't put her family in danger like that. No, she would have to come up with something else.

If only someone would walk by, someone who might help her—but everyone at the armory was attending the concert. Screaming would do no good; no one would hear her over the roar of the crowd. In fact, now that Arietta had finished her set, the live radio show was about to begin. From the other side of the stage, Millie could hear it.

*The Coca-Cola Company presents* The Victory Parade of Spotlight Bands. *And here's tonight's Spotlight Roll Call. Benny Goodman? Here! The Benny Goodman Spotlight Band? Here! The officers and men and civilian war workers of the Springfield Armory? Here! All present and accounted for in Springfield, Massachusetts, so start the victory parade marching right about here!*

The cheers were so loud and the foot-stomping so heavy that it felt as though the ground were shaking beneath them. Even Lenny loosened his hold on her for a moment to listen to the broadcast. But soon his interest faded.

"Lead the way, Mil. Let's go to Ruth's house and pick up my ring."

"I don't live with her anymore. I live somewhere else."

"With a fella, you mean?"

"Of course not! I live with a married couple. They've been very kind to me, and their children are nice to our . . . well, they're sweet." She stopped herself from speaking about Michael out loud. She didn't want to remind Lenny that there was something other than the ring that he might want to claim as his own before he left Springfield.

"Terrific," he said. "Where do they live?"

"There." With her free hand, Millie pointed to the commanding officer's house. It stood directly across from them, five hundred feet away. Even in the dark, there could be no mistaking the size or the grandeur of the building.

"I don't have time for jokes," Lenny said. "Which way do we go?"

"I'm serious," she insisted. "That's where I'm staying. My friend Lillian's husband is the commanding officer of the armory."

"You got a key?"

"Yes."

"And you're sure no one is home?"

"They're all at the concert."

"Then let's go."

Millie stepped toward the house as slowly as possible, trying to formulate a plan along the way. But the walk was too short, and her mind was a blank. Panic and fear formed a lump in her throat, and she wondered, when the time came, whether she would be able to scream.

"Let's go, let's go," he said, pushing and dragging her until they reached the front door. He let go of her arm so she could find the key in her purse, and when she opened the door, he whistled long and low. "Man, if I had my truck and a couple of guys, we could clean this place out in ten minutes flat. There's gotta be plenty of good stuff in the bedrooms." He walked through the foyer and glanced up the stairs, but before he reached the steps, Millie screamed.

"*No!*"

"What did you say?"

She had never shouted at him before. But the thought of Lenny in Lillian's bedroom made Millie physically ill. She had not imagined that her plan could have such a consequence—how foolish she had been to not think it through. He was a wrecking ball of a man, equipped only for destruction.

"You don't need to go upstairs because the ring is down here. In Colonel Walsh's office." She pointed to the door on the right side of the foyer. "In there."

"Fine," Lenny sulked, "but after I get it, I'm going upstairs."

Millie suspected that the office impressed Lenny more than he let on. The bookshelves and papers, the plaques on the wall—all were the signs of a successful, well-respected man. Lenny would never have an office like this one. He would never earn a medal or receive a letter of praise. As he wandered around the room taking everything in, Millie wondered whether he had any regrets.

"So, where is it?" he grimaced. "This place gives me the creeps."

"It's locked in the cabinet. Let me get the key." She cleared the massive desktop, moving binders and books to reach the blotter underneath. When Millie lifted it up, the brass key was still there, solid and shiny, silently waiting. She stole a glance at Lenny out of the corner of her eye, but he was busy examining a framed photograph on the wall. He was still occupied when she felt the lock of the wood-paneled door click open.

Lenny would have no way of knowing that the rifle wasn't loaded. Colonel Walsh had said she was a natural, and the months she'd spent at the shooting range had given her confidence. She would release the safety, keep one finger on the trigger, and hope Lenny would run when she aimed at his head. She took a slow breath as she pulled open the door, but when she looked inside the cabinet, the weapon was gone.

"Let's have it already," Lenny said impatiently. "I don't have all day."

As her scheme unraveled, desperation sank in. She had no alternate plan; she was out of ideas. All she could do was tell him the truth.

"The ring isn't here."

He crossed the room in three steps, his stride fueled by rage. "Whaddya mean it isn't here? What the hell are you talking about?"

"It isn't here," she repeated. "I don't know where it is."

He grabbed her again, this time by the throat.

"You sold it already, didn't you? You sold it and took all the money for yourself!"

She tried to shake her head, to form the words to protest. But he was squeezing too tightly and she couldn't get enough air. "No," she managed to say.

"Where is it then?" he shouted. "*Tell me where it is!*" He pushed her to the ground and stood over her, scowling.

She sputtered and coughed, gasping for breath. The air scratched her lungs as she struggled to speak. "I want to, but I can't," she said. "I'm sorry."

On the night he'd first hit her, Millie had known the slap was coming. Before Lenny had struck her cheek, she had felt the shift of air, she had intuited the disturbance in his movement and his mood. She felt similarly now, prescient and aware. She felt the heat of his anger before she saw his twisted grimace, she sensed him reaching into his pocket before she saw the knife, she knew just where he would stab her before his arm was raised. The violence she would fall victim to felt predetermined and inescapable. There was too much malice in him for it to end any other way.

She forced herself to look at him, to keep her eyes open. His once beautiful face was frenzied and raw. An unfamiliar tranquility descended upon her as she braced herself for the pain she knew was to come.

When the gunshot rang out, she didn't even scream.

# Arietta

The announcer warned her to keep her coat on, but she insisted on taking it off. Folks wanted to see a glamorous performer, not some middle-aged cook dressed for the tundra. Besides, she stopped feeling the cold as soon as her feet touched the stage.

From her vantage point on the platform, the audience seemed much larger than from the ground. Even with all her experience, the sight of so many people gathered together elicited a flutter of nerves in the hollow of her stomach. She placed her hand over her diaphragm and inhaled slowly. The last time she'd felt like this had been a lifetime ago.

Arietta had been six years old when the choir director at her church in New Haven arranged for her to sing at a hastily planned wedding ceremony. No one had explained the circumstances to Arietta, but the request for a young soloist came directly from the father of the bride. It was his belief that the wedding should be blessed by the voice of a child to soften God's heart toward the baby already growing in his daughter's womb.

On the morning of the wedding, before the ceremony began, the Aunties pulled Arietta into the ladies' room to retie her sash and tidy her curls. It was there that she got her first glimpse of the bride—a sullen young woman in a tight, shiny dress. When Arietta said hello, the bride scowled and stomped out. The Aunties tried to smooth things over, but the encounter left Arietta feeling apprehensive. She still hadn't recovered by the time the wedding march began to play.

"I can't sing," she said. "I'm too nervous."

She felt one of the Aunties whisper in her ear. "Listen to me, and I'm going to tell you what to do. Don't worry about all these people. Don't even look at them. Pick someone in the crowd, and sing your song to that one person."

Arietta had scanned the pews, searching for a friendly face. After a few moments, she settled on one—a woman in her thirties, with kind brown eyes and a flowered hat. Arietta never told anyone, but from the time the music began until the last note was played, she pretended that the woman she had chosen was her mother. She sang with such feeling that by the time she was done, most of the wedding guests had their handkerchiefs out. When she sang the final note, the lady in the hat beamed at her.

After that day, Arietta continued the ritual. Whenever she felt nervous, she chose one person to sing to. Until the age of twelve, she chose only women she imagined might resemble her mother. She sang her heart out to all of them, and they rewarded her with their tears. When they clapped, it was as if her own mother were clapping, and she imagined their joy to be her own mother's pride.

As she grew older and love songs made their way into her repertoire, she chose handsome young men and sang only to them. They were never as moved as the women had been, but she liked looking into their eyes and wondering what it might be like to kiss them. As time wore on, she expanded her choices, picking octogenarians or girls her own age—whoever seemed to fit the song she was singing.

Tonight, Arietta scanned the crowd for Fitz. He had pushed his way to the very first row, and his height made him easy to spot from above. With her eyes glued to his, her hesitation evaporated, and she ruled over the stage the same way she ruled over her stove. Her timing was perfect, and every movement was effortless. All too soon it was time to sing her final song of the evening.

She had never performed "Why Don't You Do Right" before, but Benny Goodman had made it famous, and she suspected it would be a big hit with the crowd. The only hitch was that she couldn't sing a song like that to Fitz—"Do Right" was about a good-for-nothing lout, and in order to do it justice, she wanted to focus on a stranger who looked the part.

The music had just started, slinky and slow, when she found the perfect match. It was clear that he'd once been a handsome man, but his good looks were spoiled by the scar on his cheek and a face full of bruises. Unlike the rest of the people around him, he appeared thoroughly uninterested in the concert and the spectacle. As the melody poured out of her, Arietta imagined that the words told the stranger's true story.

The man never realized she was looking at him. But after the second verse, his bored expression changed. At first, he looked surprised and then almost gleeful. She watched his thin lips curve into a satisfied smile and saw him push through the crowd at break-neck speed. He was moving like a man who wanted to catch up to someone.

The man's abrupt departure shouldn't have bothered her, but something about his smile sent a chill up the back of her neck. The wind shifted in the trees, and a sudden gust surprised her, ruffling her hair and causing her fingers to stiffen. From the moment Arietta had started her set that evening, she had felt perfectly warm on the raised platform; but now, all she wanted was her coat and her scarf.

For the first time in her life, she couldn't wait to leave the stage.

# Lillian

Lillian's youngest daughter, Margaret, had been whining ever since she'd arrived at the concert. First, her brothers were bothering her, then her shoes were too tight, and then the music was so loud that it hurt her ears. Lillian stopped paying attention when Margaret claimed she couldn't see; the Walsh family had the best seats in the house. They were on the side of the platform, hidden from the audience but with a clear view of the stage.

The next complaint came just a few minutes later.

"Mommy, I'm freezing!"

"If you had brought your coat like I told you to, you wouldn't be cold."

"It covered up my dress; it didn't look pretty."

Lillian's patience had long since run out. But when Margaret's teeth began to chatter, her maternal instincts took over. "Come sit on my lap and I'll warm you up," she offered. "After Arietta sings, I'll run home and get your coat." Frances offered to fetch her sister's jacket, but Lillian shook her head. "There are too many people in the square tonight, and a lot of them have been drinking. I don't want any of you walking around without an adult. Your father is checking on the guards for a bit, but I'll be back in ten minutes—fifteen at the most. Now stay up here, please, and promise to behave."

"We promise."

Lillian wove through the maze of production crew members, equipment, and tables until she reached the back of the stage. Then she descended the makeshift steps and made her way across the dimly lit square in the direction of her house.

She knew something was wrong when she reached the front door. She was certain Patrick had locked it on his way out; he had told her as much when he met her at the concert. But the door wasn't locked. It was slightly ajar.

As quietly as possible, she pushed the door open. Two voices were coming from the direction of Patrick's office. The first was a man's—unfamiliar and angry—and the second she recognized immediately as Millie's. Lillian left her shoes on the porch and tiptoed inside the foyer, sticking close to the wall where they wouldn't be able to see her. "So, where is it?" the man demanded.

"It's locked in the cabinet. Let me get the key."

The tone of Millie's voice made two things perfectly clear—the man was unwelcome and Millie was terrified of him.

*If she's unlocking the cabinet, she must want Patrick's rifle. But it isn't there.*

Lillian's senses were amplified, her nerves on heightened alert. With Millie and the man both facing away from the doorway, she scurried past the office and bolted to the kitchen. From the back of the pantry, hidden behind a sack of potatoes, she retrieved Patrick's rifle. He had brought it to the kitchen the night before for cleaning, but he'd been lazy and hadn't returned it to his office. That morning she had meant to put it back herself, but she'd gotten distracted with preparations for the concert.

Lillian rummaged frantically through the drawer next to her stove—somewhere inside it, she remembered, she had seen a single round. Patrick had confiscated it from Thomas months ago, and had slipped it into her junk drawer for safekeeping. She would have a talk with her husband later about how unsafe that was, but for now, all Lillian wanted was to find it. She groaned as she pawed through the safety pins and scissors until she saw a flash of metal behind some broken pencils.

Lillian's pulse quickened as she placed the lone bullet into the empty chamber, making sure to move her thumb out of the way before the bolt snapped shut. She couldn't remember how many years had passed since she had last fired a rifle, but she hadn't forgotten. Her father had taught her before her mother died. It had been one of the few times he had showed any patience with her, perhaps the only time he had taken any real interest. They had both been shocked to discover what a good shot she was—so good, in fact, that for the briefest of moments, her father seemed proud of her. Lillian had given up shooting shortly after that; she had been unable to stomach the thought of her actions bringing her father any kind of joy.

Once the rifle was loaded, she crept back toward the foyer. "*Tell me where it is!*" she heard the man shouting. When she peered around the corner, he was in full view, with both of his hands wrapped around Millie's throat.

Lillian released the safety on the rifle and waited. Maybe he would stop. Maybe he would leave. She sucked in her breath as the man threw Millie to the ground. Then she heard her friend whisper, "I want to, but I can't. I'm sorry."

When the man raised his knife, Lillian took aim and fired.

**The week before she died, Lillian's mother cleaned the house from** top to bottom. She arranged the books on the shelves in alphabetical order to ensure that each volume was easy to find. She cleaned out every closet and drawer, tossing out all the old underwear and donating piles of Lillian's too-small dresses and coats to the church clothing drive. She organized the pots in the kitchen according to size and finally set up the spice rack that had been languishing in the hall closet. She neatened her sewing area, polished the silver, and bought Lillian a new box of colored pencils.

The night before, she cooked Lillian's favorite Sunday dinner: homemade fried chicken, biscuits, and mashed potatoes. She made extra so there would be leftovers for Monday, enough to serve Lillian's father in the afternoon. The officers' club was closed on Mondays, so Lillian's father always ate his lunch at home.

On what would become her final morning with her mother, Lillian was running late for school. She ate her breakfast quickly, ran to her bedroom for her books, and opened her jewelry box to grab her favorite silver necklace. But when she pulled the necklace from the box, the chain was full of knots, completely enmeshed with two other pieces. Lillian handed her mother the tiny pile of jewelry and pleaded with her to untangle it. The next thing she knew, her mother's eyes were bright with tears.

"Mommy, why are you crying? What's wrong?"

Lillian could see that she was trying to smile. "I'm fine, sweetheart. I don't have time to untangle these before the school bus comes, but I promise to have them ready by the time you get home."

"Can't you *try*, Mommy? Please?"

Instead of scolding Lillian for whining, her mother kissed her cheek and tucked a stray strand of hair behind her daughter's ear. *I want to, but I can't. I'm sorry.* She hugged Lillian tightly until the bus honked twice from the end of the driveway.

When Lillian came home from school that afternoon, something was wrong. Her father shouldn't have been back from work so soon, but there he was, sitting by himself at the kitchen table. Lillian couldn't remember ever seeing him alone in the kitchen before. He always left the room as soon as he finished eating.

"Where is Mommy?"

He stared at her without answering. She was accustomed to seeing her father angry or upset, but the look on his face was different this time.

"Why is the table over there?" The round wooden table had,

in fact, been moved, pushed to the side of the room so that it was no longer centered underneath the chandelier.

"Your mother moved it."

"Why?"

"Because it was in the way." He stood from his chair. "Your mother died today, Lillian. She killed herself. I found her when I came home for lunch. The police and the ambulance left a little while ago."

Lillian heard the words, but they might as well have been in a foreign language. Nothing made sense; nothing her father said felt real or true. It was meaningless gibberish. It was a terrible lie. She ran from the room as fast as she could and slammed the door shut to her now-spotless bedroom. There, on her dresser, were all three of her necklaces, perfectly untangled and neatly arranged.

For the next several hours, Lillian sat on her bed and stared at the wall. Around eight o'clock, a schoolmate's mother knocked on her door to offer her dinner, but Lillian refused to answer. It was well after midnight when she got under the covers. Once the tears started, there was no way to stop them. She wiped at her eyes with the sleeve of her nightgown until she noticed an unfamiliar pile on her nightstand.

Her mother had left her a clean stack of handkerchiefs.

**On any other night, the sound of a gunshot coming from Lillian's** house would have been like an alarm reverberating throughout Armory Square. The neighbors would have been knocking, and the guards would have been alerted. But five thousand people were in the square that night, all for the concert she had helped bring to Springfield. From where she stood in the house, Lillian could hear them—an army of strangers cheering in the dark.

The man's body was still, facedown on the floor next to Patrick's desk. Lillian put the rifle down and helped Millie to stand. "That was him, wasn't it?" she asked. "That was Lenny?"

"Yes," Millie answered, too stunned to say more.

There were all kinds of soldiers, Lillian realized. Not only those in uniform who clashed with foreign armies but smaller, unseen soldiers who fought more familiar enemies. Lillian had been raised by a woman under siege, a woman whose struggles—both physical and mental—had formed the bleak battleground of Lillian's childhood. Her mother had been a casualty of that long-ago conflict, but Lillian had survived. Millie would too. Lillian wrapped her arms tightly around the trembling young woman. "He can't hurt you anymore," she whispered. "He's gone."

When Lillian was a child, her father had sometimes spoken of the men with whom he'd fought in the first long war—the men he'd never forget, the ones he'd called his brothers. In the wake of her own battle, Lillian felt a deeper understanding of the bond her father had described all those years ago. She and Millie were soldiers as surely as those men had been. Their connection was forever sealed. They were sisters now.

From the phone on Patrick's desk, Lillian called the armory guards. It felt like forever before someone picked up. "This is Lillian Walsh. Please send someone over as quickly as you can. There's been a break-in."

# Ruth

Ruth had just dozed off when she thought she heard knocking coming from downstairs. She glanced over at Arthur, but he was still fast asleep, so she pushed back the blankets and pulled on her robe. Before she reached the steps, the knocking had turned to pounding. Charlie was outside, a dazed expression on his face.

"Someone broke into the Walshes' a few hours ago." Ruth was out the door before Charlie finished speaking. She didn't bother with her coat. She didn't change out of her slippers. She didn't go upstairs to wake Arthur or tell him where she was going. The only thought in her mind was the safety of her sister. She ran without thinking or stopping to breathe. *Please, God, please. Let her be all right.* Charlie had to sprint across the square just to catch up with her.

Two armory guards stood by the Walshes' front door, and the inside of the house was buzzing with activity. To the right of the foyer, a handful of uniformed men were questioning Lillian and Patrick Walsh in the office. When Ruth peeked inside, she didn't see her sister, but there could be no mistaking the circle of blood on the carpet. A wave of nausea rolled over her, and she grabbed Charlie's arm. *I didn't protect her. I wasn't there when she needed me.*

"Mrs. Blum," Charlie said kindly, "that isn't her blood." Slowly, he walked Ruth toward the back of the house. They found Millie in the kitchen, standing by the back door. It was too dark to see the gardens, but Millie was staring through the glass to where the rose arbor stood.

"Mil?" Ruth said. "It's me. I'm here."

From everything Ruth had seen—the guards and the officers and the blood on the floor—her sister should have been in complete hysterics. The Brooklyn girl Ruth knew would have been sobbing loudly, encircled by a group of sympathetic supporters. But everything was different now; everything had changed. Millie stood silently, alone in the darkness. There was no one bringing her a plate of food, no one patting her on the back.

Instead, it was Ruth who fell apart. It was Ruth who needed attention, a chair, a glass of water. Sobs rushed out of her in torrents, like a newly swollen stream. She could not hold them back; she could not make them stop.

Millie asked Charlie to give them some privacy. Then she knelt beside her sister, took her hand, and waited until Ruth was calm enough to speak.

"That was Lenny's blood, wasn't it?" Ruth finally managed to ask. "In the other room, that was his blood on the floor?"

Millie nodded. "Yes. They took the body away a little while ago."

"The body? So he's . . ."

"Lenny is dead."

"He could have killed you," Ruth murmured. "He could have killed you for that ring. I should have given it to him last time. How could I have been so stupid?" She began to cry again.

"It's all right," Millie whispered. "Hush now. It's over."

"I never should have lied to you. I never should have left you. I'm sorry." Ruth wept. "I'm so sorry for everything."

•     •     •

**Ruth scanned the newspapers every day looking for some men-**tion of what had occurred. On the fourth day after the incident, a short article ran on the second page of *The Springfield Republican*.

### ARMORY SABATOGE THWARTED

*An unidentified intruder was shot and killed after breaking into the home of Colonel Patrick Walsh, the commanding officer of the Springfield Armory. The intruder threatened the life of a houseguest at knifepoint. According to the armory intelligence officer who led the investigation, the motive for the break-in was sabotage. The intruder was killed in the commanding officer's study, where he had been searching through classified papers and files.*

It was for the best that Lenny's name hadn't been mentioned. There would be nothing in print to link him back to her sister, nothing Michael would ever find that would name his father as a criminal.

At first, Ruth assumed that the slant of the article had been the Walshes' handiwork, that they had finessed the truth with the guards for Millie's protection. But when she asked her sister about it, Millie told her that Captain O'Brian was convinced that Lenny was a spy. His body was found inches away from Colonel Walsh's private desk—from piles of confidential paperwork regarding armory operations. He had snuck onto the grounds on a night he knew the house would be empty. He had intentionally carried no identification on his person. To O'Brian, the incident had all the markings of a sophisticated sabotage operation. No matter what anyone said, they couldn't convince him otherwise.

**After Millie had moved to the Walshes', Ruth had avoided Lillian** as much as possible. She turned in the opposite direction when she saw Lillian in the square, and she stopped attending the weekly meetings of the officers' wives—anything to escape an awkward encounter with her former friend.

But in the wake of Lenny's death, there could be no more embarrassment. Ruth had nothing left to hide, no more secrets to keep. A few weeks later, when Lillian resumed her weekly meetings, Ruth decided that she might as well go.

The first woman to greet her was Cecily Abbott, looking grayer and stouter than she had last February. "Mrs. Blum!" Mrs. Abbott said, taking Ruth's hand. "How nice to have you back with us."

Of course, not everyone was as warm or as welcoming. Even from across the Walshes' wide living room, Ruth could feel the weight of Grace Peabody's glare. Ruth poured herself a cup of tea and joined a circle of women deep in conversation about the latest war bond drive. Out of the corner of her eye, she saw Grace approaching.

Grace was dressed straight off the cover of *Harper's Bazaar*—in a cherry-red suit with a navy-and-white-striped blouse underneath. Her gloves were made to order, in the same fabric as the blouse—creating a dramatic and jarring effect. As usual, she had no time for pleasantries.

"What was his name? The man who got killed? I asked Lillian, of course, but she claims she doesn't know. The paper said he was carrying no identification."

"I have no idea."

Grace raised an eyebrow. "Oh, I think you have more than just an idea. It was your sister who was with him—she has to know something. What's Millie hiding this time?"

In the past, Ruth had always deferred to Grace, letting her insults go unchallenged and her accusations unanswered. But now, she grabbed Grace by the elbow and pulled her to the side of the room.

"What do you think you're doing? Let go of me." Grace tried to yank her arm free, but Ruth tightened her hold.

"I think it's time you listened to *me* for once. Do you know what my mother would have said about you? I'm going to say the words slowly, so you get the full effect. *A sheyn punim ober a beyz harts*. It's Yiddish, by the way. It means 'a pretty face but an evil heart.'"

"What are you talking about? I *said* let go!" Ruth felt Grace's arm tremble through the delicate red fabric.

"I don't *ever* want to hear you say my sister's name again," Ruth demanded. "I don't want you to talk about her. I don't want you to look at her. I *know* it was you who accused her of setting that fire. Right after Arietta saw you at the Victory dance."

Tiny droplets of perspiration appeared on Grace's forehead, threatening to ruin her perfect façade.

"I know all about Fred too—the way he attacked Millie and the awful things he said to her." Ruth paused for a moment and gestured around the room. "How many of these women do you think your charming husband has propositioned by now? With the way that man drinks? I'd say at least half."

Grace's eyes bulged with fury, but Ruth kept on talking.

"Fred might do better away from all this temptation. I hear the arsenal in Detroit is desperate for officers—all those tanks they're making have to be fitted with guns. Of course, Michigan is awfully far from your family in Boston, but you'd get used to it soon enough. I'm sure Colonel Walsh could be convinced to send him."

Grace's arm went limp. "You wouldn't dare," she whispered.

From the other side of the room, Lillian called the meeting to order. "Ladies!" she shouted, clapping her hands. "Let's all take our seats."

Ruth gave Grace's arm a final squeeze before letting go. "Oh, I would, but I'm sure I won't have to. I have a feeling that you and I finally understand each other."

# Millie

The sisters took Millie's ring to a well-known jeweler with a small shop on Main Street. Mr. Silverman's hair was peppered with gray, but his hands were as small and as smooth as a child's. "It's a very unusual piece," he said. "Let me take it in the back and examine it with my assistant."

Twenty minutes later, he returned, carrying the newly polished ring on a square velvet tray.

"The opal is particularly valuable—good clarity, no pitting, a beautiful play of color. The cut of the cabochon is symmetrical and nicely domed, and the diamonds surrounding it are of excellent quality." He paused for a moment and lifted the ring to the light. "How old did you say it was?"

"At least a hundred years old," Ruth answered. "It belonged to our great-grandmother."

"Well. I'm sure I have some customers who would be interested. I can give you eight hundred for it."

Millie chimed in, hoping to persuade him to go higher. "In New York, we were told it was worth at least a thousand dollars."

The jeweler frowned and set the ring back down on the tray.

"We don't pay New York prices in Springfield, ladies. I can go up to eight hundred and fifty, but that's the best I can do."

"What do you think?" Millie asked Ruth.

But Ruth deferred to her sister. "It's for you to decide."

"I accept your offer, Mr. Silverman," Millie announced. "You have a deal." The jeweler rapped the counter twice with his knuckles, picked up the tray, and excused himself to the back room to write a check.

When Millie first entered the store, it felt dusty and cramped, but now that the ring was out of her hands, the ancient glass cases and carpets seemed charming. The light from the fixtures that hung overhead reflected off the gems displayed along the perimeter, sending tiny rainbow beams glittering across the walls and the ceiling. Millie and Ruth stood together in the center of the room, staring up at the pinpricks of light, like children watching fireworks.

After Millie placed the check from the jeweler in her purse, the sisters stepped outside into the spring sunshine. They navigated the mass of Saturday shoppers, and Millie contemplated the freedom the check represented. She would no longer be dependent on anyone for a place to stay—she could make her own way and live wherever she pleased.

Ruth seemed to sense her thoughts. "Have you thought about what you'll do now? Where you want to live?"

"A little bit," she said. "Michael and I are ready for a place of our own."

"Well, you have a lot of choices. You could live anywhere. Even Brooklyn again, if that's what you want." Ruth stopped on the sidewalk. "But I hope you don't leave. I hope you'll stay here."

Ever since they were children, Ruth had pushed Millie away. Her disapproval was a constant that Millie had come to expect, like heat in the summertime or the turning of the leaves. But now, it seemed, there was a shift in the air—imperceptible to most, but not to her. When they stopped at the intersection to turn onto State Street, Millie knew Ruth was holding her breath for an answer.

"Of course I'm staying," Millie said matter-of-factly. "Michael and I like it here. Where else would we go?"

**On a warm day in late June, Millie moved to a house a few doors** down from Arietta. It had been the cook, of course, who had managed it for her. After one of her elderly neighbors passed away, Arietta convinced the homeowner's son that the most patriotic course of action would be to rent the two-bedroom Cape to a young widow who worked at the armory. "I know just the gal," Arietta insisted. "You won't have to move a thing; she'll rent the place furnished. Leave it to me."

Millie was thrilled to have her own place at last. Neither Ruth's house nor Lillian's had ever felt like home, and she did not want to intrude any longer on their domains. She wouldn't miss living in Armory Square, but she would miss the gardens, so she asked Lillian to help her plant some rosebushes in her yard. They would never bloom as lushly as the ones on Lillian's arbor, but Millie loved the smell of them, and they were pretty just the same.

After a full day of unpacking and scrubbing the floors, Millie put Michael to bed and settled herself with a cup of tea and the newspaper at the small kitchen table. The floral-patterned paper on the walls felt familiar—it reminded her of the DeLuca family's kitchen back in Brooklyn. Rosebuds and wisteria floated on trellises, set against a background of soothing gray green. Millie fell asleep at the table, dreaming of a plate of Mrs. DeLuca's arancini.

In the morning, she woke abruptly to a knock at her door.

Ruth was waiting on the front steps, carrying a square package wrapped in brown paper. When she saw Millie's rumpled clothes, she reached out to feel her sister's forehead. "Are you sick?"

Millie smiled and led Ruth to the kitchen. "I'm fine; I fell asleep in a chair, that's all." She smoothed back her hair and began to laugh. "The funny thing is, I think that was the best night's sleep I've had in years."

"It's the house," Ruth said approvingly. "You must feel at home here." She handed Millie the box. "This is for you."

Inside was the photograph album from their parents' apartment. "I never should have taken it without asking you," Ruth said. "I have more things at my house—Mama's candlesticks, the seder plate. You should look through everything and choose what you want to keep."

The book was filled with old photographs of relatives they barely knew—Great-Aunt Edna with their mother, their father's brother from Russia. Their parents' wedding portrait was there too, along with one of Ruth and Arthur.

"I used to love looking at this book when I was little," Millie mused. "Papa would tell me everyone's names and how they were related to us. It's a shame we have so few family photos; Mama would never let Papa buy that camera he wanted."

"Do you remember what she used to say? *If I want to know what I look like, I'll stand in front of a mirror.*"

Millie flipped through the book until she found what she was looking for—a photograph of Ruth on a sofa, holding a four- or five-month-old Millie on her lap. The children in the picture gazed at each other with mutual adoration, oblivious to the camera or to anyone watching.

Millie traced the photograph with the tips of her fingers. "This was always my favorite photo of the two of us."

"Mine too," Ruth said. "Always."

**Millie never went to another rifle club meeting. She had no stom-**ach for shooting, and she could not bear the noise. The sound from the rifle that Lillian had fired still echoed in her ears. She woke from it sometimes, bolting upright in the dark, surrounded by silence on every side. On some nights, she wandered out of her bed, thinking it was morning and that her shift had just begun. In the mist of her mind, still clouded with loss, the small kitchen table became her workstation. Her hands went through the motions with imaginary parts—her fingers like sleepwalkers over which she had no control. She took apart the phantom trigger mechanism over and over, assembling, disassembling, until the pain subsided. Moonlight wafted through the uncovered window, illuminating her face with a silvery glow. Anyone watching would have thought she was a ghost.

When Charlie realized that she would not be returning to the rifle club, he made no attempt to conceal his disappointment. "Everyone misses you," he said. "Especially me."

"Don't be ridiculous. You can't possibly miss me! I see you every day when I come through the gate."

"Would you . . . could I take you out for dinner sometime?" His eyes were hopeful, without a trace of guile behind them.

"I'd like that," she said.

He told her the story of how he came to be a guard when most young men his age had been drafted or enlisted. "I get terrible ulcers," he admitted. "The doctors wouldn't let me join up. I was embarrassed to tell my buddies, but then I found out about this job. I figured if I couldn't fight, at least I could work here."

Disappointment hadn't broken him; it had only made him more resilient.

Millie was glad he had told her. Soon, she decided, she would tell him her story—the truth about her sister, her husband, and herself. She wanted no more secrets, no more half-truths or omissions. She would try to explain to him what she had learned in his city, what she had learned from her sisters—not only Ruth but the others.

She would tell him the story of her war and how she had survived.

# Author's Note

The history of the Springfield Armory is a particularly intriguing one. It began as an arsenal, a storage place for weapons arriving from France during the American Revolution. After the war, in 1794, President George Washington endorsed a new arms factory in Springfield. The arsenal became an armory, and manufacturing began. In the early 1840s, one hundred years before my novel begins, Henry Wadsworth Longfellow visited Springfield during his honeymoon, where the racks of finished muskets inspired him to write his poem "The Arsenal at Springfield."

Although I grew up within ten miles of the armory, it took me forty-eight years to visit what now remains of its campus. In the spring of 2016, while researching the city of Springfield for my second novel, I came across the armory's Forge of Innovation website and was immediately drawn in by the articles about the women who had worked on the assembly lines as "soldiers of production" during World War II. Clicking through the site, I found recordings of interviews with former employees and armory residents. Once I heard their voices, I could not tear myself away.

Women were first employed in manufacturing at the armory during World War I, but after the war, most lost their jobs. During

World War II, the armory again turned to women to overcome the labor shortage. By June of 1943, somewhere between 11,300 and 11,800 people worked at the armory, and of that number, 43 percent were women.

I spent dozens of hours listening to their stories and reading about them: the struggling mother who'd been desperate for a job; the young woman who had taken photographs for the armory's monthly newsletter; the machine operator who had lost the tip of her finger in an accident. I listened to the recollections of a woman who had been the wife of a former commanding officer, and I read about an opera singer who had volunteered as a cook in the armory cafeteria.

The common thread in every interview was the sense of community the armory provided. Those who had been workers there spoke of armory bowling leagues and archery lessons, of midnight dances and post-shift tennis games. Those who had lived there reminisced about the midday concerts and the flower-filled greenhouses. None of it sounded like an "armory" to me. Further research revealed that the armory wasn't just a single manufacturing building, as I had always assumed, but rather a park-like campus filled with trees and gardens. It was lined with elegant homes where officers lived, tennis courts, and even a small swimming pool. It boasted not just a single factory, but facilities for research, storage, and distribution. In fact, there were so many buildings that they were given numbers instead of names.

I reached out to Alex MacKenzie, curator of the Springfield Armory National Historic Site, to arrange for a visit in July of 2016. Alex spent an entire day answering my questions and giving me a tour of the remaining grounds and buildings. Over the next two years, he continued to help me with all of my research. My most sincere thanks go to him for his patience and his kindness. I would not have been able to write this story without him.

Today, much of what was once known as Armory Square is the campus for Springfield Technical Community College. The old arsenal building now houses the armory museum. Alex walked me through a former officer's home, and let me explore the commanding officer's residence. Together, we walked the grounds, and he explained what I might have seen had I visited during World War II.

When I saw the area where the manufacturing buildings had once been located, I began to see the armory as two separate worlds—the pristine, park-like sanctuary of Armory Square and the manufacturing center of Federal Square, just across the street. The setting reminded me of the sisters in my novel: physically close, yet with distinct and opposite temperaments. Walking the grounds was a crucial piece of inspiration for me, as it influenced my creation of the sisters' narrative.

During my second visit to the armory, I pored through every issue of *The Armory Newsletter*—a monthly pamphlet that was written, illustrated, and published by employees from the fall of 1941 to August of 1943. The pamphlets were a window into daily armory life: an article recapping an employee's first day on the job; gossip pages listing engagements and weddings; sports pages detailing the scores for armory sports teams; hand-drawn cartoons poking fun at the war; and spotlight pieces about employees with special talents and backgrounds. With every edition I read, I was able to picture more clearly what it must have been like to work and to live at this remarkable place.

In writing *The Wartime Sisters*, it was my goal to offer readers a vision of the armory that was both personal and also historically accurate. The day care center Michael attends is based on the real day care center at the High School of Commerce across the street from the armory. The Army Navy "E" Award for Excellence in production was, in fact, presented to the Springfield Armory in September of 1942, and, as in my story, an unprecedented break in manufacturing was arranged in order for all employees to attend the ceremony. The "On to Victory" dance was a widely attended event, detailed in the armory newsletter with several photographs and an article describing the entertainment and refreshments. I must thank Mr. Cliff McCarthy, an archivist at the Springfield Museums, for his assistance in identifying the location of the dance: the Springfield Municipal Auditorium, now Symphony Hall.

In certain instances, I was compelled to take liberties with the timing of real events in order to move my plot forward. For example, the fire at the partially built field services building took place on January 30, 1942, but because I wanted Millie to be living at the armory during that time, I moved the incident later, to July of that year. *The Victory Parade of Spotlight Bands* radio show brought Benny Goodman to the armory for a concert on September 29, 1943. However, in the novel, I set the concert in May to improve the pacing of the story. In addition, to eliminate confusion, I did not include descriptions of a second manufacturing center—The Water Shops, which were located about a mile away from Armory Square.

Because I grew up so close to Springfield, I had childhood memories of Forest Park, Johnson's Bookstore, and lunches with my mother at the Steiger's department store tearoom. But I knew these places from the 1970s and 1980s; to be able to describe these settings as they existed in the early 1940s, I enlisted the help of old photographs and newspaper articles from *The Springfield Republican* archives.

For anyone interested in the history of the armory, I strongly encourage a visit to the site. Renovations are under way, and a plan is in place to restore some of the gardens. I also recommend the following sources, all of which were invaluable to me: *Springfield Armory, Pointless Sacrifice*, by C. L. Dvarecka, Eastern National, 1968; *Forge of Innovation: An Industrial History of the Springfield Armory, 1794–1968*, Eastern National, 2008; "Cultural Landscape Report for Armory Square: Springfield Armory National Historic Site," by Allison A. Crosbie, ASLA, *Historical Landscape Architect*, 2010; *Images of America Springfield Armory*, by Alex MacKenzie, Arcadia Publishing, 2015; *Arsenal of Freedom: The Springfield Armory 1890–1948, A Year-By-Year Account Drawn From Official Records*, compiled and edited by Lt. Col. William S. Brophy, USAR Ret., Andrew Mowbray Inc., Publishers, 1991; "The Armory at Springfield," by Jacob Abbott, published in *Harper's New Monthly Magazine*, No. XXVI, July 1852; *Postcard History Series: Springfield*, by G. Michael Dobbs, Arcadia Publishing, copyright 2008; *Our Stories: The Jews of Western Massachusetts, 2013*, by *The Springfield Republican*; and the Springfield Armory, Forge of Innovation website: forgeofinnovation.org.

Reading
Group
Gold

# THE WARTIME SISTERS

by Lynda Cohen Loigman

## About the Author

- A Conversation with Lynda Cohen Loigman

## Behind the Novel

- *The Wartime Sisters*: The Story Behind the Book

- The Real Setting of *The Wartime Sisters*:
  A Glimpse into Life at the Springfield Armory
  During WWII

## Keep on Reading

- Recommended Reading

- Reading Group Questions

*A*
*Reading*
*Group Gold*
*Selection*

Also available as an audiobook
from Macmillan Audio

For more reading group suggestions
visit www.readinggroupgold.com.

ST. MARTIN'S GRIFFIN

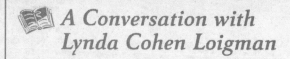

# A Conversation with Lynda Cohen Loigman

**Could you tell us a little bit about your background, and when you decided that you wanted to lead a literary life?**

Like many English majors who graduated from college in the early 1990s, I decided to go to law school. Although a lot of good things came out of that decision (I made wonderful friends and met my husband), it was clear that I wasn't cut out for a career in law. During my first year, when I was supposed to be reading about contracts and income taxation, I read *The Norton Anthology of Poetry* instead. Somehow, I muddled through three years of law school, and went on to practice trusts and estates law in New York for eight additional years.

I wanted to write, but, to be honest, I was incredibly naïve about *how* to become a writer. I didn't know anyone who wrote for a living, and I found it impossible to believe that someone like me could publish a novel. It was also true that I was terrified to fail. I could have taken creative writing classes in college, but I never did because I was insecure about how my writing would be received.

After I had my first child in early 1999, an idea for a novel came to me and stuck. I wrote a prologue for the story, but it took another thirteen years before I felt brave enough to enroll in a writing class at Sarah Lawrence College. After years of classes, the pages I had been scribbling became my first novel, *The Two-Family House*. Today, I feel incredibly lucky that my words have been able to reach so many readers. I only wish I'd had the courage to start writing earlier.

Reading
Group
Gold

**Is there a book that most influenced your life? Or inspired you to become a writer?**

When I was around ten years old, I read my mother's copy of *A Tree Grows in Brooklyn* by Betty Smith. To this day, it is one of my favorite stories. I still remember the way I felt the first time I read it, and I always hope I can make readers feel that same kind of emotional connection.

**How did you become a writer? Would you care to share any writing tips?**

The best advice is truly the simplest, and it is advice I have heard other writers give over and over again: To be a writer, you have to write. Until I took a class and pushed myself to write every day, I was not a writer. Even after I did those things, it took years (and the publication of my first novel) before I was able to overcome my insecurities and *call* myself a writer. One thing that helped was to surround myself with a community of other people who do what I do— other people who understood the creative issues I faced. Now, my novelist friends are some of the most supportive friends I've ever had.

*About
the Author*

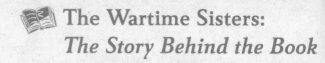

# The Wartime Sisters:
## *The Story Behind the Book*

Lynda Cohen Loigman

My favorite family stories have always been the ones m
mother and her two sisters told about their Brooklyn
childhood in the 1950s. Those tales had such an impa
on me that they inspired the setting for my first novel,
*The Two-Family House*. But not all of those family stori
were set in New York. During my mother's last years
of high school, her family left Brooklyn for the much
smaller city of Springfield, Massachusetts. Their move
was always described in the language of loss. Compare
to Brooklyn, their new city was colorless and deserted.
Where were the crowds? The knish carts? The stores? N
grandmother and her daughters were certain that they
had been dragged to the end of the earth. Their relative
from New York visited only once a year and never
stopped referring to Springfield as "the country." They
brought cans of tuna fish with them on the train becau
they were afraid they might starve.

My mother stayed behind in Brooklyn in order to
graduate with the rest of her class. Although I asked
often, she never said much about the time she spent
living with her aunt and uncle. She refused to talk
about what it was like to watch her family leave, to
know that her home was no longer clearly defined.
After graduation, she joined her younger sisters in
Springfield. Not too long afterward, at the age of
eighteen, she met my father at a dance and the two
of them married. My brother and I were raised in
Springfield at first, and then in the neighboring subu
of Longmeadow.

As a child, I was exceedingly proud of what I believe
to be my mother's exotic Brooklyn upbringing. My
father—born and raised in Western Massachusetts—

seemed to know every Jewish person in our town.
He knew all of their family histories and they
knew his. But no one knew my mother, and she
liked it that way. No matter how many years she
lived in Massachusetts, she never stopped thinking
of herself as a New Yorker.

When I first began piecing together my second
novel, I wanted to write about sisters in transition—
sisters who had left their home and were forced to
begin again. The details of my mother's arrival in
Springfield had always been hazy, and I longed for
a greater understanding of her past experiences.
I wanted to capture what the shift must have felt
like, not just for her, but for her younger sisters as
well. No one made my mother laugh the way her
sisters did, but there were arguments too—weeks
and months and years when one sister refused to
speak to another. As with most families, each sister
fulfilled a specific role in the greater dynamic—roles
I could identify, but did not know the origin of. My
mother was the worrywart, Barbara was the optimist,
and Shelley, the youngest, was always "the fun one."
Every time they got together, the same patterns
emerged, patterns that became questions I wanted
to explore: Can we ever break free from the roles
assigned in childhood? Do those who have known
us the longest really know us the best? Can our
youthful grudges ever truly be forgiven?

I decided to set my novel in Brooklyn and
Springfield, the same two cities where my own
family had lived. Although I intended to mention
the Springfield Armory only in passing, a little bit of
research planted unshakeable seeds that bloomed
into the backdrop of much of the book. I began
listening to the oral histories of female former

employees and residents, most of whom had worked at the Armory during World War II. They were lathe operators, truck drivers, teenagers, and mothers. Some were women who had lived on the grounds as children and one was the wife of a former commanding officer. learned that what I had envisioned as nothing more th a giant weapons factory was actually a bucolic campus filled with elegant homes and manicured gardens. The Springfield that existed during the early 1940s seemed a far richer setting than the one my mother's family inhabited, and I wanted my story to benefit from that history. I decided to push my narrative back twenty yea

After multiple visits to what is now left of the Armor I was struck by the contrast between the two worlds it contained: Armory Square, filled with charming buildings and rose arbors; and Federal Square, wher the factory buildings were located. Like the two side of the Armory, the two sisters in my story—Millie and Ruth—are opposites.

When the story opens, the sisters have been estrang for five years. Having lost her young husband in the early days of the war, Millie travels to Springfield to live with Ruth's family. But their reunion is not an easy one, as long-held resentments continue to feste All around them, the country they serve is at war, bu Millie and Ruth are at war with each other.

Although I am not lucky enough to have a sister o my own, I've always keenly observed my mother a aunts. Their interactions were complicated—full of ebbs and flows, high points and low. Watching the together taught me about loyalty and love, and it is my great hope to offer readers an intimate story of both the comfort and the chaos that sisterhood can be: messy misunderstandings, arguments and grudges, but also forgiveness and acceptance of ea other's flaws. By setting my story at the Springfiel

nory in the early 1940s, I hope to also highlight
strength and tenacity of women on the home
nt who worked to further our country's cause,
"soldiers of production," who gave their time
d energy as women ordnance workers. With
luck, *The Wartime Sisters* will provide both a
isfying story of family secrets and sisterhood, and
limpse into what life was like for women living
d working at the Armory in the early days of the
ond World War.

*Behind*

*the Novel*

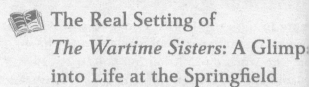 # The Real Setting of *The Wartime Sisters*: A Glimps into Life at the Springfield Armory During WWII

Women were first employed in manufacturing at the Springfield Armory during World War I, but after the war, most lost their jobs. During World War II, the armory again turned to women to overcome the labor shortage. By June of 1943, almost 12,000 pec worked at the armory, and of that number, 43 percent were wome This photograph shows a group of women workers.

Women Ordnance Workers were extremely important to Armory operations. This photo shows some of the women who worked at the Springfield Armory. They were of all ages and had all different levels of education and experience. This montage of photographs included in one of the monthly Armory News pamphlets.

of the women working in assembly at the Springfield Armory.
nings regarding proper hair and dress were given frequently.
woman wears coveralls, a hairnet, and no jewelry. Her Armory
loyee badge is prominently displayed.

*Behind
the Novel*

is a photograph of the residence for the commanding officer of
springfield Armory. In *The Wartime Sisters*, this is Lillian's house.
residence is still standing today on the Armory grounds.

During World War II, the Works Progress Administration kept several gardeners employed at the Armory. This photograph shows some of the gardens behind the commanding officer's residence.

The Works Progress Administration employed many musicians during World War II. This WPA band gave lunchtime concerts at the Armory in order to boost morale. Here, you can see Armory employees gathered around the band to enjoy the show.

DANCE

...is montage shows several scenes from the "On To Victory" Dance,
...ld at the Springfield Auditorium on February 19, 1943. Jack
...agarden performed with a 14-piece orchestra, and the singer Judy
...yne performed as well. Various contests were held, including
...itterbug contest and a contest to crown the "WOW" (Women
...rdnance Workers) girl of the evening. Over 2,600 tickets were
...ld, and the dance ran from 8:00 p.m. to 3:00 a.m. so that workers
...signed to any shift would still have time to attend. The total profits
...the dance were listed as $870.33. This money was donated for
...creational and other facilities for servicemen at Westover Field
...d the Exposition Grounds in West Springfield, as well as to Army
...nergency Relief and the Navy Relief Society.

# Recommended Reading

I love historical fiction, but I also love magical realism
and stories that tend toward the fantastical. I have a
soft spot for fairy tales and myths as well. These are t
books I have been loving most recently:

*The World That We Knew*
by Alice Hoffman

*The Golem and the Jinni*
by Helene Wecker

*The Ten Thousand Doors of January*
by Alix E. Harrow

*Spinning Silver*
by Naomi Novik

*The Sisters of the Winter Wood*
by Rena Rossner

*The Mermaid and Mrs. Hancock*
by Imogen Hermes Gowar

*Circe*
by Madeline Miller

*The Secret Chord*
by Geraldine Brooks

*Once Upon a River*
by Diane Setterfield

*City of Girls*
by Elizabeth Gilbert

# Reading Group Questions

What is it about the sisters' relationship that makes it so ripe for storytelling?

Throughout their childhood, Ruth and Millie's mother has vastly different expectations for them, especially in terms of the kind of men they will marry. Do you think their mother bears some of the blame for the poor relationship between her daughters? What about their father?

When Millie first meets Lenny, she is lonely and mourning the loss of her neighbor. Why else do you think Millie falls for Lenny? Why does she agree to marry him?

Do you think it was wrong of Ruth's mother to expect her to bring Millie with her to her new home? Why was it so important for Ruth to have a fresh start in Springfield? Did being Jewish make it harder for Ruth to fit in at the armory?

Do you think Ruth's lies to Lenny and her sister are excusable? If you were Millie, would you ever be able to forgive Ruth for what she did?

Are Millie's secrets about Lenny and her marriage more or less justifiable than the secrets Ruth keeps?

In what ways do Arietta and Lillian serve as substitute sisters for Millie? Why do you think they are so protective of her? How does the war bring these women together?

8. How does Lillian's past shape her as an adult? Do you think she would have been able to defend Millie as she does at the end of the story had it not been for her own unfortunate childhood experiences?

9. Ruth and Millie can't seem to escape the roles they took on as children. Do you think family members always fall into set patterns of behavior? Can the patterns ever be broken, or are we destined to play the same roles within our family units from childhood through old age?

10. When Millie first arrives in Springfield, she has no money and almost no luggage. Do you think Ruth truly understands Millie's predicament? Should she have been more generous? Why are class differences among adult family members so difficult to overcome?

11. How do Grace's prejudices affect her actions? Why do you think she was so jealous of Millie? Should Ruth have come to her sister's defense sooner?

12. Do you think Millie and Ruth will be able to move beyond their past grievances and have a sincere and positive relationship in the future?

# About the Author

Randy Matusow

**LYNDA COHEN LOIGMAN** grew up in Longmeadow, Massachusetts. She earned her B.A. in English and American literature from Harvard College and a law degree from Columbia Law School. Lynda practiced trusts and estates law in New York City for eight years before moving out of the city to raise her two children with her husband. Her first novel, *The Two-Family House*, was chosen by Goodreads as a best book of the month for March 2016 and was a nominee for the Goodreads 2016 Choice Awards in Historical Fiction.